I decided that I'd been wrong to call her cute. I'd been misled by her small size and rather kittenish appearance. Well, a lynx isn't very big, but nobody'd call it cute as it goes about its predatory wildcat business. I sensed that there was danger here, too. Her skin was a warm and dusky color, very smooth. She had a big mouth full of even white teeth. She had a nose that was no dainty, girlish nubbin; it was a real nose with a fine arch to it, separating a pair of strong cheekbones. And she had magnificent, large, dark eyes with lashes that could break your heart. It was an offbeat face that took a little getting used to, after years of watching TV screens filled with stock beauties right out of the glamour factory.

She licked her lips. "The *pistola* is mine," she said.

THE
FRIGHTENERS

Donald
Hamilton

FAWCETT GOLD MEDAL • NEW YORK

A Fawcett Gold Medal Book
Published by Ballantine Books
Copyright © 1989 by Donald Hamilton

Library of Congress Catalog Card Number: 88-92912

ISBN 0-449-14521-2

Manufactured in the United States of America

First Edition: May 1989

CHAPTER 1

THEY picked me up with a floatplane, which must have taken some arranging. It wasn't as if I'd backpacked into remote Alaska. Amphibian aircraft are common up there; but they're scarce down in arid New Mexico where, except for the high mountain lakes like the one on which I was camped, we've hardly got enough water to drink, let alone land a plane on. I was never told why they didn't use a helicopter; and I never asked. Foolish questions are not encouraged in our outfit.

Anyway, there was the plane, roaring in low over the ridge to the east where the sun was just about to appear, slipping in neatly, and undoubtedly giving every trout in the lake a nervous breakdown as it taxied close to the rock from which I'd been trying to catch my breakfast. When it turned into the wind, a lean young man in jeans, a blue windbreaker, and a blue baseball cap descended to the nearer float.

"Mr. Helm?" he called.

I wanted to ask whom he'd expected to find by this lost lake up in the Sangre de Cristos, Ronald Reagan? But we were both, presumably, slaves of the same cruel master, tyrannical old Uncle Sam, and there was a certain protocol to be followed. I confessed that I was indeed Mr. Matthew Helm, code name Eric. He threw a corny ID phrase at me, the flavor of the month; and I threw an equally corny response back at him. Identification confirmed, I opened a couple of buttons of my wool shirt, the thick, red-and-black-checked, scratchy kind—I was wearing jeans and hip boots at the other end—and returned to its armpit holster the short-barreled .38 Special I'd been holding out of sight behind my leg. I mean, in my line of work you don't just assume that all approaching aircraft are friendlies.

If it had been a hostile, my big, yellow Labrador pup would have been no help at all. He was a hunting dog, not an attack dog. He just stood beside me, watching with interest, his thick tail waving gently. He'd already made his professional estimate of the situation and let me know that it was a hell of a big bird, and he was under the impression that the season was closed, but if I shot it down he'd be glad to retrieve it for me.

"I'm Greer," called the young man on the float. "You're wanted in El Paso, soonest."

It was no time to protest that I still had eleven days of my month's leave coming. We're better trained than the pup is. When the whistle blows, we come. He doesn't always.

I said, "It won't take long to strike camp if you give me a hand. It's over that way a couple of hundred yards. Well, you must have seen it from the air. In front of it, I think you can bring that thing right up to the shore if your flyboy is careful."

"You'll take off with him immediately," Greer said. "I'll stay and bring out your gear and your dog. Just show me the trail down to your car, give me the keys, and tell me where in Santa Fe you want it stored and what boarding kennel you use."

I started to voice a protest but strangled it. I said instead, "So we've got another goddamn panic party."

"When don't we? Let's get moving."

Hurrying back to my little camp with the pup trotting beside me, I drew deep breaths of the cool, spring air, quite thin at this altitude—a little over nine thousand feet, if it matters. There was still snow on the surrounding peaks. There were even some snowbanks along the shores of the lake, although they'd shrunk considerably in the time I'd been there. Spring was finding its way up here; it would be well advanced down in El Paso, Texas. Well, I'd had good luck with the weather, I'd had the lake to myself this early in the season, and the fishing had been great after I'd got it through my young retriever's skull that I was capable of landing the trout I hooked all by myself, they weren't ducks, and he didn't have time to dive in to fetch them for me.

2

It had been a good, peaceful time, even if it had ended early. I looked around, fixing the place in my memory. In the business you never know which good, peaceful time is going to be your last.

Getting airborne was a bit hairy at that altitude, and we used up most of the lake before we broke loose, but the pilot knew his stuff and made it with a few inches to spare. Apart from such moments of suspense, I find the little planes more restful than the big ones. You know that one of those giant, jet-propelled monsters will go in like an overgrown artillery shell if anything goes wrong, but you kid yourself that you'll just flutter gently to earth like a falling leaf in one of the little ones if the fan up front should quit.

The pilot was one of the taciturn plane jockeys. He didn't ask me about my business, and I didn't ask him what he was doing with a seaplane a thousand miles from the sea. I spent most of the flight worrying about the pup I'd left behind, whose name was Happy: worrying that he'd run off and get lost looking for me, worrying that Greer would let him tangle with a porcupine. I didn't worry about his settling down well in the kennel once he got that far. He was a good, relaxed young dog, and he was getting used to being left here and there while the boss tended to business. Another thing I didn't worry about was the mission ahead of me, whatever it might be. When you start worrying about *that*, it's time to get a job as a night watchman while you're still in one piece.

Coming out of the mountains, we picked up the Rio Grande and followed it south down its great valley, leaving Santa Fe nestling in the foothills behind us, and passing Albuquerque under its dome of smog. I recognized a couple of places along the river where I'd hunted ducks and geese in the past; and Elephant Butte Lake and Caballo Lake. Those impoundments were pretty full this spring, I noted; our chronic water shortage wasn't quite as short as usual. Then we were settling onto another, smaller reservoir that was new to me—in that country, you can go to sleep by a running stream and wake up in the morning to find it dammed by the government's industrious hu-

3

man beavers. A gent I didn't know was waiting on the ramp. I went through the recognition routine again, and he led me across the parking lot to a shiny blue American sedan styled like a slippery bar of soap with all sharp corners and edges washed away. The Palmolive school of automotive design. I suppose they call it aerodynamics.

Three-quarters of an hour later I was in a hotel room in El Paso on the Mexican border being restyled myself. The little man with the dye and scissors had me take a shower first because he didn't like the way I smelled—that lake water had been too cold for frequent bathing. He didn't like my face much either; but he was pleased with my backwoods whiskers. Apparently he'd been afraid that he'd have to fit me with somebody else's chin hairs. He got to work, referring occasionally to a set of color photographs spread out on the small table nearby. They showed an older gent with a cropped gray beard and not too much hair who didn't resemble me very closely. At least I hoped he didn't.

While the makeup artist was doing his stuff, Mac came in. He does turn up out in the field occasionally, but it's always a surprise. He was carrying a white linen suit on a hanger, a big white Stetson or the equivalent, and a pair of white—truly—cowboy boots. There was a white Western-style shirt, also on a hanger, with snaps instead of buttons, and a bolo tie with an overgrown turquoise that wasn't quite as handsome as some that size, but what can you expect with a government disguise, the Kohinoor diamond? There were also socks and underwear.

"That's quite an outfit," I said. "You could put some sequins on it and bill me as the new cowboy Liberace. Those boots look like real toe-squashers."

"Wardrobe assures me they'll be a good fit."

"Wardrobe doesn't have to wear them."

For his own costume, Mac was sporting one of his customary gray business suits. He has them in every weight from tropical to arctic; this was kind of a medium number. A lean, gray-haired man of medium height, he looked as cold and ageless as ever. There's a theory floating around the Washington office to

4

the effect that he sold his soul to the devil in return for eternal life. I don't believe a word of it. No devil with a proper sense of self-preservation would deal with Mac for fear of being conned out of his pitchfork. He laid the clothes on the bed and studied me for a moment.

"Well, Eric," he said by way of greeting. It let me know that the makeup man was cleared, and we could talk normally. Otherwise Mac would have used my real name instead of my code name.

"Eric at the moment, sir," I said, "but who'll I be when this guy gets through with me?"

"You'll be a wealthy Texas oilman named Horace Hosmer Cody, known as Buffalo Bill Cody, or just plain Buff."

"Wealthy sounds good," I said. "Do I get an expense account to match?"

Mac ignored that as frivolous. "Mr. Cody, sixty-four, is just about to be married in the Little Chapel of the Bells, a few blocks from here. The bride is Gloria Henrietta Pierce, twenty-two, a very lovely young lady and reasonably wealthy in her own right."

"December and May," I said. "Do I gather that I'm being groomed to stand in for Mr. Cody at the altar when his child bride comes up the aisle all done up in a veil and white satin? How many people will I be expected to fool besides the girl herself? It doesn't sound very practical."

"It's an informal wedding," Mac said. "The bride will be wearing a suit and, as you see, the bridegroom's attire, although spectacular, will not be formal. No, we didn't feel you could carry off the impersonation in front of a chapel full of Mr. Cody's friends and acquaintances. The substitution will take place afterwards. The honeymoon car will be stopped in a quiet place, the real Horace Hosmer Cody will be arrested and spirited away, and you will slip into the driver's seat beside the blushing bride."

I said, "So she's in on it."

Mac nodded. "She is cooperating."

"Is he?"

5

"You will be given a general briefing shortly; later you can have the young lady herself fill in the details."

Clearly he hadn't come clear from Washington to answer a lot of questions. I said, "I suppose those are shots of the groom on the table. Do we have a picture of the bride?"

"Here."

I studied the glamorous wedding photograph. The girl was beautiful. Well, all brides are.

"Well, I've had worse-looking wives in the line of business," I said. "But why is a walking young dream like that, with money of her own, marrying a man almost three times her age? You'd think all she'd have to do was stand on a street corner and blow a whistle and take her choice."

"I repeat, she will tell you everything you need to know."

I said, "At least explain this arrest nonsense, sir. Since when do we go around arresting people?"

We're known, by the few who know about us, as a counter-assassination agency. When a homicidal individual or organization proves too much for the other fine, high-principled agencies of our government to cope with and still keep their hands clean, they send for us because we don't mind getting our hands dirty. Legally I suppose we're empowered to arrest people—under the proper circumstances, any citizen is—but it's not something we make a habit of. If you want somebody arrested, call a cop. Our methods are slightly more drastic.

Mac said dryly, "We won't be doing the arresting. We are involved simply because we just happened to have a man available who's the right size and shape for the job. Sometimes I think the rest of our government must be staffed entirely by short, fat men. When they need a tall, thin one, they invariably come knocking on our door."

I said, "Oh, God, not another beautiful friendship deal!"

"We call it interdepartmental cooperation." He picked up the phone between the beds, punched a number, and said, "He's almost ready for you, Warren. Five minutes. Room 512." Then he put the instrument down and spoke to me: "You will be under

6

the orders of the gentleman to whom I just spoke, Mr. Warren Somerset, or whomever he may deputize as your control."

"Control!" I said. "Jesus Christ, what is this, a TV superspy caper?"

The only control with whom we work is Mac himself. Sometimes it gets a little complicated, and he must feel like a juggler with a dozen airborne plates; but most of our operations are pretty straightforward, and he just points us in the right direction, gives us a gun and shove, and lets us run.

The makeup man stepped back, gave me a professional scrutiny, and said, "It is finished. As well as it can be done in so short a time. You wish to see yourself?"

I said, "I wish to see myself."

The hand mirror he gave me showed that I'd gained some years, turned as gray as Mac, and lost some hair.

"Very distinguished, no?" the makeup man said.

He was a nice enough little man and good at his job. I guess my only objection to what he'd done was that I seemed to age quite fast enough without help; I didn't need a hair-dye expert pushing me towards senility.

"Swell," I said. "Looking in the mirror, I could almost believe my name was Buffalo Bill, and I went in for cowboy boots and bolo ties."

"A fine job, Arthur," Mac said. "That's all." He watched the little man pick up his tools and bottles and hurry out; then he smiled faintly. "Mr. Somerset is going to complain that the resemblance is not really very great. I did not want Arthur to hear it. He's a very sensitive artist."

"Yes, sir." I couldn't help thinking that I'd never noticed him worrying about my sensitivity. Well, maybe I'm not an artist.

Mac spoke in a different tone, and I knew we were getting down to the business for which he'd come here. "You will do whatever Mr. Somerset requires, Eric, in the manner in which he requires it done, with one reservation. You will keep in mind that we want a man who calls himself Sábado, no description available. The reason for Señor Sábado's unpopularity does not concern you. You're about to be sent into Mexico. While you're

7

down there impersonating a loving bridegroom, keep your ears open for that name. We have reason to think that Sábado is closely involved in the problem with which you'll be asked to deal there; I'll let Warren Somerset brief you on that. However, when you have determined the identity of Señor Sábado, you are to find the man and make the touch even if it has to be done at the expense of Mr. Somerset and his operation. If you act with reasonable discretion, the Mexican authorities will be careful to look the other way. Do I make myself clear?"

I grimaced. So it was another piggyback job. Whenever he starts talking interdepartmental cooperation, you can bet there's some little unimportant errand he wants you to run under cover of the other agency's mission. Like dealing with a gent named Sábado who seemed to have made enemies on both sides of the border: We wanted him, and the Mexicans would apparently be glad to let us have him. Dead.

I said, "There's only one catch, sir."

"What's that?"

"I'm almost bound to hear the name before the week is up if I'm there that long. Sábado means Saturday in Spanish."

Mac frowned. "Indeed? It is not one of my languages, unfortunately. . . . Eric."

"Yes, sir."

"Forbearance is not a virtue. Any accomplices of Señor Sábado qualify for the same treatment. Oh, and you should be very careful. Don't take anything for granted. Things aren't necessarily what they seem."

CHAPTER 2

THEY don't build Cadillacs the generous way they used to; at least, the honeymoon heap was somewhat less than a block long. However, it was still a fairly sizeable vehicle, a sporty convertible called Allante. At the moment it wasn't at a Cadillac's dignified and silent best, since it was well-sprinkled with rice and dragging behind it a bunch of rattling tin cans.

We hadn't witnessed the ceremony or attended the subsequent champagne reception catered by the chapel management in the hall they maintained for the purpose across the street. We'd been lying in wait a couple of blocks away along the route the happy couple would take afterwards, we hoped. Mr. Somerset had determined that Buff Cody had reserved, for his wedding night, the honeymoon suite of El Presidente Hotel in Juárez, Mexico, just across the border from El Paso. There were only so many ways he could drive to get to the appropriate international bridge across the Rio Grande, and this was apparently the most likely.

The clattering white Cadillac attracted some amused attention when it appeared on schedule. Cars slowed to let their occupants look at it, and grinning pedestrians watched it turn into the grocery store parking lot where we waited. Safeway. Mr. Somerset, sitting beside me in the rear of the inconspicuous gray four-door sedan, from which he was masterminding the operation, cleared his throat in a satisfied way.

"Yes, it seems I guessed correctly. I thought he'd turn in here to get rid of the rice and junk, the first convenient area, safer than doing it at the curb on a busy street even if he could find a parking space. There was no risk; as I told you, we have him

9

covered. If he'd passed us up here, or taken another route, we'd have caught up with him and followed until he did stop. Or, if necessary, forced him to the curb; but I wanted to avoid that if possible. Mr. Cody may have become somewhat civilized in his wealthy old age, but he spent his lean younger years in some fairly rugged places. He's been known to carry a gun. It's unlikely he'd wear it to his wedding, but he could have put it in the car, and he might be hasty about using it."

I'd been waiting for an opening like that. I spoke deliberately: "A man after my own heart, it seems, sir. If you're going to use a gun at all, hasty is the only way. Waiting for the other guy to shoot first is for the birds. He might not miss."

Mr. Somerset said, rather stiffly, "That may be the attitude in your organization, Helm; but unlike you we are basically a law-enforcement agency, and our people are trained to wait until a real threat develops before employing deadly force."

I said, "How do you employ deadly force after somebody's shot you dead?"

He said irritably, "I don't know how we got on this irrelevant subject."

"Hardly irrelevant, sir," I said. "If I'm to work with you and your people, we'd better establish a few ground rules. As far as I'm concerned, a threat is a threat. I don't wait around to see whether it's 'real' or 'unreal' before I react; in fact, I don't understand what you mean by the distinction. Menace is menace, and I don't ever gamble my life on the chance that the guy may be bluffing or kidding. That's one reason I'm still here. Which means that on this job, if your boys approach me for any reason, they'd damned well better do it carefully, and empty-handed except for identification. Tell them that they do not jump out of the bushes at me and say *boo*, and they most particularly do not wave any weapons at me. I consider the muzzle of a firearm pointed my way to be a very unfriendly object, no matter what sweet things the mouth of the guy behind it is saying. I won't stop to listen; I'll just shoot the stupid bastard loose from his piece. Please pass the word, sir."

It was a little exaggerated, of course, a little flamboyant, and it was meant to be. While it wasn't the most diplomatic way of embarking on my latest career of interdepartmental cooperation, I didn't want any misunderstandings. The world is full of people who can hardly ask the time of day without brandishing a .357 Magnum. If he had any of those on his payroll and lost one, he couldn't claim I hadn't warned him. However, I had another reason for behaving objectionably: I wanted to see if he'd take it.

He started to get mad, of course. He was the head of an important government agency. He didn't like being given arrogant instructions by a mere field man like me. Furthermore, he obviously wanted to protest against my calm assumption that if I got into a shootout with one of his fine, supertrained operatives, I'd just naturally be the one to survive.

Nevertheless, he swallowed hard, and said, "Yes, we don't want any unfortunate accidents, you are quite right. I will advise my people of the difference in operating philosophies."

Okay. He needed me. Well, we'd already known that; I seemed to be the only reasonably competent person immediately available who could impersonate Horace Hosmer Cody for him. But what we hadn't known was how badly he needed me, badly enough to swallow his pride and accept the rude directive I'd given him—or at least pretend to accept it. I'd sensed it from the moment he entered the hotel room and greeted me in the overcordial fashion that people employ when meeting a member of a minority race they really think is pretty far down the evolutionary scale under circumstances in which they can't afford to show it because the guy is going to make them lots of money somehow. Mr. Somerset had stopped just inside the door to admire my disguise.

"Excellent!" he'd said. "Oh, that is very good! A very close resemblance indeed!" Coming forward, he held out his hand cordially. "You're Helm?"

"Yes, sir." I'd winked at Mac with my off eye to remind him that this wasn't the reaction he'd predicted. "Matthew Helm, sir," I said to Somerset.

I returned his handshake without too much muscle. Senior

11

officers, even senior civilian officers, love to be sirred and hate to have their hands crushed. I don't mind being tactful when it doesn't hurt.

Seeing that things were under control, Mac moved to the door, saying, "Well, there he is, Warren. I'll leave the briefing to you. I have a plane to catch."

Alone with Mr. Somerset, I took a moment to study my temporary commander-in-chief. He was a rather handsome man with a smoothly rounded face and very white teeth. Of medium height, he obviously worked hard at keeping himself tanned and trim and hated the fact that he was nevertheless a little thicker in the tummy than he used to be: not fat, not even chubby, just moderately well-upholstered and trying to conceal it. Brown hair, carefully blow-dried, probably helped out by a hairpiece although, if there was one, it was good enough that I couldn't be sure. A dark red suit—jacket and pants only, no vest—of some synthetic material that had a little gleam to it and a pink sports shirt worn with the tails out. And a stubble of beard.

It's the current fashion among the bright young people, I understand. The Happy Hobo look. Young women are supposed to look as if they'd slept in their clothes and forgotten to wash or comb their hair; young men are only in style if they appear to be recovering from a three-day drunk, still too shaky to consider using a razor, even an electric razor. But why this fairly senior bureaucratic character would fall for the gag baffled me for a moment; then I understood. He was worshipping at the altar of eternal youth. He was hoping that his thick hair, real or otherwise, his tanned face, his well-controlled middle, his sharp threads, and his fashionable chin shadow would fool people into thinking he was still one of the kids, still hip, even though he was well into his fifties.

The idea of being under the orders of a character who spent his time worrying about losing a couple of pounds, or saving what was left of his hair, or just looking youthful, wasn't encouraging since it meant he couldn't be too bright. Why brood about the years when you really can't do much about them? Nobody looks forward to senility, and I guess there were some nice things about being a kid, like the resilient muscles and snappy reflexes that went with the territory; but there are things to be said for being an adult, too. . . . Then I saw that the brown eyes watching me, estimating my reactions, were cold and clever. Mr. Warren Somerset knew exactly what I was thinking. He knew exactly the impression he was making because he'd worked very hard for it; and if I wanted to think him a youth-seeking fool, that was the point of the exercise. It would make it that much easier for him to put one over on me, if the occasion should arise—and maybe the occasion was right here, right now.

"I think we have time for a drink and a quick council of war," he said, with a glance at the gold watch on his left wrist that was the approximate diameter and thickness of a fifty-cent piece. "I see that your chief has left us the essentials. What's your pleasure?" He lifted a hand quickly. "Never mind. I've read your file, at least a carefully edited version designed for out-of-house people like me. I see no martini ingredients, so it's Scotch, I believe."

"Right, sir."

I took the glass he presented me. He was showing off, of course, demonstrating how well he'd researched this operation even down to my taste in liquor. I noted that his tipple was Perrier water. Well, maybe it was another of the youthful attitudes he was copying, or pretending to copy—these days a lot of the younger ones have the Demon Rum syndrome as badly as Carrie Nation—but maybe, on the other hand, it was one of the executive tricks they like to play to see if the underlings can be conned into drinking on duty, and if so, how much. To hell with him. I hadn't asked for employment; he'd asked for an employee. If he didn't like my personal habits he could find himself another Horace Hosmer Cody. Anyway, alcohol is a food, and it was the first nourishment I'd been offered since daybreak—hell, since supper the night before; I'd been interrupted in the process of catching my breakfast. I partook of the Scotch gratefully. Mr. Somerset waved me to a chair and pulled another around so he could sit down facing me.

"You must have been doing some guessing," he said.

"I never guess, sir," I said. "Why waste the effort of trying to anticipate what somebody's bound to tell me? Anyway, I haven't had much time for guessing. A few hours ago I was trying to interest a pan-sized trout in a small gold spinner. I've been on the move ever since." He waited as if he hadn't heard me. I shrugged and said, "Okay, I gather it's Mexico. But it isn't drugs."

He glanced at me sharply. "What makes you say that?"

"Because my chief wouldn't play if it were drugs. He says that boys and girls simply aren't gaining on it, they can't stop it any more than their predecessors could stop booze during Prohibition, and he won't risk any of his operatives in a lost cause even if it's a worthy lost cause."

Mr. Somerset laughed shortly. "Well, his attitude is practical if hardly idealistic."

He'd slipped just a little; a hint of anger had come through. They do get fanatical about it and deep down, apparently, he was one of the fanatics, although he was trying hard not to show it. Well, it's a serious problem all right, but I always wonder at people who wouldn't hand over a quarter to save a beggar from starvation—Mr. Somerset didn't look like a generous man to me—but are perfectly willing to spend millions to save him from sticking a needle into his arm.

I said, "If idealism is what you want, you've come to the wrong shop, sir." I took a slug of Scotch. It glowed warmly in my empty stomach. I went on as if I hadn't spotted his betraying reaction. "So it isn't drugs; and I doubt that the U.S. government would be sending me into Mexico to track down the lost treasure of the Aztecs or the missing gold of the Sierra Madre, although there are plenty of legends about both. And it seems unlikely that there's a sudden official interest in señoritas and margaritas. Which leaves, among the objectives usually sought below the border, only arms or politics. Or arms and politics. Although why a Texas millionaire would be involved with either, I couldn't guess."

Mr. Somerset nodded approvingly. "Very good, Helm. The answer to your question, if it was a question, is that our millionaire Mr. Cody will stop being a millionaire if he doesn't do something drastic soon—drastic and profitable. The decline in oil prices caught him seriously overextended."

"I see. So he's looking for *mucho dinero*. How does he hope to get it?"

"It seems that he had a two-pronged strategy in mind. For his long-term requirement, matrimony apparently seemed the best solution to his difficulties. However, it takes time to get married and squeeze money out of a rich wife, one way or another, so while he was working on that he looked toward Mexico for, let's say, a quick buck. I suppose I should say that his strategy was three-pronged, since he did try the usual method of obtaining instant wealth; but his attempt at drug smuggling failed and cost him part of his remaining funds. He escaped arrest, but the little adventure brought him to our attention, and he was wary enough not to try it again. His next effort . . . What do you know about the political situation in Mexico, Helm?"

I shrugged. "Not too much, I'm afraid." He gave me that waiting silence again, so after a moment I continued: "Well, they've had the same political party in power for umpty-umpteen years, each president designating his successor. The Institutional Revolutionary Party, or PRI. There are elections, but they're pretty much rubber-stamp affairs, or were until recently, when the PRI was challenged by parties both left and right and barely made it. There seems to be a lot of dissatisfaction. The Mexican economy is a shambles, and the peso was a couple of thousand to the dollar and climbing last I heard. If things don't improve, there could be some kind of a popular revolt, not necessarily at the ballot box. The old Winchester .30-30 used to be the primary instrument of political change down there; most of Mexico's history since the time of Spanish rule has come out of a gun barrel. A man with a nice lot of, say, modern M-16s for sale complete with ammo, not to mention heavier stuff . . . Well, the major opposition parties seem to be a little too stuffy and respectable for revolution, but there are other protest groups, and I shouldn't think it would be hard to find a bunch of hotheads

15

willing to use the arms. Finding a bunch of hotheads capable of paying for them would be harder, of course; and if this should be the way Cody hopes to bail himself out until his new wife's money becomes available, he'd want a cash deal. A big cash deal.''

Mr. Somerset chuckled. ''For a man who doesn't know much about Mexican politics, you paint a very clear picture. With Cody's rather colorful background in the oil industry, and his international connections, obtaining and transporting arms would not be difficult. He undoubtedly has unsavory contacts around the world. As you say, his big problem would be finding somebody who wants the weapons *and* is in a position to pay well for them; but apparently it's a problem he's managed to solve. He's come to an agreement with a minor but well-financed Mexican political group that calls itself the National Liberty Party or, in their political shorthand, PLN. We understand that the guns are on their way.''

''Where and how?'' I asked.

He hesitated. ''Unknown.''

''And I presume my job is to make it known,'' I said.

He nodded. ''Yes, that's the major objective of your mission.''

I thought about it for a moment. I could see a lot of ramifications, mostly unfavorable to success, and probably even to survival.

I sighed. ''Well, give me the gory details. I suppose the idea is that somebody'll make contact with me on this Mexican honeymoon and whisper everything you want to know in my eager ear. . . .''

It was apparently one of my better guessing days. I was pretty close, and he straightened me out on the details and gave me elaborate instructions; and here we were behind the big Safeway store watching the man whose bridegroom spot I was supposed to usurp—well, within limits—get out of the rice-sprinkled and tin-can-adorned Caddy. Bareheaded at the moment, he had exactly the lanky, dressed-up cowboy look that Arthur, the makeup artist, had made a big effort to bestow on me.

Men who spend their lives working in the sun don't generally worry about getting smooth, even, facial tans; they wear hats or caps habitually to keep their brains from frying. Although he'd made his millions, Buff Cody had the mark: the weathered face and the pale, protected forehead. Old habit made him reach behind the car seat now and bring forth a white Stetson identical to the one in my lap and clap it on his head.

The face I saw across the parking lot, the same face I'd seen in Arthur's color photographs, was that of a tough, opinionated man who'd been, as we say out west, to the head of the creek and the top of the mountain. I wouldn't expect him to have many scruples, and I wouldn't want to cross him without a club in my hand. On the other hand, he wasn't a man I disliked or despised on sight. He looked like a reasonably cheerful old ruffian. I'd expect all his sins to be large ones. He carried a little more weight than I did, but not a significant amount. His movements were those of a younger man, so I wasn't going to have to pretend to creeping senility; and he held himself straight, so a kink in the spine would not be required. The neat, closely trimmed bristle of gray beard made his face pretty anonymous under the wide hat brim. It might work out at that, I reflected. Cody went to the rear of the car to cut the strings holding the tin cans, using a pocketknife of modest size.

"That's not the kind of knife I'm carrying," I said.

"We hope you won't meet anybody who knows what kind of knife Mr. Cody carries. If he does, he'll probably also know what Mr. Cody looks like. . . . There's the young woman now."

"To hell with the young woman," I said. "I'm going to have plenty of time to look at her later."

Beyond a quick glance, I paid no attention to the girl who'd emerged from the convertible and, after smoothing down her white suit, had reached into the back of the car for a small whisk broom, with which she'd started brushing away the rice. I'm as dedicated a girl-watcher as anybody under ordinary circumstances, but the man was the one I'd have to impersonate, and this was the only chance I'd have to study him before I went into my act. . . .

17

"Able, Able, this is Baker."

Mr. Somerset reached for the microphone. "Able here."

"One man tailing bridal couple. We've taken him out of circulation."

"Nobody else interested?"

"No. The Caddy's clean now."

"Very well. You may send in the arrest team."

"Acknowledged. Baker out."

Waiting there, we saw two men, one long and one short, both in neat, three-piece suits, appear from somewhere among the parked cars and cross the lot briskly. They were marching in step, which, considering the disparity in leg lengths, took some doing. Horace Hosmer Cody, having got rid of his car's noisy decorations, straightened up and turned to face them as they approached. He looked as if he was wondering, in a normal way, who they were and what they were up to; I could detect no other reaction. He studied the IDs he was shown, started to protest, and was quickly and expertly spun around with his wrists yanked behind him, instantly handcuffed. For a man with a moderately violent background, he'd been easy to take, I reflected; but the Mutt-and-Jeff team had known its business, and I guess a man isn't at his most alert on his wedding day. The girl in the white suit stood looking after her husband of less than an hour as he was marched away. I couldn't read her expression.

"Come on, Helm," said Mr. Somerset. "I mean, Mr. Horace Cody. Let me introduce you to Mrs. Cody."

CHAPTER 3

THE girl was breathtaking in the way a work of art can be breathtaking. She would, of course, have been even more spectacular in a long satin gown, a jeweled tiara, and a veil; but she was still a vision in her smart silk wedding suit with her blond hair piled onto her head in golden swirls. Some kind of retaining spray had obviously been used to insure that not a single rebellious strand would escape. She was a moderately tall girl, nicely constructed, slender but by no means ethereal. The jacket of her suit, worn without a blouse, was cut low enough above to reveal the graceful throat and, discreetly, the upper curves of the breasts; it flared a bit below to emphasize the narrow waist and rounded hips. The skirt was slim and straight.

The elaborate wedding gown customarily worn, and the endless yards of veiling, tend to overpower the human being inside the bridal glamour, giving the impression that the face is a beautiful blank. Even in her less formal costume this young woman was, to some extent, victim of the same effect. It was hard to analyze the girl-face behind the meticulous lipstick and dramatic eye makeup, all framed by the intricately sculptured hairdo. I had to concentrate on it, feature by feature, to determine that the eyes were blue, the cheekbones were good, the nose was straight, but the mouth could probably pout given an excuse— well, many rich kids tend toward that spoiled and dissatisfied look.

Gloria Pierce, now Gloria Cody, merely nodded in response

to Mr. Somerset's introduction. She had something more important on her mind.

"You did make the legal arrangements, I hope," she said. "I would hate to think that I was really married to . . . to that man!"

Somerset said soothingly, "Have no fear; we took all steps necessary to insure that the ceremony would not be valid."

"Well, it wasn't a very nice experience anyway! I found it very hard to keep smiling at him in proper bridal fashion." She condescended to look my way at last. "What's this one's name?"

"You don't need to know his name, Miss . . . Mrs. Cody."

She sighed unhappily. "Yes, I suppose I'll have to call myself that for a while, won't I? Until this man gets your job done, whatever it is. . . . The resemblance isn't really very great."

"He isn't supposed to fool anybody who really knows Mr. Cody; we aren't playing The Prisoner of Zenda here."

"Has it been explained to him that if he takes this pseudo-marriage too seriously the whole deal is off?"

"It has been explained to him."

"Then what are we waiting for?" She spoke directly to me for the first time: "Horace always did the driving, so you'd better."

"Yes, ma'am."

I helped her into the car and went around to get behind the wheel. Since Cody was as tall as I was, the seat was already set right for my legs, and the steering-wheel adjustment was comfortable. I started the engine and studied the dials for a moment, not so much to see what they read as to learn where they were. Well, at least the bridal barge did have instruments.

"Well?" said my companion impatiently.

I waved a friendly hand at Somerset, although his friendship wasn't something in which I had much faith, and took us out of there. When the Safeway and its parking lot had vanished behind us, I said, "Helm. Matthew Helm."

She glanced at me sharply. "Your name?"

20

I nodded. "That need-to-know nonsense is a pain in the butt. Those bureaucrats get all tangled up in their own security."

She was looking around, frowning. "Where are we going? You should have kept straight at that last intersection, for Juárez."

I said, "We're not going to Juárez."

"But we have reservations—"

"Buff Cody never had any intention of picking up that hotel reservation in Juárez. He was planning to make contact with someone at dinnertime in a small Mexican town called Cananea some two hundred miles to the west. Mr. Green's Restaurant, if you'll believe it. Fine old Spanish name. We're going to keep Mr. Cody's appointment. Afterwards, he was planning on spending his wedding night with you in the Hotel Gandara in Hermosillo, about a hundred and fifty miles farther on. With luck we'll make that, too, without too much night driving, which is not recommended in Mexico."

She said, "That's around three hundred and fifty miles. I thought we'd just be ducking across the Rio Grande to our honeymoon hotel." She glanced down at her shining costume. "I'm not exactly dressed for long-distance touring."

I said, "Cody was probably counting on that, figuring that nobody'd expect him to take any vigorous evasive action with both of you still in your wedding clothes."

She said, "Now we seem to be heading north. That's hardly the way to get to Mexico."

Well, at least the girl knew her compass directions. I said, "We've lost our tail, at least temporarily. Buff Cody's tail. He was taken into custody just before Cody himself, to clear the scene for the substitution. Presumably Cody had figured out some other way of escaping surveillance. We don't know what route he planned to take to Cananea, but we're taking the interstate west, I-10. We'll run it as far as Lordsburg, New Mexico. Even though it takes us a little out of the way, we can make better time up there on the U.S. freeways than we could on the little Mexican roads south of the border. From Lordsburg—well, a few miles beyond Lordsburg—we'll cut back down across a corner of Arizona to Douglas, which is on the border. From there we'll cross over into Agua Prieta, Sonora, Mexico, and continue west on their Highway 2. Okay?''

She asked, "How do you know what . . . what Horace was planning?''

I grinned. "Don't ask. I didn't. I think there was a snitch involved, an informer. Actually, I understand you met him; he's the guy who told you some unpalatable truths about your elderly fiancé that made you decide to cooperate with Mr. Somerset.''

Gloria made a wry face. "Yes, a nasty little man, but would he know all of . . . all of Horace's plans in such detail?''

I said, "Perhaps not, but Cody's activities had already attracted attention, and I'm sure Somerset had him under close surveillance. I don't think our federal friend is a man who bothers with official authorization for every wiretap he uses; and then there are gadgets like parabolic mikes. . . . Unfortunately you see before you an obsolete secret agent. I don't know much about that newfangled stuff. My main qualification for the job is that I learned to shoot pretty good as a kid.''

"I hate guns," she said.

I managed to stifle a groan, I hoped. I was heading into a foreign country pretending to be a man I didn't look much like and messing with a potential revolution in a way that could make me a target for both sides. All I needed to make it a real suicide mission was to be stuck with one of the beautiful, nonviolent, gun-hating people as my partner.

I said, "It's going to be a long drive. Why don't you recline that fancy seat and take a nap?''

She turned on me fiercely, "Don't you dare change the subject in that condescending way! I think guns are terrible and I think men who use them are terrible. That's one reason why I had to do that to Horace! Regardless of everything else, he was my father's partner, and I've known him a very long time. I couldn't have deceived him like that, smiling at him in the chapel in front of all those people and giving him his wedding kiss like a female Judas if . . .'' She drew a long breath. "But Mr.

Somerset said he was going to import all kinds of dreadful weapons for people who planned to overthrow the Mexican government by force, as if we didn't have enough violence and enough stupid, bloody revolutions in this world already. If there was a chance of stopping it by helping Mr. Somerset, I had to do it, didn't I?''

She sounded as if she was trying to convince herself; and I thought better of her for feeling a touch of guilt—after all, whether or not he deserved it, she had deliberately used her feminine wiles to first lead a man to the altar, and then to the slaughter.

I said, ''Horace. Is that what he liked to be called by you?''

She said, ''Well, all my life I've called him Uncle Buffy, but I could hardly go on calling him that after we decided to get married; I'd have sounded like an idiot child playing at matrimony with her mama's diamond on her pinkie. And I wasn't going to call him Buffalo Bill like some of his roughneck friends, or even Buff; and in this day and age I wasn't about to go all respectful and call him Mr. Cody even if he was somewhat older than I. So we settled on Horace for him, and he called me Glory.''

''Hi, Glory.''

She gave me a reluctant smile. ''Hi, Horace,'' she said. The smile faded. ''And I do hate guns and violence. Do you think I'd have betrayed him like that otherwise? Even though he . . .'' She stopped.

''Even though he what?''

She shook her head. ''Not now. We'll talk about it later. I think I will rest a bit now. It's been . . . a lot of strain, playing Delilah.''

She used the tricky seat adjustments to allow her to lie back comfortably, first making sure that her skirt wasn't tucked up so it would wrinkle or show me anything I wasn't supposed to see. She closed her eyes. We were soon out of Texas; in that direction it terminates a few miles outside El Paso. As I followed the big four-lane highway across the arid New Mexico plains, with a steep, jagged mountain range off to the east, I saw that her breathing was soft and steady in sleep. . . .

We had no trouble at the border. As a rule, driving south into Mexico, only two classes of people have trouble at the border: the cheapskates who can't bear to part with a little cash and the highly moral folks who feel that it's terribly, terribly wrong to present a foreign official with a small monetary reward for his services. I'm not particularly tightfisted at any time, certainly not when operating on a government expense account, and morality isn't a big thing in our agency, so we went through in a breeze.

"You didn't have to be *quite* so generous!" My lovely young bride, who'd been awake since we'd made our first pit stop in New Mexico, spoke tartly as we drove away. "You're the great Mexico expert, of course; but even I could tell they'd have been happy with a buck or two apiece. A veritable blizzard of five-dollar bills was not indicated."

"That's my girl," I said. "You're doing fine. You sound just like an honest-to-God, genuine wife."

She started to make some kind of a retort, but glanced around and said instead: "You'd better pay a little attention to your navigation, mister. That doesn't look much like a main highway out of town up ahead. Unless their roads are even lousier than I remember."

She was perfectly right. I must have taken a wrong turn somewhere or, since I'd made no turns, failed to take the right one, forgetting that Mexican road signs tend to be inconspicuous when they aren't totally nonexistent. Actually, I was far from being the great Mexico expert she'd called me. Although I'd spent my younger years in the border state of New Mexico and crossed into old Mexico frequently, my knowledge of the language is rudimentary; and I hadn't been down here recently. . . . Counting back, I was shocked to realize that it had been well over ten years since, also in the line of duty, I'd last made this crossing from Douglas to Agua Prieta. Dark Water, to you.

I saw that we'd reached the ragged and run-down edge of the town. The low buildings were adobe brick from which, in many cases, the plaster had flaked off if it had ever existed. The street could be called paved, but you had to dodge the numerous and sizeable potholes; beyond the next cross street it degenerated abruptly into a dirt track leading across a cow pasture. As my ersatz bride had pointed out, it was clearly not the highway we wanted.

I made a U-turn and started back the way we'd come only to have a loafer outside a shabby cantina wave a warning hand to let me know that I was proceeding the wrong way up a one-way street. They don't mark them any more clearly than the highways; there's only an occasional, casual little arrow painted on the corner of a building or tacked to a telephone pole. I U-turned again—fortunately there was very little traffic here—and pulled up beside the gent who'd warned me. I hit the switch to bring down the right-hand window. The honeymoon heap boasted every power convenience known to man, including some I hadn't figured out yet.

I leaned across the front seat and called, "Cananea, *por favor*."

The man came forward, frowning. My pronunciation was apparently a little off; he hadn't caught the name. When I repeated it, he grinned happily, showing big, white teeth in a dark, unshaved face.

"Ah, *Cananea!*"

He proceeded to let me know, with gestures and rapid-fire Spanish, exactly where I'd gone astray and in what manner I should now conduct myself in order to rectify my unfortunate error. How they choose to speak their language is their business, of course, but they'd make it easier for dumb *gringos* if they slowed it down a bit. The elaborate sign language helped, however. I got the general idea, thanked my informant profusely, and drove away.

My companion wasn't impressed. "Terrific!" she said sourly. "People are trying to kill me, I'm coerced into doing crazy things like pretending to be the wife of a perfect stranger; and it turns out that the high-powered guide and protector they've married me to, more or less, can't even find his way through

25

the first Mexican town we hit without asking directions from a sidewalk bum!''

I glanced at her sharply. ''What's this about killing?''

She said, ''I suppose I'll have to tell you all about it, but let's not overload your feeble intelligence until it's got us on the right road.''

CHAPTER 4

I found the main road and made the prescribed turn. The town of Agua Prieta fell behind us. The Mexican landscape was bleak and rugged. It was covered with low, spiny brush punctuated by prickly cactus and thorny mesquite. That southwestern vegetation takes its defenses seriously. The highway was a narrow, winding, patched strip of blacktop that was not designed for a freeway locomotive like our Allante; but the beast had fairly quick power steering, and its suspension wasn't too soggy. I'd driven worse roads in less suitable automobiles.

The day was sunny, the sky was very blue, and the desert air was so clear that the hills on the distant horizon were as sharply defined as those nearby; there were no atmospheric gradations whatever. It was a good day on which to start on a honeymoon, but I would have preferred to pick my girl and have nothing on my mind but love. As it was, I was conscious of having been thrown into this job very low on information; and I couldn't help wondering how much of what I'd been told in the rush was the truth. Mr. Somerset with his careful, three-day whiskers wasn't a gent who inspired a great deal of confidence in me, although he seemed to have sold himself thoroughly to Gloria. But where business is concerned, there's only one man I trust—and even Mac has been known to pull a swifty occasionally. Or two or three. He was doing it now, of course. He'd thrown me into this mess with the warning that things weren't what they seemed, which is as much warning as he ever gives us; just enough, he hopes, to keep us from spoiling the operation by getting killed.

As I drove, I glanced at the girl who shared with me the fancy

27

car belonging to the man whose name I'd appropriated along with his brand-new wife. Gloria sensed my attention and gave a pull to her skirt, brushed away an imaginary smudge, and grimaced.

"It's not exactly the costume I'd have chosen for a Mexican tour, but at least I'm getting some wear out of it," she said dryly. "At one point, I was about to stuff it all into the fireplace and pour charcoal lighter all over it and watch it burn."

"Seems kind of drastic," I said mildly. "An expensive bonfire, by the looks of it."

Her voice was suddenly harsh: "How do you think a girl feels about the gorgeous wedding outfit she's picked very carefully to please the man she's about to marry. . . . How do you think she feels after learning that this wonderful man is planning to murder her for her money afterwards?" Gloria shook her head quickly. "Oh, it wasn't that my heart was broken or anything like that. Our marriage was more a practical arrangement than a passionate romance; after all, he was quite literally old enough to be my father. I'd known him all my life; he'd been Papa's friend and partner since before I was born. Good old Uncle Buffy! And all those years I'd believed in that kindly, helpful, sympathetic . . . I didn't love him, not in a romantic way, but he was an old, trusted friend, a solid rock. . . . Oh, God, you can't *stand* being so wrong about somebody, the sneaky old bastard!"

I said deliberately, "So you got back at him by preserving your expensive bridal finery to use in a phony wedding instead of burning it. You didn't let him know you were onto him; instead you got hold of the proper authorities and set him up. Or did they get hold of you?"

"They got hold of me, of course." She shook her head ruefully. "I never suspected a thing, and I wouldn't have known where to go if I had. I'm sure the police would just have treated me as a hysterical girl with the bridal jitters. After all, Horace is a wealthy and respected citizen. I didn't believe it myself when Mr. Somerset first told me, and I thought his proposition was downright wild. It wasn't until he proved to me what Uncle

28

Buffy was planning. . . . After that, I had no choice but to co-operate, did I? I had to go through with the wedding so Mr. Somerset could make this crazy bridegroom switch, although I still don't understand what it's supposed to accomplish."

I said, "Well, it's supposed to lead us to the arms somehow, but don't ask me exactly how. Presumably we'll know more after we've made contact with this character Cody arranged to meet in Cananea." After a moment, I went on: "So you'd known him all your life? Cody?"

She nodded. "Yes. He was always there, off and on, as far back as I can remember, good old beanpole Uncle Buffy, seven feet tall in his cowboy boots—well, almost—and so skinny he used to say he had to stand twice in the same place to cast a shadow. A real Gary Cooper type. He's a little more substantial nowadays, but not much. Well, you saw him. He used to bring me lollipops and ice cream cones when I was a little girl. He never forgot Christmas or my birthday; he'd always send me something wonderful even when he couldn't bring it himself, like when I was going to school in the East."

I glanced at her. "So that's where the accent went," I said. "I wondered. I haven't heard you cut loose with a single Texas you-all, not one."

She grimaced. "Yes, they did a pretty good job of beating it out of me, those eastern bitches. I don't know why they had to pick on me. Some of those honey-chile southern belles in the school talked pretty funny, too. But Papa said I'd better play along. . . . " She drew a long breath. "You know that my father was murdered here in Mexico?"

I nodded, preoccupied with the immediate traffic situation. I gauged my distances, pulled around a slow-moving semi, and ducked back into the right-hand lane in time to miss an oncoming bus. You can take a bus anywhere in Mexico a car can go and some places you'd think it can't.

I said, "I gather that after your daddy died, down here in Mexico, strange things started happening to you in El Paso. Peculiar enough that you finally took your troubles to good ole Buff Cody, your late parent's friend and business partner."

She drew a long breath. "Yes, stupid me, but how could I guess. . . . It seemed like the natural thing to do, at the time. I went to his office, and . . . and I was so scared and confused, with Papa dead like that and all those weird things going on, that I broke into tears telling him about it. He gave me his hanky to blow my nose on, just like when I fell off my pony when I was a kid; and he asked me some questions. Then he told me to run along and he'd put some of his people to work on finding out the score. He told me to be real careful until he got it all taken care of; and he turned me around and shoved me toward the door, whacking me affectionately across the rear of my smart tailored slacks just like he used to slap the seat of my dirty jeans when I was a little girl. . . . Only I wasn't a little girl anymore and suddenly, when he touched me like that, we both knew it."

"He'd never made a pass at you when you were little?"

She shook her head. "Oh, I always used to kiss him hello and good-bye, the way you kiss family. He was family, Uncle Buffy, and I'd sit on his lap sometimes, but he never . . . No, no passes, although just the other day he told me that he'd surely had a hard time keeping his hands off me all those years, I was such a purty li'l thang." She smiled grimly. "But kids don't know. God, he was Papa's friend, he was Papa's age; and it never occurred to me to think of him that way. Until that day. But we didn't say anything that day."

I asked, "How did the subject of matrimony finally come up between you and Uncle Buffy?"

She said, "Well, the first time I was almost killed after . . . after Papa died, I naturally assumed it was an accident. This crazy man in a pickup cut in and ran me into the ditch, but I was lucky, it was a shallow ditch. I was just bounced around a bit, and it didn't even hurt my little Mercedes. I didn't even need a wrecker; a couple of nice men stopped and got behind and shoved when I stepped on the gas, and she came right up to the road. I was mad, of course, drivers like that shouldn't be allowed loose, but it didn't occur to me, when it happened, that it might have been deliberate. But that night I got a phone call: 'You were lucky, lady, but we'll get you next time just like we got your daddy.' "

She stopped and was silent for a moment, clearly reliving the experience.

I asked, "What kind of a voice, male or female?"

"I thought male, but it was really just a hoarse whisper."

"Did you get in touch with the police?"

"Yes, but they didn't seem to take it very seriously. I wasn't hurt, my car wasn't damaged, and it was just another crank call, a dime a dozen. And then, a few days later, I was getting ready to get into the car after breakfast. It was a cold, mean morning and there had been some rain and sleet during the night. At the last moment, after unlocking the Mercedes, I leaned over to make sure the windshield wiper blades hadn't frozen to the windshield. There was a funny, slapping noise and a distant report; and the car jerked a little. When I looked, there was a bullet hole, right about where I'd been standing when I reached for the windshield wiper. I was petrified for a moment; then I ran back into the house and called the police again."

"Did you get their attention this time?" I asked.

She laughed shortly. "Oh, yes. Car crashes and nut calls just bore them, but a firearm seems to wake them up a bit. They came out and figured angles and trajectories and decided that the shot had come from the overgrown vacant lot a little ways up the street on the other side, but it was pretty tangled in there, and they didn't find any cartridge cases."

"What about the bullet?"

"It went right through the car from left to right. I had to have both doors fixed and it cost me quite a lot. But it missed the corner of the garage and went rambling on over the little ridge we're on. No dead people have been reported, so it didn't hit anybody, wherever it came down. The police said the holes looked as if they were .22 caliber, but they had a big argument as to whether it was the rimfire .22 or the centerfire .22. They decided that it had to be the centerfire because it was powerful enough to penetrate both doors. I hope that makes sense to you. It doesn't to me."

31

I said, "The rimfire is the little one all ranch kids used to grow up with including me. It'll kill a man, or a woman, but you wouldn't normally pick it for that. There are several center-fires to choose from, but the most likely is the .223, or 5.56mm, used in the Army M-16 assault rifle. It's certainly a killing round, although if I were doing it myself I'd pick a larger caliber to make sure." I glanced at her. "In case you're curious, the little one has its priming compound around the inside of the rim of the cartridge case, rimfire. The big ones have their primers in the center of the case head, centerfire. Now you know."

"Thank you. I don't know how I've managed to live so long without that information," she said dryly. She gave me a sideways look. "You sound as if you really know something about it."

"I've been there. On both the giving and the receiving ends."

She licked her lips. "Then you know what it's like walking down the street after you've been shot at, feeling as if every window has a gun in it aimed straight at you! It took me hours to get up nerve enough to leave the house and I thought I'd faint every time somebody slammed a car door. It was an awful day; and that night there was another phone call: 'You can't be lucky all the time, lady. Your daddy wasn't.' This time the voice was definitely masculine. I didn't even call the police again, what was the use? I just took a sleeping pill to knock myself out; and the next morning I went to Uncle Buffy, as I told you, and cried on his shoulder."

"And he patted you on the head—well, fanny—and told you to be careful, big help."

She made a face. "Yes, that's right. And that night I tried to kill myself."

CHAPTER 5

AMONG U.S. tourists you'll hear a lot of horror stories about crazy Mexican drivers, but you won't hear them from me. It's simply a conflict between two automotive philosophies: defensive vs. aggressive driving. The American driver gets into a car to be safe; progress is a secondary consideration. The Mexican driver gets into a car to get somewhere; survival is in the hands of the gods. Since I wouldn't be in the line of work I'm in if I were obsessed with safety, I find this kind of uninhibited motoring quite enjoyable; and we made good time—well, good time for that twisty little road.

I reviewed what Mr. Somerset had told me about the girl's recent bereavement. William Walter Pierce, 62, Will to. his friends, husband of Henrietta Barstow Pierce, who'd died of cancer eight years ago, and father of Gloria Henrietta Pierce, had been murdered the previous month along with a female companion, Millicent Charles, widow, 48. The crime had been committed along the highway leading from Mazatlán, Sinaloa, Mexico, to Durango, Durango, Mexico. Mazatlán is on the west coast, at sea level. Durango is about two hundred miles inland and six thousand feet up. Or three hundred and twenty kilometers and two thousand meters, if you prefer the local units of measurement.

I remembered the road in question, although it had been a long time since I'd driven it. Some six hundred miles south of us, it was the next major east-west highway crossing the mountains that form the backbone of Mexico. By major highway I mean that it was paved all the way and could be negotiated by

33

an ordinary car or truck if the driver was possessed of reasonable skill and patience. However, unless it had changed greatly since the last time I'd seen it, and the map showed no signs of that, it was no more a superhighway than the roller-coaster track we were on.

Will Pierce's Lincoln had been spotted by one of the green rescue trucks that cruise all Mexico's main roads—you see few if any speed cops but plenty of these angels of mercy, which seem like a nice twist. Actually, the *zopilotes* had been first on the scene. The Green Angels, as the rescue units are called, soon determined that the big scavenger birds really had no interest in the car, although it had been badly vandalized; their attention was focused on the bodies of Pierce and Mrs. Charles lying nearby. His wallet and her purse had been robbed of all money and tossed aside. His watch and her watch and jewelry were missing. Their luggage had been hauled out of the trunk of the car and thoroughly trashed. He had apparently tried to resist; a machete had almost severed one arm before it split his skull. She had been stripped and sexually abused before another machete stroke had almost beheaded her as she knelt before her tormentors.

The authorities had conceded that perhaps there were a few antisocial elements hiding out in the Sierra Madre Occidental but promised that the criminals would soon be brought to justice. The same authorities had stated that this tragic incident was deeply regretted, but potential tourists should note that such crimes were extremely rare and that violence was no more likely to be encountered along a Mexican highway than on a New York street. Which, to anyone acquainted with New York streets, wasn't quite as reassuring as it was meant to be.

Even at the time of my hasty briefing, I'd had some doubts about those roadside *bandidos*. Now, after hearing Gloria's story, I found it hard to sell myself on a bunch of primitive Mexican desperados who first hacked the daddy and his lady friend to death with machetes down in Durango, Mexico, and then came charging up to Texas, U.S.A., to harry the daughter with pickup trucks and sniper rifles. On the other hand, I couldn't quite swallow the notion that the attacks on two members of the same family within a few weeks had been perpetrated by two groups of criminals operating quite independently of each other.

"Well?" said my companion sharply.

"Well, what?"

"Aren't you going to ask?"

"Ask what?"

"If I really tried to kill myself."

"Did you really try to kill yourself, Mrs. Cody?"

She made a face at me. "Do I look like the suicidal type?"

"What happened?"

She said, "I'd gone to bed early. I was alone in the house. We . . . I don't have any live-in help, just a yardman, Aurelio, who works as much as needed to keep the grounds in shape, and a . . . well, I guess you'd call her a housekeeper, Teresa, who comes in time to make lunch and leaves when she's cleaned up after dinner. I couldn't sleep. I kept hearing noises the way you do when it's dark and there's nobody else in the house. After a while I just had to get up and look around."

"Unarmed?"

She glanced at me irritably. "I've told you how I feel about guns! Anyway, Papa's are all locked up in a steel cabinet he had built into the wall of his study. Even if I'd been able to put my hands on the key in a hurry, I wouldn't have known how to get the bullets into them, and I'd probably have wound up shooting my foot off. Or my head."

"Go on."

"Well, I went all through the house and didn't find anything. Anybody. I came back to my bedroom and took off my slippers and dressing gown and started into the bathroom to . . . well, to pee. There's a kind of little dressing room I have to go through, with all my dresses hanging along one wall. Just as I reached into the bathroom and turned on the light, I heard something rustle among the clothes behind me. He must have slipped into my room from the rear of the house while I was looking around in front where I'd heard the noise."

"Maybe he had a partner making a noise to draw you away," I said.

She said, "I wasn't thinking about any partners; the man himself was scary enough. The big bathroom mirror faces the door. I could see him in the glass, a big dark man who needed a shave, stepping out from among my dresses to grab me. I tried to get into the bathroom and close the door, but he grabbed my hair and yanked me back. He put some kind of a weird hold on my neck. When he squeezed hard, not choking me, just digging into the side of my neck, I blacked out. When I woke up I was in a hospital bed."

We live in different worlds. I couldn't imagine myself at any age, after having a parent murdered and surviving two attempts on my own life, not locating the key to Pop's gun cabinet and figuring out how to use one of the weapons inside—assuming I didn't already know how—and then packing it everywhere, even into the john. But I keep discovering that most other people, particularly female people, don't think that way, which I suppose is why I'm in the business I'm in and they aren't.

I said, "And they told you you'd tried to commit suicide?"

She nodded. "They had it all figured out, damn them. They'd decided that I'd been brooding about the terrible thing that had happened to Papa and Millie Charles. . . . I suppose you've been told all about that."

"Yes."

"Well, in my depressive mood, a minor car accident and a kid letting off a little .22 carelessly seemed to have given me the silly idea that somebody was trying to murder me, too. Perfectly ridiculous, of course, but you know how we paranoiacs are." Her voice was dry. "I suppose you've heard the old joke: Just because I'm paranoid doesn't mean somebody isn't trying to kill me!"

"I've heard it."

She went on: "It was all supposed to have been just too much for me, I'm such a tender bud, you understand. I'd led a nice, sheltered, happy, comfortable life and first my mother had died in that horrible way, and then my father had been killed even more dreadfully, and now people were trying to murder me, too, and I just couldn't stand this scary world I found myself in any longer. So I'd rounded up all the sleeping pills in the house and gulped them down and got into bed to die. Only, Uncle Buffy tried to call me about something and got worried when I didn't answer the phone. He drove over and saw my car in the drive so he knew I was home; but I didn't respond when he rang the bell and even banged hard on the front door. He remembered that I'd been in a state when I talked to him in his office that morning. He broke in and found me lying unconscious in bed and called 911; and wasn't I glad I wasn't dead the way I'd tried to make myself, silly me?''

I glanced at her profile as I drove. "Did you try to set them straight?''

"Yes, of course. The psychiatrist they sicced on me thought it was a healthy sign. The fact that I refused to accept the indisputable fact that I'd tried to kill myself indicated that I rejected my hasty action and wasn't likely to try again. However, there was, he said, not the slightest evidence of intruders or of a struggle; and didn't I think it was kind of a ridiculous story anyway, people hiding in my closet and cramming barbiturates down my throat?''

We were climbing now, and the narrow blacktop pavement was getting pretty bad, even more broken and patched than it had been. We'd already passed a couple of highway crews shoveling tarry gravel into the worst holes; about as effective as sticking a Band-Aid on a fatal wound.

Gloria said, "After that little encounter I gave up trying to convince the hospital people. They wouldn't listen; they just hushed me like an unreasonable child. But when Uncle Buffy came around and gave me the same maddening routine . . . Well, he was sweet, he'd brought me some flowers and a suitcase of clothes from home; but he was acting the same idiot way as everybody else. You know, as if I was pretty young and not very bright and couldn't help doing fool things sometimes, but he hoped it wouldn't get to be a habit. As if he was really pretty disappointed in me although he was trying hard not to show it.

And he wouldn't sit down and talk to me sensibly, either. He said we could talk later; right now I wasn't supposed to upset myself. . . . The old bastard really put on a convincing act, considering that he was the one who'd arranged for me to attempt 'suicide' in the first place so that he could 'save' me! But of course I didn't have the slightest suspicion of that at the time."

We met a big semi with the name TARAHUMARA painted in gaudy letters on the front bumper of the tractor, reminding me that years ago most Mexican truck drivers used to christen their roaring beasts. I wondered if this driver actually was a Tarahumara Indian. They used to have the reputation of being headhunters, I seemed to recall; and they lived in the bottom of the Barranca del Cobre west of Chihuahua City, a slash in the ground big enough to swallow a couple of Grand Canyons.

"Well, I blew my stack, I really did," the girl beside me continued. "I jumped out of bed as he was reaching for the doorknob and grabbed his arm and swung him around and screamed at him. Something like: Just because he carried his brains up where the air was too thin to nourish them properly didn't mean he had to be stubborn as well as stupid; and after two attempts on my life was he really going to swallow the third as a *suicide* try, for God's sake? Didn't he know me better than that? Just because everybody else had jumped to dumb conclusions about me didn't mean he had to!" She swallowed hard. "I *had* to make him understand! The world was going all crazy and I felt he was the only person left I could trust!" She shook her head ruefully. "How naive can you get?"

I said, "So you threw a wingding and convinced him—well, thought you'd convinced him although he really didn't need convincing—that your suicide was a phony. What then?"

She made a face. "I broke into tears, what else? It was a very weepy time for me; I'm not usually so soppy. Anyway, I went like: 'Boo-hoo, everybody thinks I'm a suicidal moron and I wish I were really dead, boo-hoo!' Words to that effect. And of course he held me and patted me and apologized for doubting me for a moment, he should have known I was a brave girl who'd never . . . Well, you can fill in the blanks. Big joke, although I wasn't in on it then." She drew a long breath. "He bent over and kissed me. It started out as a big-brother kiss, but then it changed, if you know what I mean. It startled me, and I was suddenly very much aware that my hair was a matted mess, and I had no makeup on and no shoes on and only one of those wrinkled cotton things they give you to wear in hospitals that's all open behind. . . ."

Her voice trailed off, and she sat for a while looking straight ahead through the windshield at the road winding through the cactus-and-greasewood hills ahead.

I said, "And one thing led to another, I suppose, and wound up matrimony."

She nodded. "Well, I tried to pass it off lightly: 'Why, Uncle Buffy!' And he said a bad word and told me he wasn't my uncle, he'd never been my uncle, and he had no intention of ever becoming my uncle. He said he'd had his eye on me all the time I was growing up, but he'd never stepped out of line, not once, wasn't that right? But now I was big enough, and I was sure purty enough, and if people were trying to kill me he damn well wanted me where he could keep an eye on me. . . . That was when the phone rang. Somehow I knew what it would be, and I pulled him over to it and picked it up and held it so we could both hear. It was The Voice again, of course: 'Three times lucky is better than your daddy managed, girlie, but you can't escape us forever.' " She grimaced. "It was the last straw. I'm no sturdy feminist heroine; I wanted somebody to protect me. I'd become pretty disillusioned about romantic young men my own age anyway; sooner or later I'd always see that cash-register look in their eyes. Poor little rich girl, ha! If romance was what I wanted, how could I do better than the man who'd waited for me so patiently and loyally all those years? But mostly I was just terrified and looking for shelter."

"So you agreed to marry him."

"Yes," she said. "And three weeks later I learned that all those men had been hired by him to make it happen just that way! The driver of the pickup truck, the sniper in the vacant lot, the man in my dressing room who was also, it turned out, The

39

Voice. All working hard to scare the dumb wench into Uncle Buffy's arms and bring his long courtship that she hadn't even known was a courtship to a successful conclusion.''

"The frighteners," I said. "But they weren't really trying to kill you?''

"Not then," she said. "Oh, no, it couldn't happen until we were safely married and I'd changed my will, you can guess how. But then, when the time was right, the paranoid dame would try to kill herself again. Only this time her dear, loving Uncle Buffy would be so heartbroken because he'd failed to find her before it was too late!''

CHAPTER 6

CANANEA was visible from several miles down the road, a small mining town nestling in a fold of the mountains—a northward extension of the Sierra Madre, I believe, called the Sierra de la Madera. The Timber Mountains, if my limited Spanish vocabulary can be trusted. Although they hardly qualified as Alpine peaks, they rose to respectable heights behind the town and the tall, smoking stacks of the mine. I didn't see anything growing on them but the usual sparse scrub evergreens common to that arid country, good for nothing but firewood; but maybe they produced better lumber farther south.

Gloria started preparing herself for public appearance as we approached civilization, such as it was in these parts. Actually, she had very little to do since she hadn't let herself yield much to the rigors of the long ride; no sprawling, unbuttoned, shoes-off relaxation here. She merely checked her golden hairdo, inspected her elaborate eye makeup, powdered her patrician nose, and repaired some minor lipstick wear. We entered a sprawling town of dirt streets and low mud buildings. Cheerful, ragged kids played in the dust along with scrawny dogs of indeterminate breeding. We missed the restaurant on the first pass and wound up in a rather dilapidated and unpromising residential area—not that any part of this mining community resembled Beverly Hills. I turned the Caddy around and drove back the way we'd come. I seemed to be doing a lot of backtracking on this safari.

41

"My lost pathfinder!" said Gloria dryly. "Who did you call from Douglas, just before we crossed the border?"

I glanced at her sharply. I'd made no great effort toward security, it hadn't been that important; but she wouldn't have seen me using the pay phone up the street if she'd followed instructions and stayed in the car at the filling station where we'd availed ourselves of our last opportunity to top up the tank with U.S. gas.

"Just checking with the time-of-day service, ma'am," I said. "Incidentally, you're supposed to set your watch back an hour. Mexico doesn't have daylight saving."

She laughed shortly. "You're a liar."

"Always. That's the way they train us, and I was a prize student. But I'm right about the hour."

She was watching me, frowning. She said, "I do have an interest in this operation, Matt. . . . I mean, Horace, dear. I'd like to know what's going on. Telephone call from Deming, New Mexico, where we filled up the first time—you weren't so sneaky about that one—telephone call from Douglas, Arizona, where you were supposedly laying in a supply of pesos in preparation for entering Mexico. Very mysterious. Is there something I should know that you aren't telling me, Horace, dear?" She laughed again. "Yes, I was snooping. Actually, I just meant to walk around a bit after all the driving; but seeing you at that phone made me curious, so I followed you for a couple of blocks and watched around the corner. What were you doing in that hardware store, making contact with one of your secret agents? And in J.C. Penney's? I thought the place to get foreign money was a bank."

The fact that she'd watched me didn't worry me; but the fact that I hadn't been aware of her watching me was disturbing. Either she was better at surveillance than she ought to be, or I'd been less alert than I should have been.

I said, "The gas jockey told me that the banks in Douglas won't handle Mexican money; you have to get it in one of the stores that deal with the Mexicans. The hardware store didn't have any pesos to spare, so they sent me over to Penney's, where a nice lady sold me fifty bucks' worth. At the current rate of exchange, it makes for an impressive-looking wad of bills, all covered with zeros. First time I ever handled a piece of money reading ten thousand in any denomination.''

"Anyway, it makes a good story," Gloria said. "Look, there's a cafe, but it doesn't say Mr. Green.''

"I'll go in and ask," I said, stopping the car.

The sign read CAFÉ all right, but when I got inside, I found that it wasn't an eating place at all, but just a store selling coffee. A combination of broken Spanish and broken English brought out the information that the restaurant I wanted was just down the street, I couldn't miss it.

"We can't miss it," I said, starting the car again.

"That's very reassuring," said Gloria, "considering that we've already missed it once. . . . No, look, there it is!''

She was right. Up ahead on the right was Mr. Green's Restaurant, *Buen Comer*. There was also the Blanco y Negro Bar, *Ladies, Ambiente Familiar*. And there was a motel. How we'd failed to spot this long, low, brick-front complex the first time through, I have no idea, except that it sat back a little on a street that met ours at an acute angle, and there was also a third street involved, creating a confused, wide, unpaved intersection, more like a dusty vacant lot that had presumably taken all my attention and maybe Gloria's as well. There was only one vehicle parked in front of the restaurant, an elderly red Ford pickup with Sonora plates. I stopped the Allante behind it.

"Let's try this good eating they advertise," I said. "It's about that time.''

"Are you sure we shouldn't join the ladies and sample the family ambiance in the Black and White Bar? I thought all secret contacts took place in bars.''

"Nobody told me anything about a bar," I said. "The word I got was restaurant. Come on.''

I went around to help her out, wondering if this was in character: did oil-field roughnecks, even millionaire oil-field roughnecks, hand ladies out of horseless carriages these days? I decided that the older ones probably did and still go in for this

43

kind of cowboy chivalry. The younger ones undoubtedly just snapped their fingers and told their dates, "Move the assets, baby, you're holding up the merger."

The restaurant was moderately large and encouragingly clean and empty of customers except for a single Mexican couple at a side table, presumably the owners of the pickup outside. They were drinking beer. We were early for dinner, which down there is normally served at an hour when decent American citizens are beginning to think of bed. A pleasant-looking, plump brown lady in a loose brown dress and a blue apron indicated that any place we cared to sit was acceptable to her. I picked a corner table with a view of the front door, the kitchen door, and the modesty screen nearby that was marked DAMAS at one end and CABALLEROS at the other, indicating the nature of the facilities concealed behind it.

I couldn't help remembering that not too long ago I'd visited a rest room in another country where they spoke a lot of Spanish—Puerto Rico, if you must know—and a big guy had tried to shoot me with a silenced .22 pistol. I'd had to use my knife to discourage him. I wasn't overjoyed by the knowledge that, if no contact approached me within a reasonable time, I was going to have to enter that CABALLEROS to see if he was waiting in there for me. Well, for Horace Hosmer Cody. Just what was supposed to pass between us remained to be seen. It would be the first close test of my disguise; and I hoped nobody'd been handing out photographs of the true Mr. Cody. But for the moment, if my contact was in there, let him wait. And if he was sitting at a table fifteen feet away pretending to be a Mexican peasant bringing his wife—well, on second glance, daughter—to town in their pickup truck, let him wait, too.

I said, "I'm not usually a beer drinker, but it's very good down here, it goes well with the local food, and after that drive I've got a Sahara thirst."

We settled on Dos Equis and *carne asada*. The beer was brought, along with corn chips and a spicy dip, *salsa*, that carried considerable authority. I studied the shining young woman across the table who should have been imbibing champagne in the honeymoon suite of a big-city hotel about this time, instead of slugging down *cerveza* in a backwoods eatery.

"So you have reason to think Buff Cody intended to kill you," I said.

"It's not exactly an original idea," she said dryly. "Other men, caught in a financial bind—I gather the slump in the oil industry has hit him hard—have had the bright notion of marrying a rich girl and arranging to inherit all her money as soon after the wedding as the, er, removal can be carried out without arousing suspicion." She made a wry face. "Wanted: paranoid heiress with demonstrated mental instability and proven suicidal tendencies. Who's going to ask questions if the poor screwball wench tries to kill herself again and succeeds? Well, Uncle Buffy couldn't find a suitable subject ready-made, so he manufactured one. Me. If one of his hirelings hadn't talked, he'd have been home free."

"This man who was caught, one of the three Cody had working on you," I said. "How was he persuaded to talk?"

Gloria shook her head unhappily. "It seems incredible, as if we were talking about someone I never met instead of someone who . . . who brought me bubblegum when I was a little girl. I knew that he and Papa hadn't always been model citizens, of course; they were actually kind of proud of their gaudy past, although I was always told that the details weren't fit for my tender ears. But to think of Uncle Buffy giving orders for a man to be killed, like a gangster putting out a contract . . . !" She stopped, breathless.

"Cody ordered a hit on one of his own people? Why?"

"Well, as I told you, the man was careless," Gloria said. "He was the one who'd hid in the bathroom; and he'd let me see his face in the mirror. If he were caught, I could identify him. Apparently Uncle Buffy was afraid that under those circumstances he'd talk and incriminate everyone involved including Uncle Buffy. Well, it seems that Mr. Somerset's men had them all under surveillance. They frustrated an attempt on

Dixon's life—that was his name, Marty Dixon—and the man realized that he was marked for death and made a deal. He'd tell everything in return for government protection.''

''You're sure of the man.''

She glanced up irritably. ''Yes, of course I'm sure! I not only recognized his face when I saw him; I recognized his voice. The Voice. There's no possible doubt. And he gave Mr. Somerset the names of the others: the man who'd run me off the road and the man who'd shot at me. Oil-field roughnecks who'd worked for Uncle Buffy in the past. The frighteners, you called them. That's very appropriate. Scaring me into begging Uncle Buffy for protection and at the same time giving me the reputation of being a suicidal freak was Phase One of the operation. Of course they had orders to be very careful not to hurt me—yet.'' Her voice was bitter.''I'd be worthless if I wound up with a broken neck or a lethal bullet hole before the wedding could take place. Just as Uncle Buffy was careful, himself, to save me the night I was supposed to have swallowed all those barbiturates before they could take effect. Phase One. Of course Phase Two was going to be a different proposition entirely!'' Gloria drew a long breath and rose, picking up her purse. ''I think I'd better pay a visit to the little girls' room before I eat.''

I grinned. ''In case you have trouble with the translation, you want the one marked DAMAS. Like in dames.''

She made a face at me and walked off. I finished my beer and ordered another. As I'd indicated to Gloria, it's not my favorite tipple, but in Germany and Mexico, where they do it so well, I sometimes find myself actually enjoying the stuff if I'm thirsty enough.

The lady with the blue apron brought the dinners. *Carne asada* just stands for roasted meat; this seemed to be beef and it was done pretty black, but that's customary. I hesitated. Would Horace Hosmer Cody wait politely for his wife to rejoin him? I decided he'd take at least a couple of bites to check things out, and did so, feeling slightly uncomfortable about eating with my hat on, since it was something my mother had been very strict about. In spite of its overcooked appearance, the meat was good, a bit tough but quite tasty. . . . I found myself laying down my knife and fork and getting to my feet without really making the decision and walking across the largely empty restaurant.

It had been too long. I found myself thanking Buff Cody silently for not going in for boots with over-high heels; some of that cowboy footgear feels like walking on stilts. I was also grateful for the modesty screen that would permit me to investigate the DAMAS without having the restaurant lady come running to tell the dumb *gringo* that he had the wrong door. But most of my gratitude was reserved for Mr. Smith and Mr. Wesson, whose reliable .38-caliber product I removed from its place of concealment as soon as I could no longer be seen from the restaurant. I had, of course, entered the space behind the screen from the right, the CABALLEROS side. I passed that door and knocked left-handed on the DAMAS.

"Gloria," I called innocently. "Gloria, are you okay in there? The food's getting cold."

There was no answer. I turned the knob with my left hand, standing well aside, and pushed the door back far enough to make certain nobody was hiding behind it. It was a tiled room of reasonable size for a john. It was empty. I backed away, letting that door close automatically, and looked at the other one. Well, I'd had a bad feeling about the CABALLEROS from the moment I first saw it. I stepped over to where the blast of a firearm inside wouldn't wipe me out. There was no need for conversation. If they were in there—and Gloria would hardly have entered those masculine premises of her own accord—they would already have heard me. The door was unlocked. I kicked it open and went in with it.

They were in there. It was another big-enough chamber, for a can, reasonably clean for Mexico, where surgical sterility is not considered essential to the process of elimination. They faced me from between the toilet and the urinal, which wasn't the usual kind of one-man porcelain plumbing but a tiled trough built around the corner into which a faucet poured a small stream of water, perhaps to encourage reluctant kidneys by its example.

47

I stepped inside after again making sure that no one was about to jump me from behind the door. I noted that a single golden lock had at least detached itself from Gloria's perfect hairdo and fallen into her face, which was pale and frightened.

"Drop your gun and close the door, you dirty murderer!" said the young man behind her.

CHAPTER 7

THERE was no hurry. I held on to the .38 and let the rest-room door close behind me. There was no hurry now. If he'd been a professional, it would have been over by now, and one or two of us, maybe all three of us, would have been dead; but I'd sensed that this was an amateur operation and held my fire. There was no hurry at all. Pros shoot the instant they have a clear target; but amateurs have a terrible compulsion to chat with everyone they intend to kill.

"Drop your gun or your wife dies!" he said.

I was grateful for the reference to my matrimonial status. It reminded me of who I was here. As Matthew Helm I'd have had to keep in mind the fact that in our unsentimental outfit we never play the hostage game; and that the standing orders require us, mission permitting, to take out anyone who attempts to pull it on us, no matter how many prisoners get massacred in the process. The theory is that at the very least this makes for one idiot hostage-taker fewer in a world that's too full of them; and perhaps if we demonstrate enough times that it doesn't work on us, they'll stop trying it on us.

But here I wasn't Helm, sometimes called Eric. I was Cody, sometimes known as Buffalo Bill, a totally different character driven by totally different motives. Gloria was staring at me in a pleading way, her expression begging me to do nothing rash that would bring her a bullet in the back. Her face was shiny-wet with fear.

I could see enough of the man to get a general idea of his appearance, although his height remained a question mark since he was crouching behind her for cover with his left arm across her throat. He seemed to be a rather handsome young fellow with brown eyes—I could see only one past Gloria's head, but I assumed the other matched—and more dark hair than seemed necessary. He was wearing blue running shoes, clean blue jeans, a navy blue turtleneck, and a light blue windbreaker, pretty much the same color-coordinated outfit as worn by our young man Greer who'd come for me in the mountains. The uniform of the day for bright young men used to involve gray flannel and Florsheims; now it's blue denim and Adidas. I couldn't see the weapon he was poking into Gloria's back, but her expression made it clear that he wasn't bluffing with a ballpoint pen.

"Drop the gun, Cody! I won't say it again!"

He'd already said it three times, and now he'd called me Cody. Okay, if he didn't know the real Cody, presumably the real Cody didn't know him, so it was safe to ask.

I asked, "Who the hell are you?"

"I'm Mason Charles, Junior. Yes, Charles, like in Millicent Charles. You met her; she said you'd had dinner once with Will Pierce and her and disapproved of her. Well, she didn't like you either. I suppose that made it easier for you when you sent your machete-wielding goons to slaughter your partner and any witnesses who might be along; maybe you even instructed them specifically to get rid of her, too. . . ."

"Mason Charles!" That was Gloria. "Of course! Millie talked a lot about you. . . . Look, I'm Gloria, Gloria Pierce, well, Gloria Cody now. Please, you're hurting me with that gun!"

The young man's face was grim, what I could see of it. "I know who you are, and I don't think my mother and you did a lot of friendly chatting about her offspring—in fact, you refused to meet us after they decided to get married, didn't you? You weren't going to have anything to do with her brats, isn't that what you said? You hated her and gave her a hard time even before they . . . even back when she was just your father's secretary. Don't try to kid me you and she were cozy pals now that she's dead!"

Gloria said desperately, "You're wrong, I never hated . . . !"

"Well, whatever you called it, you snooted her all to hell and did your best to break things up between her and your pop. . . . I don't know where you fit into this. I do know that you did your best to make my mother unhappy while she was alive, and now that she's dead you've married the man who had her and your dad murdered, which makes you either pretty naive or pretty callous. Either way you're not entitled to much consideration in my book; but if you behave and keep your mouth shut, maybe you won't get hurt."

His name had rung no instant bells for me, although I'd been told how Gloria's male parent had died and with whom. However, the ensuing dialogue had identified the young man fairly well. Another case of bereavement to be laid at the door of the mysterious, machete-wielding desperados of the Sierra Madre. Apparently Mason Charles had no more faith in those simple ethnic *bandidos* than I did; but there was no way we could discuss the matter sensibly here.

I said, "Look, Charles, whatever I have or haven't done, and I've got a few things buried along my back trail I wouldn't care to have dug up, Gloria had no part in them, hear? And I assure you, one thing I haven't done is set up my partner and your mom for murder. . . ."

"Your assurance isn't good enough!"

"Listen to me, son!" I snapped, as Gloria winced to the jabbing pressure of the gun muzzle in her back. "I'm giving you my word that I had nothing to do with your mother's death. . . . Hell, boy, let me finish! I'm going to prove it to you. I'm going to put up my gun and turn my back on you and walk out of here—or not, if that's the way you want it. If you like, you can shoot me at your leisure. Or you can put the piece away, apologize to the lady, and come to the table with her and I'll buy you a beer. Or a whole damn dinner if you like, while you tell me what a bastard you think I am and what's your reason for thinking so." I drew a long breath. "Well, here I go. Fire at will."

Holstering the Smith and Wesson deliberately, turning, moving to the door, I told myself that as soon as it wouldn't interfere with the operation I was going to find the young creep again and carve him into small, bloody pieces, which I would then feed happily to some hungry Mexican hogs—but that was just me keeping myself angry enough to ignore the crawling sensations along my back as I waited for the blast of noise behind me and the bullet. No shot came. I got the door open and marched out of there. When I reached the table, I sat down gratefully and finished off my beer, wishing it were whiskey, and ordered another. I'd done what I could, at some expense to my nerves; the situation I'd left behind would have to resolve itself without me, one way or another. But she was a very lovely girl, and they don't get shot very often by handsome young men, at least not until the two of them have had time to get acquainted.

The *carne asada* hadn't got as cold as I'd expected; apparently the incident hadn't taken as long as it had seemed to. I chewed my Mexican meat and waited. Presently Gloria appeared from the DAMAS side of the screen, unharmed. Young Charles appeared from the CABALLEROS side with his hands empty. I noted that he was moderately tall, although no beanpole like Buff Cody or Cody's present impersonator. He threw a look in my direction, hesitated, and strode out the door of the restaurant. I wondered if I'd been wrong about the ownership of the red pickup; but I heard no motor start up outside. Apparently Charles had been sensible enough to park his transportation some distance away, out of sight. Well, you can't be stupid all the time, although some folks try.

I watched Gloria approach. The color had returned to her face. The vagrant lock had rejoined the disciplined waves and swirls of her perfect hairdo. The stress damage to her makeup had been repaired.

"Okay?" I asked, rising to help with the chair.

She nodded without conviction, still shaken by her experience. I returned to my seat and picked up my knife and fork again.

I said, "I see that the Dark Avenger of the Sierra de la Madera disdained to join us."

She said, "You took an awful risk."

"You ain't just kidding, *querida*."

"No. I mean with my life. Not dropping that gun when he told you to. He might have shot me!"

"That Boy Scout?" I shook my head. "Not a chance. Me, maybe, if I'd remained facing him and given him time to psych himself up and tell me all about why he had to kill me. These resolute young revengers always want you to know why you're dying. But there was no way he could have killed an attractive girl no matter how tough he talked to her—except maybe accidentally while he was using that pistol as a cattle prod. And he'd never in the world have shot me in the back either. They have this thing about directional homicide. Murdering an eastbound gent, if you're east of him, is okay; but if he happens to be traveling west, it's a no-no. Once I got myself turned away from him in there I was safe as a house."

"I see." Her voice was dry. "That's why you're hitting the beer so hard, because you were so safe. Because we were both so safe."

I glanced at her sharply. She was more perceptive than I'd thought. After a moment I grinned. "Tell me about it," I said. "Start with the gun. What kind was it?"

"What difference. . . . I keep telling you, I hate them!"

"You hate them, but you don't know anything about them and can't be bothered learning. That's not much of a hate. A real hater learns everything he can about the hated enemy."

She said, "I think it was what's called an automatic. Fairly large. Not one of the little pocket things. It had a fat grip that pretty well filled his hand, and he had a good-sized hand. It had a hammer but it wasn't—what do you call it?—wasn't cocked."

I said, "Hey, that's not bad for a gun-hater. It tells us that we're dealing with, probably, one of the big 9mm auto pistols, say Beretta, or maybe Smith and Wesson. It probably holds fourteen or fifteen rounds, which is handy to know. It means he doesn't have to reload after five or six, like with a revolver. The gun is probably double action. That means the trigger doesn't just fire the gun, it cocks the hammer first—double action—so

53

you don't have to cock it with your thumb or by working the slide, which is why he didn't bother to carry it cocked." I was talking idly just to steady her down. I went on: "Okay. How did he get you in there?"

She licked her lips. "Well, you don't stare at a strange man when he's coming out of the *caballeros* fixing his pants. I just started in the other door. The next thing I knew, I'd been yanked practically off my feet and dragged into the men's room. He showed me the gun, told me to behave and I wouldn't get hurt; we were going to wait for hubby, you, to miss me and come after me. When I started to protest, he jabbed me so hard with the gun it really hurt; I was terrified that it was going to go off against my back. It seemed like forever before we heard you knocking on the other door and calling to me."

I said, "Good report. Now let's try you on something hard. How did he know?"

"Know what?"

"Everything." I shook my head irritably. "Look, we were married just a few hours ago—at least we're supposed to've been married just a few hours ago—but here's a character several hundred miles away in the wilds of northern Mexico who knows all about it. He seems to have a pretty speedy society-news service, wouldn't you say?"

"Well, we didn't come here by private jet. He could have been at the wedding and followed. . . ."

I shook my head quickly. "No. He couldn't have been at the wedding or he'd have known that the guy he was pointing a gun at just now wasn't the same guy who'd stood beside you at the altar. He might have been waiting outside in his car, watching the doors of the reception hall, say, far enough away that he didn't see Buff Cody too well when the two of you came running out in a shower of rice and drove off."

"That's right, he knew about the marriage; but he did accept you as the real Horace."

I said, "If we assume that means he was there and didn't get the news by carrier pigeon, how did he get here? We made a point of shedding all surveillance at the time you switched husbands in El Paso, remember? And we were clean as far as the border; the guy I called in Douglas said so. The chances of Charles guessing where we planned to cross and picking us up as we entered Mexico are very small; and I can swear that nobody's been tailing us along this little twisty road, at least not without a full team of three or four or five inconspicuous, radio-equipped cars that could trade off whenever there was a risk of my having noticed one of them.''

Gloria frowned. ''What are you trying to say . . . Horace?''

''I'm saying this young fellow knew too damn much. He knew we were married and he knew where to find us. How did he learn all that?''

She regarded me gravely for a moment. ''Even more important, how did he learn that you . . . that Uncle Buffy had arranged for Papa's and Millie's murders?''

I said, ''You're accepting that as the truth?''

''Shouldn't I?'' She licked her lips. ''If I accept that Uncle Buffy had his . . . his frighteners, as you called them, scare me into marrying him so that he could inherit my fortune, is it unreasonable of me to accept that he had Papa killed first so he'd have a double heiress to marry, with both Mama's old New England money and Papa's new Texas money in my name? Besides, those terrorist tactics wouldn't have worked as long as Papa was still alive to console and protect me. Of course . . . of course it makes Uncle Buffy out to be a terrible monster, having his best friend murdered, but we've already pretty well established that, haven't we?''

I said, ''Well, whatever you accept privately, publicly you're going to have to deny hotly that here's any possibility of your husband—me—being responsible for your daddy's death; that's just too ridiculous for words! Otherwise this marriage becomes totally unbelievable; you wouldn't stay with a man you suspected of being your pop's murderer.''

Gloria smiled faintly. ''Dear Horace, could we start operating on the assumption that we both have reasonable intelligence?''

I frowned at her. ''What did I say wrong?''

She said, ''Look, I know you don't think much of me. You

55

think I'm a spoiled Texas bitch and a coward to boot. Scared of guns, scared of being hurt or killed to the extent that I was even willing to marry a much older man I didn't love just because I thought he'd keep me safe. Just now you thought I should have stood in front of that dreadful pistol smiling bravely instead of all pale and sweating, didn't you? You'd be much happier carrying out this mission with a fearless little two-gun cowgirl type who could be a real fighting partner to you. . . . No, wait, let me say it all. The fact is that I don't think much of you, either. At least I didn't. I thought you were just the stupid, macho, gun-loving kind of man I detest, the kind that goes around killing things, and even people, to prove how virile they are.''

I've been shooting since I was old enough to hold a gun. I won't say I've been fornicating since I was old enough to hold a woman, because I was a backward boy in that respect; but I've still been working at it for quite a while. And with all my experience in both endeavors, I have yet to find a correlation between marksmanship and cocksmanship; but if this kind of parlor psychology made her happy, who was I to make her sad?

I said, ''Well, this marriage, such as it is, wasn't arranged for reasons of compatibility.''

She laughed shortly. ''No, but I do seem to have had you figured slightly wrong, Horace, dear. You see, I was perfectly sure you'd come smashing heroically into that awful rest room with two guns blazing, like John Wayne attacking a frontier saloon. There'd be blood and dead bodies everywhere, and one of the dead bodies would be mine—I could just see myself lying all gory on that disgusting floor between the toilet and that crazy urinal trough. But I was wrong. You handled it very quietly and intelligently and . . . and courageously, not that I ever doubted your courage, just your good sense. But I think it would be nice, although admittedly I'm not very brave, if you gave me credit for a little common sense, too.''

It was a commendable speech and increased my respect for her; but I couldn't figure out exactly what she was driving at.

I said, ''I wasn't aware that I'd doubted . . . oh.''

''Yes,'' she said. ''You don't have to point out the obvious, darling; I'm moderately bright. I could see at once that if we were going to make any kind of success of this matrimonial charade, I couldn't let that boy's accusation pass unchallenged. I mean, I know you didn't have Papa killed, because you're not Uncle Buffy; but that's just what nobody else including Mason Charles must suspect, isn't it? So I lit into him after you were gone and told him there was no possible way my darling Horace could have done such a dreadful thing, and where in the world had he picked up such a filthy lie?'' She shook her head quickly. ''No, he wouldn't tell me who'd told him, but it was obvious that somebody had fed him the information. It seems likely it's the same person who told him how to find us, don't you think?'' She laughed. ''I think that, after your commendable behavior, not at all that kind of a guilty mastermind of murder, my attack made young Mr. Charles kind of wonder if he hadn't got a bum steer about his mother's death from somebody.''

''Well, maybe it is a bum steer,'' I said. ''You say there's strong evidence that Cody arranged those phony attempts on your life; but his setting up the killing of your dad and Millicent Charles is just hearsay so far.'' I grimaced. ''Whether the boy's information is right or wrong, the big question is who gave it to him. However, at the moment we have a bigger one: Where the hell is our man, our woman, in Cananea?''

I looked up hopefully as the restaurant door opened, but it admitted two young Mexican couples, all four kids in jeans. There was considerable noise and laughter and horseplay before they settled down at a table. I noted that the man and girl I associated with the red pickup were leaving now. The girl was a slim, dark, pretty little thing with long black hair worn loose down her back. She was wearing a shapeless black dress and bright red slippers, rather dusty and badly scuffed, with high, slim heels. She walked a bit gingerly, as if the bright pumps didn't fit very well; I had a hunch that, as soon as she'd left civilization behind, she'd kick them off and go barefoot. The man, a good many years older, was in jeans and a work shirt; a blocky gent with a leathery Indian face. They dropped no messages and went out without having looked my way. No contact there.

I made something of a production of figuring the bill and tip and translating the pesos into dollars for Gloria's benefit. Actually, although it looked like the national debt, it came to less than ten bucks, not bad for two pretty good dinners, several beers, and a fairly generous *propina*. It became obvious that none of the four young Mexicans was going to approach us; they were engrossed in their own laughing conversation. I sighed, got up, and helped Gloria with her chair; Buff Cody was going to have a real reputation for courtesy in this part of the world.

Outside it was still daylight, but the sun had dropped a noticeable distance toward the western horizon. The low light made the shabby little town of Cananea look quite picturesque, with shafts of golden sunshine striking through the dust raised from the unpaved streets by the passing cars and trucks, mostly vintage vehicles. I noted that the red pickup was gone. It had been replaced by a very battered jeep, presumably belonging to one of the kids inside. No one seemed interested in us standing there in our wedding clothes beside our expensive American convertible.

I drew a long breath. "Scratch one rendezvous," I said. "As we Texans say, a water haul."

"What do we do now?"

"We were given no fallback routine; but we do have a hotel reservation in Hermosillo. Maybe that's the fallback; maybe our contact just wanted to check us out first, here. Anyway, I see no alternative."

"Well, wake me when we get there. That beer made me sleepy. I'll be glad to get out of these clothes and into a comfortable bed." She glanced at me sharply. "Alone."

"*Sí, señora. No amor. Qué lástima.*"

"What was all that garbled Spanish?"

"I just said it's a pity."

"Down, Rover."

But she was smiling faintly as she got into the car. I closed the door on her and went around to slide behind the wheel. I

58

started the engine and checked the dials and the rearview mirror. . . .

"Glory, dear," I said.

Something in my voice made her sit up and look at me sharply. "What is it?"

"Pass me a Kleenex, please. Somebody seems to have been messing with my mirror."

I pointed. Soaped on the left-hand outside mirror of the Cadillac were two numbers and two letters: *KM95*.

CHAPTER 8

Driving off into the sunset, I didn't turn my head to look back, but I did use the mirrors. They showed nobody back there who seemed interested in our departure, only a bunch of dirty kids beyond the restaurant, playing some kind of a game that involved a lot of running and shouting. They displayed plenty of healthy energy, even if their moms didn't wash their little faces quite as often as would have been considered proper north of the border.

Nevertheless, I had a hunch somebody'd hung around long enough to see if I'd spotted the message. If so, he would have seen me cleaning it off the mirror, presumably having read it first. Or she would. The pretty little lady in the shabby black dress and the red shoes? Or her peasant companion? The pleasant, dumpy woman with the blue apron who'd served us? One of the four jean-clad kids from the jeep? What about Mason Charles, Junior; could that whole performance in the rest room have been faked for reasons still to be determined? If so he'd taken some awful chances with guns; we could easily have wound up in a Wild West shootout. No, I didn't really think it was Charles. Probably our contact was somebody who'd been careful not to let himself, or herself, be seen; but I wished he, or she, had been a little less cryptic and let us know what the communication meant. Correction: the meaning was fairly clear, it was the precise application that had me puzzled.

"What does it mean?" Gloria asked. "What's KM?"

"Karl Marx, of course," I said. "Come on, Mrs. Cody!"

She threw me a resentful glance. "Well, I suppose it must

stand for kilometers, but . . . Ninety-five kilometers, that's about fifty-seven miles, isn't it? But fifty-seven miles from where?''

Our relationship had changed somewhat since she'd analyzed it for us. In a sense we'd made a deal: she'd combat her natural inclination to consider me a dangerous, macho meathead if I'd refrain from treating her as a brainless, gutless society bitch.

I said, "A kilometer is roughly six-tenths of a mile, check. And in the absence of indications to the contrary, I've got to assume that we're supposed to measure our distance from right here in Cananea." I pushed the button to set the trip odometer back to zero. "The catch is, if I remember my geography correctly, ninety-five kilometers will take us well past the little town of Imuris, where we're supposed to turn left—south—on the main highway that comes down from Nogales, on the Arizona border, and goes to Hermosillo, Guaymas, and the whole west coast of Mexico. But that's a hell of a busy road; I kind of assumed we were sent this way, instead of through Nogales, because somebody wanted privacy. . . .''

"Matt, look! Sorry, I meant Horace. But look!''

I looked ahead where she was pointing. There, at the side of the highway, was a small, square, white, official-looking post. Painted on it in black was: *84KM*. I shook my head at my own obtuseness. As I drove, I'd been vaguely aware of the roadside mile markers—well, kilometer markers—but I simply hadn't made the connection.

As we passed it, Gloria said eagerly, "Obviously we're not supposed to drive ninety-five whole kilometers from here; we're simply supposed to find the ninety-five-kilometer post. Which way have the numbers been running?''

"They started at Agua Prieta and they've been getting bigger ever since.''

"Well, it seems as if we only have eleven kilometers to go. About seven miles. Let's go!''

She was all caught up in the wild excitement of it; she, a mere amateur, had solved the riddle and saved the day for the stupid pro. I let the fancy automatic transmission—I hate the damn things—work its way up through the gears, if gears are what those slushboxes have inside them. We passed some enormous heaps of orange-brown gunk from the mine and headed up into the wooded hills. Excuse me, the Timber Mountains. The road climbed to a pass called Puerto de Cananea, 1840M. About 5500 feet. It wasn't real mountain-goat country, there were no spectacular cliffs or peaks, there was just a lot of evergreen landscape standing more or less on end. Beyond the pass the country was more arid, and the vegetation was much less dense, although it seemed odd that the slopes facing the wet Pacific Ocean should be the ones lacking moisture.

The highway builders had made no effort to move the mountains out of our way in U.S. road-building fashion. The highway followed the folds and dips and precipitous slopes faithfully, the pavement was atrocious, and as we labored out of one ravine and plunged into the next I'd be blinded by the sun that was sinking rapidly ahead of us. Some of the kilometer posts were missing. Number ninety-two appeared on schedule, but ninety-three was not in its appointed place.

"There's ninety-four," said Gloria. "What are you doing?"

I'd put my foot down and the Allante was gaining speed. "We had a date in Cananea, and a man with a gun was waiting for us. I think we'd better just blast on past this rendezvous and see what's there. You watch on your side, and I'll watch on mine."

Doing about sixty, which was all that road was good for, I saw the kilometer post a couple of hundred yards before I reached it. There are very few marksmen who can figure the correct lead for a target traveling at eighty-eight feet per second that only presents itself for an instant, and there were no marksmen waiting. There was only a small dirt road running up the side of a hill and, parked just off it, barely visible through the brush, an old brown van. No enemies waiting in ambush but, on the other hand, no cheering crowds, no welcoming band.

"Anything on your side?" I asked as I took the next curve fast.

"Just brush and trees and cactus."

"One brown Dodge van on mine. Nobody around it, but I couldn't see inside it."

"Matt, aren't you going back?"

I didn't remind her that I was supposed to be Horace around here; I was debating whether or not to pass a slow-moving Arizona Chrysler with a sticker on the rear bumper that, translated, read I LOVE MY DOG. However, LOVE was represented by a red heart, and DOG by a picture of a German shepherd, a somewhat unreliable canine in my opinion; but then I'm a Labrador man myself. I hoped our man Greer had got the pup to Santa Fe all right and that he was settling down well to kennel life. I remained in line behind the slowpoke, since I wouldn't be following him long.

I spoke without looking at my companion: "From now on, please do exactly as I tell you. For a start, unbuckle your seatbelt. We'll be unloading fast. . . . No, please, there's no time for a question-and-answer session now! We can talk later."

I didn't have to unbuckle my own claustrophobia straps because I wasn't wearing them. Maybe they're okay for peaceful civilians, but in the business your life can just as easily depend on your ability to get out of a car fast as on your ability to stay in it. Gloria had choked down a protest, but her expression was hostile again. So much for détente.

She said stiffly, "I hope you know what you're doing, because I certainly don't. And please remember that I'm hardly dressed for acrobatics."

I said, "How you're dressed, and how I'm dressed, is one of the few things we've got going for us right now. . . . There, I see a good spot up ahead, I hope. Stand by to disembark. Bring your purse. Leave the car door open."

The rearview mirrors were clear for the moment. I slowed and swung the Allante onto a small dirt road that headed over a low hill to the right. The dog-loving Arizonians disappeared around the bend ahead. When I got the car to the top of the rise, pitching and bucking in the ruts, I found that the track didn't go anywhere; it just stopped at a wide, level, open spot surrounded by brush and littered with cans and bottles and other trash. Maybe it had once been a parking space for the machinery that had built the road. I stopped, set the parking brake, and switched off, leaving the keys in the lock. Getting out, I reached in back to get a sturdy paper bag displaying the name of the hardware store I'd patronized in Douglas, Arizona. Gloria was moving, but in a hesitant way, as if reluctant to leave the luxury car for the great outdoors.

"Out!" I snapped. "Back to the highway on the double. . . . Dammit, I said leave that door open!"

She reached back to yank it open, more vigorously than necessary, and walked off stiffly, but stopped to look back at the white convertible, which had the hastily abandoned look of a ship after the crew has taken to the lifeboats.

Gloria turned to me in protest. "But we can't leave it in this garbage dump, and not even locked! It'll be stripped by morning!"

I said, "What does it take to keep you moving? Come on!"

I took her arm, not very gently, and hurried her down to the highway and across it. One of the ubiquitous Mexican buses went roaring by heading east, leaving a stink of diesel.

"Matt, I really don't like the way you . . ."

"You can tell me all your don't-likes in a few minutes, sweetheart. You left some good girl-tracks over there, real beauties. Now I want you to put a nice, clear, high-heeled print of your left foot in that soft spot, facing the highway, as if you were moving toward a parked car. . . . For Christ's sake, this is no time to worry about a little dust on your shoe! Now a dainty right toe-print here . . . Swell, even a city boy ought to be able to read that sign like the Last of the Mohicans. Now grab this paper bag and hang onto it, along with your purse. I'm going to pick you up and carry you so you don't leave any more pointy little heel marks."

"Look, this is absolutely crazy. . . ."

I said, "If you prefer, we'll let you clamber around this landscape in your stocking feet, but it looks mighty stony and uncomfortable and hard on the nylons. . . . Okay, put your arms around my neck and hang on tight, but don't drop that bag."

Lifting her, holding her, I grinned at her flushed and angry face, very close. "Ain't it hell what a man will do to get a dame into his arms?"

Behind us, as I made my way down into the roadside ravine with my warm but resentful burden, I heard a big semi going by to the east, followed by a passenger car of some kind. I didn't turn my head to look. In spite of her fashionably slender look, she'd turned out to be a substantial girl. She was all I could manage to carry, and I didn't want to stumble and drop her. She'd leave marks that would be hard to erase; besides, she was mad enough already. Some westbound traffic went by on the road above and behind us. We were well down the slope now, too far down to see or be seen; but I found myself listening closely. I didn't hear a vehicle stop. At the bottom of the gully, I set the girl on her feet.

"Matt, if you don't explain this minute . . . !"

I said, "Just stand there; don't leave any more footprints than you have to. I've got to go back and fix a couple of places where I slid. Thank God Cody didn't go in for very high-heeled boots."

She licked her lips. "He was thinking of me, he said; he didn't want to tower too high above me at the altar."

It seemed like oddly considerate behavior for a would-be murderer. I said, "A real sweet guy sometimes, huh? Don't move, I'll be right back." When I returned, carrying a branch of desert juniper that I'd used to brush away the more conspicuous traces of our descent, she started to speak angrily, but I cut her off: "That paper bag, please."

She handed me the sack and watched me produce a small canteen full of water, a little pocket telescope, a compass, and a couple of folded pieces of paper. The canteen went onto my belt; the other items into my pockets.

"Matt, if you think I'm going to . . . !"

I remembered that I'd suspected that her beautiful mouth could develop an unbecoming pout. I'd been right, and her voice had acquired a typical spoiled-brat whine to go with it. She'd been fun to have along when she'd eagerly spotted the mileage marker, like a clue in a happy treasure hunt; but she was getting tiresome now.

65

However, I tried to speak patiently. "I don't think we have much time, Gloria. Please be quiet and listen. There's not much cover here, and I'd like to put a little more distance between us and the highway. Besides, I want to be up on the ridge where I can see what's happening. But I'm not Superman and I can't carry you up, it was hard enough bringing you down. So I'd appreciate it if you'd make the climb under your own power. Please? Watch where you put your feet. Stay on your toes as much as possible and try not to let your heels dig in. Okay?"

She shook her head violently. "No, it's not okay! I'm not going to move another step in this ghastly wilderness until you tell me exactly what you think you're doing!"

I said, "Dammit, I'm trying to save our lives, baby! Please start climbing."

"No! Not until you explain. . . ."

I didn't want to hit her—that is, sure, I wanted to, a little, she was a stubborn, infuriating bitch, but I didn't know how she'd react to physical abuse. Anyway, she'd told me the proper weapon to use against her. If she hated and feared guns, hell, I'd give her guns. At the sight of the .38 her face changed shockingly.

I said, "Either you move or you get shot, sweetheart. After listening to all this gripe, gripe, gripe I don't really give a damn which you choose. Just make up your cottonpicking little mind. . . . Okay, that's better." I drew a long breath as, after a momentary hesitation, she turned sullenly and started to climb. "A little to the left now. Swell, you're doing fine."

She had to lift her hem considerably in order to negotiate the steep hillside. I should have found the view intriguing as I climbed along behind and below her. I'm usually a sucker for a neat derriere in a smoothly fitting skirt, slender legs in sheer nylons, and, for a bonus, occasional glimpses of a lacy slip or petticoat. I could excuse my lack of reaction by saying that I was too busy with my juniper broom, brushing out the traces of her progress and my own, one-handed; but the fact was that having to threaten her had made me feel lousy. I don't like, at

66

any time, waving guns stupidly at people I have no intention of shooting. I particularly don't like it when it works too well.

I mean, this girl should have known that, no matter how much she annoyed me, I wouldn't fire. For one thing, I had orders to preserve her, and for another, after all the trouble I'd taken to hide our tracks, I obviously wasn't going to cut loose with a cannon blast and let everybody within miles know where we were. But instead of spitting in my eye defiantly, as she should have, instead of calling my bluff and leaving me standing there foolishly holding my silly firearm, she'd surrendered abjectly at the sight of it. I remembered the gray terror on her face in the washroom in Cananea, and I remembered again that this was the girl who'd let herself be frightened into marrying a man almost three times her age. Lovely as she was, and bright and pleasant upon occasion, she was clearly lacking something in the courage department. Well, when they're beautiful enough I guess they don't have to be heroines.

"Easy, now," I said at last. "The old Indian fighters never silhouetted themselves on the skyline. Cut around through that notch to the left. . . . Are you okay?" She'd slipped to one knee.

"Well, I just ruined a stocking, but I don't suppose that means anything to you." She started upwards again wearily. Her voice was bitter, as well as noticeably breathless from her exertions. "You might at least have let me change out of my wedding gown, such as it is, before dragging me on this mad mountain-climbing expedition."

I said, "I told you, that's just the point. Cody was counting on it in Juárez, the fact that nobody'd expect him to make any violent evasive maneuvers as long as you were both in your chapel clothes. Well, I'm hoping it'll work here, too. But if we'd suddenly turned up in jeans and hiking boots, they'd be ready for us to do something drastic, and we'd never shake them."

"Shake who? I didn't see anybody at that kilometer marker, and you said you didn't either."

"That was their mistake. They should have had somebody waiting to greet us at the rendezvous with a big smile and an outstretched hand, but I guess nobody wanted the job. The guy would have been taking a certain risk, and sacrificial goats are hard to come by these days. So, seeing nobody, we were supposed to pull up into that little road behind that decoy van and get out to investigate it, at which point they'd spring their little trap. Probably they pulled some stunt just like that, arranged some kind of a secret boondocks meeting, to get your daddy and his lady friend off the highway where they wanted them."

"You're just guessing. You can't know . . ."

I said, "I know that when I get that funny itch between my shoulder blades it's time to get the fuck out of there. That's how I've stayed alive longer than most in this business."

She threw a glance over her shoulder. "You haven't said who you think it is. It can't be Uncle Buffy himself; we saw him arrested in El Paso."

"I don't know who he's got doing his dirty work for him here, but I'm looking forward to finding out." I checked back to see how high we'd come. "That's far enough, I think. Let me get up there with you and take a look. . . . Swell, now lie down behind that bush, please."

We were on the side of a little knob that lifted us above the level of the brush and low trees on the far side of the ravine out of which we had climbed. There was a good view of the road. We could even see over the ridge on the other side of it into the open space where we'd left the white Allante, looking very expensive and deserted among all the litter. There were no other vehicles in sight until a bus roared by on the highway, going west.

"You can't be serious!" Gloria said.

Kneeling, I looked up at her, still standing there in her white suit like the Eddystone Light. She might have been a little more conspicuous with strobe lights in her hair, but not much. I was fed up with her; besides, there was action below. A brown van was just coming into sight from the east. Gloria was saying something about how I couldn't possibly expect her to lie down on the *ground*, dressed as she was. I reached out and yanked her feet out from under her. She sat down hard, and the pitch of

68

the hillside brought her sliding down to me with another interesting display of nylon pantyhose and lacy lingerie. I told myself this was no time to be admiring a lady's intimate apparel, and I grabbed one arm and twisted it around so she was glad to roll over onto her stomach and flatten out behind the bush I'd indicated. I took off my conspicuous white Buff Cody hat, tucked it under the bush out of sight, and lay down beside her and showed her the gun again.

I said, "Now lie perfectly still and stop all this nonsense. Jesus Christ! You have a trained man assigned to you. You're told one of his jobs is to keep you alive. And by God, when he tries to do that job, you're so dumb you fight him every step of the way. Think about this: if your idiotic chatter and moronic behavior cost me my life here, I'll be damned sure I take you with me. Now be quiet and watch!"

Down on the highway, they were taking their time, leaving no stones unturned and no side roads unexplored. I knew the Cadillac wasn't visible from the highway, but they investigated the little track as a matter of routine. Thorough.

I spoke softly to the sullen girl beside me: "We can figure a two-way radio and some kind of roadblock prepared for us ahead, which was why I didn't dare drive too far past the contact point. You always have to assume the other guy has a few brains, in this case enough to provide himself with a backup in case Plan One misfired. So the boys at kilometer ninety-five called ahead to say we must have smelled a trap because we'd driven past them without stopping. Then the boys waiting to take us if we got past ninety-five reported back that no fancy Yankee convertibles had reached them. Obviously we'd stopped somewhere in between, and our friends in the van down there have been coming up the highway slowly, checking both sides to find out where we disappeared to. . . . Aha, they've found us!"

The van had pulled up behind our Allante. The rear doors opened and half-a-dozen men got out—correct that, two of them were women, although it was hard to tell the difference. They were all dressed like farm workers, a few in the white pajama suits of Latin *paisanos* straight out of Central Casting, others in dark shirts and jeans or other work pants. There were big straw *sombreros*, and there were the kind of freebie caps that advertise feed or beer or machinery. Mostly the men and women were pretty dirty and ragged, but the weapons they carried gleamed cleanly in the low evening sunshine.

I whispered to the unresponsive girl: "Quite an assortment of firepower. Ammunition supply must be a problem. I see everything from a .45 Colt Auto to a 9mm Uzi to a specimen of the gutless old .30-caliber carbine that must be one of the most useless firearms ever invented but for some reason everybody loves it. . . . And there's *El Jefe* in nice clean khakis; and just look at the tool he's carrying, in addition to another .45 in a fancy holster on his left hip. We've got us a southpaw villain, it seems."

A moderately tall man, wearing a long-billed khaki cap to match his sharply pressed shirt and pants, had emerged from the van's right front door. Even in the most romantic Mexican movies, most Latin leading men are fairly substantial; but this hero wasn't carrying too much extra weight. I'd brought out the little telescope that had been provided for me. It was sharper than you'd expect for as small as it was. It showed the khaki-clad gent to me clearly as he stepped forward to take the keys out of the Caddy's ignition. He went back and opened the trunk, clearly not well enough acquainted with fancy automobiles to know that you don't need a key for that operation nowadays; all you have to do is push a button on the dashboard. He stood there studying the closely packed luggage.

"He's trying to figure out if there's anything missing," I said. "He wants to know if we—particularly you, since women aren't supposed to be able to get very far in high heels and nylons—if we grabbed any practical clothes when we lit out of there so fast we didn't even pause to lock the car behind us. But that's a neat packing job and it looks undisturbed. You and Cody really had your honeymoon chariot loaded."

She was watching the distant scene. "What in the world is he *doing*?" she asked.

The man in the khakis was hauling some of the bags out of

the trunk, perhaps to see if anything was hidden beneath them. He didn't set them down, he simply tossed them aside and watched them hit the ground as if hoping they'd burst open, but they were good pieces and remained closed. One set was tan with brown piping; the other was dusty rose. His and hers. At last the khaki-clad gent picked up a medium-sized, rose-colored suitcase right-handed, tossed it high into the air and, with a powerful swing of the machete in his left hand, sliced it open as it came down. I remembered being told that the luggage of Will Pierce and his lady had also been demolished. Gloria gave a gasp at the sight of her intimate honeymoon garments spilling out and fluttering away across the trashy clearing. Distant whoops of laughter reached us as the whole crew, except the driver, who remained in his seat, surged forward to join the party.

"Note the weapon our friend is using," I said softly. "We may not have found who ordered your daddy and Mrs. Charles killed, but maybe we've spotted the gent who did the actual killing."

"But they're *destroying* . . . !"

The head man had stepped back to watch the show in a tolerant, boys-will-be-boys manner. I studied the dark, clean-shaven face, rather handsome in the Latin manner, until I knew I'd recognize it if I saw it at close range without optical equipment and passed the glass to Gloria.

"The *jefe*," I said. "Anybody you recognize? No? Well, make sure you'll know him the next time you see him. And as many of the others as you can."

"Matt, they're just . . . just *vandalizing* . . . !"

"There's not much we can do about it."

"But why? What's the point?"

"Just be glad it isn't you," I said. "Think how they vandalized your pop and his girlfriend."

Gloria gave me a shocked look; apparently I should have been more respectful of the dead. Down across the highway, they were trashing the Cadillac thoroughly. Other machetes had come into play, slicing up the soft top, smashing the lights, carving up the upholstery, chopping up the tires—that took a little doing, but they made it—and even hacking up the body metal. They were also, of course, looting the luggage and demolishing everything that couldn't be pocketed or carried away. Soon the car was a total wreck, and the area looked as if the trunk had exploded, blowing fragmented suitcases and rags of clothing, male and female, in all directions.

At last the man in khaki called them to order and gave them their instructions, finishing with a wide sweep of his machete that encompassed all of northern Mexico. I couldn't hear the words, and I might not have understood them if I had heard them, but the meaning was obvious: *You've had your fun, now find me the lousy* gringos, *pronto.*

"But I don't understand!" Gloria whispered plaintively. All the sulky resentment had gone out of her as she watched the scene across the way. "I just don't *understand*! Our rendezvous . . . Why would anybody send us into a . . . a deathtrap?"

I said, "Isn't it obvious? I wasn't really selected for this bridegroom spot because I was such a bright and competent fellow. I was selected because I'd make a swell dead body that, after a little judicious machete work by our friend over there, could be buried as Horace Hosmer Cody, another unfortunate victim of those murdering Mexican *bandidos* who specialize in Texas millionaires and their dames."

CHAPTER 9

STRANGELY they had only one tracker worth a damn. You'd think that among a bunch of mountain ruffians there'd be hardly anybody who didn't know how to work out a simple trail; but they obviously weren't hunters, they'd had no training as military scouts, and they didn't think in those terms at all. Anyway, by the time they'd finished doing a job on the car and luggage and got themselves organized, they'd milled around so much that there were no clear footprints except theirs left near the vehicles. The khaki-clad leader never even looked at the ground; he just sent them off to hunt for us in every direction, apparently figuring that, dressed as impractically as we were, we couldn't have got far.

They might never have found our tracks, the tracks I'd been careful to leave for them, if it hadn't been for one man, the one who'd driven the van, who'd finally got out where I could see him clearly. Another Little Boy Blue, in jeans, blue work shirt, and a short blue denim jacket, except that he was a Big Boy Blue. He must have been close to my six-four in height, and in width he had shoulders that just had to give him trouble going through small doors. He was the kind of specimen that, when you meet him in my line of work, you toss aside the .38 and reach for the .44 Magnum if there isn't an elephant rifle handy. He wore no hat and his light hair was cut quite short, giving him a bullet-headed look. Some kind of a revolver was stuck into the front of his pants, but it was obvious that he didn't take it very seriously. With those shoulders, and hands to match, he didn't need to.

He exhibited no signs of Latin blood that I could see at that distance. As far as we were concerned at the moment, he was the one to watch, even though I got the impression that finding us wasn't really his job; he served the headman as driver and bodyguard and hadn't been included in the search-em-out orders. But there were apparently brains inside all the beef; and after a while he got bored watching his *compadres* thrashing around mindlessly in the sparse, spiny brush, so he got out of the van and wandered down the dirt road toward the highway, finally spotting the mark of one of Gloria's spike heels. Then he found another. Reaching the paved highway, he made a cast along the shoulder to the east and then, returning, to the west, discovering no more of those distinctive feminine shoe signatures. He was looking across the road thoughtfully, obviously considering an examination of the other side, when the man in khakis called to him, remonstrating with him. It was hard to tell through the little scope, but I guessed that the bossman was the typical kind of paranoid big shot who isn't comfortable without at least one gun at his side in addition to his own. With a couple of hostiles on the loose, *El Jefe* wanted his protection sticking close and paying attention to his job instead of wandering around looking at the ground.

"Shouldn't we be running?" Gloria whispered.

I shook my head. "How fast can you run, dressed like that? And how far? How fast can I run in these damn boots? We'd just leave them a clear trail to follow. Those guys look pretty durable; I don't think either of us is in good enough shape to outdistance them. We may as well just keep an eye on them from here and see if they fall for the phony trail we laid for them. If they don't, if they spread their search pattern wide enough to find us here, well, it's a better spot for a fight than some I've seen." I grimaced. "Hell, I've got five in the gun and a couple of five-shot refills. There are only eight of them. No sweat."

Gloria gave me a glance of annoyance; apparently she didn't appreciate gallows humor, if that's what it was.

She licked her lips. "If they catch us, they . . . they'll kill us like they did Papa and Millie Charles, won't they? Both of us?"

"I would judge that to be the object of the exercise, yes, ma'am."

"Oh, God, they're coming across the highway now!"

She sounded as if it was the end of the world; actually I was happy that Big Boy had talked his southpaw boss into letting him continue his researches. They crossed the highway together. After a little, they discovered the tracks I'd had Gloria make by the edge of the pavement. The big man was suspicious of the dainty footprints and started to look farther, but he was called back impatiently. *El Jefe* had decided to buy the scenario I'd sketched out for him: the beautiful young *gringa* and her elderly husband, after leaving their fancy car in a breathless hurry, not even stopping to lock it, had stood by the roadside and flagged down a bus or other vehicle and ridden it back east the way they'd come, crouching down so they wouldn't be seen from the brown van that soon passed them from the other direction. It was too bad, *qué lástima*, but they were obviously miles back down the highway by this time. Further search was clearly futile; and with a lot of illegal arms showing and the demolished Cadillac sitting there to incriminate him, the man in khaki was suddenly hot to evacuate the premises and gave sharp orders to that effect.

Big Boy Blue was obviously not so certain that the answer they'd found was the right one. Heading for the vehicles, he paused at the far side of the highway. Somehow I knew what was coming next, and even though I was lying in the shade and facing north, so there could hardly be any reflections, I lowered the little telescope hastily and checked to make sure that Gloria and my big white hat were out of sight. Then he'd turned to look straight at me. The distance was about a quarter of a mile and without the scope I had no chance of reading his expression, but I knew that he knew I was there, not from footprints or other evidence, just because that's where he'd have been if our situations had been reversed.

He stood there for a moment, obviously debating whether or not to make a final attempt to persuade his nervous chieftain to delay long enough to throw a few men across the ravine and have them scout the ridge. Then he shrugged resignedly, swung away, and hiked up to the van parked in the clearing behind the wrecked Cadillac. A few minutes later, all aboard, they were driving away, back toward Cananea and points east.

I heard Gloria's breath go out in a long sigh as the van disappeared from sight. She lay beside me for quite a while with her face buried in her arms.

"Are you okay?" I asked at last.

She raised her head to look at me, dry-eyed, clearly hating herself for having been scared and me for having been a witness to her fear. She didn't answer my question but sat up behind our bush and started to give a modest pull to her skirt. She stopped, aghast at its soiled condition. She made as if to scramble to her feet to determine the full extent of the catastrophe, but I put my hand on her sleeve.

"Easy. The men at the roadblock up the way may have got radio instructions to come by and see if they can catch us doing a victory dance to celebrate our escape, or just standing by the roadside trying to pick up a lift. Let's give them another few minutes. . . . Down! There they are."

It was a small white Japanese station wagon, not new, with a badly bent rear bumper and plenty of dents and scratches. There were two men in front and two in the rear. They turned up the little road across the way and pulled up behind the Cadillac as if they'd been told where to find it, as they undoubtedly had. The driver got out and walked up to the convertible and kicked one of the wheels, and I saw that I'd been wrong again, this was a woman, Mexican, short and stocky, with stringy black hair, but that means nothing nowadays. Some of the most glamorous fashion-magazine models look as if they'd been shampooed with crankcase oil. Her sturdy figure strained, in the obvious places, the faded cloth of the green coverall she was wearing. She carried a small machine pistol, make unknown, slung from one shoulder.

Returning to the station wagon, she paused to pick up something, and held it against her substantial figure, modeling it for the benefit of the men in the car: a lacy, black garment designed for minimum female coverage and maximum male stimulation. Everybody laughed. I heard Gloria give a sniff of indignation at this display of her underwear. The sturdy lady in the coveralls tossed away the lingerie and climbed into the beat-up wagon. It drove off eastward, as the van had done.

I rose and clapped the Stetson on my head. "Now let's get the hell out of here."

Getting to her feet with my help, Gloria glanced down at herself and was horrified by what she saw. "Oh, God, just *look* at me!" she gasped.

I said, "What are you complaining about? I don't see a single bullet hole or machete slash. I never contracted to preserve your pretty costume, just you. Stop fussing and come on."

She was trying to pull herself tidy and brush herself clean. "But where? How? We haven't got a car. . . ."

"Oh, yes, we have. It's about three miles southwest of here." I took out the two folded papers that had come with the survival kit I'd picked up in the Douglas hardware store, selected one, and unfolded it. "Southwest, yes. Say two point seven miles." I got out the little compass I'd been given, and pointed. "That-away."

She was watching me, frowning. "You arranged . . . ?"

"That's what I'm for, arranging."

She looked in the direction I'd indicated. The view wasn't encouraging, just the same steep, brushy landscape through which we'd been driving.

"Three miles! I can't possibly . . ."

I said, "Sure you can, if you just stop worrying about your lousy clothes. Hell, that's the bridal outfit you were going to douse with kerosene and set fire to because you didn't like the attitude of the groom, remember? You were going to write it off then; well, write it off now. There'll be something for us to wear when we reach the car. Do you want me to break the heels off your shoes and chop the bottom off your skirt for better leg action, like in the movies?"

"No, thank you! You've done quite enough to me already!"

She turned and marched off stiffly down the back of the ridge

77

in the direction I'd indicated. I went after her but soon moved into the lead so I could pick the easy routes for her; she had absolutely no eye for country. At first I also tried to give her a hand in the bad places, but she rejected my help irritably. When we stopped, it was still light enough to read a map. Sitting on a stone of convenient size, I took a look at the one I'd been given. Actually, it wasn't a map but an aerial photograph—rather, to be completely accurate, a small piece cut from a larger aerial photograph. Having been brought up on topographic maps, I still have trouble deciphering the stratospheric snapshots that have largely replaced them; but the ground covered here wasn't too hard to figure out. The photo fragment displayed an inked arrow for north and a straight ink line on which were marked four mile divisions for distance. It showed the winding, paved, east-west highway we'd left. It also showed an even wigglier little unpaved mountain track coming up from the southwest. It ran within a few miles of the highway for a short distance and then swung down to the southeast.

Where the track ran briefly parallel to the highway, an X marked the location of the car that awaited us. However, we'd spent too much time on that ridge, not that I'd had a choice. I'd had to make sure they accepted the false trail I'd laid for them and weren't coming after us; I'd been warned to shed all fleas and ticks before I picked up the car. Now I glanced at our position on the aerial shot and at the sun. It had been a long day for me, starting at a lake up in some other mountains almost five hundred miles away in another country; and there was some of it left, but not much. Say at most an hour before it became too dark to walk without risking a broken leg or neck.

"What's the matter, are we lost again?" Gloria's voice was tart, if a little shaky from her exertions. "Buffalo Bill, ha! It's a good thing you don't have to make a living as a sightseeing guide; I'm sure you'd wind up showing your busload of tourists the wrong city."

It was no time to let her pick a fight with me. I said mildly, "The car should be a little over a mile that way."

"How do you know?" she snapped. "How could you arrange

to have a car put in just the right place when you didn't know where the ambush was going to be? And what was that other map you had?"

I said, "If it was in just the right place, you wouldn't be griping your head off about having to hike several miles through the boonies, would you? We figured, going this way, west, they wouldn't want to operate too close to Cananea; they'd want us to get beyond the pass before they took us. But they'd want to catch us while we were still in this rugged country, and there's open farmland not too far ahead, so we kind of split the distance between the pass and the end of the rough stuff."

"And the other map?"

"Shows where the other car is located, the one we didn't need, as it turned out, about five miles east of Cananea, in case they laid for us before the rendezvous, or sent us back instead of forward. Or sabotaged our transportation so we'd need new wheels. Satisfactory, Mrs. Cody?" When she didn't speak, I went on: "If this photo is correct, there's a mean arroyo over that ridge ahead. The light's going to start fading on us any minute now, and we want to be out of that hole while we can still see, so we'd better keep moving."

She said, "No."

"What do you mean, no?"

She said sharply, "I mean, I've had it, Mister Secret Agent! I'm totally bushed, I look like the wreck of the Hesperus, I'm full of thorns like a pincushion, and my feet hurt. You can play in your damned arroyo if you want to. This is as far as I go, damn you; I don't care if it means spending the night sitting on a rock!"

I looked at her. Badly winded, she'd flopped on the ground beside me when I stopped, heedless of her clothes and dignity. Her grubby skirt was bunched up immodestly, showing a remarkable expanse of lovely, scratched legs more or less covered by tattered pantyhose that hadn't been exactly opaque even before they got torn. I found myself studying this display longer than I should have. It was a very odd thing. Back when she'd been a regal vision of perfumed, immaculate loveliness, she'd affected me no more than an expensive Barbie doll. I still didn't like her very much but, perversely, I found her more desirable with her fragile feminine armor in disrepair. I reminded myself that I was here to protect the dame, not rape her; and that a gentleman never, never takes advantage of a lady in distress who's totally dependent upon him. . . .

I rose. "Come on, let's go."

She didn't move. Her jaw was set stubbornly. "I won't resist if you want to pick me up and carry me as you did before. I won't give you the satisfaction of demonstrating your superior masculine strength. But you can't make me walk one step farther!"

I thought of the gun. It had worked before, but I hadn't liked waving it at her then and, tired and disgusted as she was now, she might call my bluff. I stood looking at her a moment longer, wondering what the hell she was up to. I mean, even if she was exhausted after hiking less than two miles, which I doubted, she wasn't a girl to take eagerly to sleeping on the desert without benefit of bed or plumbing. But I was tired of trying to understand her perverse ways. I drew a long breath and hauled her to her feet and tried to drag her along, but she refused to walk, she just allowed herself to collapse into an untidy heap at my feet. I reached down for her again, and stood her up again, and slapped her hard.

"Come on, you stupid bitch, start walking, or I'll knock you out from under what's left of that fancy hairdo!"

It was a mistake. Slapping people around just because you're mad at them is always a mistake, particularly when the people are women. I don't mean that I have an overpowering sense of chivalry. If they come at me with knives, I'll gut them just as fast as if they were men; if they shoot at me, I'll shoot back without hesitation; but somehow that's different from knocking one around angrily, a girl who'd had a rough time already, a girl for whom I was kind of responsible, a girl who—let's face it—attracted me sexually, just to make her walk somewhere, even for her own safety. We glared at each other for a moment. I saw two tears make dark tracks down her cheeks, bearing some of her remaining mascara.

"Damn you!" she whispered. "I should have known it was coming! You've done everything else to me, haven't you? Threatened me with a gun, scared me to death, rolled me in the dirt, dragged me through rocks and brush. . . . But you aren't satisfied with turning me into a walking scarecrow, you dirty sadist, you've got to beat me up, too. Well, go ahead, hit me again, knock me down, kick me. . . . Come on, come on, finish the job, beat me to a pulp . . . !" She took a step forward and slapped me hard. "There! What more excuse do you need? The dangerous wench attacked you, didn't she? So slug her again, defend yourself . . . !"

She swung at me again, and she had a couple of shots coming, so I stood there and took it; but then the last thin thread of control snapped, and she lunged at me hysterically, clawing for my eyes with chipped red nails. I turned aside and gave her a shoulder to work on while I disposed of my gun before she thought of trying for it. To be sure, she'd told me she hated them; but my experience has been that they hate them only until they find use for them. I couldn't help remembering that the last girl gun-hater I'd known had wound up emptying my own weapon at me, missing with all five, but you can't count on that.

With the .38 safely laid aside I turned back to deal with Gloria. She was sobbing as she clawed at me, and she'd already managed to rip the shoulder of my jacket and draw blood from my ear; she'd have pulled out a lot of my hair if I hadn't been wearing it pretty bald thanks to Arthur, so there wasn't much for her to grab up there. As it was she wasn't doing my scalp a bit of good. I got one wrist and then the other. She was still doing her best to annihilate me. She knew where a knee would hurt and tried to put one there. She attempted to drive a spike heel through my instep. I parried those attacks successfully, but then she butted me in the face and hurt my nose, so I hooked a foot behind her ankle, threw her down, and pinned her.

Her eyes stared up at me wildly out of her tear-wet face. Gradually she relaxed under me. I released her. An odd gleam came into the blue eyes, and she reached up with both hands and grabbed my head and pulled my face down to hers, kissing me hard enough to hurt, while her body moved fiercely against mine. There was no word spoken. We dealt with the clothing problem breathlessly and got the job down without tenderness. Lying there afterwards, I was aware of her freeing herself from my arms and sitting up beside me. A choked sound made me open my eyes, but she wasn't crying. She was looking down at me and laughing harshly.

"The big hero!" she sneered. "The great guide who can't find his way through a simple little Mexican village. The tough, experienced secret agent who falls like a ton of bricks for the old careless-skirt trick and a little physical contact. It's a good thing you never met the real Mata Hari, darling. Susceptible as you are, she'd have had you jumping through hoops as well as betraying your country!"

Well, I'd known she had something in mind when she stopped like that. So she'd taken revenge for the humiliations she felt she'd suffered at my hands by seducing me. I rolled over and closed my eyes again, feeling pleasantly relaxed and spent. It wasn't the worst vengeance I'd ever endured.

CHAPTER 10

I awoke in full darkness to find her still stirring around. You'd think, having fixed it so that we had to spend the night here, she'd at least take advantage of the stop to get some rest; but she was sitting on a nearby rock making sounds of annoyance. It took me a moment to realize what she was doing: she was trying to put her pantyhose back on by moonlight, having a hell of a time because the illumination was poor and the garment was so badly damaged that her toes kept coming out the holes.

I glanced at my watch and saw that I'd had a couple of hours sleep, all I was entitled to under these conditions. Actually, I thought we were pretty safe at the moment; but that's what the gents with all the gold braid thought at Pearl Harbor. I got up and pulled myself together and brushed myself off a bit, checked the gun I'd retrieved, and went to stand beside her. She didn't look up.

I asked, "What's the point? There isn't enough left of them to keep you warm, if they ever did."

Still without looking at me, she said, "My mother always said that nice little girls wear panties. Or pantyhose."

"If you want to be a nice little girl, you go about it in funny ways."

"Please don't!" she said. "I was just so scared and tired and dirty and fed up with being dragged around and ordered around. I . . . I just got mad and used the only weapon I had, the weapon any girl has. . . . Oh, shit!" Frustrated, she yanked off the shredded tights, wadded them up, and hurled them into the night.

She fumbled in her purse, brought out a comb, and started fighting her hair savagely, pausing to say, "I thought, if I got my stockings and shoes back on and my clothes brushed off a little and my hair combed out, I'd stop feeling so goddamn *primitive*, like a battered cave girl sleeping happily by the fire in her greasy furs after having a wild old time out in the bushes with the tough boyfriend with the club. At least she didn't have to brood about the runs in her nylons, lucky girl. Well, neither do I, now. . . . Matt?"

"Yes?"

"Tell me what we're doing here. Tell me what it's all about."

I said, "When I find out, you'll be the first to know."

She tugged irritably at the comb. "Ouch, that hurts!" she said. "No, don't give me that bullshit. You know. You knew kilometer ninety-five was a trap. You knew there'd be other men waiting farther on in case we didn't stop there. You even knew that they'd be coming by to check on us after the first bunch had left."

"I've had some experience with traps," I said. "Once we were in it, I knew pretty well how it had to function. As for how I knew it was there, all contacts are potential traps; but Mason Charles gave me the final word on this one."

"I didn't hear . . ."

"Oh, it wasn't what he said. It was the simple fact that he was there. That he knew where to come to waylay us. We discussed it earlier, remember?"

"We didn't come to any conclusions."

"We decided that he couldn't have tailed us to Cananea. Somebody must have told him where to go so he could make a fast run by a shorter route and beat us there. And there's really only one man who could have. The one who was so careful to make sure that nobody—well, nobody significant—saw Horace Hosmer Cody Number One, the genuine article, being replaced by Horace Hosmer Cody Number Two, the phony, me, in that Safeway parking lot. From things I overheard, I knew that somebody'd been spotted following you and Cody from the wedding chapel, and that he'd been picked up to get him out of our hair.

Obviously it was young Mason Charles trailing the man he suspected of being responsible for his mother's murder. And obviously after we'd taken off for points west, Mr. Mason Charles was turned loose again with the names *Cananea* and *Mr. Green's Restaurant* burned into his vengeful little brain. Sure, there was already a deathtrap set west of town; but you don't turn down gifts from the gods. I was wanted dead and here was a boy eager to do the job, so send him along and let him take a crack at me first. If he didn't manage it quite right, there were undoubtedly men standing by to fix things properly, like using his gun to blow my face off after he'd shot me down. As good as a machete job and just the thing a maddened son might do to avenge his raped and mutilated mother, emptying his piece into the bastard's head. A very neat solution, and they'd have themselves a dead, unrecognizable Cody to bury without upsetting the authorities with another *bandido* job." I grimaced. "A couple of dead Codys, since they could hardly leave you alive to talk. A stray bullet wouldn't be implausible with all the shooting."

Gloria shivered slightly. "Only it didn't work."

"So back to Plan One. Grab a hunk of soap, quick, and write *KM95* on the Cadillac's mirror and radio the boys to stand by, the mark is on his way after all."

She was silent for a moment, then she said, "Mr. Somerset."

"That's right. It has to be Somerset, doesn't it?"

"But it's impossible. He works for the United States Government."

"Ha ha," I said. "Say something else funny."

"But it doesn't make sense," she said. "He told me that, while he had no suitable agents available, the head of another government agency had offered him a man who could handle the impersonation, a competent man who'd pretend to be my husband and protect me. That sounds as if there had been a consultation, doesn't it; as if your mysterious organization, whatever it may be, was in on the plot, too. Either that, or your boss was badly deceived."

"My boss doesn't deceive easy."

85

"Then . . . then you have to face up to the fact that he, well, offered you as a human sacrifice."

I grinned in the semidarkness that gave our bleak surroundings a very eerie look. It takes a lot of moonlight to really brighten things up, and the fractional heavenly body above didn't give it to us.

"What the hell kind of an outfit do you think we are, Mrs. Cody?" I asked. "We're all walking human sacrifices. Nobody really expects us back when we leave the office in Washington, or wherever the briefing takes place. As a matter of fact, I was warned. I was told that things weren't what they seemed, be careful. My hunch is that somebody's been keeping a suspicious eye on Mr. Somerset's current operation, whatever it may be; somebody in another branch of government. I'll bet that when Somerset started looking cautiously for a substitute Cody, I was volunteered so fast it would make your head swim. Our highly placed governmental person wanted to have a man in there who could find things out and break things up; and my chief elected me as finder-outer and breaker-upper."

"But if your boss was aware that you were supposed to be murdered . . ."

"Somerset would hardly have told him that, sweetheart. Somerset might have covered himself by saying that the man selected for the impersonation would be running some risk; but risk is the name of the game. And don't kid yourself about my chief, he wouldn't hesitate to send one of us into a trap if he had some reason for wanting to see what it looked like turned inside out. Hell, we're supposed to be survivors; we're supposed to be smart enough to know when we're being set up; we're supposed to be able to cope. With practically anything. Just because a twerp like Somerset may have homicidal plans for us doesn't mean we run home to bed and pull the covers over our heads, shaking in abject terror. We've dealt with lethal creeps before."

"And it hasn't made you very modest," she said dryly. She hesitated. "You said Mason Charles tipped you off, or his presence in Cananea did. But you must have arranged for the cars,

86

that elusive car we haven't caught up with yet, before you ever saw him. Those telephone calls up in the U.S. before we crossed the border . . ."

I said, "I said Charles gave me the final confirmation. I'd had suspicions before that, enough to take a few escape measures. I called from Deming to have it set up; when I checked in Douglas they told me what had been arranged and where to make contact. That hardware store. I got my final instructions there and the bag of basic stuff I needed."

"Suspicions?" she said. "What made you suspicious?"

"I'm always suspicious when a bureaucrat is nice to me," I said. "They do like to throw their weight around, particularly when dealing with us field men, to show that we may think we're tough but we don't scare them a bit. But Somerset was just as sweet as sugar, even when I gave him a hard time. It was obvious that he needed me badly. It was also obvious that he felt he could tolerate my rudeness because he had something in store for me that would punish me for my lack of respect."

She shook her head. "That seems like a vague reason for taking such elaborate precautions."

"He also made a mistake," I said. "When he was recruiting me, he'd given my chief the impression that he had nobody in his own agency suitable for the job, just as he told you. That had to mean nobody tall enough to impersonate Buff Cody, since a guy like Somerset would never admit, even to himself, that our people are more competent than his. But do you remember those two operatives of his who turned up in that parking lot to arrest the real Buff Cody and whisk him away?"

She frowned. "I don't understand what you . . . One was quite short, wasn't he? The other . . . oh!"

I nodded. "The other was well over six feet tall. With no more makeup work than was done on me, he'd have made a swell Buff Cody. So why didn't Somerset use him and keep it in the family? I figure it was because, while I doubt that he tosses and turns at night, kept awake by concern for the safety of his people, he's an economical man and he isn't going to sacrifice one of his own trained and experienced and trusted agents to get a dead body he needs when he can borrow a suitable stumblebum from another agency.'' I shook my head ruefully. "He shouldn't have let me see that guy. That's when I got really uneasy; uneasy enough to decide that it wouldn't hurt to set up a parachute operation in case we had to bail out fast."

Gloria sighed. "It still seems a little clairvoyant to me."

I said, "We're very strong on ESP. And there are no tricks those computer commandos can pull that haven't been pulled on us before."

"If you're such a great mind reader, tell me why Uncle Buffy wants people to think he's dead." Then she went on quickly: "Well, obviously it's because he's done something so terrible that he has to drop out of sight. I suppose it must be the way he arranged for Papa and Millie Charles to be killed and the fact that Millie's son has found him out."

I said doubtfully, "You think that Somerset went to all the trouble of setting up a phony Cody, me, to be murdered, just so the real Cody could disappear and take up a new life as, say, John Jones?"

Gloria said, "You don't sound convinced. Why not? The government is always arranging new identities for gangsters and racketeers, isn't it?"

"Yes, in return for important testimony in court, but what's Somerset getting out of Cody that's worth all the effort?" I shook my head. "How do we know it's Cody who wants everybody to think Cody died down here in Mexico?"

"What do you mean?"

I said, "What if it's Somerset who wants people to think Cody's dead down here in Sonora?"

"Somerset?" She was startled. "Why would he want that?"

I said, "He'd want it if Cody was really going to be dead up in Texas."

"I don't understand!"

88

I said the same thing in different words: "Somerset would want it if he planned to kill Cody or have him killed."

"But that's crazy!"

"Think about it. If that's the situation, Somerset can hardly just issue a casual press release to the effect that this millionaire U.S. oil man was terminated, for reasons that are classified, by U.S. agents working under the direction of a certain Warren Somerset. And on the other hand, although I'm sure Somerset has ways of doing it, Horace Hosmer Cody can't just vanish. He's too prominent and, if what I hear about his finances is correct, he owes too much money; there'd be too many people trying to find him. But suppose somebody named Cody is murdered below the border, shot by a vengeful boy or chopped to death by vicious bandits. The identification is positive, the burial is immediate, and Mr. Somerset can proceed with his little homicide in perfect safety, eradicating a gent who no longer exists."

Gloria licked her lips. "But that would mean that we've been doing Uncle Buffy a terrible injustice!"

"It doesn't follow," I said. "There *were* three phony attempts on your life, designed to make you marry him for protection, weren't there? And there's no doubt in your mind, is there, that Buff Cody was responsible; and that once you were Mrs. Cody he intended to have you killed? The fact that somebody planned to murder him, too, and may very well have done it by this time, doesn't make him Mr. Clean." I frowned thoughtfully. "Let's say Cody and Somerset were together in a big deal of some kind, very sensitive, no publicity permitted. But we've already been told, even by Mr. Somerset himself, that Cody was running guns into Mexico; well, suppose Somerset was actually a silent partner. It wouldn't be the first time an important U.S. official got his pinkies dirty in a foreign arms deal. Somerset would probably claim, they all do, that he did it for highly patriotic reasons; but after all the recent scandals—hell, there was another one just the other day, remember—it wouldn't make him popular if it came out. Now let's say that the operation fizzled somehow; and that Mr. Somerset, afraid of being connected with it publicly, is wiping the record clean in proper Washington fashion, only he's not just shredding papers that might incriminate him, he's shredding people as well.''

"You mean you think he's the one behind Papa's murder?''

I said, "Let's forget, for the moment, Cody's little plot against you. We can call that a private money-making scheme, irrelevant to the main action. Cody was just going to eliminate one person. There's much more ambitious homicidal talent around. . . .''

Gloria interrupted: "He could just have asked!'' Her voice was soft and bitter. "All Uncle Buffy had to do was ask for the money he needed; he didn't even have to marry me. I'd have given it to him. I trusted him!''

I said, "Well, apparently he didn't trust you to be generous to the full extent required. But skip all that. It's small potatoes. Who cares about one lousy heiress, more or less, when big international affairs are involved? It seems likely that Somerset, covering his tracks, is wiping out everybody who can connect him with this arms deal, and if he also has to slaughter an innocent agent for camouflage purposes, a nice friendly chap like me, it's just too damn bad.''

Gloria protested: "But Papa and Millie Charles, how could they endanger Mr. Somerset, if you're suggesting that he's the one responsible for what happened to them?''

"What was your pop doing down in Mexico, anyway?'' I asked.

"I don't really know.'' She hesitated. "We were . . . we weren't on speaking terms. I'd made some remarks about the propriety of his traveling openly with a woman from the office— she was just a secretary, you know; but she'd thrown herself at him from the moment she was hired. That was when he told me he was going to marry her! I'd never dreamed it had gone that far. I pleaded with him. I said, sleep with her if you have to, even make the grand Mexican tour with her, I take it all back, but please, please don't make her my stepmother. It didn't go over real big, if you know what I mean.''

"I can see that it might not,'' I said. "Well, let's make a

guess as to the purpose of the jaunt. Let's say that your daddy had got wind of Cody's big arms deal and came down here to investigate, afraid that his money-hungry partner would get them both into serious trouble. And apparently he stumbled onto something Somerset couldn't afford to have known, so he had to go. Mrs. Charles just had the bad luck to be traveling with him. And having arranged for the removal of Will Pierce, Somerset would be afraid that Cody would guess who'd done it, so Cody had to go, too."

I felt Gloria shiver slightly beside me. She said after a moment, "But if you're right, that's one crime we've been attributing to Uncle Buffy—and Mason Charles has, too—of which he wasn't guilty. I should have known he'd never do anything to Papa after all the years they'd been together!"

"Well, it's still to be proved, one way or the other," I said. "But if I'm right, we're two more human documents for the hungry Somerset people-shredder. He can still use a dead Cody body down here; and in any case he can't have me testifying about what he tried to do to me. And he can't have you running loose and talking, either."

Gloria was silent for a little. "I don't know what made me . . . made me do that," she said at last; and we weren't discussing Mr. Warren Somerset any longer. "I don't usually . . . Believe it or not, but I'm not usually *that* much of a bitch. Do you think it was being such a total, grimy mess—in my eight-hundred-and-fifty-dollar wedding suit, for God's sake!—that released all my baser impulses? Like a little girl getting a weirdo charge from playing in the mud in her pretty party dress?"

I grinned at her in the moonlight. We'd never be friends, and I doubted that we'd ever be lovers again; the worlds in which we lived were too far apart. But there was a kind of understanding between us now that hadn't been there before.

I said, "If you want analysis, lady, see a psychiatrist. I'm just a poor damn gun-toting government employee, and I'm going to get some sleep."

CHAPTER 11

ACTUALLY, as I said, I'd had all the sleep to which I was entitled. After she'd settled down, I just lay there and listened to the night. You learn to handle the long night watches without either dropping off completely or going ape from boredom. We had a midnight coyote serenade for entertainment, but the girl did not awaken. The incomplete moon slid off the sky to the west, very gradually. At last the rugged horizon became faintly visible in the east and a gray hint of daylight found its way into our hollow. Gloria stirred, threw a slightly embarrassed glance my way, rose, and tiptoed off gingerly to find shelter behind a convenient bush. When she returned, smoothing out her crumpled silk suit as best she could, I made a point of waking up elaborately and making the same pilgrimage. I came back to find her sitting on her favorite rock, once more combing her hair. I decided there was something to be said for my temporary baldness.

"I know we haven't got much water," she said, "but could we spare just enough to dampen a Kleenex so I can mop this smeary makeup off my face and look a little less like a circus clown?"

"I think it can be managed," I said, unlimbering the canteen. "Here. You can take a reasonable drink for breakfast and use a few drops for your *toilette*, as we Frenchmen call it." I fingered the neat beard Arthur had made of the camping-out whiskers I'd brought him. "One good thing about this Cody disguise, I don't have to worry about shaving."

Gloria laughed. "Just the same, you look like a tramp who's

92

been sleeping in the woodshed. A lot of woodsheds. Well, so do I.''

We were chatting a bit too brightly to cover up the memory of what had happened between us last night. The fact that, in daylight, we both looked like castaways on a desert island was another source of embarrassment. When she'd finished cleaning up, I clapped my smudged white ten-gallon hat onto my head, waited briefly for her to stuff her dirty bare feet into her grimy white pumps, and led the way southwards. We made it through the big arroyo, and I was glad we hadn't tried it in the dark. I'd hoped for a little water at the bottom, but there was no stream at the moment, although it was obvious that torrents rushed along the eroded channel after heavy rains. On the crest beyond, I spent twenty minutes glassing the basin ahead—it took awhile because the powerful little telescope they'd given me had only a very limited field of view.

"What are you looking for?" Gloria asked. She was sitting a little below me, shoes off, massaging her bruised feet.

I shrugged. "Anybody," I said. "Anything. I'm just taking the standard precautions. Now we'll move up about a quarter of a mile and make another area check. Talk only in whispers and keep your head down, please."

We made a cautious approach to the next vantage point I'd chosen. I left Gloria well below the top, in charge of my conspicuous hat, while I crawled up, bareheaded, to where I'd have a good view.

She whispered eagerly, "Can you see the road yet? Can you see the car?"

"Yes and yes. You can move up here quietly if you want to."

It was a fairly large valley with a brushy gully at the bottom. Beyond, the ground rose steeply to a high escarpment. Partway up the slope, the road we wanted was notched into the hillside like a narrow shelf. On it, partly screened by some roadside bushes and a couple of scrawny little trees, was parked a small silver-gray station wagon that I recognized, through the 'scope, as a four-wheel-drive Subaru of fairly recent vintage. In that rugged country, I'd expected to be given a jeep-type vehicle or

93

maybe a husky four-wheel-drive pickup; but the Subaru had the reputation of being a fairly tough little beast that would do the job if you didn't ask too much of it in the way of road clearance. To the right of the car, just as the aerial photo had indicated, the road disappeared around the hillside to the southwest, heading down toward the coastal plain. To the left it wound up the steep slope that was just touched by the rising sun and lost itself in the mountains to the southeast.

I passed the scope to Gloria and aimed her in approximately the right direction. Except for the motionless wagon over there, like a small, silvery beetle perched on a distant bookshelf, there wasn't another vehicle in sight. We could no longer hear the rumble of traffic on the main highway behind us, and it was very quiet on our ridge: that early-morning hush you seldom experience unless you're hunting something. Or something is hunting you.

"Have you got it focused for your eye? Okay, follow the road to the left from where it comes around the bluff. . . ."

She said irritably, "It's like peeking through a keyhole; I can't even find the road. . . . Oh. Yes, I see the car. It's not very big, is it?"

"What did you expect on that goat-track, a stretch Mercedes?"

"Just so there's a pair of jeans on board, that's all I ask. And a pair of comfortable shoes." She handed back the telescope. "Well, what are we waiting for?"

I took a small drink from the canteen, capped it, and gave it to her. I took off my jacket and laid that across her lap. Then I reached into my pocket, found the little compass and the folded aerial photograph, and placed them on top of the coat.

"You're staying here while I scout things out," I said.

She stared at me indignantly. For a moment she was Lady Gloria of the sculptured hairdo again: "My dear man, aren't you overdoing the Dan'l Boone nonsense?"

I said, "Stay right here. I'm going to circle that station wagon and make sure nobody's lying in wait over there. I'm leaving you the telescope, the water, the map, and the compass. If the coast is clear, you'll see me come out on that road to the left of the Subaru and wave my arms for you to come on over. Give me two hours. Even if you hear shooting, wait out your two hours. If I come out *alone* and give you the signal, get over there. If there's anybody with me, or if I don't show up by . . . well, make it ten o'clock, head for the highway. Walk due north, just follow the little needle; it's shorter that way than the slant-wise way we came in, and it looks to be easier. With luck you can hitch a ride west to Hermosillo. The Hotel Gandara. Some-body'll be watching for us. He'll see that you're taken care of.''

I moved off without waiting for her response, going wide to the right, the west. My choice of directions was dictated by the fact that the hostile forces had last been seen withdrawing to the east, towards Cananea. That meant that if anybody had explored that dirt track this morning, he'd probably picked it up east of us. But if he hoped to find a car awaiting us, he wouldn't want to drive up to it or past it, leaving his fresh tire tracks in the dust to warn us. He'd therefore leave his vehicle to the east and scout ahead on foot. The area west of the Subaru was therefore the least promising, which was why I took it first. You want to check out all the unlikely spots for unpleasant surprises before you close in on the likely ones. . . .

An hour later I'd made my circle. I was tired, thirsty, dirty, ragged, and disgusted. Gloria was quite right, this Dan'l Boone business could be overdone. I'd found no sign of anything hu-man, let alone hostile. But they brainwash you thoroughly at the Ranch in Arizona where agents are constructed and recon-structed as required; I made the last approach to the Subaru with infinite care, and it was a big waste of time. I even looked in-side the car, gun in hand, to make certain nobody was lying in wait there. That is, I checked what I could see, but the space be-hind the rear seat was equipped with a kind of roller-blind cover to protect the luggage from larcenous eyes. A man could be hiding there waiting for the right moment to let the spring-loaded sheet of plastic snap back and come out shooting. I didn't believe it for a minute, but old habit made me carry out the farce to the end. I found the key where I'd been told it would be, in a little magnetic box under the left front fender. Pistol at the ready, I flung open the tailgate and slipped the roller-cover from its catches; and of course the trunk was just as empty of people as the rest of the car. I drew a long breath and stood there for a moment taking inventory of the goodies that had been provided for us.

There were clothes and boots and weapons and a big plastic cooler that presumably held food, but at the moment I was particularly interested in the insulated gallon jug of water. It had been a long, dry hike. However, my conscience reminded me that Gloria was out there awaiting my signal fearfully. Before I indulged myself with drink and food and clean clothes, I'd better set her mind at rest and get her moving this way. I holstered the .38 and straightened up. . . .

"Please to make no sudden movements, Señor Cody." The voice from behind me was soft and heavily accented. "Turn now, *por favor*, but slowly, maintaining the hands clearly in view."

When they get the drop on you like that, you always ask yourself: *Is this the place?* I mean, if they intend to kill you, you may as well go for it while you still have a gun and your hands free, regardless of how much artillery they're pointing at you. You'll take some lead, maybe too much lead, but you were scheduled anyway; and at least you've got a chance of taking some of the bastards with you on the long safari. So you wonder if you've finally found the spot for your George Armstrong Custer act, otherwise known as Helm's Last Stand.

It's always a tough call; but in this case I'll admit that the politeness of the man behind me influenced my decision somewhat. Of course, I've known some very courteous human monsters; nevertheless, it's easier to surrender to a man who's nice about it than to a blustering blowhard who tells you how many gory pieces he's going to blow you into if you move one finger wrong. There was also the fact that nobody was supposed to be there. I'd checked, hadn't I? I'd scouted the area thoroughly. I would have said I couldn't possibly have missed anybody. Now

I had to live long enough to see what kind of invisible men they grew in this part of the world.

I said, "It's your deal, señor."

I turned slowly, hands at shoulder height. It didn't make me feel any better to learn that I hadn't just overlooked one man; there were four of them. There was one consolation, however; they bore little resemblance to the ragtag bunch that had tried to trap us the evening before. I hadn't fallen into the hands of *El Jefe* and his machete freaks.

These were small, sturdy, brown men in identical camouflage suits. They were wearing cocky little berets, also in camo. Elite units of the Mexican Army, perhaps, but I seemed to recall that the Mexican military caliber is 7.62mm. These men were carrying U.S.-made 5.56mm M-16 assault rifles, the same kind of weapon that had probably punctured Gloria's Mercedes, back when Buff Cody was working on scaring her into matrimony. All four men had broad Indian features and were either clean shaven or naturally beardless. Three had ropey black hair worn fairly long. The fourth man, the one who'd spoken, had a more civilized haircut. They all had badges on their berets, dull black so as not to reflect the light and betray the wearer's location; but his was more elaborate than the others. It was presumably an indication of rank, as was the .45 automatic pistol he held—his assault rifle was slung across his back. The piece in his hand was a lightweight Colt Commander, a compact version of the old 1911 Army pistol. He holstered it and stepped forward to relieve me of my revolver.

He spoke in his careful English: "I am Lieutenant Ernesto Barraga, of the *Fuerza Especial*. My orders are to capture you alive, which I have done, and to convey you to *El Cacique*, which I will now do. We will use this vehicle since it is available. As you say in the U.S., it beats walking. I will drive. You will sit beside me. A man in the rear will have you covered at all times. Since it is a small automobile, we will leave the other two to follow on foot." He stared at me hard for a moment. "Please do not try to escape. I would much prefer to deliver you intact according to my instructions. Even if you should get away

97

without a bullet in you, which is very unlikely, these men would run you down in short order. In this country, with such men, one needs no bloodhounds; they are the best trackers on this continent."

I said, "I can believe it. At least you all slipped up on me very competently. I usually hear people coming." I hesitated. "If I may ask, who is *El Cacique* and what is the *Fuerza Especial*?"

"Any questions you have, about the Special Force or other matters, will be answered by my superiors, if they choose. Please get into the car."

He spoke to his men in a language that meant nothing to me, except that it was neither English or Spanish. One continued to cover me as I climbed into the right-hand seat. One of the others seemed to be carrying some radio equipment; he paused to lower an antenna before placing his electronic backpack in the rear of the wagon; then he took his place in the back seat, behind me. Barraga stuffed his assault rifle into the rear and got behind the wheel and started out. Surprisingly he was a gentle and careful driver; there's something about a vehicle with four-wheel drive that seems to turn most drivers into spring-busting madmen. It was a clear day with a cloudless sky and a very bright sun; I hoped Gloria was hoarding her water supply carefully, but she hadn't impressed me as being strong on self-discipline. I wondered what she'd think when she saw the station wagon drive away, probably that I was deserting her. Since there was nothing else for her to do, she'd undoubtedly start limping angrily toward the main highway in her impractical shoes. I hoped she'd make it.

We proceeded downhill past the point where I'd crossed the road on foot earlier in the day and entered territory that was new to me. The road lost altitude rapidly and eventually crossed a wide wash where all four tires of the Subaru had to throw sand like paddle wheels to drag us through. We climbed around a shoulder of the ridge beyond and turned off the main road. An even smaller and rougher track brought us to a grassy meadow

98

and an encampment composed of two wall tents, not very large, and a motor pool.

One of the tents was easy to identify. Apparently this was mealtime—late breakfast or early lunch—and men in camouflage suits were lined up at the door and walking away with trays of food. The field kitchen. A sentry in front of the other tent indicated that it probably served as headquarters for *La Fuerza Especial* or at least this part of it—maybe there were similar units elsewhere. If sleeping was done here, it was apparently done mostly on the ground. Well, as Gloria and I had learned, in this dry climate it wasn't an unbearable hardship.

The motor pool consisted of four Chevrolet three-quarter-ton Suburbans, the big station wagons sometimes known as carry-alls. They had auxiliary air-conditioning units on the roofs—with that long wheelbase, the dashboard cooler isn't effective all the way back—and they had dark glass in the windows and four-wheel drive. Next to them stood a van that was identical except that it lacked the auxiliary AC and had two fewer doors and windows only in front. It was presumably the supply train for this miniature army. The vehicles were not painted in military camouflage or olive drab; instead they were civilian white, brown, blue, green, and tan.

Little groups of men were sitting cross-legged in the sunshine eating off their laps. I was pretty certain, although I couldn't see them, that there were others out in the brush standing guard. Lieutenant Barraga was no Latin exhibitionist; he felt no need to call attention to his captured vehicle by gunning it through camp with wheels spinning and dirt flying. He just drove up sedately and parked. I'd played the docile-prisoner game before, so I sat still while everybody else disembarked.

"Now we will see *El Cacique*," Barraga said, after retrieving his assault rifle. He opened my door and motioned me out. "Walk ahead of me to the tent that is more near, *por favor*."

We passed a small bunch of men eating in the shade of one of the trucks, an exercise in optimism since with the sun almost overhead the shade didn't amount to much. The food seemed to be tortillas and beans, not my favorite dish but it reminded me

99

that I'd eaten nothing since the *carne asada* of the previous evening. There was also, it seemed, a choice between coffee and Coca-Cola. Beer would have gone better with that food, but I suppose you can't serve beer to military personnel on duty; although as I recall the British Navy used to fight pretty well on rum.

"What have you there, Lieutenant?"

The contemptuous question was obviously spoken in English so I would understand it. The speaker, emerging from the tent ahead, was a tall man with Spanish features, a small black mustache, the usual camouflage uniform, and a beret badge that was even fancier than Barraga's.

"This is Señor Horace Cody, Captain," Barraga said. "Señor, this is Captain Luís Alemán."

"I think we can dispense with the social formalities, Lieutenant Barraga," said Captain Alemán. He looked at me without liking. "So this is the subversive arms smuggler we have been seeking!"

I'd forgotten that I was supposed to be a merchant of death here. It wasn't a very good piece of country for me, I reflected. One gang, knowing I wasn't a bankrupt oil millionaire named Cody dabbling in weapons to retrieve his fortunes, was trying to butcher me with machetes. And now another group of gents, who believed I was that arms-smuggling Cody, was pointing automatic weapons at me. I restrained the impulse to tell the tall captain that he couldn't have been seeking very hard or he'd have found me sooner, like at the border.

He spoke sharply, "Why are his hands free? Tie them immediately. . . . No, behind him!" When Barraga had whipped a length of rawhide around my wrists, Alemán said, "That is better. I will take him to *El Cacique*."

"Yes, Captain."

Then Alemán was giving me a violent shove toward the nearest tent that, with my hands lashed behind me, would have had me on the ground if I hadn't been expecting something of the sort. You can always tell the shovers and the slappers. They're the ones who aren't quite sure who they are and what they are, and it shows in their eyes. They have to keep proving their toughness at other folks' expense.

"Inside, you!"

He waved the sentry aside and gave me another push that sent me stumbling through the door of the tent. He followed me in and swung me around and backhanded me across the face.

"Where is it?" he demanded.

CHAPTER 12

EXCEPT for the two of us, there was no one in the tent. As I'd guessed, it was an office of sorts. GHQ. A sturdy folding table with metal legs and a plastic top functioned as a desk, well loaded with paperwork. There was a typewriter and a portable radiotelephone set. A folding metal chair was set up behind the desk, and a couple of others waited in reserve against the side wall of the tent. There was a narrow folding cot along the rear wall, behind the desk chair. It was neatly made up. An expensive, closed suitcase stood at the foot of it—an unmilitary touch, I thought. On an expedition like this you'd expect everyone to operate out of duffel bags and leave the fancy luggage home. On the other hand, rank confers certain privileges everywhere.

Getting no answer to his question, Alemán took another swing at me. The forehand wasn't as bad as the backhand since I didn't get the knuckles or the stones of the rings he was wearing, but I made it look spectacular, flinching away from the blow and letting myself lose my balance and go down. They always enjoy knocking you down; and when they're beating on you, you want to keep them happy. If you make them sad, they may actually hurt you.

"*El Cacique* has stepped out for a few minutes," the tall man said, standing over me. "I intend to have this settled before he returns. *Where is it?*"

I felt a little blood running from my nose; I made no effort to sniff it back. They love the sight of blood—other folks' blood—and the human body holds several quarts. I could spare a few drops for public relations.

"Where is what?" I asked. "Dammit, I don't know what you're talking about, Captain!"

"Do you think I am so foolish?" he demanded. "We want the shipment of arms, Cody; waste no time pretending you do not know where it is! The arms intended for the rebels. We know they were landed on the beach at Bahia San Cristóbal. Four trucks transported them inland. We know there was the cross-double, as you Yankees call it. The rebels did not have the money they claimed to have, the money they had promised, so they tried to take the weapons without pay. But when they opened the trucks, they were empty. Fearing such treachery, your agent, Jorge Medina—you see, we know much about your clandestine operations—had hidden the cargoes before proceeding to the rendezvous."

"Medina?" I said. "I don't know any Medina."

"That is strange, since his lady friend watched you visit him and arrange the smuggling. She is very bitter about the way you involved him in your criminal activities and sent him to his death."

"They killed him?"

"You know this very well. Yes, they questioned him, but they were rough and clumsy. Medina died at their hands, apparently without giving them the information. But do not try to make me believe that he was not operating under your instructions and that you do not know where he concealed the materiel!" Alemán shook his head sharply. "No, do not waste my time with more denials! Obviously the rebels learned that much from your man, that you also knew the location. That is clearly why they have turned their attention toward you. They tried to intimidate you, first by killing your partner, Pierce, and his woman, and then by attempting the life of his daughter, for whom you obviously have a certain regard since you just married her. Finally, when you would not yield to this manner of pressure and tell them what they wished, they tried to capture you for interrogation."

He was talking to intimidate me by showing how well-informed he was, which was fine for me, since he was telling me useful stuff I hadn't known. But I had a problem: I'd been sent down here by Mr. Somerset to die as Horace Hosmer Cody; could I do anybody any good by continuing to live as Horace Hosmer Cody? I decided that I might as well stick with the impersonation for the time being, since Alemán wasn't likely to believe he'd got the wrong man and stop beating on me, no matter who I claimed to be.

I said, "Oh, is that what they were doing? The way they were brandishing those machetes, I thought they had the same treatment in mind for us that they'd already applied to my partner, Will Pierce, and his lady friend."

"You know quite well what they were after!"

"Look, you-all are barking up the wrong tree!" I reflected that I was sadly underqualified for this assignment; I wasn't any better at talking Tex than I was at talking Mex. "I never arranged for any shipment of arms, hell, no! I'm a respectable businessman; where would I get arms? I never knew anybody named Medina, and I sure God don't know where any guns are hidden. . . ."

All of which was the exact truth, of course, except for my being a businessman and respectable; but it didn't help me much. Alemán stepped forward and kicked me in the side as I crouched there in abject terror. Fortunately he was wearing reasonably flexible jungle boots instead of rigid military brogans, but while I didn't think any ribs were damaged, it drove the breath out of me for a little.

"You force me to take measures I do not like!" he snapped. "I think you will be less stubborn in a moment. . . . Bring her in!"

The tent flaps parted, showing three figures silhouetted against the outside light. The outer two were soldiers or whatever they called themselves here. The middle shape, supported between them, was feminine and familiar, but it seemed to be considerably more tattered than I remembered it.

The two men bore Gloria forward and dumped her onto the canvas floor of the tent and marched out again. With my hands still tied behind, I kneed my way clumsily to her side, as she struggled to sit up and made it. She wasn't in very good shape.

104

For a moment, looking at her, I thought she'd also suffered a beating. Then I realized that her scratches and scrapes were not attributable to fists or clubs; she'd just been forced to do a lot of heedless scrambling through rocky and thorny places by people who hadn't been as careful to pick the easy routes as I had. My jacket seemed to have got left behind, but she was wearing my Buff Cody hat. Too large for her, the big Stetson should have given her a comic look; but she was too dirty and battered and nearly naked to be funny. I was relieved to see her pull at her rags in an effort to cover herself as she sat there. Not that I was greatly affected by what showed and what didn't—I'd already made its acquaintance—although Alemán, behind me, was undoubtedly licking his lips salaciously; but if she could worry about modesty her condition couldn't be too serious. Still, while the big hat had protected her from painful sunburn, her face had a haggard look I didn't like, and her lips were dry and cracked.

"Easy," I said. "Easy, Mrs. Cody. Who let you out in that skirt?"

I'd been afraid she'd call me by the wrong name, but she got the message. She managed a weak smile. "Who let you out in those pants, Mr. Cody, dear?" She tried to lick her parched lips, as she regarded me more closely. "Horace! You're hurt!"

"What's a little nosebleed between friends? Are you all right?"

There was awkwardness between us now that we were no longer alone in the wilderness; we'd spent a day and a night together and had learned to know each other a little too well in some respects and not at all in others.

"Now there's a really *stupid* question!" she said. "Do I look all right? If you really want to know, aside from being utterly destroyed, I'm simply dying of thirst. They wouldn't give me . . ." She drew a long, shuddering breath. "I was watching the road, waiting for you to show, and suddenly they were just there, behind me, waving guns at me; and then they made me walk so fast! It was miles and miles through that barbed-wire brush, and I kept falling down in these crazy shoes, God, I'll never wear another pair of high heels as long as I live! I tried to break them off like you offered to once, but you were talking through your hat, mister. It's some kind of crazy space-age plastic that King Kong couldn't break and they wouldn't lend me a machete to chop. . . . They'd just yank me back to my feet and order me to keep up and drag and shove me along when I couldn't. I'd used up all the water hours before, well it seemed like hours, and they wouldn't give me . . ."

The captain, standing over us, interrupted: "The lady exaggerates. My men carried her most of the way. They are trained to water discipline, of course, and they know where to find it in this country if they really need it. They do not carry canteens in the field so there was none available for her."

"Well, there's some available here in camp, isn't there?" I said. "Aren't you going to let her have some?"

"Of course." His voice was expressionless. "As soon as you tell me what I ask, the lady will have all the water she requires, enough to bathe in if she so desires."

"You bastard!"

Calling them names is always pointless, of course, and it can earn you some quite unnecessary bruises. However, I had to keep in mind that I wasn't an experienced agent here, with years of practice at keeping my temper. I was an arrogant, hotheaded Texas millionaire who'd be bound to make with the indignant dialogue. In fact, under the circumstances, I was sure that the real Buff Cody would have gone into much greater detail about the captain's ancestry.

Captain Alemán smiled thinly. "Eventually, as her thirst increases, I am certain that the pretty señora will persuade her loving husband to yield. I can wait!"

"You're a low-down, stinking coyote!"

It sounded pretty corny to me, but he found it convincing enough to give me a backhand crack to the side of the face. One of his rings nicked me above the right eyebrow and produced a little more blood for his pleasure. It was pretty much the same situation as I'd met in the men's room in the restaurant in Cananea. Normally, whether the girl was threatened with execution or dehydration, Superagent Matthew Helm, code name Eric, would not have been permitted to deal; we can't roll over and play dead every time somebody grabs a hostage off the street. However, to maintain my cover as Horace Hosmer Cody here, I was entitled to consider the welfare of my bride; I was merely concerned with the timing. Could I yield convincingly now— well, as far as I knew how to yield—or should I wait until I had a few more cuts and bruises and he'd knocked Gloria around a bit, brought out the knife he was bound to produce, and promised to spoil her face if I didn't talk? I mean, I'd been here before. The moves are predictable.

Gloria stirred impatiently. "Horace, I'm really *awfully* thirsty, darling! What can he possibly want you to tell him that's more important than . . . than me?"

I hesitated, a man struggling toward a reluctant decision. "All right, baby, but I'm afraid you won't like what you hear. . . . I really don't know where the arms are hidden, Captain." I shook my head quickly. "Now don't get violent again, dammit! I'll admit I arranged for the guns and the ship, isn't that enough for you?"

"Where did you obtain the munitions?"

I said, "I got them very indirectly through certain foreign channels, that's all I can tell you. I don't know exactly where the middleman I used over there got the merchandise. I didn't ask; I didn't want to know. I'm a respectable businessman like I said; I couldn't afford to be directly connected with anything like that. Jorge handled this end of it. He fronted for me here in Mexico; he dealt with the revolutionaries and arranged for the trucks and drivers."

I was making it up as I went along, mainly from what he'd already told me, but I thought I was pretty close. Illicit arms operations generally follow a certain pattern.

"Go on."

I said, "Jorge warned me that those wild-eyed dissident bastards didn't look too reliable; we'd better take some precautions, like caching the stuff until we saw their money, even if it meant a lot of work unloading and loading again if the deal was straight. He said he'd let me know as soon as he'd scouted the route and picked a good spot, but he never did. Next thing I heard, he was dead. Hell, that's why I'm down here, spending my honeymoon looking for a bunch of lousy guns!"

I looked significantly at Gloria, and she took the cue, saying in a shocked voice, "Horace! Were you actually dealing in . . . You were going to use me, our marriage, our honeymoon, to hide what you were . . . You know how I feel about guns!"

It was soap opera of sorts, but she was a pretty good actress; her anger and distress were reasonably convincing.

I said defensively, "Sweetheart, I have a lot of money tied up in those arms; money I can't afford to lose and, as my wife, neither can you."

Captain Alemán broke in: "Enough of this! You are lying to me, or at least withholding information. Possibly you were never informed of the exact location; but you would not be here in Mexico if you did not have some idea of where your agent would have hidden those weapons. At least you know whom to ask and where to start searching. I have listened to your evasions long enough. My patience is at an end. You force me to resort to more drastic measures!"

He spoke over his shoulder and reached a hand through the tent flaps; I'd guessed wrong. It wasn't a knife. When he stepped forward he was holding a big machete, a rather beat-up looking and tarnished old blade that looked as if it had been used for cracking cement blocks. He put his foot against my shoulder and kicked me away from Gloria and stood over her for a moment, making a thing of testing the edge with his thumb.

"Not very sharp, unfortunately. I regret this very much, beautiful señora, but you must blame your stubborn husband, not me." He reached down and whipped the oversized hat off her head and tossed it aside. He dug his fingers into her matted blond hair, pulling her head back against her knees, and he laid the edge of the heavy weapon against her cheek. "As I said, not very sharp, it will make a ragged wound and an ugly scar, impossible to repair. Do not procrastinate further, Señor Cody. You have told a part of the truth, now give me the rest. Tell me how to find those arms!"

There was nothing to do. I simply didn't know enough to continue lying plausibly. I didn't know the location of the place on the coast, Bahia San Cristóbal, where he'd said the guns had been landed, and I didn't know the inland delivery point where the trucks had been found to be empty and Cody's agent, Medina, had been tortured and killed. There was no way I could stall by inventing a plausible fictional hiding place somewhere between those two geographical points. Hell, I didn't even know what Mexican state or states we were talking about.

Gloria's face was pale under the dirt. A little thread of blood wormed its way down her cheek. She didn't protest or plead, perhaps because she was afraid that just the movement of talking would cause more damage, or perhaps because she realized that it was useless. She just stared at me without hope, knowing that, not being Cody, I had no idea where the damned arms were hidden, so I couldn't save her. . . .

"That will do, Captain!" The voice spoke sharply from behind me. "We do not make war upon women."

A man in civilian clothes marched past me. He helped Gloria to her feet. Alemán stepped back, lowering the ugly blade.

"Sir . . . !"

"You may go, Captain Alemán."

"Sí, señor!" Offended, Alemán tossed aside the machete and marched out.

"He is a good man, but he gets carried away." The newcomer was examining Gloria's face. "Only a scratch, señora. As he said, the weapon had a very rough edge. There will be no mark; to make certain, we will clean it and bandage it in a moment. I am the one they call *El Cacique*. Chieftain, in your language. You are Mrs. Cody?"

"Yes, that's right."

"And this is Mr. Cody?"

El Cacique turned to look at me; and I knew him. I'd encountered him before in the line of duty here in Mexico. From his surprised expression, quickly controlled, I saw that he recognized me, too, in spite of the years that had passed and the disguise I was wearing; and that he knew perfectly well that I wasn't anybody named Cody.

You might say that was one impersonation that had never really got off the ground.

CHAPTER 13

"IT is a pleasure to meet you again, Mr. Cody. Cigarette? No, I remember, this Mr. Cody does not smoke. . . . This Mr. Horace Hosmer Cody who is known as Buffalo Bill for some mysterious Yankee reason that will have to be explained to me."

We were sitting in the front seat of one of the three-quarter-ton Suburbans—the white one, if it matters—with the motor running and the two air conditioners gradually dispelling the heat that had built up inside the closed vehicle. Maybe that was why this one had been chosen for our conference, because a white car doesn't get as hot in the sun as a darker one. I knew that the gloomy window glass prevented the men eating in the meadow outside from seeing in, but it was hard to believe since I could see out perfectly well. We'd left the tent to Gloria and her personal cleanup campaign.

I said, "The original Buffalo Bill was a frontier scout, and later a star in a Wild West show. He had the same surname. I imagine young Horace Cody was a tough kid and didn't much like the sissy name he'd been given. Horace, for God's sake! He was willing to go along with what the other kids called him in a joking way, so the nickname stuck. I guess you could call it an example of Texas humor."

"I see. Very dimly. Do you mind if I smoke?"

I said, "In our racket, when we die, it's seldom from second-hand carcinogens."

"Or even first-hand ones. I find the habit very satisfying. As you say in your country, who wants to live forever?"

I said sourly, "The old bad-guy/good-guy routine. The bad guy holds the rusty machete to the lovely heroine's face and the good guy comes charging in crying that he doesn't make war on women. Corny! You ought to be ashamed of yourself, Ramón."

He laughed. "I did not know with whom I was dealing, friend Matthew, or I would have found a better approach. Would you care for a drink?"

"I can't remember the last time I refused."

He passed me a small silver flask with the cap off. Out here in the Mexican boonies, I'd expected some kind of ethnic tipple like tequila, or maybe even corrosive mescal or pulque, but it was very good, smooth Scotch. Well, I suppose that could be called an ethnic tipple, too; I guess they all are, and only ethyl alcohol itself can be considered truly international. I took a judicious slug and passed back the flask with appropriate thanks, sat there while he drank, and had another one, feeling the liquor easing the strains and bruises of the long morning.

In Mexico, you never come directly to the point, and we had all the time in the world, so there was no need for any rude *gringo* haste.

I said, "This is quite a collection of rolling stock you have here."

Ramon laughed. "We did not wish to attract attention by employing obvious military vehicles. As a matter of fact, I asked for trucks and vans of various makes and styles, but apparently a *político* had a friend who sold Chevrolets and had a surplus of these left from the previous year that he wished to dispose of profitably. You know how it is." He shrugged. "At least they are of different colors and have the dark windows so that we do not flaunt the fact that we are transporting men in uniform along the public highways. It is not total camouflage, of course. The people in whom we are interested know who we are; but it diminishes public curiosity."

"And just who are the people in whom you are interested, Ramón?"

He laughed and didn't answer. I had not, of course, called him by name the moment I recognized him, or reminded him of old times, or embraced him fondly—well, that would have been quite a trick with my hands tied. But we don't recognize people unless they make it clear that they want to be recognized; and after that first flicker of surprise he'd treated me as a stranger. I was merely the husband. He was more interested in the lovely, distressed wife. Well, that figured. He'd always been a ladies' man.

After applying a neat Band-Aid to her cheek—it really wasn't much of a cut—and seeing that she had plenty to drink and that her other needs were taken care of, he'd produced a small automatic pistol and ordered me to precede him out of the tent, leaving Gloria alone with a washbasin, a washcloth and towel, a five-gallon jerrycan of water, the feminine clothes that had been provided in the Subaru, and his assurance of complete privacy.

As an afterthought, he'd made me wait at the entrance briefly while he took care of something he'd forgotten: he went back to his suitcase and produced a bar of scented soap, fragrant enough to make the whole tent smell like a florist's shop when he opened the plastic case for her. They have some effeminate tastes down there, and I have no desire to smell like a flower, even in the bathtub, but you'd better not underestimate them on that account—I noticed that, while he'd been just as solicitous as he could be, he hadn't left her the machete. He'd gathered it up casually and passed it to the sentry outside the tent door. Then he'd marched me at pistol point, hands still tied, to the big white station wagon, indicating clearly to anyone interested that I was a dangerous prisoner with whom no chances were being taken. Once inside the vehicle, however, he'd brought out a small pocketknife and cut me free.

His name was Ramón Solana-Ruiz. He was a short, stocky man with a brown face and a full head of glossy black hair. He could have had some Indian blood but I'd never asked; you never know, with this racial nonsense, if they're going to be flattered or insulted. He was wearing a dark but summerweight business suit with a faint stripe and an immaculate white shirt. There was a silk tie with a discreet pattern in green. I remembered that

113

he'd never gone in for casual clothes much. The city outfit didn't look as out of place here as it should have, but I couldn't help wondering how he kept his black shoes so shiny in this dusty area.

Years ago we'd been in more or less the same line of business for our respective countries; and in the line of business he'd saved my life once, on a deserted islet in the Gulf of California. In the line of business I'd done him some favors that might be considered to even the score—except that I don't ever forget folks who save my life, any more than I forget those who try to take it. The last time we'd met, Ramón had indicated that he was through with our kind of work; he'd had a very rough time on a previous mission, and his nerves weren't up to it any longer. That had been quite a while ago, and I hadn't expected ever to see him again; we don't keep track of old business acquaintances with Christmas cards and social visits. Now I'd found him down here playing chieftain to a warlike tribe of little men who could move through these mountains like ghosts. *El Cacique*, for God's sake!

He must have sensed what I was thinking, because he said, "Hey, how you like my Yaquis, *amigo*."

I grimaced. "Hell, I'm supposed to know my way around the boonies, but the little bastards made a monkey of me. I never knew they were there until they had me." I glanced at him. "I thought you people exterminated your Yaquis around the turn of the century."

He laughed. "Yes, like you people exterminated your Apaches. Perhaps they are not all full-blooded Yaquis. What is that strange term you use north of the border, Native Americans? I found it hard to believe when I first heard it. Such an insult. Is calling a man a native not like calling him an ignorant primitive, a brutish aborigine? The Native Americans are restless tonight, hey? But very well, we will follow Yankee custom in this as in many other things and call my men Native Mexicans." He laughed again. "You will be happy to know that my Native Mexicans report that you move quite well in the brush—for a clumsy *gringo*."

114

I grinned. "Thank them for me. I'll treasure any compliment from those slippery little gents, even a qualified one. But where did you get that Alemán clown?"

Ramón shrugged in the elaborate Latin manner. "He is my second-in-command and my liaison with the Army. My own military experience is far in the past. He makes a useful executive officer, he knows the current regulations, he is good at administration and discipline, and the Army does not like independent commando units, even small ones that are fully authorized. There have been too many independent armies in Mexico's history. So we have one of their officers as, what do you call it, a chaperone? To see that we do not misbehave."

"Politically, you mean?" When he nodded I studied him for a moment. "Not to be snoopy or anything, but I'd still like to know why you're prowling these mountains with a bunch of trained Indian scouts. What is this commando unit of yours fully authorized to do?"

He smiled thinly. "Perhaps I will answer you—after you have told me what you do in Mexico using the name of a man who is currently very much *persona non grata* here."

And that brought me up against a question I'd been anticipating, for which I had no official answer: How much could I tell him? I mean, he was a good man and an old friend of sorts; but he had his country and I had mine.

I said, "Before I start lying to you, I'd like to ask a few questions, if you don't mind."

"Ask."

I gave myself a moment to line things up in the right order inside my head. "First, what do you know about a man who calls himself Señor Sábado?"

He studied me thoughtfully. "You are, of course, aware that it is what we call one of the days of the week. Saturday."

"It's about all I know," I said.

"What is your interest in this Mr. Saturday?"

"It's merely a name I was told to watch for—I suppose I should say, listen for. But I was informed that if something

115

should happen to said Sábado your government wouldn't order black armbands to be worn and flags to be flown at half mast.''

"That is correct." Ramón smiled thinly. "Let me put it this way: We have not been able to determine the identity of Señor Sábado, but the name has come to our attention in a context that leads us to believe that an accident to the gentleman—even a very serious accident—would not, to use your figure of speech, justify a day of national mourning, quite the contrary.''

Well, I've heard less elaborate ways of passing a death sentence, but it confirmed what Mac had told me in El Paso: the Mexican government would put no obstructions in the way of my shadowy mission and might even cooperate to a degree.

I said, "Now tell me how Lieutenant Barraga came to address me by name—well, by the name I'm using here.''

"We are, of course, very interested in those missing arms, and in everyone connected with them. When we heard—we have our sources above the border; maids and waiters hear a great many things—when we heard that 'Mr. Cody' intended to spend his honeymoon in Mexico, we made arrangements to protect him from the fate met by his partner, Pierce.''

"Some protection!" I said.

Ramón laughed shortly. "My men, watching, reported that the elderly millionaire gentleman was not, it seemed, quite as helpless as his bald head and gray beard would suggest. I suppose the skill with which you made your escape, as well as the vehicle that was so conveniently supplied you, should have led me to suspect your identity—''

I said, "I've met some backwoods characters in their eighties who could walk me into the ground. The real Cody could be tougher than you think, and he's certainly got the resources to get a little Japanese station wagon planted anywhere he needs it.''

Ramón shrugged. "In any case, you were doing quite well without help; I saw no reason to interfere. I merely gave orders to have you and the lady brought in the following morning. It seemed unnecessary to interfere with the happy couple's wedding night, even though it had to be spent under fairly uncomfortable conditions.'' He gave me a sly glance; I wondered what those damned Yaquis had reported to him. ''Although not as uncomfortable as if General Mondragon and his men had caught you. The interrogation to which they subjected Cody's partner, Pierce, and his lady, was rather brutal, I understand.''

''I didn't know that,'' I said, frowning. ''You mean they worked over Mrs. Charles and Gloria's dad before finishing them off?''

''Worked over?'' Ramón frowned at the unfamiliar phrase. ''Oh, yes, it was very ugly work. I had forgotten that Mr. Pierce was the papa of the young lady at present calling herself your wife. A very lovely person, congratulations.'' He paused and went on: ''Yes, the full story was not released. Officially it was felt that a rape and two machete deaths were adverse publicity enough for our country without adding torture to the list of horrors.''

I said, ''Heavy questioning would indicate that his captors had reason to think Pierce had some information they wanted. I presume it involved the missing weapons everybody seems to be chasing.''

Ramón said, ''Yes, Mr. Pierce was apparently conducting a private investigation into his partner's illegal affairs. With what you call inside information—I understand he had been associated with Cody for years—he seems to have made a discovery here in Sonora that led to his capture, questioning, and death. At least certain people obviously thought he was carrying information worth killing for; but indications are that they failed to extract it from him, just as they had failed earlier with Cody's accomplice Medina.''

I said, ''So your idea was that, having missed out twice, these unpleasant folks decided to grab Cody himself and put him through the wringer and see what they could squeeze out of him, arms-wise.'' I hesitated. ''Who the hell are these people? You mentioned a General Mondragon. I suppose he's the man I saw, the handsome chap in khakis with an outsize Yankee bodyguard. At least he was giving the orders to that gang of bandits.''

''You are guessing correctly,'' Ramón said. ''But we must

117

not call them *bandidos*. They are noble revolutionaries who are going to bring democracy and freedom to my poor, oppressed country.''

I said, "Yeah, with machetes."

Ramón laughed shortly. "Is there another way? This is Mexico, my friend. Here, political change has always come with the machete. Or the rifle. Or the cannon. Well, the machetes we have always with us, but we can keep the rifles and cannons to a minimum. Now explain, *por favor*, what you do here, and in that elderly disguise."

I hesitated. It seemed unnecessary to go into all the complicated motivations and machinations behind my stage appearance as Horace Cody, so I gave him a slightly edited version.

"Cody's under arrest in El Paso, for attempted murder. He's being held incommunicado, I hope. It was thought that, if I made this honeymoon jaunt in his place, somebody might get in touch with me—or, hell, try to kill me—and give us a line to those arms." Well, it wasn't too far from the truth.

"And the young lady? Is she a—what do you call it?—a 'ringer,' too?"

"No, she's the real thing."

"She must be a brave girl. How did you get her to cooperate?"

"She's the victim Cody intended to murder, after marrying her. For her money."

"I see."

I said, "So your people picked us up when we crossed the border and followed us to Cananea. Your boys must be as good on the road as they are in the brush; I wasn't aware of anybody behind us."

He shook his head. "You didn't overlook them. It wasn't necessary to follow, *amigo*. We knew where you would be hit; Mondragon and his band have been under loose surveillance for months."

It didn't seem diplomatic to point out that his boys apparently weren't quite perfect; supposedly protecting me, or Horace

118

Cody, they'd apparently missed young Mason Charles and his ambush in the restaurant john.

Ramón was still speaking: "That is our function, about which you asked earlier: to keep track of this embryo paramilitary force and any others that may appear up here in the north, while letting them think themselves unobserved. These particular heroes are the action arm of the PLN, the National Liberty Party, which as you may know is a small, very noisy, opposition movement."

I said, "Yes, I've heard of it."

"Unlike the more respectable parties of the left and right, the PLN has made little real impression on the political scene. Its overt, legal, political activities are, we think, only a screen for its illegal ambitions. Like violent overthrow of the government."

I said, "The government being the Institutional Revolutionary Party for which you work."

He shook his head. "Do you work for your Republican or Democratic parties? I work for Mexico, *amigo*. And I do not think my country needs to be torn apart by a bloody rebellion armed by foreign profiteers." Having put me in my place, he smiled thinly and went on: "To be sure, the present administration is not one of angels. But I see no shining wings on the others, either. In any case, politics is not my business."

I said, "So why just watch these hotheads playing their murderous little games? Why not bring in the troops and wipe them out?"

He made a show of being shocked. "What fascist talk is this? Are you suggesting that we should murder our brave but misguided fellow citizens? Is that the democratic American way of dealing with dissension?" He laughed grimly. "It is true that Mexicans have been killing Mexicans for centuries, always with the finest political motives, but I and those above me would like to avoid serious bloodshed here, if possible, not only for humanitarian reasons, but because drastic action on our part against Mondragon could well create a national hero, martyr, and trigger the very uprising

119

we are trying to avoid. At the moment, as you saw, they have only weapons enough for a handful of them and rather a strange collection of firearms at that. They will not constitute a military threat unless they are properly armed. It is my duty to see that this does not happen.''

"And in the meantime you let them chop up American millionaires and Cadillacs undisturbed. Shedding *gringo* blood and crankcase oil doesn't count.'' I grinned. "Forget it, I'm kidding. Tell me more about that joker, the one who was running that ambush.''

Ramón said, "The left-handed officer you saw, Carlos Mondragon, calls himself a general; revolutionary armies have more generals than they have soldiers. Mondragon has no real military training but that, of course, has been true of many leaders in Mexico's past. Benito Juárez did not commence his career as a soldier. Mondragon sees himself as another brave commander of revolutionary armies and patriotic savior of his country. The political head of his party, he is a compelling orator and very popular.''

"It looked like a half-baked operation to me," I said. "Mondragon, at least, couldn't seem to keep his eye on the ball. He let his men horse around helping themselves to our belongings and chopping up what they couldn't use and busting up the car while we slipped away.''

"It is the way he maintains his popularity, catering to the men. The world is full of incompetent people who are convinced that they can run a restaurant, write a novel, or conduct a revolution." Ramon grimaced. "They are all half-baked operations until they catch fire, if I may use the word. Then they become great popular causes. My mission here, to put it another way, is to make certain that this one does not ignite.'' He shook his head. "Unfortunately somebody in your country seems to be willing to spend considerable money to fan the spark of dissension that now exists into the leaping flame of revolution.''

I hesitated, because this was an awkward subject. "How much money? Do you know?''

He answered readily enough, "We estimate that the total sum involved was approximately two million, four hundred thousand dollars. Our information is that a down payment was made of one third, or eight hundred thousand dollars. This must have been paid by the PLN to Señor Cody, or he would not have ordered the munitions. At that, he must have added some of his own money to make the purchase; his Asian suppliers would not have shipped until they had cash in hand. Cody would have expected to be reimbursed, with a massive profit, when the final payment was made by the PLN; but as we know, Mondragon never paid but instead tried to take the weapons by force. Apparently his source of funds failed him."

"Or they got greedy and tried to help themselves to both the arms and a million six."

Ramón shook his head. "With that much money lacking, there are many possibilities, but we feel that the most likely theory is that their financial backer simply refused, or was unable, when the time came, to pay over the additional sum."

I asked the critical question: "Do you know his name, Ramón?"

Ramón hesitated, and then spoke without expression: "Will it surprise you when I tell you it is this man who calls himself Sábado? And while we have not been able to establish his nationality, I think we can both guess the nationality of the funds he is distributing."

I studied his face for a moment. "You can't be saying that a certain large country just to the north can actually be spending money to interfere in the politics of a sovereign Latin American nation. What an outrageous suggestion! Who ever heard of such a thing?"

He gave me his thin smile. "You said it, my friend. I didn't. Even if I had proof, I would say nothing. There is enough anti-Yankee sentiment here already. I would merely continue to try to prevent those arms from reaching the rebels, maybe I should say the would-be rebels."

I frowned thoughtfully; but it didn't make sense to me. I said,

"I'm a political moron, Ramón. I thought our two countries were getting along reasonably well, considering everything. What would be our motive for upsetting your apple cart?"

"Apple . . . oh, yes, I understand." Ramón grimaced. "The motive? You know what the motive is, *amigo*. Always the same one. We do what we can to get along with you, but we will not stop the world for the sake of a little white powder. We will not turn our country into an armed camp for the sake of a pretty weed. We will not forget the falling price of oil, and our rising inflation, and our starving citizens, and concentrate our limited resources on saving a few idiot *gringos* from taking pleasure in chemicals that no one is forcing them to smoke, inhale, or inject into their veins. No matter what we do to assist this crusade of yours, it is never enough. So it seems that people in your government, some people, have decided, with or without consulting higher authority, that if our present government will not cooperate properly with this noble jihad of yours, they will force upon us a government that will. Mondragon has undoubtedly sworn a sacred oath to give the highest priority to helping you eradicate this evil traffic if he is assisted to power."

I drew a long breath. "Well, it's no crazier than some other unauthorized undercover adventures we've heard about. Even after the earlier scandals, the U.S. government still seems to be thick with freewheeling gents ready to implement their own foreign policy with secret funds—the media seem to be licking their chops over a new revelation daily. Maybe the most recent furor in Washington was what scared off the moneybags in this operation when it was time for the final payment, leaving the PLN boys no choice, if they wanted the arms, but to try to take them by force. Only Jorge Medina was a little too smart for them and died a little too soon. And Cody was left holding the bag. Instead of the profit he'd hoped to make on the transaction, which would keep the wolf from the door until his new wife's money became available, he was even stuck for the dough he'd shelled out for the arms in addition to the down payment the

PLN had given him; and thanks to Medina's caution he didn't even have the arms. So he decided to come down here and find them; maybe he could sell them to somebody else and get his money back. Only Señor Sábado didn't want anybody stirring things up down here; as far as he was concerned, the longer the buried weapons stayed buried, the better for him. He was going to wipe the whole operation off the record, and if that meant wiping out Buff Cody and snoopy Will Pierce and any ladies who happened to be associated with them at the time, that was just too fucking bad.''

Ramón said, a little impatiently, ''That is all very well, my friend, but we really have only one interest in this business: the missing shipment. If it stays lost, very well; but it must not be found except by us. Found and, preferably, destroyed, but at least put out of the reach of this revolutionary rabble, one way or another. Our Mexican rabbles, properly armed, can be quite formidable, as any history book will tell you.''

I looked at him for a moment; then I grinned. ''So ask, *amigo*.''

He regarded me grimly. ''You are the best man to look for those arms. As Horace Cody, you may have access to contacts that we do not have.''

''Maybe. But since I'm not really Cody, I could have trouble finding them. I'll need all the information you have available.''

''It will be yours.'' He laughed shortly. ''Very well, I will make the request a formal one. Señor Cody, as a great favor, will you be so kind as to maintain your masquerade and employ it, and your unique talents, to determine for us the location of the missing munitions. I, and my country, will appreciate very much your assistance in this matter and will make certain that you suffer no legal consequences for any action you may be forced to take in our behalf.''

I said, ''You've got yourself a deal, *amigo*.''

''Oh, just one more thing.''

I restrained a grimace. There's always just one more little thing. ''Shoot,'' I said.

"This Mondragon. As I have said, we must not harm him, and we certainly cannot allow him, a Mexican national, to be harmed by foreigners. But if General Mondragon should come to grief in some way that could not be attributed to either of our nations, I can guarantee that the person responsible would not regret it."

CHAPTER 14

THE city of Hermosillo, some hundred and fifty miles south of the border, is the capital of the state of Sonora. It has a population of roughly a quarter-million people, a university, and a towering new Holiday Inn. At least it was new to me. Just beyond it is the old Hotel Gandara.

Failing to recognize it at once in the shadow of its unfamiliar neighbor, I drove past and had to U-turn to get back to the entrance. I seemed to be doing a lot of that lately. Actually, I'd been looking for the pleasant little hostelry I remembered from years ago, set in the middle of large, well-tended lawns and gardens. I'd never stayed there overnight, but from time to time I'd used it as a lunch stop on the way to Guaymas and points farther down the west coast of Mexico—it was just the right distance if you'd spent the night in Tucson, Arizona. I remembered it as having a wonderful, quiet dining room with white tablecloths, an elegant headwaiter, and excellent food, a true oasis in a desert of shabby enchilada parlors.

Now they'd built sprawling, one-story motel units all over the lovely, unprofitable lawns. In the middle of this clutter, the main building still stood, but inside it the formal dining room was gone, replaced by a bunch of casual tables in a kind of sunken passion pit with a fountain. What they'd done, of course, was to turn a first-rate Mexican hotel into a second-rate Holiday Inn. I had a hunch that, given a choice, I'd have done better to patronize the genuine article next door, where they really knew the Holiday Inn business.

I had to hand it to the man at the desk, however; he didn't let himself show any curiosity when I let him know that I'd come on my honeymoon without my bride, but I'd take the suite I'd reserved for us anyway. He checked the list, deadpan.

"Mr. and Mrs. Horace Cody? *Sí*, it is here, guaranteed, but we were expecting you last night, señor."

No rude curiosity, but a hint of reproach. I apologized for my tardiness and said that I appreciated their holding the accommodations for me, and of course I was prepared to pay for the full two days of the reservation even though I'd arrived one day late. This put me back into favor; but I could see that some interesting theories would be circulating among the hotel help concerning the elderly *gringo* who'd claimed the honeymoon suite so belatedly, alone. A newlyweds' spat, perhaps, and it must have been a spectacular conflict considering the beat-up state of the gray-bearded one's face; his señora must be quite a tigress, *amigos*. . . .

Unexpectedly, in view of my getting-lost record on this Mexican jaunt, I drove straight to the right unit without any detours or misadventures. I pushed the button on the Subaru's dashboard to unlock the tailgate—my newly acquired heap had almost as many power conveniences as the demolished Cadillac, surprising for a fairly rugged little wagon with four-wheel drive. My worldly belongings, as far as Mexico was concerned, were contained in a light blue canvas carryall with piping and handles of some kind of darker blue plastic that was supposed to look like leather and didn't. Well, the canvas didn't look much like canvas either.

As I approached the motel door, bag in hand, I found that I was relieved not to have the girl with me, although it was a waste of a perfectly good honeymoon suite. Still, I missed her in a way, and I hoped I hadn't left her too worried and frightened after Ramón and I had worked it out over tortillas and beans and coffee brought us by a dark-faced commando.

"I would rather hear your thoughts on the subject, *amigo*," he'd said when I asked him just how big an assortment of what kind of arms he was hoping I'd help him keep out of the hands of the would-be *insurgentes*. "Let me see if your reasoning parallels ours."

I shrugged. "I don't know a hell of a lot about military hardware," I said. "But if you want me to kick it around . . . four truckloads? What kind of trucks? Big semis?"

"No, they were not the large articulated vehicles. Those could not have been maneuvered on the small dirt road on which they were found. With the bodies of Jorge Mcdina and the four drivers lying nearby."

I said, "They killed the drivers, too? Interrogation?"

"Yes, they had also been questioned brutally, like Mcdina. But apparently Medina had been clever and changed drivers after hiding the shipment, so those men knew nothing. Either that or they were very heroic, which seems unlikely. In any case, we know that they did not talk, or Mondragon would already have the arms."

I wanted to ask the dimensions of the trucks involved, but he was obviously testing me to see if, perhaps, my brains had atrophied since we'd last met. I worked it out in my head and, for four moving-van-type vehicles, not too large, got the rather startling answer of roughly six thousand cubic feet of merchandise weighing, if the drivers didn't mind straining their heaps a bit, around one hundred tons. This translated to something like three thousand assault rifles, a million rounds of ammunition, with space left over for some heavy machine guns and missile launchers and a reasonable quantity of grenades.

I said, "Wow, we're getting into some pretty impressive figures here! I didn't realize you could fight a war from just a few lousy trucks."

"It is what we fear," said Ramón.

I drew a long breath. "Three thousand guns is a lot of guns. Can the underground arm of this National Liberty Party come up with three thousand men to use them? And if so, can three thousand men take Mexico?"

"Fidel Castro took Cuba with eighty-two men, *amigo*."

"Well, for a start. As I recall, he picked up a few reinforcements as he went along. But Mondragon is no Fidel, from what

I saw of him. And your government may not be run by perfect angels with shining wings, but they're no Batistas. At least I don't think you have the heritage of oppression and hatred that makes instant armies spring out of the ground like mushrooms.''

Ramón sighed. "But there is inflation and poverty and dissatisfaction, although I will deny that statement if you ever quote me. And this is Mexico, my friend. Traditionally, in bad times here, an ambitious *politico* who has a plausible cause and some rifles to offer has always found men to shoot them.'' He shook his head. "No, the PLN can probably not find that many men at the start, but more will come to them if they have any kind of success. And, no, it is not likely that they can take Mexico, although Mondragon does have a considerable following among the people. I do not, myself, think these men can win, but I have been wrong upon occasion. Even if they lose, however, they can turn my country into a battlefield, at least the northern part of it. Wounds can be inflicted that will bleed for generations. But it will not happen without the rifles.''

I was beginning to think that my companion might really belong to that rare, endangered species called patriot. Well, there are still a few of them around, even in our dark and dirty business.

I said, "So let's find the lousy guns and remove them from circulation, one way or another. How are you planning to explain releasing us to search for them, a subversive Yankee arms smuggler and his moll?''

"The young lady stays," Ramón said. "I require her with me so that I can display her as a hostage for your good behavior. I will report to those who must be informed that I have made a bargain with you. I have promised you that your crimes, to which your wife must be considered an accessory since she accompanied you willingly, will be forgiven if you carry out this mission successfully. Mr. and Mrs. Cody will simply be escorted to the border and sent back into the *Estados Unidos* with a warning never to return.''

I regarded him for a moment. It was pointless to ask what

would happen to us if I was not successful. It would depend entirely on his political power and his political position. He wasn't a vindictive man, but he wasn't a sucker for friendship, either, if friendship was what we had. Faced with a failure that threatened his career and an armed revolution that could destroy his country, I didn't think he'd risk very much to save me or my female associate, in spite of his promises, if somebody, say Captain Alemán in his role of political officer, demanded our blood.

All this was between us, unspoken, as he asked, "Where do you intend to start?"

"I can give you a better answer after you've told me what you know."

Later, when he'd finished briefing me, and I'd made some suggestions to which he'd agreed, I said, "Okay, let's put the show on the road. I'm the doting older bridegroom terrified by the threats you've made against my young bride. How could I bear to let you stick her into one of your filthy Mexican dungeons, you lousy greaser bastard?" I drew a long breath. "Let's go see her so I can explain it to her."

We found her eating her lunch at Ramón's desk. She finished her coffee with a gulp and rose to face us. "I hope you don't mind," she said. "I never was much of a picnic girl; I don't like eating off my lap."

"It is perfectly all right, señora." He smiled. "I apologize for the crude facilities of my camp, but you seem to have made good use of them."

Actually, the improvement was startling. She'd discarded the forlorn remnants of her wedding costume and cleaned herself up carefully. She'd even washed her hair. Still damp, and stripy with the marks of the comb, it was beginning to return to gold at the ends as it dried. She was wearing a new gray chambray work shirt, stiff new blue jeans and blue-and-white jogging shoes over white gym socks. The damp hair, and the tape on her cheek—and another patch on the heel of her right hand—not to mention the other scrapes and scratches, made her look like somebody's kid sister, a tomboy brat who'd just been washed off and patched up after getting mauled in a game too rough for her. It was hard to reconcile the rather wholesome picture she made now with the image I carried in my head of the disheveled but seductive glamour girl who'd conned me, not altogether against my will, into a violent moment of passion on the mountain.

She licked her lips. "What . . . what's going to happen to us now?" she asked.

"I'm going out to save the world," I said. "Well, at least the Mexican part of it. You're staying here as hostage for my good behavior."

"You will be quite safe, señora," Ramón said.

After a doubtful moment, she gave him a slow smile that had nothing tomboyish about it. "Oh, yes, I am sure I will be, Mr. Cacique. . . ."

Now, in Hermosillo, I realized that I was stalling at the motel door. There's always that sense of foreboding as you enter a new phase of an operation: you've survived the early threats and traps, now what's waiting to kill you? I drew a long breath, turned the key, slammed the door back, and threw my little canvas bag into the room, hoping that the carpet that received it, and the pajamas in which I'd wrapped it, would preserve the expensive bottle inside.

Inside the honeymoon suite a gun fired.

CHAPTER 15

THE girl was wearing a rough *serape* thrown back over her left shoulder, leaving her gun arm free. There was something familiar about her, but I didn't take time to make the connection, although she hadn't shot again.

Figuring that no pro of any competence would let himself be tricked into shooting at a decoy bag, I'd made the kind of tumbling dive and roll into the room that can work when you're up against amateur opposition; the amateur will shoot behind, always. You hope. But there had been no more shots. I'd come up into a crouch with the .38 ready, and there she was, holding a small automatic pistol awkwardly. If it had been aimed anywhere near me I'd have fired, but it was pointing in a vaguely upward direction, as if she didn't quite know what to do with it. Responding to the threat of my gun, she held it away from her gingerly as if she'd picked up a dead rat by the tail. I saw her fingers start to relax.

"No!" I snapped. "Don't drop it, dammit! Put it down on the big chair, gently. *Pone la pistola . . .*"

Hollywood to the contrary, you don't go around dropping loaded automatics unless you're looking for an interesting variation on Russian roulette—when they bounce they tend to go off in any direction. I was still trying to figure out the Spanish for lay that pistol down, baby, when she reached behind her to place the weapon on the seat of the chair in which she'd presumably been waiting when I startled her to her feet. She did it without looking, without taking her eyes off me. I knew her now; she was the girl of the shabby black dress and the high-heeled red shoes I'd seen, with an older male companion, in Cananea.

She licked her lips. "It is as I thought before! You are not . . ." She paused, frowning. "I was told the reservation was in the name of . . . But you are not that Cody, señor!"

"Maybe not," I said, "but let's not shout the news all over Hermosillo."

I maintained a poker face, and I hoped a poker voice, but her voice had given her away: it had been louder than it needed to be. She was pretty good, she didn't once look toward the door leading into the other room of the suite, but she might as well have. It seemed unlikely that she'd jacked up the volume because she thought I was hard of hearing. On my feet now, keeping her covered, I sidled toward the outside door and listened to make certain nobody was charging up to ask who was shooting whom in here. No one seemed to be interested, which is often the case with a single, muffled, small-caliber report that could be a back-fire or somebody slamming shut the trunk lid of a car.

I closed and locked the door. I motioned the girl aside and moved past her cautiously to gather up the pistol lying on the chair cushion. It was a cheap little weapon; a nickel-plated, hammerless auto so trashy that the manufacturer hadn't even had enough pride in it to stamp his name clearly on the slide— perhaps he was afraid of bending or cracking the flimsy metal if he hit it too hard. The caliber had come through in readable fashion, however: .22 L.R., for Long Rifle, the little rimfire round I'd once discussed with Gloria. I found the catch, released the magazine, and pulled back the slide to eject the round from the chamber. I stuffed it into the top of the magazine, returned the magazine to the gun, and pocketed the weapon with the chamber empty.

The girl was watching me. She looked a little restive. Well, any attractive girl would, seeing a strange male paying more attention to a lousy pistol than to lovely, irresistible her; but I thought she was listening hard for sounds from the bedroom— this was the living-dining-kitchen area of the suite, with a cooking and eating corner sheltering behind a low room divider serving as a bar, and a social area holding a couple of comfortable chairs, a cocktail table, and a sofa that could presumably sleep an extra person or two when unfolded. If you and your bride wanted an extra person or two along on your honeymoon.

It was time for stocktaking at last, and I had my look. I'd got the impression in Cananea that she was kind of a cute little thing with her cheap, loose, knee-length, black dress, her pretty bare legs, and her high-heeled red shoes. In faded denim pants she gave a different impression. There was a long-sleeved black jersey which she filled adequately but not spectacularly. The heavy, gray-brown *serape* she wore over it gave her a slightly barbaric look that went well with the glossy, rather coarse black hair that, hanging loose down her back, was almost long enough for her to sit on. She was still wearing the scuffed red shoes with the high, slim heels, and I still got the impression that she'd have preferred to kick them off and go barefoot.

I decided that I'd been wrong to call her cute. I'd been misled by her small size and rather kittenish appearance. Well, a lynx isn't very big, but nobody'd call it cute as it goes about its predatory wildcat business. I sensed that there was danger here, too. Her skin was a warm and dusky color, very smooth, and her small face looked crowded at first glance, as if her features had outgrown the space allotted to them. She had a big mouth full of even white teeth. She had a nose that was no dainty, girlish nubbin; it was a real nose with a fine arch to it, separating a pair of strong cheekbones. And she had magnificent, large, dark eyes with lashes that could break your heart. It was an offbeat face that took a little getting used to, after years of watching TV screens filled with stock beauties right out of the glamour factory.

She licked her lips. "The *pistola* is mine," she said, in a tentative way.

I shook my head. "No longer, sweetheart. Any gun that fires at me is mine if I live to take it. Spoils of war."

"But I was not shoot at you! You just frighted me so it go off, boom. And then I saw you were not Cody and did not shoot again."

"But if I had been Horace Cody . . ."

"Then I would have kill you! That is what I come for. I am good shot; but it is the suspense, *sí*? All the waiting, and then the door bang open like that and something fly through the air. . . . I just pull the trigger before I mean. Very stupid. I did not even hit your valise."

"Damn good thing, too," I said. "Do you know what a fifth of J&B costs down here?"

"J. and B. ?"

"Never mind," I said. I regarded her for a moment. There was only one person she could be, of those I'd heard mentioned in connection with this mess, but it was safer to ask: "Who are you, señorita?"

She hesitated but decided that there was no reason for her to remain anonymous. "I am Antonia Sisneros. Do you know that name, you who are not H. H. Cody? Do you know why I hate the man you pretend to be?"

I said, "You are the lady friend of the late Jorge Medina, who worked for Cody, right?"

She grimaced. "Friend, yes. But no lady, not when my man is made to be kill! Where is real Cody?"

I asked, "How do you happen to know him by sight? When did you see him?"

"He visit Jorge in Guaymas where Jorge live; they must consult. About certain weapons. It was many days ago. I was with Jorge when Cody come. I was supposed to leave much before, but the love, it does not watch the clock. I was send away quick when he come to door, made to sneak by back door like thief, it make angry. They do not trust me to see this man, so I will see him! I wait over street until he comes out. It is dark, but I see good enough to know that it is not you. Very much luck, or I shoot you."

"Very much luck," I agreed. "Cody was arrested in El Paso a couple of days ago. I don't know where he is now."

"And you take his place? You do not look very like!"

I shrugged. "I wouldn't say this impersonation is the world's greatest success story. Well, I did find one sucker who seemed to believe in it; maybe there's another somewhere. I keep hoping." After a moment, I said, "I was given your name, Miss Sisneros. I was going to look you up when I got to Guaymas tomorrow. I was going to ask your help."

Between us, Ramón and I had figured out that she was probably the best lead we had. Meeting her unexpectedly like this had involved a certain risk, and if I'd come through the door first instead of my bag I might have some holes in me, but it was certainly convenient. I was trying to decide if it wasn't, perhaps, just a bit too convenient.

"Help?" she asked. "What for do you need my help?"

I said, "The deal your friend Medina discussed with Cody, the night you saw him, went through, as you know. The weapons were landed on the coast. Medina hid them. He was killed by men trying to learn where."

"And you wish to find, too?" She shrugged. "I know nothing of the hiding. I know that he should never have been given such a work. He was beautiful man but weak and much afraid. This selling of bad weapons, this working with *insurgentes* against the government, it make him very much fright, very much not happy. It make him dead. This Señor Cody, he promise much money if help, much threat if no. He has great fault for this. He should not make frighted man to be crooked and be kill. For this I will shoot him. I will shoot also the cheating general who not pay money promised but instead have my Jorge hurt until he die. You will try to stop?"

"Hell, no," I said. "Shoot all the generals you want and all the real Codys you want, lady, just spare this phony one. But actually, since Horace Cody is in custody up in the U.S., you'll play hell trying to get at him, so you'd better concentrate on Carlos Mondragon."

I felt quite Machiavellian as I said it. The answer to one of my problems had dropped into my lap; if Mondragon was killed by an angry young woman avenging her lover, the Mexican populace could hardly blame their government or the Yankees. Ramón would be happy and cover up any crimes I had to commit. Now all I had to do was maneuver the kid into position and, while I was doing it, locate the missing arms and identify the mysterious Señor Sábado and deal with him.

Antonia Sisneros made a grimace of distaste. "Carlos Mondragon! One who talks much, promises much. One who will free us all from one terrible government and give us instead another terrible government. His. Like hole in head, is that what you say? That is how we need his murdering revolution!" She drew a long breath. "But *insurgentes* hiding in their own mountains . . ." She shrugged. "Not easy to find, señor. Not easy to kill."

I said, "Killing is not my primary job at the moment. My job is the arms. But I have a hunch I'll have no trouble finding those men when the time comes. They'll find me. They'll be watching me search, hoping I'll lead them to the hidden weapons cache, hoping to move in when I locate it. You're sure you don't know where your boyfriend hid the stuff?"

"Ha, I am woman, I cook the food and keep clean the house and make the love. My Jorge no tell woman about weapons, that is man business. I know nothing of the hiding."

I wasn't sure she was telling the truth. She had a very good little poker face, but it did not seem advisable to pursue the subject until I'd investigated the room next door.

I said, "Okay, I'll take your word for it, but before we proceed, maybe you'd like to give me that *pistola* under your shirt. It looks like a big one. If it slides down your pants leg, it could give your toes an awful whack. . . . Careful, now!"

She had some difficulty getting the weapon out from under her jersey and the tight waistband of her jeans, worn without a belt. Well, snug as they were, there wasn't much chance of her losing them, even without support. She gave me the gun reluctantly.

"It is mine. I take. It is very good gun, very expensive."

It was nice to find someone with a sound respect for guns as property. You meet a lot of characters, many with badges, who wouldn't dream of stealing a hundred bucks from your wallet but think nothing of casually depriving you of personal property in the form of firearms worth many times that; and you're supposed to accept this kind of larceny calmly. It was refreshing to find someone who didn't.

Her second weapon was, as she'd said, a good one, around six hundred bucks retail: a big new 9mm Beretta automatic, the one with the fat grip and the magazine holding fifteen rounds and the self-cocking trigger mechanism that saves you from having to jack the slide back, or even cock the hammer, to fire the first round. It was fully loaded with a cartridge in the chamber. As I looked at it, something stirred in my memory, as if I'd seen this gun not too long ago; but the picture wasn't clear.

"From whom did you take?" I asked. She shrugged and didn't speak. I said, "Why don't we ask your friend in the next room to join the party?"

She laughed. She had a pretty laugh. "But they cannot join," she said. "I tie good."

I looked at her for a moment, still wondering about her. I mean, now that I'd survived the initial encounter, I could say that it was lucky she'd come to Hermosillo to meet me, saving me from having to hunt her up in Guaymas. Or was it? And what about the Mexican spitfire act and the heavily accented English? Well, things do break your way sometimes in the business, and Hispanic ladies are notoriously temperamental, and a lot of people aren't fluent in languages not their own. Nevertheless, she wasn't a kid I intended to turn my back on until I knew considerably more about her.

She'd tied very good, however, just as she said. They lay together on the big honeymoon bed in the rather ornate bedroom, a man and a woman, thoroughly trussed with strong rawhide that reminded me of the stuff the little Yaqui lieutenant had produced to tie my wrists. I wondered how much Indian blood Antonia Sisneros carried. The woman lay facing me very uncomfortably, with a gag in her mouth and her wrists and ankles lashed and then drawn together behind her with more rawhide so that there was no possibility of her walking, hopping, or even crawling anywhere. She was a woman I didn't know, but she had good sense. She'd presumably tested her gag and bonds earlier and decided that there was nothing to be gained by

137

thrashing around fighting them. She just lay there watching us with cold blue eyes that said she'd endure any indignities she had to endure, but she didn't have to like them—or forgive them.

The man beside her was one of the you-can't-do-this-to-me kids. He'd already mussed the bed badly with his fruitless struggles; now he had to flop around some more to show us how mad he was, and how he was going to tear somebody limb from limb when he got free. He made some angry gaa-gaa noises through his gag. I knew him. I'd met him in a certain men's john two days earlier. He was the young man who belonged to the pistol I'd just taken from Antonia.

The last time I'd seen him I hadn't got a look at the gun, because it had been poked into the back of my supposed bride, but afterwards I'd figured out what kind of a weapon it had to be from Gloria's inexpert description. He was young Mason Charles, the one man I'd fooled with my disguise so far, the dedicated avenger who thought I'd arranged to have his mother killed along with Will Pierce on the Mazatlán-Durango highway.

Antonia looked down at her two prisoners rather fondly, as if they were property of which she was proud, and at the moment you could say they were.

"No problem," she said. "I wait for Cody. I hear them come and I hide. I do not know if friend or enemy of Cody. If friend, I want no interfere. If enemy, they cannot have, he is mine. So I take gun away and tie good, hey?"

CHAPTER 16

I was relieved to find that my fifth of Scotch (750ml by local measurement) had survived intact in the canvas bag in spite of making a crash landing after flying a dangerous mission under fire. I placed it securely on the bar but reminded myself that there were a couple of small chores I should perform before I could relax.

First I found and pocketed the empty .22 cartridge case. Then I located the bullet hole under the windowsill. It was fairly inconspicuous but unmistakable, so I worked on it a bit to make it look like an irregular chip knocked out of the plaster rather than a neat, round hole. I used the little, all-stainless Russell knife I'd already employed to release Antonia's captives. It was a replacement for a favorite Gerber I'd lost on a previous assignment—destroyed, along with the lethal lady who'd taken it from me, when a certain terrorist headquarters blew up, never mind how.

The ex-prisoners were still pulling themselves together, ignoring the Mexican girl who was watching them with malicious pleasure, getting all the mileage she could out of their humiliation. An interesting little girl, a striking little girl in her offbeat way, but not necessarily a nice little girl. I found ice and beer in the diminutive kitchenette refrigerator. The glasses provided were flimsy plastic wrapped in even flimsier plastic. I peeled them and asked for orders. Antonia voted for beer; the other two admitted, grudgingly in the case of the man, that a spot of J&B wouldn't be unwelcome. Mason Charles went on to explain to me how unfairly he'd been tricked and disarmed by that little Chicana tramp. . . .

The as-yet unidentified woman looked at him sharply, silencing him. "Cool it, Junior," she said. "Apologize."

I remembered that he'd originally introduced himself as Mason Charles, Junior. He said quickly, "The hell I'll . . . !" Then, surprisingly, he shrugged, drew a long breath, and turned to Antonia. He made her a ceremonious bow, and spoke elaborately: "My humble apologies, señorita. Please allow me to withdraw that unfortunate remark."

It wasn't the most sincere apology I'd ever heard, but the Mexican girl accepted it with a mocking little curtsy that went oddly with her faded jeans; but at least it showed she knew how.

"It is forgotten, señor," she said.

The nameless woman was rubbing her rawhide-chafed wrists. She took the glass I offered her with a curt nod of thanks. Lean and moderately tall, she was one of the short-haired girls who look a bit like boys, except that the boys mostly wear it to their shoulders nowadays. The light brown hair was trimmed closely enough to her head to display her ears and the nape of her neck. She was wearing white jeans tucked into high brown boots with moderate heels. A man's blue shirt hung outside her pants, cinched in at her waist by a concha belt that must have weighed several pounds and cost several hundred bucks, maybe several thousand. The prices of that silver stuff are getting stratospheric. There was also a very good squash-blossom necklace.

She was handsome in a severe way, but she didn't do anything for me. I guess I prefer soft, skirted females to hard, panted and booted ones. This one was in her late twenties, I judged, and she looked tough—well, call it competent—with a square jaw, a firm mouth with long, thin lips on which she wore no makeup, a thin, straight nose, and a good tan. Looking at her, I realized that I was being stupid. She not only looked a bit like a boy, I knew the boy she looked like. He was standing right beside her. Well, at least she wasn't the susceptible kind of dame, past her girlhood and aware of it, who'd deliberately pick that kind of

140

handsome, immature young stud to travel with. Who gets to pick their siblings?

Still watching the lady, I shoved a glass down the bar toward Mason Charles. "Brother and sister?" I asked.

The woman nodded, but it was Charles who responded dryly: "After I told her over the phone about our . . . well, encounter, Jo decided she'd better come down to keep her baby brother out of trouble."

The woman murmured, "Charging around a foreign country with an illegal gun, shooting the wrong people."

Mason Charles protested: "He calls himself Cody, how could I know he wasn't? You didn't really know it yourself until this girl told us just now. And anyway, I didn't shoot him, did I?"

Disregarding him, I spoke to the sister, "Jo for Josephine?"

"Jo for Joanna," she said. "Joanna Beckman, but Beckman doesn't live here any more, thank God."

I studied her for a moment. "You objected to your brother's shooting the wrong people. Are you in favor of his shooting the right people?"

"Like the people who killed our mother?" She shrugged. "It's not a big thing with me, Mr. Cody or whoever you are. I don't have the burning yearning for retribution that Mason does. Maybe the mother-daughter bond isn't quite as strong as the mother-son bond, if you know what I mean. But my brother feels he has to do it, and I guess I've kind of got into the habit of looking after him. Little Mother Jo."

"Ain't that the everlasting truth," Mason Charles said ruefully. He grinned. "Well, I suppose somebody had to, after Pop rolled his pickup on a county road in the rain. I was all of four years old at the time. Jo was ten. She kind of took over the house, and me, while Millie went to work to support us—she liked us to call her Millie; we only called her Mom or Mother to tease her." His mouth tightened. "God, she was so . . . she was such a wonderful person; and after all those years she had to spend slaving in those lousy oil company offices, just when it looked as if things were finally going to break right for her, that slimy, gun-smuggling sonofabitch set her up for murder!

141

Just because he was afraid of what his partner might have learned poking around down there in Mexico and thought some of it might have rubbed off on her!" He made a wry face. "But it seems I've been practicing my Mad Avenger act on the wrong Cody!"

Jo Beckman said, "I knew there had to be something funny going on. That's why I came down here to see for myself. . . . According to Junior, you behaved in such a reasonable and civilized way in that rest room that I couldn't help wondering if he wasn't making a horrible mistake. I thought I'd better come down and see this paragon of courage and self-control with my own eyes before . . . before something irrevocable happened."

"You mean, before your brother took another crack at me and killed me?"

She shook her heard. "No, before he took another crack at you and you killed him." She was watching me steadily. "Of course, I didn't want him to have it on his conscience, shooting the wrong man; but I was more afraid . . . He's pretty good at targets, and he's done quite a bit of hunting, but it's not the same thing, is it? Making neat little bullet holes in paper and shooting deer and antelope, and maybe an elk or two, doesn't really qualify an amateur to go up against a professional, does it?"

I frowned. "What makes you think I'm a pro?"

She laughed shortly. "What else can you call a man who'll calmly size up a tense situation involving firearms—and it had to be *very* tense from what Junior said—and then trust his judgment to the extent of putting away his gun and turning his back on a loaded weapon in the hands of . . . I guess I really knew, the minute I heard it, that you couldn't be Cody, although it took me a while to accept it because it seemed so very far out. But no macho, self-made Texas millionaire would ever walk away from a scene like that, even with his wife's life at stake. What, run from a wet-nosed kid with a toy pistol when he had a gun of his own? Sorry, Junior, but what I'm trying to say is that it would never happen, no matter who got killed!"

I said, "So you told your brother over the phone that I couldn't

142

be the man he wanted. And I suppose he told you you were nuts.''

She laughed ruefully. "Well, you can hardly blame him. He'd seen a tall, bald, gray-bearded man all dressed in white go into a church in Texas and come out with a beautiful bride. A few hours later he saw a tall, bald, gray-bearded man in white go into a restaurant in Mexico with the same beautiful bride, a girl Junior recognized although we don't move in the same social circles as the former Miss Pierce, and she'd made a point of not getting to know us in spite of the fact that her father and our mother were . . . Well, never mind that!''

I glanced at Antonia, who'd stirred uneasily. "Did you wish to say something, señorita?''

She shook her head. "No. No, I have nothing to say. It has already been said: You are not Cody. But I would like another *cerveza*, please.''

I opened one and gave it to her. I turned to the boy. "Unlike Miss Sisneros, you obviously didn't know Cody by sight.''

"No, we never met any of the people Millie worked with," he said. "Except Will Pierce, after . . . Well, when they started talking marriage, Millie brought him home to meet us, but the proud daughter stayed away. I only recognized her because I'd seen her picture in the paper." He shook his head angrily. "Dammit, how could I guess somebody'd switched Codys on me? The man at the wedding had to be Cody; no phony could have fooled all his friends at the wedding reception. And hours later, in Cananea, there was Gloria still playing the loving bride; if she continued to accept you, why shouldn't I?'' He grimaced. "I told Jo she was out of her tree. I told her she was hallucinating, and she'd better stop smoking that strong stuff and settle for cancer and emphysema.''

"That was when I decided I'd better come down here,'' the sister said to me. "It was all wrong! You were behaving all wrong and so was Gloria. The fact that she wouldn't listen to a word against you and defended you hotly against Junior's accusations . . . I mean, a young girl madly in love with a boy her own age might shut her mind to any hint that her beloved wasn't

143

perfect, but one who'd deliberately married a man so much older, well, you'd expect her to see him more clearly—clearly enough to be just a bit uneasy when she heard him accused of dreadful crimes, clearly enough to want to hear a bit more before launching into indignant denials. But young Mrs. Cody didn't. Junior said she just lit into him the minute the door closed behind you."

The boy laughed. "She surely did. Whew!"

Jo Beckman said, "It wasn't natural, not for a girl like that."

"A girl like what?" I asked, a bit sharply.

Even if it had only been a brief midnight incident initiated by her, you tend to feel protective—maybe the word is possessive—about a girl you've slept with; and I do hate to hear females running each other down. Not that males haven't been known to do a bit of backbiting on occasion.

"All right, all right, I'll admit I'm prejudiced," Jo Beckman said. She was looking at me knowingly as if she'd just learned something about me; and perhaps she had. She went on: "All I really know about Gorgeous Gloria is what I've read on the society pages and what Millie used to tell us about Will Pierce's snooty debutante daughter giving her a hard time." Jo shrugged. "Well, to be fair, I suppose any girl, particularly an only child, is going to find it traumatic when her widower daddy starts fucking his secretary and talking about marrying her. But I really wouldn't have expected Miss Gloria, brought up wealthy and spoiled the way she was, to put on such a touching demonstration of loyalty. Childlike faith isn't very big in society circles; but Junior said she showed no hesitation, no suspicion, no doubts at all, no uneasy curiosity about her daddy's death, just total anger at the suggestion that her wonderful new husband could be involved in any way. It couldn't be for real. It had to be an act."

Mason Charles said defensively, "She was damn convincing. It never occurred to me she could be lying."

His sister said, "But that's just the point. She was damn convincing because she wasn't lying. She insisted that this wonderful man hadn't had her daddy killed. Well, this wonderful man hadn't. Cody had, but this man wasn't Cody and she knew it, so she could proclaim his innocence with perfect sincerity. Obviously she was doing her best to help him with his impersonation. It was the only answer that worked, loony though it seemed." Jo frowned at me. "Which brings up the question, why would she help you pretend you're her husband? It's got to mean she's working against him. Why? We know what we've got against him, Millie's murder. We know what the señorita has against him, the death of her man, what was his name, Medina?"

Antonia spoke: "His name was Jorge Miguel Medina de Campo."

"Whatever," the tall girl said. "But what was Glorious Gloria's motive? And please don't try to tell me she was charging around a foreign country with a strange man who was pretending to be her husband simply because she'd learned about her would-be bridegroom's gunrunning project, and it was against her fine, nonviolent principles!"

I said, "Well, the guns were part of it; but she'd also learned that once she was safely married to him, Cody planned to kill her for her money. We can go into the details some other time."

Jo said sharply, "That's more like it! I can see her getting very upset about a threat to her own lovely skin."

I said, "Miaow, miaow."

Jo flushed slightly. "All right, I told you I was prejudiced. Even if there was nothing personal between us, I just can't stand those useless, pampered beauties."

I asked, "What's your feeling on the subject of munitions smuggling?"

She shrugged. "That's a pretty dumb question, Mr. Cody or whatever your real name is. It depends on whom the munitions are being smuggled to, doesn't it? If George Washington had been running short of muskets and lead and gunpowder at Valley Forge, and we could have got a shipment to him, wouldn't we have been all for it, even high-minded Gloria Pierce or whatever *her* name is now? I suppose you can find equally worthy causes nowadays if you look hard enough. To say that guns are

145

always evil is to say that nothing's worth fighting for." She grimaced. "God, Soapbox Beckman strikes again!"

Mason Charles said, "Did Cody really plan to marry Princess Gloria and then murder her? The man must be a real monster!"

I said, "It seems to be pretty well established that he had an elaborate plot going, first to scare her into his arms and then to dispose of her after she'd made a will in his favor, which she'd undoubtedly have done if she hadn't been tipped off to his plans. His connection with your mother's murder, and Pierce's, is a little more tenuous. He gained by them, of course, to the extent that Pierce was a threat to him; but as you probably heard me tell Miss Sisneros, the murders were actually committed by the people for whom the shipment of arms was intended, a movement calling itself the National Liberty Party that plays feebly at Mexican politics to make itself look harmless and ineffectual while secretly it's making plans to take over the government by force. The name to remember is Carlos Mondragon." I hesitated. "Talking about names, does the name Sábado mean anything to anybody? Señor Sábado? Mr. Saturday?"

I was watching the Mexican girl as the most likely source of information on this subject. She looked blank, and Jo Beckman shook her head without hesitation.

"Charles?"

He shook his head. "I was just going to say it when you did, that it's the Spanish word for Saturday."

"Yes, I know." I changed the subject. "So your mother was going to marry Will Pierce? That was the break you said she'd got at last?"

The boy nodded. "Yes, she was pretty happy about it; but they had to put off the wedding for this Mexico trip. Will had just learned, somehow, that Cody was involved in some kind of a shady deal down here that could be disastrous for the partnership. Apparently it wasn't the first time Cody had got greedy and almost ruined them. Will had to rush down here to investigate the situation and, if possible, repair the damage. Millie insisted on going with him; she called it her honeymoon-in-advance."

146

"Some honeymoon!" Jo Beckman said grimly.

I said, "Keeping weapons from self-styled Latin patriots is about as safe as keeping meat from hungry lions. I'm surprised Pierce would let her come along."

Brother and sister both laughed. Jo Beckman said, "You didn't let or not-let Millie do things, right, Junior?"

Señorita Antonia Sisneros, rather rudely ignored by the three of us at the bar, had taken her second beer to the big chair in which—with her prisoners gagged and hog-tied on the honeymoon bed in the next room—she'd awaited the arrival of Horace Hosmer Cody earlier. She was listening with interest. I didn't take her heavy accent too seriously. I had a hunch she understood most of what was going on, even though we were employing pretty rapid-fire English.

The tall girl went on: "Actually, she insisted on going because she thought Will needed her to keep Cody from putting one over on him if they met down here. Because they'd been partners for years. That means a lot to a Texan. In the early days they'd sweated and suffered and fought side by side; they'd got rich together; and while sobersides Will might occasionally get pissed off at his freewheeling partner's get-rich-quick schemes, it would never occur to him that Cody might deliberately betray him, let alone, well, hurt him. If there was a confrontation between the partners, Millie wanted to be there to make sure Will didn't trust Cody's friendship too far. Well, you know what she told us just before they left, Junior."

I asked, "What did she tell you?"

Charles answered: "That's what put me on Cody's trail in the first place. Millie wasn't worried about hungry lions or dangerous revolutionaries, just Buff Cody. She told us she felt that, with a lot of money at stake, he could be really dangerous. She said she didn't believe for a moment that friendship would keep him from taking violent action if he thought his partner was about to interfere with his profitable smuggling plans. She said she'd do her best to keep Will from sticking his neck out, but if anything happened to them down in Mexico, we could assume that Cody was responsible and it would be nice if we could get the authorities on the case somehow." He gestured helplessly. "But when . . . when it did happen there wasn't anything . . . What could we tell the police? That our mother had hated Mr. H. H. Cody and thought he might kill her and her lover, Cody's partner; and now they were dead? What action do you think they'd take on evidence like that against a big man like him, particularly since it had happened out of the country? So I started following him around and discovered that . . ." He stopped abruptly.

"What's the matter?" I asked.

"I'm not supposed to talk about it."

I grinned. "About what? About the fact that a certain Federal agency already had him under surveillance?"

There was sudden suspicion in the boy's voice: "How do you know that? Oh, of course . . ." He frowned, trying to work it out, remembering now that the Federal agents who'd been following H. H. Cody had taken him, Charles, into custody, and assured him I was Cody, and given him back his gun, and sent him after me after swearing him to secrecy. "If you're not Cody, who the hell are you?" he demanded.

"Same government, different agency," I said. "I'm afraid we're not always a band of brothers. In fact, we sometimes work completely at cross-purposes. Sad, but that's the way governments are."

"I suppose you can prove that!"

"That I'm a government agent?" I said. "Oh, sure, I always carry my little tin badge even when I'm pretending to be somebody else, just to make sure anybody who shakes me down will know I'm a phony. Be your age, *amigo*!"

That was a mistake. It reminded him that he was the youngest one here—at least, if Antonia didn't have him beat in years, she did in experience. It made him think I was patronizing him; and maybe I was, a little. His ego had already taken considerable punishment recently. He'd come down here, armed, to avenge his mother, feeling ruthless and dangerous; but two days ago a man had simply ignored his gun, and today a girl had taken it away from him. And now they were all ganging up on him to

148

sell him a highly implausible yarn about an unlikely impersonation for which there was no real evidence but his bossy older sister's questionable logic and the word of a little *mestizo* wench whose morals and veracity were highly suspect.

I'd forgotten the sensitive pride of a kid that age—well, a male kid that age. I'd probably been just as touchy, but it had been a long time ago. It wasn't a good frame of mind for him to be in if we were going to work together, and I opened my mouth to say something soothing, but the ringing of the phone on the bar interrupted me. I picked up the instrument.

"Yes?"

"The yellow dog was delivered safely to the boarding kennel."

"I'm happy to hear it," I said. So it was Greer, the young agent I'd met briefly by a mountain lake, identifying me by giving my dog's location and hearing me respond with Happy's name. "Go on," I said.

"You've got company outside."

I sighed. I'd hoped they'd let me run until I found out what they wanted to know. "How much company?"

"I've spotted three of them."

"U.S. or Mex?"

"Two U.S., one Mex. Do you want help?"

"How much help?"

"Just me and my piece at the moment. Reinforcements are a couple of hours away."

I said, "We can probably cover the back and front. Take anybody who tries the side window. I'll need you to help bury the bodies afterwards, if any; but don't come charging in without plenty of warning. The troops may be just a bit trigger-happy."

"Gotcha. Greer out."

CHAPTER 17

REPLACING the phone, I reflected a bit cynically on the fact that our man in Hermosillo had waited until now to alert me. He'd presumably been watching earlier, when I arrived. He'd let me walk in, all unsuspecting, on an armed Mexican beauty, junior grade, not to mention the brother-and-sister team—he couldn't know they'd been immobilized. I decided that it was just another example of the reasoning that had sent me on this mission in the first place: I was a trained and experienced operative, and I wasn't supposed to need a nursemaid unless the odds got too outlandish. At that, Greer hadn't been quite as optimistic about my capabilities as Mac, who'd apparently figured I could handle without assistance any deathtrap set for me by anybody. Flattering, but a bit frightening. Greer, on the other hand, had left me to cope with three amateurs on my own, but he'd decided that I might need a friendly warning, and maybe even a friendly gun, when a trio of pros got into the act.

Correction: while the U.S. pair he'd mentioned was undoubtedly professional, the status of their Mexican ally remained to be determined.

I became aware that my companions were watching me expectantly, awaiting explanations, but I left them on the hook a little longer while I reviewed our defensive perimeter in my mind. One wall was safe, shared by the other half of this duplex motel unit, with no connecting door. On the other side, the protection of the large living room window had just been assigned to Greer, and an earlier peek into the bathroom had told me that the window in there was too small to admit anything but a monkey. Which left the front, which I intended to defend myself, and the rear, where large French doors opened from the bedroom into a small patio that was probably not impregnable, although I hadn't checked for any gates.

I spoke to the Mexican girl: "Here's your gun. Go into the bedroom. If someone breaks in from the patio unarmed, hold him. If he's armed and Mexican, talk to him, stall him if you can; we've got some clout locally, but I don't want to strain it by damaging any Mexican citizens I don't have to. But if he's armed and American and gives you any trouble, it's okay to shoot him. Understood?"

"*Yo comprendo,*" she said.

"There's no shell in the chamber," I said.

She jacked back the slide of the little pistol, let it snap forward smartly, and set the safety. She grinned at me. "There is now, señor," she said, and was gone with a flick of her *serape*.

Jo Beckman was frowning at me. "Do I gather that you're expecting an invasion?"

She sounded skeptical. Considering that she and her brother, one of them armed, had entered the premises illegally and found Antonia already present with a gun, I couldn't see why she'd be surprised that still others might have the same idea.

I said, "That's right. There have been two attempts on my life already, if we include Junior's noonday try in Cananea. I'm a real unpopular fellow."

"You, or Horace Cody?" She frowned. "I mean, are they trying to kill you because they know you're a fake or because they don't?"

This tall, lean lady might not do much for my virility, but I had to admire the way she'd gone straight to the heart of the puzzle.

I said, "It's very complicated, and we haven't got time to go into it now. If you and your brother get into that corner over there, you should be reasonably safe if it comes to shooting."

She studied me for a moment longer, shrugged, and moved toward the spot I'd indicated; but the boy didn't follow her. He looked toward the bedroom.

"Those French doors back there aren't much. That's the way we got in, easier than opening a milk carton. Suppose I go give the little lady a hand." He glanced at the pistol butt showing at my waist and held out his hand. "How about my gun?"

Well, it was understandable. Antonia was close to his own age, a pretty girl who wasn't his sister, and she'd made him look bad earlier by taking his weapon away. Clearly he wanted a chance to demonstrate to her that he wasn't the ineffectual stumblebum she'd made him appear.

I shook my head. "Sorry, Charles. No gun."

He stood perfectly still for a moment, shocked and insulted; then he threw another glance at the door through which Antonia had gone. He protested: "You gave *her* back her gun!"

I said, "She's seen the real Cody, and she knows I'm not him. And your sister has convinced herself that I'm a genuine phony. But you're not quite sure, are you? You're thinking Jo could be wrong, and Antonia could be a plant I put in here to lie for me, and I could just possibly be H. H. Cody after all, running a great big elaborate con game with you as the mark." I shook my head again. "So, no gun."

He made an angry sound in his throat, wheeled, and marched off toward the bedroom. I started to call him back but checked myself. Wherever he was, with his present suspicious attitude, he was trouble. Maybe it was better to have him one room away from me than in the same room behind me.

Jo Beckman said, "That wasn't very nice of you."

"Lady," I said, "the last time I came across your kid brother I promised myself that, next time we met, I was going to treat myself to the pleasure of beating the living shit out of him even though I normally disapprove of fisticuffs. But look at him, there isn't a mark on him. Be satisfied with that, don't ask for nice."

Actually, I remembered, I'd had pleasant visions of carving the gun-waving punk into bloody little pieces for the hogs, but it was no time for meticulous accuracy.

The tall girl laughed. "Have we time for another drink?"

"A wench after my own heart," I said. "Two Scotches, coming up."

I went to get her glass and returned to the bar. As I was pouring the liquor, Jo Beckman said, "I really don't understand what the hell is going on. Just exactly who are you, what are you trying to do, and who's trying to stop you? Junior and I heard what you said to the Mexican girl about a missing shipment of weapons for a revolutionary organization, but . . ."

She was interrupted by a knock on the door. A woman's voice spoke, heavily accented: "Please, I have the towels for the bathroom."

"Just a minute."

I walked over and placed one glass in Jo Beckman's hand. It was, I noted, quite steady.

She said softly, "I was in the bathroom right after you cut us loose. There are plenty of towels."

"Sure." I raised my voice. "Coming!"

Walking over there, drink in hand, I paused to take a couple of slow sips before reaching for the knob. I was giving Greer time, I hoped, to get into position from wherever he'd made his call, presumably one of the nearby motel units. Then I pulled the door open.

She had the towels all right, a sizeable pile of them. Smiling at me apologetically over them, she stood in the doorway, a chunky brown woman in her thirties with short, dark hair that looked as if its last shampoo had been considerably longer ago than yesterday. Motel maids no longer go in for picturesque full skirts and white peasant blouses down there to please the gringo tourists; she was wearing baggy, faded jeans and a loose gray work shirt with the tails out. If she was actually a maid bribed to perform a small chore for the opposition, she undoubtedly found the costume more practical for making beds and scrubbing floors; but visually it was a dead loss on a sturdy figure like hers, making her look like a sack of potatoes. Well, in certain areas, melons.

"I am sorry to disturb the señor," she said, still smiling a bit hesitantly. *"Un momentito, por favor."*

"Help yourself."

I stepped aside for her. She came forward, and I gave the

door a left-handed push to close it behind her. At the same time, I threw my drink into her face right-handed, plastic glass and all, and carried through with my right hand by chopping down hard on the pile of towels. I felt a solid object under the layers of absorbent material and heard it thump on the carpet as she lost her grip on her burden. She started to grab for it, but my left hand shoved her forward, my foot tripped her, and things started happening very fast.

I was given no chance to deal with the gun on the rug, if it was a gun. The woman exploded into action. I was suddenly busy sidestepping a skilled backwards kick that would have had my knee bending the wrong way if it had landed. Even with a faceful of whiskey, she'd recovered instantly from her stumble and lashed out like a vicious mule—the first blackbelt motel maid I'd met, to my knowledge.

Even if I could have taken her, there wasn't time for a lot of *Hah-Hah* stuff; my attention might be needed elsewhere in the suite at any moment. I backstepped quickly, therefore, to give myself shooting room, and got out my .38. The woman had whirled to stalk me with her hands raised, karate fashion, ready to crack cinder blocks, bricks, or me. Her whiskey-wet face was still smiling in an intent, meaningless way. She wasn't a bad-looking woman, really, if you liked them husky, and she had very white, very even teeth.

I realized abruptly that I'd seen her before. She'd been wearing military-style coveralls, and I'd seen her at a considerable distance, carrying a submachine gun of unknown manufacture as she examined the wrecked Cadillac, and then making a funny thing of modeling some of Gloria's underwear for the benefit of her companions in the beat-up white station wagon she'd been driving. I didn't particularly want to shoot her, but it didn't look as if she intended to leave me much choice; she was going to rush my gun to keep me busy while her associates closed in. . . .

The window across the room to my left crashed in. A man's voice I didn't know yelled in standard Hollywood cop-show English: "Drop the gun! Freeze!"

I didn't even take time to look. I just gave him the standard response: I pulled the trigger and threw myself to the floor. The crash of the short-barreled S. and W. was deafening in the closed room—well, not quite closed, I guess, now that the glass was broken. A gun roared over there, and something tugged at the shoulder of the windbreaker that had been among the clothes I'd found in the Subaru to replace my grimy and ragged wedding costume. I rolled desperately, knowing that I had no chance to beat his second bullet, whoever he was; but against expectations I got myself pointed in the right direction without being shot. When I tried to pick him up over the sights, his face and his revolver were no longer staring at me over there. He was hanging in the window frame with his head and shoulders inside the room, and his gun was lying on the carpet below his dangling hand. There was enough glass left in the frame to do him no good at all, wedged there, but he seemed to be in no condition to object. Behind him was a face I knew.

"Easy, it's me!" Greer said quickly. He was holding a revolver of his own, gripped for striking rather than shooting. "This one should be out for a while; how about yours?"

"She should be dead. I didn't have time for any fancy marksmanship."

Greer looked, and said judiciously, "Well, I'd say she wasn't going anywhere in a hurry."

There was broken glass all over the carpet, and the unconscious man was bleeding on the windowsill and down the wall where I'd been so careful to camouflage Antonia's little .22-caliber bullet hole after conscientiously picking up the tiny cartridge case, but nobody was going to return this room to normal now without calling in the redecorators. I remembered that I'd also been trying to avoid harming any Mexican nationals, but the phony motel maid, sitting on the floor limply with her back and head supported by the big chair favored by Antonia, didn't look good.

Getting to my feet cautiously, keeping her covered just in case, I said, "What about the rear. . . . Hey, Antonia, are you okay?"

The Mexican girl answered from the bedroom cheerfully: "I

am very okay, and Señor Charles is very okay also; but we have a very pretty man here. He behave him good now. Do you want?''

"Bring him in." I remembered Jo Beckman. She was still standing where I'd left her, still holding the drink I'd given her. As far as I could see, she hadn't spilled a drop. "What about you?" I asked.

She licked her lips. "I'm all right, but I think that woman is badly hurt."

"Well, curb your Florence Nightingale instincts until I've checked her out."

She made a wry face. "You flatter me, sir. At the moment I'm too grateful for not having wet my pants to worry too much about anybody else's problems." She drew a long, shuddering breath, and took a drink from her glass. She rubbed her left ear, which had been aimed toward the gun in the window. "So that's a gunfight! All I can say is that it's a damned noisy business!"

I stepped over to examine the seated woman, but the front of her gray shirt wasn't gray any longer; and her brown eyes were staring across the room at a stylized motel-type picture of a little brown Indian boy and a little brown Indian girl—I always wondered who paints those things—and seeing nothing. Well, I had my answer. She'd been a pro all right. I suppose it was as good an epitaph as any.

"Dead?" It was Jo Beckman's voice. When I nodded, she asked, "Did you have to?"

I said bitterly, "Hell, no, I'm an antifeminist, I just knock them off any time I get the chance, like vermin."

"I'm sorry, I didn't mean . . ."

I grimaced. "If I hadn't shot her, what the hell do you think she'd have been doing while I was ducking her partner's bullets? You saw that lethal kick she unleashed. She'd just have stepped over to where I was crawling around on the floor, taken one fancy karate chop at me, and cracked my neck like a broomstick." I shook my head grimly. "I wish to God these jerks would stop watching TV and forget that idiot *freeze-drop-the-gun* routine!"

Greer, waiting outside the broken window, wasn't interested in the oratory for the defense. He said, "Whatever you want to do, Mr. Horace Cody, you'd better do it fast, before the shooting brings out the Mex marines."

I said, "First let's get that specimen out of the glass before he slices himself in two." I was working things out in my head as I crossed the room toward the unconscious man. I went on: "We're going to have to get a little political pressure working here or we'll all wind up in the *cárcel*. If you get to a phone before I do, the contact is 17-45-55 and ask for *El Cacique*. The number has some kind of priority, so you shouldn't have any trouble getting through. Use my code name for ID. . . ." I stooped abruptly, realizing that, preoccupied with the casualties, I was overlooking the fact that something that should have happened, hadn't: the backroom boys and girls hadn't appeared. I stepped back from the window. "Antonia, what's the problem back there?"

"No problem." It was the boy's voice. "Our guest tried to get tough, but we gentled him." There was the sound of a blow. "Come on, you! Behave yourself good, don't make a liar of the lady."

I watched them appear. The prisoner was of Superbowl proportions, big in every direction. He was no taller than my six-four, but he must have weighed close to three hundred against my two, with shoulders that would have split my windbreaker right down the back if he'd been silly enough to try it on. An unfashionably short haircut made him look bullet-headed, and his nose had been broken at least once, but the odd thing was that he was obviously by no means a brainless bruiser. In fact, in his early twenties, with clear blue, guileless eyes, he looked like kind of a nice boy. A nice *big* boy. He was dressed in jeans, like everybody else in the room, with a light blue jersey topping things off. On the front of the outsized jersey was stenciled: LOVE! I suppose it was a disguise.

I knew him, of course; I'd seen him through the little telescope a short time before I'd seen the woman I'd just shot. He'd been playing driver and bodyguard for General Carlos Mondragon.

Big Boy Blue. Behind him, covering him with her little .22, came Antonia. Mason Charles followed along, holding a .38 revolver with a four-inch barrel like the one the unconscious man had dropped on the floor, clearly the standard weapon for that organization. The boy gave me a challenging glance: if I wouldn't give him back his own gun he'd damn well get a gun somewhere else, and did I want to make something of it? I backed up to give them room, letting the challenge pass. The big young man in the lead spotted the dead pseudomaid on the floor.

"Oh, Christ, did you have to kill her? She was just doing her patriotic Mexican duty by giving us a hand."

"Hand, hell, it was a foot that almost did me in," I said. I holstered my own gun and scooped up the revolver belonging to the man in the window. I laid it, with Mason Charles's Beretta, on the bar. I said, "Maybe you'd like to give my friend some help getting your friend out of the window before he comes to and thrashes around in all that glass and guts himself like a herring."

Concerned about the dead woman, the big guy hadn't even noticed the unconscious man. Now he stared, shocked, and started to speak angrily but controlled himself. He stepped forward and studied the situation briefly.

"Lift him straight up," he said to Greer. "Now ease him this way gently, keep his legs high, let me take the weight. . . ."

I left them to it. I always like to keep track of all the local artillery, and I remembered that there was still one firearm unaccounted for, buried in the disorderly pile of towels that had been dumped by the front door.

"Watch him, keep him covered," I said over my shoulder to Antonia and Charles as I moved that way.

"Not to worry, we've got him," the boy said.

I kicked around a bit and located the piece. As I bent over to pick it up, there was a warning cry from the Mexican girl. I turned to see Mason Charles's weapon aimed straight at me, and Antonia throwing herself that way in an attempt to knock the revolver aside, but the big young man whose name I still did

158

not know, who'd just placed his unconscious associate tenderly on the floor, leaped like a great cat from that position and swept her aside. I was making my dive for the carpet for the second time that evening; but this time I wasn't fast enough. The left side of my head received a violent blow that filled my vision with a white glare and drove a strange, tingling sensation through my whole body. I was still hearing the crash of the gun as I fell and a triumphant, boyish voice saying:

"Good-bye, Mr. Horace Hosmer Cody!"

I felt unconsciousness sweeping over me and receding and washing back over me again, like waves attacking a beach on an incoming tide, but I hung on grimly. There was something I had to do, something I'd been trained to do, something that had been hammered into me ruthlessly: *We give no freebies!* Nobody's immortal. They can take any of us any time they want us, but they have to pay. They damn well have to pay.

He came, of course, to gloat over his first kill. Afterwards, no doubt, he'd rush to the bathroom to puke like the lousy little amateur he was—well, I wouldn't have been jackass enough to turn my back on a pro. At that, it had been a piss-poor performance on my part; after all, I'd sensed that the mother-fixated young avenger was strictly unreliable.

"No!" That was the voice of a woman whose name I'd been told, now forgotten. "No, not again, Junior! Damn you, you've shot the wrong man!"

I felt his foot turn me over. There was no feeling in my right side and no strength in my right hand, but it didn't matter. That's why we use cross-draw holsters worn over the left hip so they're available to either hand. I let myself roll with his nudge and saw him above me, not just one of him but two, a symptom of anything from a mild concussion to a bullet in the brain and to hell with it. I simply closed one eye to get rid of one target and put my bullet into the middle of the other. The crash and recoil of the snub-nosed Smith and Wesson was too much to bear. I let the surging black tide carry me away.

CHAPTER 18

I woke up strapped into a vibrating projectile hurtling through an endless blackness. I was frightened because I didn't know whether the blackness was inside or outside me—didn't know whether there was nothing to see or whether something was out there, and I was just incapable of seeing it. The thundering pain in my head made the second seem a likely theory. Then a wonderful blaze of light filled the world for a moment and was gone with a blast of sound.

"Fucking semis think they own the road," said the woman driving the car softly, without any real anger. She was clearly speaking to herself.

I recognized her voice. She was the one whose name wasn't Josephine. I had no idea what she was doing there or, for that matter, what I was. Where we were was another problem that would have to be solved eventually. I'd left myself lying dead on the bloodstained carpet of a motel room in a Mexican town called . . . called . . . Anyway, after surviving the best homicidal efforts of the best and brightest professionals in the business, I'd let a vengeful young amateur take me by mistake. Dumb, dumb, dumb! I'd died and somebody had raised me from the grave, presumably the woman beside me. The way my head ached, I wished she hadn't bothered.

Somebody'd tucked my S. and W. back into its hidden holster inside my waistband. I seemed to have a bulky bandage on my head. The straps I'd been aware of weren't really doing much of a job; most safety harnesses don't function well with the seat fully reclined. The car was my Subaru wagon—well, it was mine for the moment, unless the lady had decided to take possession. I was in no condition to contest any claim she cared to make. But I could see now and recognize the dimly lighted dashboard and be grateful that there was only one of them. I remembered having had double vision earlier, although I had no idea how much earlier. I also remembered a numbness in my right side, and it was still present as the curious tingling sensation you get after a cold day in the duck blind or on the ski slopes when the half-frozen flesh gradually thaws out in front of the fire in the warm lodge. The toes and fingers on that side seemed to be back in operation, although I wouldn't have wanted to present them with any demanding tasks like kicking a football or playing a Mozart piano sonata. Not that I'd ever been expert at either chore, at the best of times.

"Did I get him?"

The words surprised me; I hadn't been aware that I was going to speak or even that I remembered how.

The woman turned her head briefly. "So you're back. If you're going to be sick again, let me know so you can do it outside the car."

"Did I get him?"

She gave an angry little snort. "You keep asking that, you bloodthirsty bastard. How many people do you have to kill a night to keep you happy?"

I said, "I can't remember your name. Something like Josephine . . . Okay, I've got it. Joanna. Joanna Beckman."

"Can you remember yours?"

"Sure. Helm. Matthew Helm."

She laughed shortly. "Well, at least we've got *that* out of you even if we had to practically blow your head off to do it. Can you remember the name you were going under in Hermosillo?"

There were warning signals flashing in my aching brain; maybe I shouldn't have been so ready with my name, since I apparently hadn't given it to her before. I must have had a reason, or must I? Maybe I just hadn't got around to it when I got shot. Maybe she'd never asked. Anyway, my memory was still

161

very hazy in spots, I needed information to clear it up, and I wasn't going to get some without giving some.

I said, as much to myself as to her, "Hermosillo. I was groping for that name, thanks. I was going under the name of Cody there, Horace Hosmer Cody. And the name of the young man who shot me was Mason Charles, Junior. You called him Junior. I turned my back on his gun twice, and it was once too many. Now tell me, did I get him?"

"Don't you remember?"

I said, "I remember making a very tricky left-handed shot from a very awkward position, with my whole right side nonfunctional—temporarily, I'm happy to say; it seems to be clearing up now. I'm fairly sure I hit him, but I departed the conscious scene at that point so I don't know how hard I hit him."

"And that's all it means to you? You just want to know if your marksmanship was adequate!" She made a small sound, a gasp or a sob. "Goddamn you, he's my kid brother! I raised him from a pup!"

I spoke deliberately: "I wouldn't boast about it if I were you, the way you goofed his education. You should have taught him important things like not taking shots at government agents or, if he had to, shooting straight enough to put them down for good." I raised my right hand, the tingling one, pleased to discover that I could do it quite easily. I touched the bandage on my head, which seemed to be a towel of some kind. "This sort of peripheral marksmanship is guaranteed suicide."

She started to respond angrily but checked herself and gave a little bark of laughter instead. Well, I'd had a hunch she'd respond better to brutal honesty than to fake remorse and sympathy.

She said, "At least you're a consistent monster. And now we know whom you're working for."

"Hell, I told your brother that when we were discussing the outfit that had held him for a while in El Paso. Same government, different agency, I said."

"So it's really a sort of intramural shooting match with the U.S. taxpayer footing the ammunition bill for both teams." She grimaced. "As usual, the government's right hand doesn't seem to know what the left is doing."

I said, "Actually, it's a four-way battle royal, with the Mexican government and the would-be revolutionaries also in the ring, to change your metaphor slightly."

"He was very badly hurt," she said. "Junior. If you must know. A very ugly stomach wound. It was obvious that he'd die without proper medical attention. *Fast*, proper medical attention. That's why you're here."

I licked my lips. "The logic escapes me."

She said, "I made a deal with your friend, the one who calls himself Greer. I don't suppose it's his real name, any more than yours is Cody. He didn't give a damn about Junior; all he cared about was getting you away to a doctor he knew locally who'd keep his mouth shut. He wanted you out of there before the police arrived—fortunately, like all cops everywhere, they were taking their sweet time about it. Greer wanted to be sure that, if you survived your wound, you could carry on with your mission, and if you didn't, you could be buried discreetly elsewhere, and he wouldn't have to explain your presence in that suite. I think he was actually carrying out instructions he'd received over the phone. He'd made a quick telephone call, I assumed to the number you'd given him."

"So you made a deal," I said. I was finding it hard to concentrate.

"Yes, I examined you and told him that, although I couldn't be sure without X-rays, I didn't think you'd really need a doctor unless you had a considerably worse concussion than I thought; all you required was some rest and a bit of TLC and somebody standing by to get you to a hospital fast if you started developing certain symptoms, which I didn't really expect. I said I'd get you out of there and take care of you if he'd make sure my brother got to an operating table immediately with a good man in attendance. I'm not a surgeon myself, I told him, but I'm certainly doctor enough to take care of a thick-skulled moron with a little crease in his scalp."

I tried a cautious grin, but it hurt too much for me to maintain it. "People always say you can't hurt us Scandihoovians by shooting us in the head. And if I'd said that about some other races I can think of, you'd accuse me of being a dirty racist. So you're an M.D.?"

She shrugged. "Kind of, sort of. I do have a degree in medicine, but actually I'm a child psychiatrist."

"I'd never have guessed," I said. "I thought child specialists were supposed to be nice, gentle, sympathetic folks." She smiled faintly at my insult; maybe it was a favorable symptom. I asked, "How did my young pal Greer manage to get control of things? Last I remember, the home team was in bad trouble and the visitors were marching down the field for the TD."

"The little Indian girl," she said. "Or whatever she is. Sisneros. While you and Junior were bleeding all over the rug, and the big boy and I were trying to determine the extent of the damage, she got hold of that gun you'd been after, the one belonging to the so-called maid who'd brought the towels."

"Why would Antonia need it? I remember seeing her own in her hand."

"Hers was empty. Apparently Junior had recognized the big fellow when he came in through the French doors as one of the agents he'd met in El Paso. His name is Rutherford, incidentally, Marion Rutherford. Can you imagine a two-ton character like that going around calling himself Marion? Actually, he doesn't; he's known as Tunk Rutherford, probably derived from tank, like in Sherman tank. Or maybe that was the noise he made hitting the opposing football team in his college days. Anyway, Junior decided to change sides I guess, assuming he'd ever been on yours. He grabbed Sisneros from behind so Rutherford could disarm her. Then they emptied her gun but let her keep it because you'd have become suspicious if she'd been without it. With Junior covering her from behind, she pretty well had to cooperate while they pretended to march Rutherford in to you as a prisoner. . . . Well, you know how it went from there."

"So afterwards, being mad at the way she'd been treated, the little girl got a loaded gun and, I suppose, got the drop on the big guy and opened the front door to let Greer join the party;

164

and everybody lived happily ever after." I glanced at her. "And what were you doing while all this was going on? Whose side are you on, Mrs. Beckman?"

She said grimly, "I'm looking for one I can bear to associate with. I haven't found it yet. Now you'd better rest and let me concentrate on my driving."

I said, "They say you should never drive Mexican roads at night. The cattle think they have the right of way."

"Go to sleep. If I hit a cow, you'll know it."

I closed my eyes and listened to the murmur of the engine and the rumble of the tires on the lousy Mexican pavement and the occasional rush of a passing car and the throbbing of my head. Greer seemed to be handling things okay, and apparently he'd got in touch with Ramón, who'd help him clean up the mess. . . .

When I awoke again, I was in a real, stationary bed, not a reclining, jiggling car seat, and there was sunlight at the windows. Vision: normal. Tingling: none. Headache: agonizing, but not much worse than a serious hangover. Sitting up, I found that my right arm didn't like to push very hard; it was functional but rather tired. I swung my legs out of bed and stood up cautiously; the project turned out to be quite feasible, but my right leg felt equally weary. However, I found that I could manage a few steps without falling on my face.

It was a bare room furnished with a double bed consisting of a mattress, a spring, and a wooden frame that looked homemade. There was a bureau and a small wooden table by the window, flanked by a couple of slat-seat wooden armchairs that looked like porch furniture and aroused in me no desire to curl up in one and continue my perusal of *War and Peace*, which I'd started in college and never finished. There were no pictures on the white-plastered walls. A couple of small, well-worn rag rugs, one on each side of the bed, protected the feet of the occupants from the shock of morning contact with the colorful but cold Mexican-tile floor.

The top drawer of the bureau was empty; the next one down held some female-type bathing suits and underwear, not very sexy; even the pantyhose seemed to have been selected chiefly for durability. Size Q for Queen; a sizeable lady apparently. Equivalent male garments filled the bottom drawer. Shorts size 34. T-shirts size 38. No pygmy, but the queen-size wife would have him outnumbered. A similar division of space was apparent in the closet, where room had also been left on the rod for the use of a visitor. My own canvas bag, unopened, was on the floor.

I started to pick it up, but bending over that far turned out to be not such a good idea, so I left it there. A visit to the bathroom was essential, however. It was apparently a communal facility; entering, I was confronted by another door that presumably led into another bedroom. I didn't feel strong enough to investigate; but I did have a look around the small, tiled cubicle that housed the plumbing. The shelf above the washbasin held a toothbrush and a small tube of American toothpaste—Crest, if it matters. The toothbrush, wet, had obviously seen recent employment. There was also a comb with a few light brown hairs in it, not very long. The medicine cabinet held some male shaving gear and some female cosmetics on the upper shelves, the lower one again having been vacated for the use of visitors.

The mirror on the cabinet door showed me a long, thin gent with a bloodstained brown towel wrapped around his cranium and dried blood on his face. Those scalp wounds do tend to pour it out in large quantities. I was in my underwear—apparently my high-powered medical attendant had balked at inserting me into pajamas—and it was pretty gory, too. Not an attractive figure, but alive. I hadn't earned it, but I wasn't about to turn it down.

I performed the obligatory function and made my way back into the bedroom. The bed looked very good to me, but I still had no idea where the house was located, so I moved to the nearest window and adjusted the slats of the Venetian blind so I could see between them. It was a rather bleak, sand-and-cactus landscape out there, with some scattered, small residences that didn't employ the mud-brick architecture used in most Mexican villages in this part of the country and weren't as old. There were some arid-looking hills on the horizon. I was at the rear of the house, which seemed to be at the edge of this desert community with few habitations beyond it. I moved to the other window, at the side, and peeked out; in this direction was a solid row of little houses, and between them I caught glimpses of blue water glinting in the sunshine. It looked like a not too high-class California beach development, but even if we'd driven all night it seemed unlikely that we'd made it up into the U.S. and clear over to the Pacific Ocean.

"Get right back into that bed!"

She was standing in the doorway holding a glass of water and a small bottle of Tylenol. Her expression puzzled me: equal parts of indignation and apprehension, although what she had to be apprehensive about, I couldn't understand. She was wearing a blue tank top upon which she made no unreasonable demands and white shorts in the flaring, floppy style that makes any but the skinniest woman look fat. She was built narrowly enough to get by with them, but it seemed to me she was rushing the season a bit; the morning seemed chilly for shorts and bare shoulders. On the other hand, her temperature was her own business; and the shoulders weren't as bony as I'd expected, and the long, lean legs weren't totally unattractive either.

"*Please* get into bed and stay there, Mr. Helm," she said.

"Let's stick with Cody," I said, as I obeyed her orders. "I haven't got much out of this impersonation so far, just a cracked skull, but there's always tomorrow."

"Don't count on tomorrow if you're going to start running around before we know how badly you're hurt. . . . Here, take these."

"Okay, but it's like spitting at a forest fire. A couple of lousy little pills aren't going to touch it."

"It's really bad, is it? Do you have any other symptoms beside the headache?"

It didn't make sense. I mean, I was the man who'd shot her brother, perhaps killed him, and here she was full of tender concern about my health.

She went on, "I know you probably feel messy and uncom-

167

fortable, but please don't dream of taking a bath. As soon as I've changed your bandage I'll bring some warm water and . . ."

I said, "Beckman."

She said, "A sponge bath and a pair of clean pajamas—I saw some in your bag—will make you feel much better. Then I'll fix you something to eat. . . ."

I had it at last. I said, "Beckman, you have a very guilty conscience. Why?" Standing over me, she looked away and didn't answer. I said, studying her handsome, averted face, "That was a lot of crap you handed Greer and me last night, wasn't it? I've had a little time to think, and I've been hit on the head before, and my impression is that there isn't a doctor in the world who can take a quick look at a bloody groove in a man's scalp and know anything except that the bullet bounced instead of penetrating. I could have had a cracked skull and a brain full of blood and bone splinters, and the best surgeon in the world couldn't have told the difference without an X-ray. Certainly a lousy pediatric wigpicker couldn't. You lied to Greer to get his cooperation. You weren't the least bit sure I was going to be okay, but you were willing to take a chance on my going into convulsions, or a coma, or dying on you, just so your back-shooting brother got the attention he needed. Beckman, I'm ashamed of you. Hippocrates is ashamed of you. You should be ashamed of yourself. Now get this crummy turban off me, and let's see what the damage really is."

CHAPTER 19

THE healing process took a while, particularly since the tall lady doctor really did have a bad attack of the guilts and insisted on making amends for gambling with my life once by taking no more chances with my health. She kept me bed-bound long after the headache subsided and the right-side weaknesses departed. I submitted to her ministrations in a docile manner, feeling strangely remote and unconcerned. So there was a load of arms to be found and a gent called Saturday to be dealt with, and maybe, if it could be discreetly arranged, a guy named Mondragon, and so what? They'd keep. According to Jo, there wasn't a phone in the house, but who cared? There wasn't anybody I wanted to talk with anyway.

I wasn't even greatly interested in the lady who was taking such meticulous care of me. I mean, she was pleasant enough company when I wasn't reading—the owners of the house kept stacks of well-thumbed paperbacks around—and she wasn't physically repulsive by any means, but I had no real urge to grab her and pull her down to join me in the big bed. I wasn't even seriously concerned about where we were. There had been the initial stirring of curiosity that had led me to peek out the windows, but our exact geographical location seemed a matter of minor importance. Gradually I learned from Jo that we hadn't made California after all that first night out of Hermosillo, although we had reached an arm of the Pacific. We'd driven a mere sixty-five miles west to Kino Bay, on the body of salt water known to the Mexicans as the Sea of Cortez. The Gulf of California, to you.

There had long been a Mexican village here, now called Old Kino; then *gringos* had discovered the lovely white beach and the fine fishing. A transient settlement of trailers and campers and motorhomes had grown up, but gradually it had been replaced by more permanent vacation homes, strung out for a mile or two along the beach road, starting above the old native village to the south and ending at the bluff that terminated the beach and halted further development to the north. From Jo's conversation, as the days passed, I got the impression, although I wasn't interested enough to ask, that the relatively new community of Kino Bay supported a motel or two and a few restaurants as well as extensive facilities for recreational vehicles.

On the fifth or sixth or seventh day—I hadn't kept very good track of the time—she came back from one of her daily shopping expeditions with her bag a little heavier with loot than usual. I sensed an air of excitement about her, but I wasn't curious enough to ask. After checking on me, she headed into the kitchen to start her dinner preparations a little earlier than usual; then she came back into the master bedroom and threw some clothes onto the bed.

"Get dressed," she said. "I'm tired of looking at you horizontal. Let's see what you look like vertical."

"Yes, ma'am," I said.

"First take a bath and trim that beard a bit, or at least scrape the fuzz along the edges."

"Wow, are you sure my heart can stand the excitement, Doctor?"

"Never mind your heart. Your head is my concern; cardiology isn't my field. I haven't a bit of worry about your heart anyway; I know it's made of stone. So it probably won't make you jump up and down with joy to hear that Junior's going to make it. I just got through to the hospital in Hermosillo again. It's been close, but he's going to be all right."

I said, "I'm glad for your sake, Jo."

She said coolly, "Do I gather that it isn't a great load off your mind? When you shoot people you'd just as soon they'd stay

170

shot, is that right?'' When I didn't speak, because she was quite correct, and I didn't owe her brother a damn thing except a headache, she shrugged. "Like I said, solid granite. Get yourself cleaned up and dressed while I see to the chicken. I thought we could use a change from all the fish we've been eating, even though it's very good and fresh here.''

It felt strange to be moving around pretending to be a more-or-less normal human being for a change instead of an invalid. Taking care to keep my head bandage dry, I showered and then scraped my face a bit with the Schick razor, complete with blades, that had been left in the medicine chest by my unknown host, the man with the size 38 undershirt. The tall, gray-bearded character confronting me in the mirror looked like a dull and tired fellow, hardly the type to get into the kind of bullet trouble indicated by the rakish bandage on his head. If the truth were known, he'd probably just cracked his head on a low door.

My supernurse had washed the blood out of my clothes. I dressed myself in the blue denim shirt and pants provided by a grateful nation. The jogging shoes that had also been put into the Subaru were a little tight, and the socks were those lousy one-size-fits-all numbers that invariably cramp the toes of anyone with feet at the upper end of the size scale like mine. After fingering the small bullet-tear in the shoulder of the windbreaker, I put that on, too. It was still early enough spring to be chilly in the evenings, even at sea level this far south. It was kind of like leaving the nest and learning to fly again. Properly clad for the first time in almost a week, if you want to call jeans proper, I ventured out of the room, savoring the reckless thrill of exploration.

Except for the master bedroom and the bath, I had up to now seen nothing of the house to remember—I hadn't been very interested in houses when I arrived. I found myself in a living-dining room with a table set for two to my left and a sofa, a cocktail table, and a couple of big chairs grouped around a good-sized fireplace to my right. A fire burned in the fireplace, giving the whole place a cozy look although the furniture was cheap and rather shabby. The burning wood gave out occasional cracks and snaps. It seemed to be the hard, heavy, local stuff called ironwood that comes in such nice twisty shapes that it always seems a pity to burn them since a sculptor should be able to make something of them; and many local sculptors do. I noted a sideboard on which stood a small ice bucket, a couple of glasses, a bottle of soda, and another bottle I recognized; Greer must have tucked it into my bag before sending me off with the medical lady.

I could hear Jo Beckman working in the kitchen behind the closed door to my left. I poured myself a drink of J&B and stood sipping it, feeling light-headed and strangely dissociated from my surroundings. The room had glass doors looking out onto a patio that was protected from the street by a man-high wall. There was a small rock garden featuring local shrubs and cacti. Somebody'd been working in it recently, weeding and raking, and it pretty well had to be Jo since there had been nobody else around. For a child specialist the girl had unexpected talents. There was also a tiled terrace out there equipped with some black-iron furniture: a round table, and four chairs that looked more comfortable than the hard, wooden, veranda stuff in the bedroom.

"Oh, there you are!" Jo came in carrying a bottle of wine, which she set on the sideboard. "You can make yourself useful and open that. It's supposed to breathe a little, isn't it, or is that the red? I never can remember. Corkscrew in the top drawer. Then make me a drink, not too stiff. Let me get this fucking apron off; it makes me feel like a goddamn housewife, but I'm a slob in the kitchen and I didn't want to spot my dress. Back in a minute."

I wrestled the wine cork out and got her Scotch prepared, remembering that she'd taken it straight with just a couple of ice cubes the last time I'd served her, in Hermosillo. She came out to accept the glass from my hand and sip the contents gratefully. She was actually wearing a dress, as she'd said, the first time I'd seen her in one. It was a simple, long-sleeved sheath of fluid black jersey that clung to her in interesting ways. It was held in at the waist by the heavy concha belt I'd seen before. The squash-blossom necklace was also very much in evidence. The gleaming silver looked very dramatic against the matte black dress.

I whistled softly. "May I call you Slinky, ma'am?"

"It does make me look a little like a femme fatale, within my limitations, doesn't it?" She laughed. "But it's very practical, unwrinkleable, totally washable, and packs like a dream. Let's not let the fire go to waste, I'm very proud of it. One match. Generally I need a blowtorch to start the damn things."

We took our drinks over to the two big chairs. When she was seated, I noted that she was wearing nylons and black pumps with moderate heels; like most tall girls, she didn't go in for real stilts. Even so, they did nice things for her ankles, and I found myself thinking of her, for the first time since I'd been shot, as woman instead of doctor or nurse. Maybe that was the idea.

"Tell me about the little man with the big wife," I said. "The people who own this place."

"How did you . . . ?"

"I'm a detective of sorts, remember?" I grinned. "Size 34 shorts, queen-size pantyhose."

Jo laughed. "Hal isn't really so small, just skinny. He's a doctor at the clinic, a dermatologist. Harold Schonfeld. I'll admit Ziggy is fairly substantial, a massive German hausfrau type, but nice."

"The clinic, is that where you've got your office or whatever a child psychiatrist works out of?" I asked. When she nodded, I asked, "Where is it?"

"Tucson, Arizona. The Desert Pines Clinic."

"And what does one do around here when one hasn't got a cracked head?"

"If you mean the Schonfelds, mostly they fish. They bring their two boys down several times a year, with the boat on a trailer; it's only a day's drive. That is, Hal and the boys fish; Ziggy hates boats and doesn't think much of catching fish although she's great at cooking them. She putters around the house and garden and gets a tan on the beach. Between visits they lend the place to friends, like me. It was my official excuse for coming down. R and R as they say in the Army; and don't think my work isn't a real battle at times.'' She grimaced. ''I could hardly tell them at the clinic that I was taking a week off to make sure my baby brother killed the right man and not the wrong one.'' She shook her head ruefully. ''I really thought we'd convinced him you weren't Buff Cody.''

''He didn't want to be convinced,'' I said. ''We'd all been giving him a hard time. Back in Cananea, I'd left him standing there holding his gun and feeling foolish—in front of a pretty girl, no less. So Big Sister Jo comes down to make sure he wipes his nose and changes his socks, as if he were still a little boy; and in Hermosillo another pretty girl takes the gun away from him and hog-ties him, right in front of said B.S.J., who later makes casual remarks about a wet-nosed kid with a toy pistol! By this time, he's ready to kill somebody, anybody, just to make people take him seriously. Along comes the big guy called Tunk, who treats him and his vengeance mission with great respect, I'm sure, and tells him he's been perfectly right all along: 'Don't let them kid you, Mr. Charles, he's Cody all right, your mother's murderer; give me a hand with this feisty Latin wench and we'll go get him for you!' So he did.''

Jo sipped her drink, regarding me thoughtfully. There was red evening sunlight at the westward-facing glass doors behind her; we'd had fine weather all the time we'd been here, not that it had done me much good, confined to the big bed with an adamant jailer to see I stayed there. Jo drained her glass and rose.

''Maybe we'd better tackle that chicken. I've had enough Scotch for now, since there's wine coming; and I think you have, too.''

''Yes, Doctor.''

At the table, she made me carve, took a bite of chicken and nodded her acceptance.

"Well, it's edible," she said. She glanced at me across the little table. "I don't understand you, really. You seem to be reasonably intelligent, not too obnoxious, and quite brave. . . ."

I sighed. "I know that approach; I've heard it before. After telling me what a swell person I am, you spring the big question: 'What's a nice girl like you doing in a wicked house like this?' Right?"

A little color came to her face. "I suppose so. Well, what are you?"

I grinned. "Exactly the same thing you are, Doctor Beckman."

"Oh, no!" She looked up quickly, shocked. "No, that's a ridiculous thing to say!"

"Is it? You deal with the ones the parents and the schools and the cops can't handle. Am I right? Well, we deal with the ones the other undercover services and the cops can't handle. You have your tools and techniques; we have ours. What's the big difference?"

She licked her lips. "The difference between life and death, I should think."

I touched the bandage on my head. "And that's often just one hundred and fifty-eight grains of lead, if the guy is using the standard .38 caliber police load." I shook my head. "Now we're just talking words. But the fact is that I do what I'm good at just as you do what you're good at. At least I hope you do. If you do, that makes us both lucky. The world is full of people stuck in jobs that don't suit them at all."

She said, "I know what the rewards of my work are, but what satisfaction can there be in your . . . profession? Is it the danger that drew you to it? And keeps you in it?"

I shrugged. "To some extent. I never gamble with money, because neither winning nor losing money means a hell of a lot to me. But when I gamble my life, that's something else again. The biggest goddamn crap game in the world. It's a compulsive thing, and very few women seem to have it. Maybe that makes them more sensible than men, I don't know; but I can tell them they're missing something.''

"And that's all it is, just the thrill of danger?'' She was watching me curiously across the table. ''You don't say anything about patriotism and risking your life for your country.''

I said irritably, ''If we're going to talk a lot of bull about patriotism, I'm going to need another drink.''

She laughed. ''As a psychiatrist, I've observed that the only people who like to talk about how patriotic they are, are the ones who aren't. We may as well have our coffee comfortably by the fire; and an after-dinner drink sounds good. Why don't you bring in a few more logs and fix our drinks while I get the coffee? The wood is just outside the door to the left.''

Out on the terrace, away from the warmth of the fireplace, there was a little bite to the night air, and the stars were very bright although not as bright as they'd been by that mountain lake in New Mexico where I'd been nine thousand feet closer to them. I gathered up an armload of wood and managed to close and lock the sliding glass door behind me as I carried it inside. The fire had burned down while we were eating. I arranged some fresh wood on the glowing coals, according to my private theory of fire building. Every man has his own. I poured our drinks and brought them to the cocktail table; then I returned to the fire to make sure it was taking hold all right. I stood there for a little, watching the small blue-and-yellow flames spring up around the new wood. I heard Jo come into the room behind me.

"It looks as if you know something about building fires, unlike some people. Come drink your coffee.''

"I've spent a lot of time cooking over campfires,'' I said. ''Hell, they pulled me out of a mountain camp for this operation.''

She'd arranged herself comfortably at the end of the big sofa. She patted the space beside her and leaned forward to pick up a steaming mug that had a Disney figure on it.

"Cream or sugar?"

"Both, please."

I sat down and she placed the mug into my hands. We sipped our coffee in silence for a while, watching the rapidly reviving fire. I was much more aware of the woman sitting decorously beside me on the sofa, both of us fully dressed, than I had been in bed with her, skimpily clad in shorts and tank top, bending over me sponging my naked back.

Jo spoke lazily: "Were you camping alone?"

"I had my dog with me."

"What kind of dog?"

"Labrador. Yellow."

"We always had dogs when I was girl but somehow, with college and med school and everything, I got out of the habit."

I said, "Jo."

"Yes, Horace."

"What did you have in mind, research or therapy?"

There was a little silence. I didn't look at her. The fire snapped sharply as the new wood blazed up.

The woman beside me gave a strained little laugh. "You're a real bastard, aren't you?"

"It's the majority opinion."

"Was I that obvious?"

I said, "You forget, while you were studying anatomy and psychology, or a little before that, I was majoring in assassination with a minor in seduction."

"You mean, other girls have wined you and dined you and snuggled up to you afterwards in front of the fire with motives strictly immoral?"

I said, "Sad to relate, ma'am, I have actually met deadly ladies who employed sex as a professional weapon, if you'll believe such wickedness."

Jo said stiffly, "I assure you, vengeance was not on the evening's program; I have no knife for your back. For one thing, Junior really is getting well although you have only my word for

177

it, and for another, as I've told you, even if he wasn't, I'm not the vengeful type.''

"I know. I wasn't worrying about that. I just thought I'd save you some playacting.''

"Thanks loads!" She drew a long breath. "All right, I guess I was pretty stupid to try the old Mata Hari routine on a pro, but it just seemed . . . well, as you said, therapy. You've been lying around here like a zombie, no interest, no curiosity. A blow on the head will do that sometimes, cause a certain amount of dissociation, but I couldn't turn you loose like that, to do what you'll probably have to do; you'd get yourself killed. You needed to be waked up, shaken up. . . . Well, maybe I'm not sexpot enough to get the job done, if it can be done that way, but it would have been an interesting medical experiment. Oh, don't think I was being altogether scientific, or unselfish. Ever since the divorce . . . Messing around with married colleagues isn't for me, and there aren't all that many good unmarried ones around. And celibacy gets old after a while. And doesn't every woman, particularly one with psychiatric pretensions, want to know what it's like to sleep with a dangerous man who carries a gun and even uses it upon occasion? As you said, research.'' She'd been talking at the fire. Now she turned to look at me. "I'm sorry. It was a crazy idea. But taking care of a man for a week does tend to put crazy ideas into a woman's head. If he isn't completely revolting and she isn't ready to murder him by the end of that time . . .'' She shrugged and got to her feet, standing over me. "Well, I'd better go do the dishes. Thanks for not letting me make a complete damn fool of myself.''

I said, "It's not too late.''

She looked startled; then she laughed shortly. "Now you're the one who's crazy! If there was ever any little flickering flame of romance around here, you just did a good job of blowing it out.''

I said, "Romance, shomance. It was a nice buildup, but it was as phony as the name I'm wearing: wine and firelight and love. Do you really have to have it dressed up like in the

178

paperback romances our queen-sized landlady reads? Can't we just be two adults who, after spending a certain amount of time together, find each other interesting and acceptable, even though there's no great emotional involvement and may never be?''

She licked her lips. ''You're a cold-blooded bastard, aren't you?'' Then she laughed softly. ''But an honest one. I guess it's a relief not to have to go through the slaves-of-breathless-passion routine. Well, you call it. Your bedroom or mine? I don't recommend mine, it's kind of a boys' dormitory, and two people are apt to fall off one of those lousy little cots.''

''And I'm pretty tired of mine; but this is a nice big sofa. If you get rid of all that priceless hardware and I discard my .38, I think we can manage on it.''

We did.

The crash awoke me. Instinctively I freed myself from the warm arms holding me and threw myself off the sofa, raked up the Smith and Wesson I'd placed ready on the floor, and rolled clear, aware of Jo sitting up behind me. Her black dress was almost invisible but her white face and bare legs showed clearly in the red glow of the dying fire. There was another crash outside; I realized that somebody had blundered into the woodpile a second time. Then he was at the door, knocking. Midnight assassins don't normally knock. As a rule they don't lurch noisily against woodpiles either. I drew a long breath and moved that way cautiously.

I could see him through the glass door, waiting out there, steadying himself against the doorjamb. He was a tall man in a dirty white suit and a grimy white Stetson hat and scuffed white cowboy boots; a tall old man with a short gray beard. When he took off the hat to peer in through the glass, I saw that his hair was also gray, and he didn't have much on top.

I heard Jo whisper, ''My God, it's you! I mean, it's Cody, the real Cody!''

Gun ready, I unlocked the door and pulled it open. Horace

179

Hosmer Cody stood there for a moment, hat in hand; then he fell forward across the threshold. I saw that the back of his soiled white jacket was soaked with blood that looked black in the night.

    I checked him for weapons first and found nothing. I was aware of Jo coming over to help me as I pulled him inside. I retrieved the hat he'd dropped on the terrace; then I rolled the door closed and locked it. I found the right pull cord and covered the expanse of glass with the threadbare brown drapes I hadn't bothered with earlier, trusting, wrongly as it had turned out, to the privacy afforded by the high patio walls outside. I turned on the living room light. Jo was kneeling beside Cody. She'd shoved the sleeves of her black dress above her elbows, and there was blood on her hands.

    "It looks as if he was shot in the back two or three days ago," she said, looking up at me. "The wound seems to have been bleeding intermittently ever since. He's got an amateurish bandage under his shirt; he probably strapped it around himself. Apparently he got the hemorrhage stopped several times, but he always managed to start it up again, the last time probably within the hour. I think he just fainted from cumulative loss of blood, although he also seems to be running a temperature. I can't find any broken bones; I'd say it's safe for us to move him, at least as far as the bedroom."

    "Try to work on him right there for the moment," I said. "I've got to get outside and scout the neighborhood; see how he got here, and if he brought company with him. Has he got any keys on him?"

    Jo protested, "The man is badly hurt! We can't just leave him lying . . . !"

    "Hell, he makes you a better patient on that tile floor than bleeding all over the Schonfelds' bed; we'll tuck him in after you get him patched up. And you'd better change before you get blood all over your dress."

"To hell with my dress. . . . Oh, all right, if you're so worried about my wardrobe, get that damned apron from the kitchen and put it on me." When I returned, she stood up and, holding her reddened hands away from her, let me wrap her in the outsized apron belonging to our landlady. She looked at me and grinned abruptly. "Talking about clothes, darling, I hope you aren't planning to carry out this reconnaissance mission outdoors wearing nothing but a shirt and a revolver."

I realized that I'd charged off to repel boarders in a strictly bare-ass condition, which still remained. We regarded each other for a moment. A little color came to her face. What had started out as a polite exercise in practical biology had become considerably more passionate than planned. By the time I'd disposed of my gun and shoes and socks and pants and shorts, and she'd removed her jewelry and shoes and pantyhose and called me over to give assistance with her dress, the sensible and unromantic attitude with which we'd embarked upon this experiment had become difficult to maintain. Unhooking the top of her dress in back and trying to work the long, rebellious zipper—I always wonder how they get themselves undressed without my help— I'd found myself kissing the nape of her neck instead and realizing that it was quite a nice, long, slender neck, and that I'd been wanting to do that for several days, in a vague sort of way. But there was no vagueness about my present desires. They were sharp and urgent. She'd made a small, purring sound of pleasure and turned in my arms to be kissed properly.

"Ah, to hell with it!" she'd breathed, when I started to undress her again after some time had passed. "We'll just give it the sex test, darling; check on how unwrinkleable it really is. . . ."

Now, by the time I had my clothes back on, Jo had removed the unconscious man's stained jacket and was peeling off his bloody shirt. She looked up as I came to stand over her.

"There are his keys," she said, jerking her head toward a

nearby chair. "You have a pocketknife; I saw it when I washed your clothes. Leave it with me, please, if you can spare it. I may have to cut the bandage off him; it seems to be stuck pretty badly in places. Be careful, darling."

I put my knife on the chair and picked up the keys. "I'll be back as soon as I can, but don't panic if it takes a while. Is there a patio gate? Well, there's got to be; he got in."

"Yes, it's to the left as you come out on the terrace."

"Lock the door behind me. If he comes to, hit him on the head with something. Remember who you've got there."

She looked startled. Seeing a hurt man, functioning instinctively as a trained healer, she clearly hadn't given a thought to the fact that the warm body on which she worked belonged to the enemy, the man responsible for her mother's death, the man her kid brother had come to Mexico to find and kill. I gathered up the keys and examined them. The split-ring carried the blue plastic tag of an El Paso auto dealer: *Herrera Oldsmobile-Cadillac*. However, the keys did not come from a passenger car but a GMC truck, presumably something Mr. Herrera or one of his Cadillac salesmen had taken in trade. Well, at least it gave me a notion of what I was looking for.

But I didn't go after it right away. With a gallant gesture toward Jo, like any brave knight riding out to dispose of a few dragons, I slid behind the draperies, unlocked the glass door again, eased it open far enough to let me slip through the crack, and rolled it shut again cautiously. I had to avoid, not only the woodpile, but the logs Cody had knocked off as he stumbled weakly against it. The gate was the hairy bit. If somebody was waiting out there with a gun I'd be moving right into his sights when I came out, but there was no painless way of going over the broken-glass-protected wall, and I wasn't in very good condition for wall-climbing, anyway. I eased the gate open, slipped through fast, and met no blinding muzzle flash, deafening report, or shocking bullet.

A concrete driveway ran along the side of the house. Ahead of me was a small, weedy, vacant lot and another house about the size of the Schonfeld vacation mansion. To my left was the dull, vaguely silvery shape of the Subaru station wagon parked in front of the kitchen door; to my right was the beach drive and, beyond some larger houses over there, the water. This late at night—well, it was only eleven-fifteen but that's late for rural Mexico—there was hardly anybody around. I watched a lonely set of headlights pass along the beach road. I moved in the other direction, past the Subaru, toward the open ground I'd seen from the rear bedroom window. I took fifteen minutes to check around the house; then it was time to determine where Cody had left his transportation.

I found it easily enough, on my first cast to the north. There were few vehicles parked on the street in this community and it stood alone, no Japanese toy truck but a husky U.S. three-quarter-ton pickup with four-wheel drive, dark red in color. Texas plates. Having located it, I still had to determine if someone else was interested in it. Hunkered down in some bushes up the street, I gave it an hour. It remained an ordinary, slightly beat- · up pickup truck parked on one of the small side streets off the main beach road. At last I said to hell with it and stepped out of hiding and walked over there boldly. No bells, horns, or whistles sounded when I unlocked and opened the door; no lights flashed; no bombs went off. Inside the cab there was dried blood every-where and fresh blood on the tan vinyl seatback as if, at the wheel, Cody had hit a bad bump or been forced to make a violent maneuver not many miles back up the highway and had started his wound leaking again. There was a bag containing three apples, a six-pack of beer with two cans remaining—Coors, if it matters—an open bag of potato chips, half a package of Oreo cookies, and a lot of trash like empty beer cans and candy wrappers and the debris from drive-in hamburgers. A cheap black raincoat shared the floor with the garbage; presumably he'd used it to cover his blood-stained suit when he had to appear in public. Otherwise, aside from the food and drink, there were no personal belongings of any kind, either inside the cab or in the truck bed.

Well, unless you count guns as personal belongings. They were in a paper bag tucked into the narrow space behind the

pickup's seat, three of them, all standard Colt .38 Special revolvers with four-inch barrels. Two were fully loaded and un-
fired. The third was also fully loaded, but the barrel and four
chambers of the cylinder were dirty. There were four fired cartridge cases in the bag, and two loose, loaded rounds; plus one
empty six-shot speedy-loader and two full ones. Apparently the
old man had managed to separate three guns and loaders from
their owners somehow. He'd got into a firefight and got off four
shots with one of the liberated weapons. Before hiding all the
guns away, he'd dumped the cylinder of the one he'd used and
slapped in a full load of six. Good firearms discipline for a gent
with a hole in the back. Where he'd obtained all the weapons
and spare ammo was an interesting question, and I had a hunch
the answer would be equally interesting. However, at the moment the important thing for me to keep in mind was that, although he'd had weapons and ammunition readily available, he'd
come to the house unarmed, indicating that his intentions had
probably not been hostile.

Nobody interfered with me as I took inventory; there seemed
to be nobody around. After all the time and trouble I'd taken to
reach it, I decided that the best thing to do with the truck was
just leave it right there, guns and all, for the time being. Hiding
it might have been better, but I wasn't in good enough condition
to lose it out in the boonies and make a long hike back; and I
didn't know enough about the town to find an empty garage or
barn in which to conceal it. I locked it up again, therefore, and
headed back to base by roundabout ways, making my approach
from the south, very cautiously. When I could see it clearly, the
house looked just the way I'd left it, with the kitchen windows
lighted and a vague glow inside the patio walls indicating that
the living room illumination, only partially blocked by the
drapes, was still spilling out through the big glass doors.

The patio gate was inviting. I'd had a lot of exercise for a man
who'd spent the past week in bed. Some of the exercise had been
very pleasant, but I was getting tired now. Nevertheless, I made
my way to the rear where the bedroom windows were dark and
slipped past them to get a look around the far corner—and pulled

back quickly. Okay, the old hunter/hunted instincts could still be relied on after all. One Buff Cody, the true or the false, had visitors coming. There were two of them, and they were about to tackle the patio wall on this blind and gateless side. Watching silently, I saw the smaller shape fling a rug or blanket over the broken glass. The larger one put his back to the wall and made a step of his hands, and hoisted the smaller one to his shoulders.

It was no place for loud firearms. They saw me charging at them, of course, but there wasn't a hell of a lot they could do about it. The lower man was pretty well immobilized and, perched on the big one's shoulders, the smaller man on top was trying to get a knee up on the wall in a rather gingerly manner, clearly not quite sure that the rug was going to protect him from the sharp glass if he put his full weight on it. He turned to look my way, but he had no chance to jump clear before I smashed his support out from under him. The man I hit, while not overly large himself, felt solid and muscular. The small one came down on my legs. I kicked him away and rolled to my feet before the bigger one and kicked that one in the face as he started to rise at last and got my gun out, hoping that I could use it to stabilize the situation without actually killing anybody noisily. . . .

"No!" gasped a girl's voice behind me. "No shoot, Meester Cody! Is me, Antonia!"

CHAPTER 21

THE patio was silent when I entered it. I managed to detour around the fallen firewood without getting involved with the spines of the cactus garden. I knocked on the big glass door.

"It's me. Let me in."

There was a long enough pause for apprehension to start building, then the curtains billowed and Jo appeared, making her way between them and the glass. The lock rattled, and the door slid aside.

"Enter, me."

The brightly lighted living room was a shock to my dark-adapted eyes. Jo was standing well back. I noted that she'd discarded her big apron and her slinky dress; she was dressed for action in shirt, jeans, boots and silver. I'd seen the costume before, of course; but the object in her hand was new to me. Well, at least in these surroundings. It was a heavy automatic pistol that I recognized, after a moment, as one that I'd last seen in Hermosillo. Her brother's gun, or a reasonable facsimile. She held it with the muzzle pointed ceilingwards, her finger off the trigger and outside the trigger guard, the way you hold a loaded gun everywhere but in Hollywood. That was fine, I was glad to see she knew that much about firearms; but I'm usually very careful about keeping track of the guns around me. The fact that I hadn't been aware that there was another weapon in the house in addition to mine wasn't reassuring. Watching her tuck the piece inside her waistband, where it was concealed by the loose shirt and the silver belt, I reflected that I really did seem to have spent the past week in a daze. I noted that my flat little stainless

187

Russell knife, folded, lay on the small table at the end of the sofa.

Jo licked her lips. "I heard some noises outside. I was afraid. . . . I didn't expect you to be quite so long. I was getting worried. Did you have any trouble?"

"Well, I almost shot that damn girl again," I said.

"Which damn girl? You have so many." She laughed and stopped laughing. "Oh, you mean Sisneros? She's out there?"

"With a friend or an uncle or something. Anyway, she calls him *tío*. *Tío* Ignacio. I guess it can either mean uncle or just any older gent toward whom the speaker feels respectful. I'd seen him with her before, in Cananea."

It had been a little tricky. Although I didn't think he was combat-trained, the man was tough and might well have a knife. The girl was impulsive, to say the least, and undoubtedly carried at least her cheap twenty-two, reloaded. But we got it sorted out without casualties, and it turned out that, far from wishing me harm, she'd come here to save me from the true, wicked, dangerous Horace Cody.

"That nice boy Señor Mason Charles send us to help," she said, after retrieving her *serape* from the top of the wall, shaking it out, and putting it back on. "Not help you, he cares nothing for you, who shoot him; but he has concern for the tall, cold sister. He said you still much sick, much weak. No good for protect. He said Señor Greer tell him Cody escape and come this way. Señor Greer say somebody asking about the sister at her hospital in the *Estados Unidos*, and he thinks Cody learn where you are."

It had taken considerable persuasion before she'd agreed to wait outside with her tough companion. Now Jo was frowning at me, puzzled.

"How did they find us here?"

I said, "Apparently she's been visiting your brother in the Hermosillo hospital. She thinks he's a nice boy. When he heard Cody was loose—Greer told him—he told her where we were and asked her to protect us. You seem to have given him the impression over the phone that I'm still in pretty bad shape, too

188

bad to look after us.'' I grinned. ''Well, maybe I was, until you awoke me with a kiss, like the Sleeping Beauty.''

She colored a little, and asked, ''Do they know that Cody's here?''

''That's why I found them climbing the wall instead of knocking on the front door. They'd spotted his pickup by its Texas plates and found some fresh blood by the gate; *Tío* Ignacio seems to be something of a tracker. They guessed he'd got inside and figured they'd better sneak in from the rear and case the situation before revealing themselves.''

''Where are they now?'' Jo asked. ''Why didn't you bring them in?''

I said, ''You forget what the little spitfire is really after. We made a deal. She knows I'm hungry for information, and she's giving me a chance to question the guy before she shoots him.'' I grimaced. ''They're waiting out in the Subaru. I'm supposed to let them know when I've finished with him.''

''But you're not *really* going to . . . ! We can't let her murder a helpless old man!''

''That's not the way you described him before,'' I said. ''Don't borrow trouble, Jo. After we've talked with him, maybe he'll shape up as such a bastard you'll be perfectly happy to let her have him, helpless or not. After all, what do we know good about him? Nothing.'' I glanced at the man who was still lying on the floor where I'd left him, now covered by a blanket. ''How's he doing?''

She hesitated. ''I . . . I had to take the bullet out of him. You keep your knife nice and sharp, darling. As good as a scalpel any day. There it is. I . . . I cleaned it up for you afterwards.''

I pocketed it and knelt beside Horace Hosmer Cody. A strong pulse beat in the side of his neck as he lay there facedown with his head turned to the side. After determining this, I pulled back the blanket so I could see the bandage. She had him pretty well mummy-wrapped, and the layers of gauze were clean and white.

''It's a good thing you laid in a big stock of medical

supplies for me in Hermosillo," I said. "Did you get him to take some of those antibiotics you've been feeding me?"

"Yes, Doctor." She laughed shortly. "You've got to hand it to him, he's a tough old bird. Didn't move a muscle while I was whittling on him; but when I was through I saw that his eyes were open. 'Did you get it out, girl?' he whispered. I said I had. 'You got a foul mouth on you for an educated lady,' he whispered. 'Or do all doctors cuss like that while they're operating?' Then I gave him some capsules and a drink of water, and he passed out again, and I ran to the bathroom and was very, very sick. I never had any ambition to be a surgeon. Well, let's put our elderly baby to bed. I guess the best way is to slide that blanket under him and pick it up by the corners. . . ."

Somehow I was reminded of lugging Gloria Pierce Cody around the mountains, although she'd made a lighter and more pleasant burden. Jo and I got the man who was young Mrs. Cody's real husband—at least until she got the marriage declared void—unloaded onto the bed. I put my pajamas on him, and that wasn't easy, although they fit him just fine. We really were pretty much the same size, not surprising since that was the reason I'd been selected for this idiot mission in the first place. Jo finished tucking him in with the bedside expertise that seems to be standard with the medical profession, all branches. We stood looking down at him, our very own patient.

"Can you bring him around?" I asked.

"I don't think it would be good for him."

"Antonia isn't going to be good for him either. She isn't going to wait out there forever. We'd better hear what the guy has to say for himself, if anything." I grimaced. "If you can't think of anything better, well, maybe he'll react favorably to alcoholic odors; I'll get the bottle and wave it under his nose like smelling salts and see what happens."

"I don't think J&B is exactly what's medically indicated here, darling. Let me fix him something in the kitchen instead; then we'll see if we can't bring him around to drink it."

We'd started for the door when there was a whisper from

behind us: "See to it that the little lady gets a stiff shot of whiskey even if she won't let me have one, mister." Jo and I glanced at each other and turned to look at the patient, who was watching us from the bed. He whispered, "She's damn well earned herself a drink, even if she did swear like a roundup cook while she was cutting me."

I walked back to him. "How are you feeling, Mr. Cody?"

He whispered, "About like you'd expect, son. You look like a man who's packed a little lead under his skin once or twice; so why ask dumb questions?" He studied me for a moment. "Hell, they didn't do half a bad job of fixing you up to look like me, did they?"

I said, "Thanks, you're almost the only one who's thought much of the resemblance so far."

He licked his lips. "I heard you talking. Who's Antonia?"

"A young lady who doesn't like you very much and hopes to kill you," I said, watching him closely. "I gather you were never introduced to her, but she was the girlfriend of the late Jorge Medina and holds you responsible for his death."

"Medina?" He looked puzzled, as if he'd never heard the name or, in his weakened state, had forgotten it. He moved a shoulder in a cautious shrug. "Well, tell the girl to pick a number and wait her turn. Seems like the whole world don't like me much these days." He watched me curiously for a moment. "Your real name is Helm?"

"Yes. Matthew Helm. Who told you?"

"I heard them talking, the ones that grabbed me, right after the wedding. Never met such a loose-lipped bunch of fellers; a man might have got the idea it didn't matter what he heard because they was fixing to kill him anyway. Place they held me, I heard a lot I guess they didn't expect me to live to tell." His lips formed a ghost of a smile. "Cocky young sprouts, figured there was no danger from a scared and feeble old codger like me. I tell you, I was downright pitiful, boy; got so I could hardly walk for pure senile terror; got it so bad they even had to help me to the bathroom so I wouldn't piss my pants. Excuse me, ma'am. Grabbed a gun from one and disarmed a couple more but a feller barged in who purely wanted to be a hero, and that's when the shit hit the fan. I had to leave two of them dead. Getting away from there, I never heard so much shooting hitting nothing since Gene Autry fit the Indians. All holding their little pistols in both their sweaty little hands. Hell, if a man can't hit what he's aiming at with one hand, he'd ought to give up shooting. Only slug that hit me was one that bounced off a wall. I guess I was lucky at that. Been a direct hit, it'd have tore me in two instead of running around the ribs and stopping under the arm-pit."

I said, "You've been playing possum on us."

"Wouldn't you, boy, in a fix like this?" He regarded me for a moment with blue eyes several shades paler than mine. "You don't look real dead to me. Good thing for me; they were just keeping me alive waiting for word that you'd been killed. Supposed to've happened before that first day was out. They was mighty upset about how you kept on spoiling their plans by keeping on breathing; they wanted you dead and buried with a nice gravestone over you down here with my name on it. Poor old Buff Cody, damned if he didn't go and get himself kilt by some dirty Mex *bandidos*! And I'd be dead, too, right up there in the States, but there'd be no stone for me. Did you keep my girl-wife safe?"

"Gloria?" I said. I told myself he was an evil old man, responsible for many crimes, but I found it impossible to lie to him, even by omission. I spoke carefully: "It depends on what you mean by safe, Mr. Cody."

He knew what I was saying, and he gave a little snort that was meant to be a laugh. "Wasn't asking about your love life, son. Or hers. Young folks will be young folks. But she's alive, and you're keeping her well protected?"

"Yes."

"Seems like those fellers just ain't much good at killing people, hard as they try, don't it?"

"Or maybe we're pretty good at surviving, Mr. Cody."

"Hell, call me Buff," he whispered. "All my friends do."

"What makes you think I'm your friend, or you're mine?" I asked.

He didn't speak at once; he just lay there watching me slyly. Because he knew, damn him. He knew that, now that we had talked, although we might wind up killing each other eventually, we were bound together by certain ties. For one thing, we had a lady in common, legally his lady, at least for the moment. Apparently he didn't hold it against me; but it was a debt I owed him, and he'd be the man to keep count. And for another thing, we were both survivors; and regardless of his morals, regardless of his crimes, I couldn't work up too big a hate against a sexagenarian smart and tough enough to deceive a bunch of trained young agents into thinking him harmless, shoot his way clear of them, and drive several hundred miles with his life running out of a ragged hole in his back. And the gray old fox knew that, too.

He whispered, "Maybe friendship's too strong a word, son, but we've got enemies in common. Amounts to practically the same thing. Same fellers trying to kill us both. I figured if I could find you down here, we could work together."

"How did you find us?"

"Man in my business has got to have connections," he said. "I left a trail of bloody phone booths clear across the U.S. Southwest tracking you down. No trouble learning you'd got as far as Hermosillo; then there'd been some kind of a shooting. Word was you'd been hurt, and you and a Mrs. Beckman, Dr. Beckman, had disappeared. Maiden name Charles. Has a brother, Mason Charles, now in the Hermosillo hospital, who seems to've shot you for me by mistake, and who's probably still fixing to kill me when he gets out, or so those chatty fellers said while I was listening harder than I let on, all the time complaining how my rheumatiz hurt something awful and keeping an old man shackled up like that was downright wicked cruel— I'll be damned if they didn't take pity on the poor old codger and take the bracelets off after awhile. They thought it was real comical, the way they'd set that angry boy on my trail. Or yours. And the mother he was trying to avenge was Millie Charles, who was my partner's fancy lady, and purely hated my guts because I didn't appreciate how sweet and pretty and innocent she was; and who got herself murdered with Will a few hundred miles south of here. Probably by those same Mex outlaws who was all set to kill you—if you believe in those busy *bandidos*."

Jo, beside me, made a small sound of anger. "We know who those murderers are, Mr. Cody, the revolutionaries to whom you were selling arms. And we know who arranged for them to kill my mother and Will Pierce!" She swallowed hard. "And she wasn't anybody's fancy lady, damn you; she loved your partner and was going to marry him! And now you'd better shut up and get some rest. . . . Well, since you're conscious, I want to get some liquid into you first, to replace what ran out of you. Probably straight whiskey!"

"Beer, ma'am," he whispered. "Just good Coors beer."

She made a face. "As far as I'm concerned, they can pour that lousy stuff right back into the horse. Stay quiet now, while I warm some bouillon for you. If you start yourself bleeding again after all I went through to patch you up, I'll shoot you!"

We watched her march out, closing the bedroom door firmly behind her. The man in the bed chuckled.

"That's a lot of woman."

I said, "You still haven't said how you found us."

"Had somebody find out where she worked and got somebody in Tucson to check the Desert Pines Clinic. Dr. Joanna Beckman was taking a week's vacation in a place in Kino Bay lent to her by some folks named Schonfeld. 'Seaview Cottage,' half a mile up the beach road on the right-hand side, name on wall, can't miss it. Kino Bay isn't a full seventy miles from Hermosillo; seemed likely that, with a wounded man on her hands, she'd head right here. My only trouble was lasting this far. With no load in the bed, that damn truck Herrera got me—that's my car-dealing *primo*—bounced me around like the old plowhorse I learnt to ride on; kept knocking things open back there. Not that it was likely to heal over, anyway, with the bullet still in there."

He grinned at me. ''And to save you asking, Art Herrera owes me a few, beyond the high-priced Caddies he's sold me; and I just happen to know some folks who cross the border regular without checking in and out, who had reason to oblige me and fix me up with stickers and papers. Wouldn't hold up if anybody really looked; but I didn't figure I could make it through the legal tourist-permit routine, the way my back was.''

I said, ''I'd think, with your connections, the first thing you'd do was find a discreet doctor to patch you up.''

''That's what you'd think, and that's what those fellers would think who was after me. They have pretty good connections themselves—you'd know more about that than I do—and they'd have every doctor I knew covered, discreet or indiscreet; probably every doctor in this whole damn border country. Didn't figure it was worth the risk. With two dead and maybe a couple more wounded, they'd be coming after me hard. Wasn't as if I had a bullet in the lungs or the guts; I could feel it sitting right there under the skin. If worse came to worst, I'd have bought myself some razor blades and got in front of a mirror and tried slicing it out of there myself, even though it was a hell of a place to reach.''

I said, ''And now for the sixty-four-dollar question, Mr. Cody: just what the hell do you want me for?''

He grinned at me wolfishly from the pillow. ''I want you for doing your job, son.''

''And what do you think my job is?''

''I figure it's finding a bunch of weapons that got kinda mislaid here in northern Mexico. You want them and I want them, so why don't we just pool our resources, like the man says, and find them together? Once we got them, we can fight over what's to be done with them.''

I looked down at his drawn, whiskery face for a moment and reminded myself not to let the faded eyes and the gray hairs fool me. That mistake had been made quite recently by other men who thought they were smart and tough; and a couple of them had died. They probably weren't the first.

I said, "Do you really think I'd work with you, you old prairie rattler?"

He gave me his best smile to date; I've seen a more trustworthy grin on a trained killer Doberman.

"Now that I see you, boy, I think you'd work with the devil himself if he could help you get what you was sent for. And figure on outsmarting him once you got it."

The trouble was, he was perfectly right.

CHAPTER 22

STANDING in front of the fire, bare to the waist—I seemed to be forever exposing one end of me or the other here in Kino Bay—I held up my arms so Jo could wrap the long strip of cloth, torn from a bed sheet, around my chest.

"Tighter," I said.

"You won't be able to breathe."

"Don't argue with the patient, doctor; there isn't time. The sizzling señorita isn't going to wait out in the cold forever, and there are a few more things that need to be cleared up before she comes barging in." I gestured impatiently. "Go on! I want it bulky enough to show a little under my coat and shirt and tight enough to remind me that I'm a poor, feverish, wounded old man. . . . Swell." I waited for her to fasten the cloth in place with safety pins. "Now take that cheesecloth coronet off my head and replace it with just enough tape so my brains don't leak out. I want to be able to get that lousy Stetson on. Fortunately he's the kind of guy who practically wears his hat in the shower."

"Brains?" she said. "What brains?"

She replaced my head bandage with a small, taped dressing and watched while I buttoned Buff Cody's fancy wedding shirt over the chest wrappings and pulled on his white suit jacket. After getting the bloodstained garments off him, Jo had run them through the washer-dryer in the kitchen figuring that they couldn't look worse than they already did. Not being wash-and-wear, the pants and jacket hadn't taken kindly to the treatment, but Jo had mashed them into some kind of shape with Ziggy

Schonfeld's electric iron, and I wasn't planning on exposing them to any more fancy wedding receptions anyway. At least the blood had washed out, and the bullet hole in the back of the jacket wasn't conspicuous. In return, I was leaving the old man the windbreaker with the bullet-torn shoulder; it should make him feel right at home. I tried on the battered white hat cautiously. The pressure on the partly healed furrow in my scalp wasn't comfortable, but I could live with it. The revolver holstered inside my waistband wasn't an authentic part of the disguise. I buttoned the jacket to cover it.

"How do I look?" I asked.

"You are crazy," she said. "Absolutely nuts!"

"Well, you're the psycho expert; you should know."

"He's sending you into a trap."

"That's how I make my living, being sent into traps."

"What makes you think you can trust him?"

"For one thing, the fact that he's in bed weak as a kitten and you've got a gun."

"Well, you're not in such red-hot shape yourself, buster."

I said, "Gosh, and here I thought I was doing pretty well." I saw a little color come to her face, and I grinned. "Medically speaking, I'd say the treatment was a success, Doctor. It might even catch on. Beats electroshock all to hell."

She said rather stiffly, "I don't know. I still think you're suffering from something, the way you accept everything that man tells you. . . . My God, darling, that's Cody in there, Buffalo Bill Cody, Horace Hosmer Cody! The man responsible for my mother's death, and Will Pierce's; the old man who was going to marry a young girl who trusted him and then have her murdered in cold blood so he could have all her money!"

I said, "That's what everybody seems to think."

She stared at me. "Can there be any doubts, after all we've been told?" She hesitated. "You must have talked it over with Gloria. What did she tell you about Buff Cody?"

"That he was a wicked old gent who'd deliberately arranged to frighten her into marrying him with eventual murder in mind.'' I shrugged. ''Oh, she believes it, sure. And your brother is sincere in his hate, and the evidence is overwhelming. Buff Cody is a sinister, scheming, murdering, gunrunning old son of a bitch who should be strung up to the nearest cottonwood with no prayer for his rotten soul since he obviously doesn't have one. Just the same . . .'' I stopped.

''What's the problem?''

I said, ''The problem is simply that none of that, none of what we've heard, fits the old man in the bedroom. Now that I've seen him up close, I just don't believe it.''

She shook her head sympathetically. ''Like I said, my well-considered professional diagnosis is: nuts. That'll be a hundred and fifty dollars, please; you can pay the receptionist as you go out.''

I said, ''Something's very haywire here. I don't say the gent in my bed is an angel. I'd hate to play poker with him, and if I had an oil deal going with him I'd want a regiment of high-priced lawyers on my side. And I don't say he wouldn't run a few illegal guns in a worthy cause or even just a profitable one. But there are two things he'd never do. He'd never raise a hand against his partner of many years, the man who shared his march to success, unless that man betrayed him unforgivably; and even then he'd take the necessary action himself and not turn the job over to a bunch of machete-wielding revolutionaries. . . .''

''And the second thing?'' Jo asked when I paused.

I said, ''That Horace Cody in there would never, ever harm a young girl who depended on him, the orphan daughter of his dead partner, a kid he'd known since her childhood.''

''But you just told me she's convinced he did. Or was planning to.''

I said dryly, ''What convinces Gloria isn't something I take too seriously.''

''But she's known Cody all her life. You've talked to him for about ten minutes. Yet you think you know him better than she does.''

199

I said, "Sure. Why not? We're both westerners, but she was brought up in the big white house on the hill with the dull rich folks and the polite servants, while I grew up around the corrals where the interesting characters hung out. I've known several tough old gents like that one in there. I know they'll skin you in a horse trade as soon as look at you and give you their last dime if they like you and apologize because it isn't a quarter. And Gloria has never had to gamble her life on her judgment of people. I have."

Jo said, "I'm supposed to be a pro at judging people, and I don't trust that old goat one little bit."

I grinned. "Your trouble is that you've been trained to draw your conclusions from the clinical data. But there are times when you have to throw the numbers out the window and go on instinct. My instinct says our Mr. Cody, the one in there, had nothing whatever to do with the machete slaughter down on the Mazatlán-Durango road and never had the slightest intention of murdering his child bride. And if he's not guilty of either of those things, maybe he didn't even run any guns, although, as I said, he's probably quite capable of that."

"But he's asking you to help him find them."

"Everybody wants those damned arms; that doesn't mean everybody was involved in bringing them into Mexico. I want them and I wasn't. I don't know what the old goat is up to; I just have a hunch that my best bet is to play along with him." I drew a long breath, glanced uneasily toward the kitchen door through which Antonia could be expected to come any minute, and settled my borrowed hat on my head. "Well, we're running out of time; let's see if he's thought of anything else to help me."

"Help!" Jo snorted. "All he'll help you to is a bullet. Maybe the next one will hit you in the ass and really hurt you. I'm told the dinosaurs kept their brains down there, and you're pretty prehistoric in some respects."

I grinned and went to the bedroom door, opened it gently, and slipped inside. The old man in the bed opened his eyes and reached up weakly to feel the spectacular new head bandage we'd given him.

"Fool thing," he said. "If they find this place and get in here, what difference does it make if they think I'm you or me? They're out to kill the both of us."

I shrugged. "It's probably a waste of time, but I was trained to be thorough. If I'm out there impersonating you as well as possible, you might as well be in here impersonating me as well as possible. It probably won't buy us anything, but you never can tell in this business and, hell, all it cost is a little surgical gauze." After a moment I went on: "I'm going to get you some protection here; but they'll supposedly be protecting me and my damaged skull, now that this safe house seems to be pretty well compromised. If you and Antonia could find it, somebody else can. Remember that you're a guy suffering from a bad concussion. Meanwhile, Buff Cody, with his clothes hastily washed and his wound patched up, will be heading out into the desert in his trusty red truck." I posed before him. "Think I'll pass?"

He looked up at me searchingly and nodded. "Those clothes look like they fit you pretty good, even the hat and boots. But you'd better wear that bolo tie of mine; it's my lucky piece, and anybody who knows me knows I wouldn't leave it behind, no-how."

I was aware of Jo, who'd come to stand in the doorway, turning away; a moment later she was back, handing me the braided, silver-tipped, leather tie with its big silver-mounted turquoise. I'd left the cheap one I'd worn for my masquerade when I changed out of my own beat-up, white wedding costume in Ramón's camp.

"There's a man I'm supposed to be looking for," I said. "While you were being held, did you hear them mention the name Sábado?"

Cody frowned. "Not Sábado. But I did hear them refer to a Mister Saturday once or twice."

"In what connection?"

"Can't really say. I mean, I just heard the name go by me. Like I said, there was a lot of talk."

201

"Was the speaker being serious or funny?"

"Kind of funny. Like he was calling a feller my height, or yours, by the name of Shorty, or referring to the boss as Old Sourpuss. You know the way a bunch of the boys will make up fool names for everybody. Is it important?"

"Not at the moment," I said. "So let's go over what you told me once more. I'm to take your truck and take the road north along the coast and find a man named Arturo. Last name?"

"Don't know as he's got one. Never heard it if he does."

"There are only two things wrong with that program I can see at the moment," I said. "First, the only road shown on the map doesn't run along the coast; it cuts well inland. It doesn't return to the coast until it hits a flea-spot on the paper with the fancy name of Puerto de la Libertad, at the mouth of the Rio Lobos, seventy-five miles north of Kino Bay. Second, it all seems to be empty country, rocks and desert. There's nobody out there. The map shows no sign of habitation, nothing. So just what are you expecting to gain by sending me out into the empty desert to find a man who doesn't exist, Mr. Cody?"

The old man grinned. "There's always somebody out there, son. And you look like a man who knows enough not to trust any fancy maps. Hell, if Will Pierce and I had trusted to the crap they draw on maps we'd still be wondering where our next meal was coming from. . . . Shit, I keep forgetting. Will's not worrying about his meals these days." He cleared his throat. "Damn, we had us some times, Will and I, I can tell you, until we went and got ourselves rich and spoiled all the fun."

After a moment, I said, "There's a lake on the Jicarilla Apache Reservation in northern New Mexico called Stinking Lake. Good spot for duck hunting, but you'd never find it if you followed the gas station maps or even the state tourist map. They've had the roads up there all wrong as long as I can remember."

"Well, there's a jeep track runs up along the coast. Jeep track, hell, if I know my locals they make it in ordinary pickup trucks and maybe even beat-up old Yankee Cadillacs. Anyway, it goes at least twenty-five miles north, I'm told, to a little fishing village some say is called El Mirador. Others say El Mirador's the name of another village up there that dried up and blew away and this one's got no name. Anyway, name or no name, that's Arturo's village."

"Arturo is a fisherman?"

"I gather that's what he calls himself, and likely he catches a fish now and then when he's got nothing better to do. But mostly . . . You know what kind of fish is a square grouper?"

I grinned. "Sure, it's a bale of marijuana," I said. "But I heard the term in Florida, where fishermen often find them drifting after some smuggler's boat has jettisoned a load when the Coast Guard got too close. I never heard it used on this coast."

"It's used. There's other stuff comes through, too; stronger stuff. Don't approve of the trade myself, but I was raised not to run to the school principal with everything I saw. Or the police. I take care of my conscience and let the other fellers take care of theirs. Anyway, I was given to understand this Arturo knows everything goes on in this part of Mexico."

I asked, "Is this El Mirador place, where Arturo lives, by any chance located on Bahía San Cristóbal, where the arms were landed?"

"Nobody lives at Bahía San Cristóbal far as I know. But if anything gets landed there, I've been told, Arturo's the man to tell you about it. Any trucks that went to Bahía San Cristóbal or came from there, he'd have known about them. He might even have heard the names of the drivers. Hell, he might be the man who recruited them in the first place. I figured it was a starting place. Arturo might have a clue to where that shipment was hid. You shouldn't have no trouble getting there in that truck of mine; that's why I picked it off Herrera's used-car lot." He gave me a mean little grin. "No trouble except that it'll damn near beat you to death like it almost did me. Goddamn beefed-up suspension. Don't have to worry about locking the front hubs for the four-wheel drive. They're automatic; and the lever for the transfer case is right by the gearshift, marked good and plain. Left some pistols behind the seat I took off those fellows. Didn't want to come in here armed and maybe get myself shot; but if you could see your way clear now to leaving me one . . ."

"I found them," I said. "But Dr. Beckman doesn't trust you very much, *amigo*, and she's the one who'll be mostly looking after you while I'm gone, so I think I'd better keep your guns for the time being. As I said, there'll be some people watching out for you. They'll have enough guns."

He turned his head painfully to look at Jo. "I suppose a lot of folks, including your brother, been telling you what a wicked old man I am, ma'am."

"Not to mention my mother," Jo said.

Cody smiled thinly. "Didn't get on with Will's lady at all, and that's a fact."

"She told us, if anything happened to her or Will down here, you'd be to blame, Mr. Cody."

"Hating women do say the damndest things; and your ma purely did dislike me, young lady. Maybe because I'd seen Will make a fool of himself about women like that before, and I tried to warn him against her." He grimaced. "You'd think an old man like me would have learned better, wouldn't you? Should have known I'd just make Will stubborn mad and the lady a bad enemy."

Jo hesitated. "Why . . . why would you want to warn your partner against my mother, Mr. Cody?"

The man in the bed shook his head minutely. "No profit in my talking against your ma, girl. I think you know the kind of woman she was. Maybe the boy don't or don't want to admit it—boys get funny ideas about their moms—but you're a smart young lady and you know. No need for me to badmouth her to you."

Jo licked her lips, and said stiffly, "I don't know what you're talking about. My mother was . . . was a fine person and you're just trying to . . . You haven't really explained why you came here. You must know lots of people who'd be willing to help you, at least for a consideration, yet you came crawling to a man you didn't even know. . . ."

"A man who owed me," Cody whispered. "Ask him, he'll tell you. He stood by while they arrested me; watched them put the handcuffs on me. He drove off with my car. He took my young wife. He even took my name. Waiting in that place they held me, I figured to look him up some day and get back some of what he took, out of his hide maybe. Then I heard them talking about the way they'd tried to kill him a couple times and he'd got away from them and even got one or two of them doing it. So maybe he wasn't such a bad feller after all; leastways he was tough and on the same side as me, against them. Figured if I could find him, a man who was in my debt like that, a man with the same interests you might say, we could work something out. Like we're doing."

Jo gave an exasperated little sigh. "They ought to give special courses in male psychology. No woman would think like that." She frowned. "This Arturo you're sending him to, is he old and blind or something?"

"I'm told he's a middle-aged gent; don't know about his eyesight. . . . You're wondering how your man's going to fool him? I never met Arturo, ma'am. All I know of him is what I hear from . . . well, let's say from folks who had business dealings with him."

"Drug dealings?"

The old man moved his shoulders in a minute shrug. "I figure it's my job to make one gent named Cody do what I think is right. It's not my job to make the whole world do what I think is right. Or not do what I think is wrong. Too many folks minding other folks' business these days, ma'am."

The air was getting pretty thick with philosophy. I said, "To get back to business, what you're saying is that you don't really know this Arturo. And he doesn't know you. So even assuming that I can deceive him into believing I'm you, what have I gained? What lever can I use to make him talk . . . ?" I stopped, listening.

"You forget, you're in Mexico," Cody said. "Money'll get you damn near anything in Mexico. Well, it's the same back home, but they ain't so blasted hypocritical around here. . . . Something wrong, son?"

"Easy now," I said softly. "We're about to have visitors. Take it very easy, Mr. Cody, don't make them nervous."

Jo said quickly, "But if it's Antonia, she's coming in here to kill Mr. Cody. Are you going to let her? You *can't* let her!"

The old man said dryly, "I surely do appreciate your friendly concern, ma'am, but it seems a mite inconsistent."

I said, "Nobody's going to kill anybody. Just stay perfectly still and don't startle them. . . ."

There was a sudden ripping noise as a knife slashed away the screen at the open window. The twin barrels of a shotgun parted the worn curtains, faded green with a pattern of white in this room. For a moment I thought I'd made a serious error, perhaps a fatal one, since neither Antonia nor her weatherbeaten sidekick had carried a shotgun when last seen; and if I'd let the wrong people get the drop on us, we were in serious trouble. Then I saw *Tío* Ignacio's weathered face behind the big hammers of the ancient doublegun. I'd wondered why Antonia, an impatient type, had waited so long before crashing the party; but apparently, not trusting my cooperation, she'd taken time to let Ignacio provide himself with heavier artillery, either from their car or from a friend or relative in Old Kino, probably the latter since, if they'd had a shotgun along, they'd have brought it to the house in the first place. I noted that the hammers of the antique weapon were cocked.

"Pasa adelante, guapa," said the man at the window.

I was aware of Jo, in the doorway, stepping aside to let Antonia come in. The Mexican girl stared at me for a moment defiantly. Flinging back her *serape* with a dramatic gesture that freed her gun arm, she turned toward the bed, raising the little .22 I'd been wondering about. A couple of tense seconds passed, but the weapon did not fire. Instead, the

206

Mexican girl made an odd, hissing sound and swung the gun muzzle toward me.

"Ees joke, perhaps?" She spoke through clenched teeth. "This man, he is no Cody, no more than you! You make big Yankee joke with Antonia, maybe?"

CHAPTER 23

I'D rather tackle a vanload of armed revolutionaries than the Mexican telephone system in the middle of the night. Fortunately I managed to arouse the manager of the new motel up the beach—La Playa de Kino, *playa* meaning beach—and a U.S. fifty-dollar bill changed his indignation to cooperation. As Cody had said, money is very effective in Mexico; particularly, with their current rate of inflation, American money.

Señor Saiz's efforts at the motel switchboard finally got me through to our man in El Paso, Texas, whom I didn't know and probably never would know. The Lone Star Improvement Corporation, twenty-four-hour service. Up in Texas, three hundred and fifty miles from Kino Bay, Lone Star juggled some electronics and telephonics and finally connected me with Greer, sixty miles away in the Hotel Gandara in Hermosillo. Not the most direct route of communication; but I had to keep in mind that I expected, and even hoped, that there'd be people coming after me, and whatever price I paid the manager for his silence, they could probably outbid me.

For Horace Cody, wounded and on the lam, to call a hotel in Hermosillo, a city where he had no obvious connections—particularly that hotel—would have raised questions in their suspicious little minds. For him to call an oddball company in El Paso, his hometown, shouldn't. He was a rich man, and they'd figure it was one of his tame corporations, perhaps a front for some kind of shady business. He could be calling for assistance, or money, or information, or political influence to be used in his behalf. They'd consider it normal fugitive behavior. I hoped. . . .

We'd had an interesting time back at the Schonfeld house, of course, after the Mexican girl's announcement. I'd noted that Cody himself had taken it calmly enough; but Jo had reacted with a gasp of incredulity and started to protest. However, there'd been other problems to be solved of more immediate importance than a mere question of identity, so I'd cut her off.

"Antonia, how about asking your uncle to park the artillery? That ancient *escopeta* makes me very nervous; I'd hate to have him pull the trigger and blow himself up."

"No blow, very good gun." The Mexican girl laughed shortly and made a gesture. *Tío* Ignacio withdrew the long shotgun barrels and the curtains fell back into place before the window, hiding the damaged screen. Antonia looked at the little pistol in her hand, shrugged, and tucked it inside her waistband. "So. Now explain this so-funny joke, *por favor*."

Jo had exploded at last: "But it's ridiculous! This has got to be the man who married Gloria Pierce with my brother watching the chapel from across the street. Isn't it, Matt? Isn't he? He's the man you traded places with, the man you've been impersonating, isn't he? You can't tell me somebody went to all the trouble to fix you up like that, complete with gray hair and beard and bald spot, just so you could impersonate a bad impersonator; that would be just too mad for words! Not that the whole thing isn't pretty wild anyway!"

I looked at the old man in the bed with the phony bandage on his head.

I said, "What do you say, Mr. Cody?"

He regarded me for a moment. "What do you know, son?"

I said, "I know that I came charging into a motel room where Señorita Sisneros was waiting for Horace Cody with a gun. Startled, she let go one wild shot, but she didn't shoot again because she recognized instantly that I wasn't him. Now, my disguise isn't perfect, sir, but it isn't *that* bad. In fact, you thought it was pretty good, didn't you? So how the hell did a young woman under stress, catching a brief glimpse of a man in violent motion, a man carefully made up to resemble the man she wanted to shoot, manage to make the decision that he was the wrong man and hold her second shot?'' I waited for him to speak; when he didn't, I went on. "Later, Mrs. Beckman described the tall, gray-haired, gray-bearded Horace Cody her brother had been following. Antonia started to protest but decided against it. I think it would be interesting to hear *her* description of Cody, don't you, sir?''

He nodded, and spoke to the Mexican girl: "Do I understand that you met Horace Cody, señorita?''

"No meet.'' The girl's voice was sullen; clearly she wasn't sure she wasn't being ridiculed. "I was send away when Cody coming. But I watch across street, I see him come. My Jorge such a lovely fool, do stupid things; somebody must watch he no get in trouble.'' She shook her head sadly. "When I hear what he is plan to do for Señor Cody I try to stop, but he will not stop. He say we make rich. Who wants rich and dead?''

The old man nodded. "So you got a good look at Horace Cody when he came to make a deal with your Jorge? Jorge Medina, is that right?''

"Medina, yes. And I see Cody good, when he come and when he go.''

I said, "How about describing him for us.''

She looked at me suspiciously, still wondering if she wasn't being made the butt of some kind of a strange *gringo* joke; then she shrugged.

"*Sí*, if you wish. When the medical señora was talk about the tall man with the *barba* and the *cabeza pelada*—the head with not much hair—I am wish to laugh. So much boolsheet I never hear. And this old one, this so-tall one here in the bed, he should be Señor Cody, hah? I see Señor Cody good. He has not much tall, never one hundred and ninety centimeters like this *viejo* who takes the name. Not small man, no, but eighty kilos and a hundred and seventy-five centimeters, maybe. He has no bald; the hair is much for such an age, maybe sixty years.

210

I think maybe *peluca*, yes? Wig, you call? Brown, no gray. The face is shave very careful, no *barba*, no *mostacho*. Very careful the clothes, also. No big hat, no boots with the toes and heels, no cowboy thing around neck with big stone, very like the man of business, what you call conservative, hey? That is Señor Cody who come to Guaymas to send my Jorge to die. That is Señor Cody I will kill, hey?''

There was a silence in the room after she'd finished, then Jo burst out: ''But that's not Mr. Cody she's describing. That's Will Pierce!''

I looked at Cody, but his face was expressionless.

The Mexican girl asked sharply. ''Pierce? That is not a name I hear. Who is this Señor Pierce?''

Jo ignored her, speaking to me: ''Junior and I made fun of Will's rug and his three-piece suits to Millie, and she slapped us down hard; if he wanted to look young for her, wasn't that nice, and weren't we as tired as she was of Texas men who dressed and talked like superannuated cowboys?'' She glanced quickly at Cody, a little embarrassed. ''I mean . . .''

The old man spoke at last: ''No need to apologize, ma'am.'' He grimaced and looked at me. ''But she drove old Will plumb crazy, that Millie woman did. Seen it happen to other older fellers who got themselves infatuated with young girls, but Mrs. Charles was no young girl; still, she was a handsome, well-preserved female, I'll hand her that, and he had her beat by more'n a dozen years, and it graveled him. He had to have himself a diet and a hairpiece, and even visits to a tanning parlor, as if we hadn't had enough sun in our younger days to last us this lifetime and the next.''

I asked, ''Did you know, sir?''

''That Will was using my name down here?'' He shook his head grimly. ''Not for certain, not for a while, but I started hearing about places I'd been I hadn't been and things I'd done I hadn't done. If you know what I mean. It went against the grain to set the hound dogs sniffing after Will, after all these years; but I came to it at last and what I learned wasn't easy to take. There was a drug deal first, going to make him millions,

211

but it went wrong somehow, and he almost got caught. Scared him out of that business, and a good thing, too; but I reckon that was where he made the connections for this arms deal that was going to have him rolling in greenbacks. . . . Will was always like that; anybody could sell him pie in the sky if they just said if it was blueberry or apple so it would sound like they knew what they was talking about. But he was a good partner in the field, and he saved my life at least once, which made it mutual; and he had the goddamndest nose for oil in the ground of any man I ever met. Long as he stuck to finding it and let me handle the business of cashing in on it and making the money grow, he did fine.'' Cody grimaced. ''Only we had that fight I told you about, about the woman, and after that he wouldn't listen to me, not even when I told him oil was going to drop through the floor and what we should do about it. So I bought him out, Cody and Pierce is all mine now, although not many folks know it. And Will took his money and put it in all the wrong places and lost most of it when the bottom fell out, there in Texas. Real massacre, and he was one of the massacrees. And with that woman egging him on, I reckon he got downright desperate, trying to get his stake back playing with drugs and arms like he did.''

''And using your name.'' I looked at him. ''Is that why you came down here, to set the record straight?''

''What record?'' The old man looked me straight in the eye. ''Nothing on any record, son. A few people, including maybe some government people in a couple of governments, kinda think now that Buff Cody's even a worse bastard than they thought before, if you'll excuse it, ma'am; but there isn't a damn thing they can prove, and I'm not about to smear Will's name to whitewash mine, particularly now he's dead. In most places I do business, having a crooked reputation is an advantage, and I never cared much what folks thought of me anyway.''

Jo asked, ''Then what did you come down here for, Mr. Cody?''

''Hell, some fellers done killed my partner, ma'am—or leastways the man who was my partner for forty years, even if we did break up at the end over a woman."

She looked baffled. "You mean that after what he did to you, you still feel obliged to . . . to avenge him?"

Cody drew a long, painful breath. "Man's a damn fool to criticize a friend's woman; no better way to end a friendship. Maybe if I'd kept my mouth shut about her we wouldn't have broke up the team, and I could have kept him from throwing his money away, and he wouldn't have felt obliged to try the fool ventures he did in order to recoup his losses. And to sign my name to them out of anger." The old man drew a long, painful breath. "Anyway, my reputation can stand being called a drug dealer and an arms dealer; it can't stand being called the kind of man who does nothing when his partner of forty years has been chopped down by a bunch of machete-swinging hooligans. Soon's I grow back a little of the blood I'm missing, I'll take care of those big-hat *insurgentes*. I figure if I can find those weapons they want so bad, or you can, and blow them up with dynamite or give them to the government, that'll put a spoke in their wheel and make them wish they'd never heard of Will Pierce. After that I'll go after a political gent named Mondragon I'm told bosses this revolutionary gang who did the killing and may have taken a swing or two at Will and his lady himself."

Driving away from there I'd had a lot to think about; but what bothered me most was a discrepancy: apparently, contrary to what I'd been told, Buff Cody had not lost much if any of his money; he'd had no need for a rich wife's fortune to bail him out. Yet there seemed to be clear evidence, still unrefuted, to show that he was the one who'd sent his frighteners to drive Gloria into a panic. I could see no way the blame for that could be switched to Will Pierce; and it seemed unlikely that Gloria had made up all those things that had happened to her: the accident, the gunshot, the almost-suicide. As I'd told Jo, I couldn't believe now, having met him, that the old man really had eventual murder in mind, but everything indicated that he had given the

213

girl a very bad time, and it seemed completely out of character for him. However, the conference had used up most of his remaining strength, and I couldn't afford to hang around until he recovered enough to satisfy my curiosity. . . .

Unlike the motel manager, Greer seemed happy to be awakened in the middle of the night, meaning that after a week of standby duty he was bored out of his gourd. We established that the state of my health was satisfactory and that Washington had sent no recent queries or instructions.

"The Charles boy is going to make it," he told me over the phone. "Too bad. Pistol-happy little creep!"

I found it rather touching that he felt more vindictive about my being shot than I did.

I said, "Yes, his sister got through to the hospital this afternoon. She told me. Any further word from *El Cacique*?"

"No. But he seems to have plenty of clout; he got the lid clapped on here like Reagan putting the hush on Grenada. The courtesy of the local authorities you wouldn't believe. It had me shaking worse than if they'd tossed me into the Black Hole; a polite cop always scares the shit out of me. Oh, and your *Cacique* friend said to tell you your bride remains safe, and he finds her a most charming young person."

It'll probably go down as another serious mark against my character, one of many, that I received this information with a certain amount of relief. Apparently Gloria had taken our crude mountain affair no more seriously than I had. The fact that Ramón now found her charming indicated that she'd been as quick to look elsewhere as I had, or even a little quicker; he wouldn't have been singing her praises if she'd slapped him down.

"Well, he always was a ladies' man," I said. "I'm glad to hear he hasn't lost his touch. How soon can you get down here?"

"Kino Bay? Normally, I gather, it's an hour's drive; call it an hour and a half in the dark, Mexican roads being what they are. I should be there by . . . call it five o'clock. Where do I go and what do I do when I get there?" When I'd told him, and given him the background, he said, "Do I understand that you want

214

me to arrive with bells and whistles and make a big production of guarding the house?''

"You've got it. Let everybody know that I'm still in that bed, still in bad shape, and that with my secret hideaway compromised and everybody milling around it—this evening you could hardly tell it from Times Square, with all the traffic in and out—you figure I now need close protection until I get back on my feet, if I ever do. Have Washington send you a couple of men or borrow them from Ramón if you think it'll help you look convincing."

Greer hesitated. "If you'll excuse my asking, what's the point? So they think Agent Helm is laid up in Kino Bay at death's door, heavily protected, unreachable, and the man they're chasing up El Mirador way is the same Mr. Cody who got away from them in El Paso, so what? They'll still be after him to kill him. You."

I said, "Cody asked the same question. The answer is that if they know I'm me, an experienced fellow operative with a certain reputation, I flatter myself they won't take any chances dealing with me. But Cody's not a pro, and he's a fairly elderly party. Sure, he's a tough old bird; sure, he made saps of them once; but if they think I'm him they'll still come after me as if they were chasing an aging amateur, just a little optimistically and carelessly. It could give me an edge when I need one." I laughed. "Let's just say that after all the time I've messed around with this idiot impersonation I want to get something out of it."

The motel manager was wearing a maroon brocade dressing gown over red silk pajamas. He was a short, plump, brown-faced individual with thick, slick, black hair he'd taken time to brush neatly into place before joining me. Or maybe he wore a nightcap to bed to keep it undisturbed. I gave him an additional fifty, although I had a hunch that old Cody, while he'd willingly pay what things were worth, wasn't too generous with handouts. But the folks following him weren't likely to be aware of that—they'd know his bank account to the last half cent and every scar on his body; but they wouldn't waste much time on vague stuff like his psychology—and the large bills so casually distributed did a good job of convincing the manager that my shapeless white suit and battered white hat and smudged white boots were mere affectations; he was in the presence of real Yankee money.

"I apologize for disturbing you, Señor Saiz," I said.

"Por nada," he said. "I am happy that I could be of service, Señor Cody."

I'd parked Cody's pickup in the lot at the rear of the motel, but I went out the front and circled the place cautiously. They'd have spread the word to all their contacts in this part of the world, and they had more of them than we did. Sooner or later somebody'd pick up Cody's trail. He, or she, would pass the word to the big brain controlling their operation, and he'd give the kill order again, and Mr. Cody would have them breathing down his neck again. My neck now. Which was exactly what I was planning on, but I didn't want to make the mistake of assuming it hadn't happened already. . . . The moon was down now, but when I came around the corner of the building and peeked through the ornate shrubbery I could see that somebody was sitting cross-legged on the hood of the parked red truck.

It didn't seem like very hostile behavior, and the figure was small enough not to be too much of a burden to the sheet metal. I reached for my gun anyway and watched for several minutes, checking the surroundings for indications of an ambush; then the seated figure gave a very feminine toss of its head and I could see, even in the darkness, that the tossed-back hair was glossy black and quite long. I drew a long breath and walked forward.

"How the hell did you get here, Antonia?"

"Was not far. I guess you come here for *teléfono*. I walk."

"In those heels?"

This evening she was again wearing the scuffed red pumps in which I'd seen her a couple of times before.

"I take off. I carry the moccasins here." She patted a lumpy area of her serape, and went on: "Arturo have not much English. You have not much Spanish. I speak both very good; I come with."

I looked at her sharply. "How do you know Arturo doesn't speak English?"

"Jorge take me to El Mirador one time."

"Medina took you to meet Arturo?"

"Not much meet. I stay in peekup. Man business. You know. Woman stupid little thing not to bother stupid little head." She shrugged. "Good to make man feel big and smart, no? But I see. I hear. Arturo knows many people who care not much for honest or dishonest. He get the four bad men who drive the *camiones* for Jorge. Yes, I know El Mirador. I know Arturo. So I come with, no?"

CHAPTER 24

WE made slow progress in the dark. The pavement ended
at the bluff—solid black against the starry night sky—that also
terminated the beach at the north end of the settlement, like a
roadblock thrown up by a giant bulldozer. From there we followed a small dirt road that angled inland to scramble over the
massive obstacle and drive into the apparently uninhabited valley beyond. At least, with Kino Bay left behind, there wasn't a
light to be seen anywhere.

Except for the fact that its cab was reasonably luxurious—
well, after we'd shoveled out most of Cody's garbage and
scrubbed out most of his blood—the GMC three-quarter-tonner,
unlike many of the lighter, half-ton jobs, made no soft conces-
sions to passenger comfort. On the other hand, it gave the impression of being totally indestructible, it had plenty of power,
the headlights were excellent, and the dashboard actually
mounted a businesslike display of instruments instead of enter-
taining you with cute little twinkie-winkie lights in the manner
of too many cars nowadays.

I'd probably have missed the turnoff if I hadn't had the girl to
warn me it was coming up, since the so-called coast road was
even less impressive than the main, inland, north-south highway—meaning the rough dirt track—that we'd been following.
The new thoroughfare was merely two ruts across the desert. In
this dry weather, it should be passable, but I shifted into four-
wheel drive anyway just to make sure I knew how.

"What's a *guapa*?" I asked after a while.

I guess she'd fallen asleep beside me in spite of the jarring ride. She stirred and asked, *"Qué dice?"*

"Sorry, didn't mean to wake you."

"Is okay."

I said, "When your uncle called you into the bedroom after shoving his shotgun through the window, he addressed you as *guapa*. I don't know the word."

She laughed. "Very good word for you. Means 'pretty one.' Say to all the girls. Maybe they slap you the face. But maybe not." She glanced at me. "You fuck with the tall *muchacha*?"

"None of your damn business, small fry," I said.

"Okay, you fuck with her. I bet she not so good as me."

I said, "It's too bad that we'll never know, isn't it?"

She gave me again that big, white, flashing grin. "She your lady now? I could take you away, I bet, but it is still too soon after Jorge, I am not interest."

"Well, it's nice to know what to expect," I said. "And what not to expect. Talking about expectations, are there any surprises along this road, like sudden arroyos or soft sand dunes?"

"No, Jorge make it easy in his little peekup from Japan that have not even the four-wheels drive. In such a big strong *camioneta* like this one, *no problema*. But maybe Arturo shoot. Not very nice man. But maybe he talk. What you wish I ask him if he talk?"

"The drivers," I said. "I think they've got to be the starting place. Your friend Medina used two sets of drivers for his trucks, apparently. Eight men. The first quartet was presumably the bunch you heard him ask Arturo to recruit for him. I figure those men drove the four trucks up to Bahía San Cristóbal, loaded them with arms from the ship, and then drove them on to Medina's secret hiding place. They unloaded the weapons there, and Medina undoubtedly had them take the empty trucks a reasonable distance from the cache so nobody could guess where they'd been. Then Medina paid those four men off and sent them away after, presumably, swearing them to silence. If I could find them, or even just one of them, I might be able to get a lead on those armaments. You don't happen to know any pertinent names or addresses, by any chance?''

"No, but maybe Arturo tell. I will ask. You have money?''

"Yes.''

"For money, maybe he tell. And maybe he just kill and take money anyway.''

"The possibility had occurred to me,'' I said dryly. "Well, the way I figure it, Medina was being very cagy. He didn't trust that first crew of his to keep its mouth shut under duress, so he got rid of it before entering the danger zone and had a second bunch of drivers standing by who couldn't be made to spill anything because they didn't know anything. They drove those empty vans to the mountain rendezvous to meet the guerillas commanded by that great orator and self-styled revolutionary general, Carlos Mondragon. And that's where the four trucks were found, with all four men lying beside them, tortured and dead. Along with the man who'd hired them, your lover Medina, who'd probably thought he was reasonably safe because they couldn't afford to get too rough with him or they'd lose the information in his head and with it the weapons. Only Mondragon or one of his henchmen didn't know his own strength. . . . Oops, what do I do here?''

"*A la derecha,* to the right,'' Antonia said, as I slowed uncertainly at a fork in the track I was following. "Other road go straight to beach. That Mondragon I will kill very soon with much hurt, very slow.''

There was a hint of light in the sky over the shadowy moonscape inland; we'd have daylight soon. As always, the vague sharpening of the horizon in the east made the darkness seem more impenetrable where we were. The headlights appeared to be drilling a tunnel for us through solid blackness. A jackrabbit flashing across the path of illumination ahead at full throttle was a startling sight, reminding us that we were not the only inhabitants of this dark underworld.

I said, "Too bad they killed Will Pierce before you could get to him; you could have had a lot of fun with him, too.''

"Yes, they owe me, is that what you say? Señor Pierce was

mine!'' Then the girl glanced at me with sudden suspicion. ''You make joke of Antonia, hey? You think is funny I want to kill?''

I said, ''Hell, no. Blast Mondragon all you want, if it'll make you feel better. There are too many people in the world already; we can spare a few of those who won't behave themselves properly. But toasting him over a slow fire first, I don't know. I've always felt that if you're going to kill something, whether it's a duck, a deer, or a man, you ought to make it quick and clean. Oh, sometimes you've got to stretch it out a bit if there's information to be extracted, but you don't have to like it.''

''Fonny man,'' she said. ''Has sentiment, *mucho corazón,* very nice! Maybe I will take away from that female *médica.*''

The dawn broke abruptly, as it does in that part of the world; one moment we were jolting blindly down the narrow beam of our headlights, the next there was pale light all around us, growing rapidly brighter. Our first sight of the village was from the high ground inland. I stopped to use the mini-telescope I'd tucked into my overnight bag way back when I'd packed my gear in Ramón's mountain camp. El Mirador, if that was its name, was on the shore of a rather pretty little bay—well, pretty if you don't equate scenic beauty with lush vegetation. This was still a rugged, arid landscape. The road ran down the long slope from the hills to a scattering of mud huts with a few beat-up cars and pickup trucks parked among them. Beyond, I could see three fishing boats moored in a small inlet. I passed the spyglass to Antonia.

''I wonder they don't use this bay for unloading their goods, whether drugs or weapons.''

''Is too shallow for ship, only small boat can use.''

''Which house is Arturo's?''

''On the hill, the big one, *muy grande.*''

It didn't look *muy grande* to me when I got the telescope back, just two huts joined together by a covered breezeway; but that made it twice as large as the one-hut establishments in the village below, and I guess it all depends on the frame of reference. On the bare, dusty premises was a tan four-wheel-drive pickup that looked larger than ours, I guessed a one-ton job, dirty but reasonably new and otherwise in good shape; and a big, battered, gold-colored American sedan old enough to have fins on it. There were also three rusty, wheel-less wrecks from the dawn of automotive history. I've never yearned to own a bunch of nonfunctioning cars and display them in my yard, but it seems to be a fairly common compulsion.

We got back into the GMC and drove down there. Several dogs of indeterminable breeds made halfhearted passes at us, barking as if their hearts weren't in it, as we drove through the dusty space in the center of the little community. You could hardly call it a town square, or a *plaza*, but perhaps they did. I could see no people at all. There was, however, a small goat in one yard. More dogs came out to greet us as we ground up the hill to Arturo's house. There was a rusty iron gate in front, in a barbed wire fence that had largely fallen down on both sides of it. I parked in front if it and got out awkwardly, the bulky bandage reminding me that I was supposed to be a wounded man. I hobbled around the truck to help Antonia out.

"Sooch a gentleman!" she murmured.

"We're being watched; why not put on a good show?" I said. "When we get out of here you can open your own damn doors, baby. If we get out."

"There is Arturo."

He was standing in the breezeway; and I had a sudden impulse to laugh. I guess I'd been expecting to see a dramatic figure of some kind, tall and Mephistophelian perhaps: the sinister local *jefe* of crime. I suppose I'd also expected him to be surrounded by heavily armed henchmen. What I saw was a single, chunky, bowlegged little man with a big, black mustache in a round, brown, friendly face that smiled a big welcome at us. He was wearing work clothes that had seen better days. He looked a little like one of the plump, baggy-pants comedians they love in Mexican movies, and like them he had a big hat on, shapeless and sweatstained, which he swept off with a flourish as I let Antonia through the gate and she went up the foot-hammered dirt walk toward him.

I stopped to let her make the first social overtures; also to close the gate again. I'd been brought up in ranch country where custom dictates that, even if it serves no useful function, you leave a gate the way you found it. A couple of the dogs came up to investigate me. I let them sniff my hand and told them they were great dogs and they believed me. I get along well with dogs; it's people who give me trouble. But Antonia was beckoning to me, and I left my instant canine friends and marched stiffly up the walk to join her in front of the little man.

She said to him, "This is Señor Horace Cody." Apparently Arturo did know some English because she used that language. She went on, speaking slowly and clearly to me, but obviously hoping that Arturo would also understand what she was saying so he wouldn't think we were plotting against him: "I have explain to Señor Arturo that you are truly Señor Cody. I have tell him the one who was here before is your partner who use your name and trick you like he trick my Jorge, like he trick Arturo himself. I have say you wish much to find men Jorge use to do that bad man's business."

I said, *"Buenos días, Señor."*

"Buenos días."

He held out his hand. I remembered that they don't go in much for the Big Grip down there; we barely touched palms gently. He started to speak, in Spanish, with gestures. When he was through, Antonia translated.

"He say please excuse he not speak much good *inglés*. He say his house is your house. He say he is very happy you come all this way to see Arturo. He say a friend of his present him with some mescal of own making, very not legal, but here is no policeman, and he thinks it is very fine mescal. It would please him much if you would taste and see if you agree." She hesitated. "You must say yes or is big insult."

I said, "There's nothing like a little mescal for breakfast. Tell him I'll be honored to join him in a drink."

The little man waved us through the breezeway where some battered chairs, no two alike, were scattered around a covered patio of weathered concrete. As we sat down, a middle-aged brown woman in a shapeless brown dress brought out a bottle without a label and some shot glasses. The bottle was clear, and the liquid inside was very pale. There were other men around us now, although I didn't know where they'd come from; tough, wiry, brown-faced men. There wasn't a firearm in sight; it was strictly a social occasion.

Arturo passed me a glass and lifted one of his own, speaking in Spanish: *"Por todos mal, mescal. Por todos bíen, también!"*

Antonia translated: "Is old saying: For all things bad, mescal. For all things good, the same."

"Say, that's real sharp. The universal cure and celebration. I'll have to remember that." Living near the border, I'd only heard it about a hundred times before, and Buff Cody undoubtedly had, too, but this seemed to be a good place to play stupid. "Do I sip it or slug it down?"

"Slug is okay."

I saluted Arturo with my glass and drank it off, as he did the same. The mescal was strong but smooth. Some of it goes down as if they hadn't got all the spikes off the cactus from which they made it; but this was all right, for mescal. That took care of the hospitality, and it was time for business. I sat and listened to Antonia talking with Arturo, catching an occasional word like *hombres* and *camiones*. Four or five men and several dogs stood around saying nothing.

At last Antonia said, "He say one hundred dollars."

"Do I bargain?"

"Me, Antonia, I have bargain. You pay."

"It's a deal." Actually, it was too good a deal. If the man really had the information I needed, I'd have paid several times that. I made a show of having to search my wallet for enough American money, coming up with four twenties, a ten, a five, and five ones. It didn't seem advisable to flash any hundreds or even fifties around this place. "Here you are."

I gave the money to Antonia, who passed it to Arturo, who counted it carefully; then he began to talk. I listened to the names he rattled off, which I caught after a fashion, at least the last names, confirmed when Antonia repeated them: Delgado, Ruiz, Miera, and Bustamente. But the directions lost me. Even when Antonia told them back to make certain she'd got them right the Spanish crackled too fast for me to follow it. All I could make out, because it was spoken several times, was the word *cordillera*, meaning mountain range. A final slug of mescal and Arturo's gentle handshake, as we stood up, put the seal on the bargain. The little man was smiling at us, innocently pleased to have been of assistance.

"Vaya con Díos, señorita, señor."

We walked down to the pickup in silence; even the dogs didn't bother with us any more. I heard somebody start to laugh back at the house and stop laughing abruptly. I remembered to make a painful production of climbing into the cab. Nobody followed us away from there.

CHAPTER 25

"FONNY man, Arturo," Antonia said as we left the village behind. "When I come with Jorge, Arturo very rude, have many men with guns, behave to Jorge very tough, very dangerous. This time, with you, so much nice. I think he play treeks, no?"

I was glad to hear her say it. I mean, I still had some doubts about that heavy Spanglish accent and about the girl herself. After all, she'd wished herself off on me deliberately, and all I knew about her was what she'd chosen to tell me. However, the fact that she wasn't trying to sell me Arturo as just a happy country boy was certainly a point in favor of her honesty. My Scandinavian ancestry didn't qualify me to understand the Mexican mental processes of a gent like Arturo very well, but Latin or Nordic, Catholic or Protestant, black or brown or red or yellow or white, I know a cheerful con man when I see one.

"I think he plays tricks, yes," I said. "Let me have it, quick, what he told you about those truck drivers he recruited for Medina."

"You hear names?"

"I think I caught most of them, but give them to me again, please."

"Those men name themselves Santos Delgado, Enrique Serafin Ruiz, Eloy Miera, and Bernardo Bustamente."

"And the place? Did he tell you the town in which they live? Do they all come from the same town?"

"He say they all together. He say you find in place call

Piedras Negras, means black stones, in the Cordillera Santa Anna, how you say, Mountains of Santa Anna?''

"Named after the well-known general? Quite apart from his performance at the Alamo, he was kind of an all-around political bastard, wasn't he?''

"Our General Santa Anna very great man," she said, "and very great bastard, yes.''

"And where is this *cordillera*?''

She pointed ahead. "Other side Cerros Vaqueros, there, is Valle de Santa Anna, where other road go. Road to Bahia San Cristóbal and Puerto de la Libertad.''

"The one we turned off just outside Bahia Kino?''

"*Sí*, that one. Other side valley, big mountain. Cordillera Santa Anna. We climb over Cerros Vaqueros and down across valley to road, drive north seven kilometers, turn into *cordillera* on road not so big, find Piedras Negras. Big stones, what you call conspicuous, no can miss.''

I said, "Oh, God, not another one!" When she looked at me questioningly, I said, "I've spent most of my life searching hopelessly for places I can't miss. . . . Never mind, it was just a dumb *gringo* joke. And that bunch of hills up ahead is Cerros Vaqueros, the Cowboy Hills?''

"That is what Arturo call them. He say much steep but he make in *camioneta* with four-wheels-driving easy.''

I studied her a moment and asked the big question: "Did he say why he was so eager to help us locate a couple of million bucks worth of armaments instead of finding and cashing in on them himself? I mean, he must guess, even if you didn't tell him, why we're trying to track down those men.''

"No tell, but Arturo say. Proud man, he say. Drugs okay. Weapons no okay. Against principle, he say.''

It wasn't fair to laugh; the sneaky little guy might actually have meant it. They all pride themselves virtuously on having something they won't do.

"I'm not sure I believe that story," I said.

Antonia grinned. "Besides, guns much dangerous to sell, government no like. Drugs, every people want, who can stop?

227

Only foolish policemen try, not very hard. But guns make government angry, make tough, make much trouble for business of Arturo.''

I said, "Okay, that makes more sense. But I have a hunch he isn't above cashing in on those guns without going near them. I think he sold what he knows to the opposition before peddling it to us.''

"Opposition?''

"The *norteamericanos* who were hunting Cody and are now, I hope, hunting me, thinking I'm Cody. Not that they'd kiss me on the cheek if they knew I was me: but Cody, Will Pierce's former partner, is the guy they really want to silence like they did Pierce himself. I'm just a minor annoyance, an actor they'd hoped to use who had the bad taste not to stick to his script. I was gambling that they'd take a little more time to pick up his trail, my trail now. I was betting that we'd have them behind us, driving up here; but I seem to've lost my bet.''

"My trail, *igualmente*,'' Antonia said. "Equally mine.''

"I'm not forgetting it,'' I said. "Anyway, judging by Arturo's helpful, overhospitable behavior, I'd say the opposition has been here ahead of us and bribed him to make things easy for us to go where they can dispose of us at their leisure. It isn't too surprising that they got here first, considering the revolutionary connections they've got. Among their guerilla friends there are undoubtedly several unsavory characters who know all about Arturo, crime's little Mister Big in these parts.''

"Oh, yes, many bad peoples know Arturo.''

I went on: "When the boys fell for Cody's senile-citizen act and lost him up in the U.S., they must have figured out that he'd head for this part of Mexico. After all, that was where he'd been planning to go at the time of his arrest. He'd been starting out to investigate the activities and death of his partner, using his honeymoon as a cover; and it now appears that El Mirador is where Will Pierce came first. So they beat us here and paid Arturo for information and cooperation. The larcenous little creep was undoubtedly happy to take their money, plenty of it no doubt, and then screw an additional lousy hundred bucks out of us, and ply us with mescal and information, and send us driving off with his blessing—*Vaya con Díos*, indeed!—right into the enemy's arms, or guns."

"So what you say we do, *hombre*?"

"Just what they expect us to do, up to a point," I said. I grimaced. "My gambles haven't been paying off well lately. A week ago I took a chance that young Charles wasn't going to shoot me and he practically blew my head off. And today I figured I'd have the hunters behind me so I could ambush them, and instead it seems they're in front figuring to ambush me. But if at first you don't succeed . . . I think we'll gamble that the boys with the guns, since they know where Arturo's going to send us, and since they think I'm old Buff Cody and not hotshot agent Helm, will do it the easy way. They won't set up along the road to take us, a risky moving target—without heavy weapons, shooting at people in cars is always chancy—they'll just wait for us at the place to which they know we're coming."

"You mean Piedras Negras."

I nodded. "Did Arturo say how far to the junction where we head into the hills?"

"He say four kilometers from El Mirador."

"One and a half to go, then," I said, with a glance at the odometer. "El Mirador. What the hell does it mean, anyway?"

"Mirador is balcony, or high place from which one watches."

"I didn't see any high places except that little hill on which he had his house, but who says names have to make sense?" I glanced at her. "So Arturo told you Will Pierce visited him and pretended to be Cody, just as he did with Jorge Medina."

"*Sí*, Señor Pierce, who call himself Cody, come to El Mirador with Yankee woman, not so young but *muy bella*, Arturo say. Very nice the hair, the makeup, the clothes; but much complain. Road bad for beautiful big car, dust bad for pretty white *pantalones*, too much hot she say, and sit in the car with the *aire acondicionado* while men talk on *portal*." Antonia grimaced. "This in *primavera*, spring, many days ago, not even so hot as now! She should stay summer and see real hot!"

"Maybe she's seeing it where she is now." When Antonia

229

glanced at me uncomprehendingly, I said, "What's Spanish for hell? *Infierno?* The dame is dead along with her gentleman friend. They were killed by Mondragon and his henchmen two or three or four days—I haven't got the chronology of their trip quite straight—after they paid that visit to Arturo. Two questions come to mind. First, what did they want from Arturo, did he say?"

"They want what you want, the drivers of the *camiones*. He say he give them what he give us: the names and Piedras Negras."

I said, "That's odd, because right after coming here—well, maybe they had time to explore as far as Piedras Negras, but not much farther—Mrs. Charles and Mr. Pierce seem to have lit out for points south. The place where they were murdered is some eight hundred kilometers down the coast and a hundred inland, around five hundred miles of driving. Could they have found a clue to the arms that took them that far afield? It doesn't make sense. There's a lot of pretty rugged country right around here. I'd think there'd be any number of suitable hiding places within, say, thirty miles—fifty kilometers—and your Jorge and his trucks and his second batch of drivers were found in the mountains not too far east of here." Actually, Ramón had told me, the four vehicles and the five bodies had been found just off the little mountain road on which he'd had his encampment. "If Jorge actually hid the stuff way down Mazatlán way, he must have done a hell of a lot of driving with that convoy of trucks, with more to look forward to when the deal finally went through. It seems unnecessary for him to have spent that much time on the main roads, not to mention unsafe. After all, just a small accident could have brought them to the attention of the cops. But if he didn't lug the goods way down there for concealment, what the hell were Pierce and Mrs. Charles doing there?"

Antonia gave that inimitable Latin shrug that indicated, in this context, that she had no theories to offer. As I drove along slowly, trying to work things out in my head, I found myself distracted by thoughts of the late Millicent Charles, who, after making the same excursion we were making, had met such a brutal death with her lover, so many miles to the south. The true Millicent Charles had clearly been a somewhat different person from the widowed mother, brave and loving, whom Mason Charles had tried to sell me. Even her daughter had half-admitted that dear Millie hadn't been quite perfect; and Buff Cody obviously considered the dame a rapacious female menace who'd hypnotized Will Pierce and turned him against his partner of a lifetime when said partner tried to speak a few sage words of warning. It seemed likely that she'd been more or less responsible for Will Pierce's financial troubles; her hatred for Cody was probably what had caused Pierce to reject his partner's investment advice and lose his shirt.

Then, after helping him to financial ruin, dear Millie had apparently made it clear that she wasn't very fond of bankrupt millionaires, and if Will wanted to keep her, he'd damn well better pull up his socks and *do* something about it. She'd presumably put enough pressure on the lovesick sexagenarian to send Will Pierce looking for money in strange and illegal places; always assuming that she hadn't actually suggested, or maybe even planned, his ill-fated forays into crime. Maybe she was also the one who'd had the idea of his doing the dirty work under the name of Cody, the man she hated because he'd seen right through her. Perhaps I was being unfair, but the evidence seemed to indicate that the mother of Mason and Joanna hadn't been the nicest lady in the world, although I gathered that, for her age, she'd been one of the prettiest. . . .

"Alto!" At Antonia's command, I halted the truck. She pointed to a rudimentary road running up into the hills to the left. She asked, "Is four *kilometros* now?"

"Three point seven. Close enough." I studied the marks in the dust. "Looks as if there'd been some traffic here. I make out at least two different treads. Well, let's give it a try and hope there'll be room enough up there to turn around if it gets too bad."

It was quite a drive. I've put in more time in sports cars and other rapid vehicles than I have in four-wheel-drive machinery, since most of my boondocks experience was gained on the back of a horse or backpacking on foot. Fortunately this wasn't a true off-road situation requiring an expert. I did have a track of sorts to follow, and there was no question of coping with deep snow, tricky mud, or even soft sand, although some of the arroyo crossings weren't as firm as I'd have liked. Mostly it was simply a matter of using the low-low granny gear judiciously, not so much for its power as for the fact that it let me take the bad spots very slowly without slipping the clutch. I concentrated on picking a route that wouldn't high-center the tall GMC and was glad I hadn't had to try it in the lower Subaru which, while competent enough in other respects, might not have cleared some of the obstacles we had to straddle.

Then the top was in sight. I found good cover for the truck well below and sneaked up to the crest cautiously, to look out over a desolate basin sloping down from our hills and then up to a higher mountain range beyond: the Valle Santa Anna and the *cordillera* of the same name. Way over there near the foot-hills was a red-brown line across the yellow-brown landscape; and I spotted a plume of dust moving along it. The telescope told me it was kicked up by a big, old, empty, flatbed truck heading south along the unpaved road. I warned myself not to get paranoid, every vehicle in northern Mexico wasn't hostile; but I watched it out of sight just the same.

Antonia had joined me. She was calmly running a comb through her long hair. "Road much not good, goddamn, but we make, no sweat. Very good man. Shoot good. Drive good." Standing there, the little girl looked up at me and grinned her great, big grin. "Love good?"

"I don't think this is the right time to check out my virility, small fry."

"Very brave with gun. Very brave with car. Very cheecken with girl, ha!" But it was just her manner of friendly kidding; and in a moment she stopped grinning, looking off to the east and north where Arturo's instructions would take us. "Still think men wait at place with black stones?"

"Well, if they're anywhere around here, they're keeping themselves well hidden. There were at least half-a-dozen places back along the road where we'd have been easy targets for an ambush. I guess we can take it that they're letting us come through as I'd hoped." I glanced at her. "Antonia."

"*Sí*, what is it?"

"This is as far as I'd better drive," I said. "I'll take it on foot from here. You can wait in the truck or come with me as you choose, but if you come and there's trouble you're on your own, and if you lag behind I won't wait for you."

"Sooch a proud man!" she said. "We see who makes lag, ha!"

with exactly one sorry on the word—we lagged, to get to
oppose our resting spot. However, it was only a few hours
past eight o'clock when Antonia turned major the clock but
pointed east.
...
...
...
...

CHAPTER 26

WE made our way north along the ocean side—well, the Sea of Cortez side—of the Cerros Vaqueros. It was rough going. The girl had tucked away her pretty pumps and switched to moccasins. She followed silently behind me. Whenever I looked back, she was right there, never more than half-a-dozen paces behind me. Her dark little face was always carefully expressionless, but I found myself regretting my macho remark about lagging, which I guess was the idea.

It occurred to me that I really wasn't picking my female hiking companions very well. One I'd practically had to carry through the wilderness, and this one looked as if, impatient with my clumsy progress, she wanted to carry me.

There was also the fact that the girl continued to make me uneasy. We'd divided up the handguns and ammo before starting out. That gave her enough firepower to take on the whole revolutionary army, such as it was; and I don't like having people with guns behind me whom I don't altogether trust. She was cute and sexy, she was bright and cheerful, she was proving herself to be stoical and enduring, and I had no doubt that she was brave; but she came from a background I could never understand, and the atavistic instinct that had saved me many times before still warned me that, small and attractive though she was, she was dangerous. Whether she was just generally a dangerous young lady, or specifically dangerous to me in this particular situation, remained to be seen.

I was navigating by time. Figuring our speed over that rugged terrain at two miles per hour, I calculated that it should take us

234

until roughly eight-forty on my watch—two hours—to put us opposite our destination. However, it was only a few minutes past eight o'clock when Antonia tapped me on the shoulder and pointed east.

"I think far enough," she said. "I think Piedras Negras there. We look?"

I studied her face for a moment, wondering how much more she knew than she'd told me. If anything. Maybe I was borrowing trouble. After all, some people have a sharper sense of country than others, and my primitive time-and-velocity calculations weren't infallible. We could have made better progress than I'd estimated. Or Arturo could have been dealing in short kilometers.

"Sure, if you think so," I said.

I led the way to the top cautiously, by way of a brushy notch that afforded good cover. We crawled to a vantage point from which, still hidden, we could look out across the valley. As Arturo had said, you couldn't miss them. Apparently there had been a prehistoric volcanic disturbance in the mountains across the way, accompanied by a lava flow that had hardened as it cooled, like black fudge, and had then been split into jagged blocks by centuries of erosion, bite-sized candies for a rock-eating giant, casually spilled out of a great bowl in the mountainside opposite. From the north-south road that was clearly visible over there, presumably the same road we'd seen on our first view of the valley, lower down, a small track ran up into the disorganized jumble of black stone blocks.

I said, "If there's a village, it's got to be right up in those rocks. We can't cross over to it here without being seen, the damn valley is too open. It seems to get narrower up above, and I think I see better cover there, so we'd better keep going another kilometer or so. Then we'll slip across and come back down the foothills on the other side. We can hope they won't be expecting trouble from the north. A superannuated gent like pore ole gray-whiskered H. H. Cody, plumb exhausted from being chased from country to country, feeble from loss of blood, wouldn't be likely to make any wide five- or six-mile mountain detours, even assuming that he was still capable of getting around on foot. What do you say?''

There was no answer. I looked sharply at my companion; she was staring across the valley with odd intentness.

I asked, ''Do you see something? Have they got a man watching in those rocks?''

''*Qué dice*? Oh . . . oh, yes, I think I see man moving. Not see now.''

I didn't think she'd seen any man, but I said, ''Maybe it's not such a bad idea to rest and watch for a bit, see if anybody goes in or out. Hell, we've got all day.''

I got out the telescope, and we settled down comfortably in the brush. Antonia slipped off a moccasin and picked a thorn out of her foot.

''You have plan, Cody?''

I said, ''Well, I think I'm probably going to kill somebody, if you want to call that a plan. I'm getting a little tired of being ambushed and hunted. I think it's time to do some ambushing and hunting. Maybe I can make somebody mad enough to do something stupid.''

''Somebody? What somebody?''

''Well, I'm hoping for a mystery man called Sábado, but I'll settle for your friend Carlos Mondragon, if you're still of the same mind about him.''

''If you mean I kill him, I am still of mind. You think I find that *político* here?''

I shrugged. ''I think trapping Cody is basically a *gringo* operation, but they do like to use guerilla manpower when they can, like when they laid for me near Cananea, and even earlier when they arranged for the killing of Will Pierce and Millie Charles way down east of Mazatlán.''

''You think they make follow those two clear to Mazatlán; and then, on road to Durango, *poof*?'' She made a chopping motion with her hand.

''*Poof* is right,'' I said. ''Actually, that pursuit may have been Mondragon's own idea. He knew that Pierce was looking for the arms; hell, since Pierce hadn't been paid for them, they were still his, weren't they? His ticket back to financial respectability, maybe, if he could find somebody else, somebody with money, to buy them off him. Mondragon was undoubtedly informed of Pierce's visit to Arturo and his jaunt up this way, with the pretty lady in the white pants. It seems likely that he was as intrigued by the couple's subsequent mad dash south as I am. He couldn't help but think that Pierce had spotted something at Piedras Negras that gave him a clue to the whereabouts of the weapons and that he was heading south to check it out. I figure Mondragon loaded his murder crew into his little brown van and went after the couple to see what they were up to. When it began to appear they were leading him on a chase to nowhere he moved in on them, in his usual impatient fashion, tried his usual crude, muscular brand of interrogation, and wound up, as usual, with some dead bodies and no information."

Antonia said, "Not much bright, this Mondragon."

"Well, he's desperate; if he's ever going to get his revolution off the ground, he's got to have those arms. Of course his Yankee paymaster, who didn't give a hoot about the weapons now that the whole deal had gone sour, found the killings quite satisfactory. It wasn't feasible for him to silence everyone connected with the ill-fated arms deal; but he could at least take care of those who were likely to make trouble for him north of the border. As far as he was concerned, the only good Pierce was a dead Pierce, and the same went for Cody after he had the bad judgment to let it be known that he was going to spend his honeymoon in this area, presumably snooping. I figure the paymaster—call him Sábado—made a new deal with Mondragon: 'Take care of all these embarrassing Yankee characters for me, wipe them off the map, and you're welcome to the damned weapons if you can find them.' Which means, I figure, that Mondragon is right over there across the valley somewhere, waiting for us with his merry machete-men so he can carry out his part of the bargain. You may get a shot if you can figure out the right place to lay for him." I glanced at her. "Of course, it's likely to be risky. It could even get you killed."

She shrugged in the inimitably fatalistic way they have. "All peoples die. You let Antonia look though glass, please?"

"Sorry. Anytime."

I watched her as she adjusted the telescope to her vision. She looked cute trying to squinch her left eye closed as she peered through it; but something about her expression wasn't cute at all. She passed the instrument back without speaking.

I asked, "Did you see anything?"

"*Nada*. No *hombres*. Only birds. Maybe we go now, hey?"

She backed off the crest and started away at a good clip. I paused to take a final look through the little scope. I couldn't see any birds, except for a hovering buzzard, and you always see those. I couldn't see any *hombres* either. I had to hurry to catch up with Antonia. She made no move toward letting me resume the lead; she just kept loping along ahead of me in her lithe and silent way. She seemed to know where she was going. She found a twisting pass through the hills that took us over into General Santa Anna's valley, which we crossed by way of various arroyos and brushy gullies that hid us, we hoped, from any lookouts posted up high to the south of us, if they should bother to look our way. There was, as I'd said, no reason why they should. We hoped.

Then we were in the Santa Anna foothills and climbing. The week-old bullet crease and the days of inactivity were telling on me seriously now. The phony chest bandage impeded my breathing. Cody's clumsy boots didn't help, and maybe the fact that the kid was half my age gave her an additional edge; but I was damned if I was going to be outwalked or outclimbed by a lousy little Native Mexican wench wearing paper-thin moccasins and wrapped in a lousy blanket. I plugged along grimly in her wake.

"So. Now very careful. We look from top."

Following along breathlessly, I'd almost run into her when she stopped. She pointed to the top of the ridge we'd been climbing, where it came to a knobby point.

"From there see Piedras Negras, I think," Antonia said.

"Would they be likely to have a sentry there?"

"*Sí*. Could be man other side. Bad place for climb but good place for look." She hesitated. "I go?"

"Sure, you're quieter in those moccasins," I said. "You scout it out, since you obviously want to. But if there is a sentry, let me deal with him. I've had more sentries to practice on, probably, than you have. . . . Oh, just one thing. A favor, Antonia."

She made the inevitable Spanish response: "It is yours."

"I'd like to borrow your .22."

She frowned. "You want my little automatic gun you say no good? You make joke?" she asked. When I didn't speak, she shrugged. "I say is yours, okay, is yours. Here." Watching me hide it, she laughed with comprehension. "I see, you need very small gun for the boot. *Muy bueno!*"

Then we stood for a moment, facing each other. She was very foreign to me in that moment. In the next hour—hell, in the next few minutes—she might betray me completely, or she might lay down her life for me, and I wouldn't be surprised either way. She removed the *serape* and gave it to me to hold. Without her high heels and the bulky blanket she was almost tiny.

She gave me her beautiful big grin. "Not much lag, hey?" she said slyly.

"Don't rub it in. Just go away and let me finish catching my breath," I said. "Antonia."

"*Sí*."

"Be careful."

She rose on tiptoe and kissed me lightly on the cheek and was off up the slope, silently, fading from sight in the sparse brush almost at once. I sat down to wait, a little chilly in the shade of a bush since I'd worked up a good sweat on the way up. The same buzzard was still circling lazily over Piedras Negras, or where I figured Piedras Negras ought to be. He'd been joined by a friend. Or maybe they were two brand-new *zopilotes*. I guess all buzzards look alike to me.

I examined the *serape* she'd left with me, lumpy at one end with her small red shoes; there were pockets in the coarse material to hold them. There was also a partial box of high-speed

239

.22s, but I left it there; no sense packing a hideout gun and then lugging extra ammo where it would be found by the first man to shake me down. Not that I expected to be caught and searched, but it was in the realm of possibility. . . .

"There is one man." Antonia had returned as silently as she'd departed. "Sit against rock, smoke cigarette, I smell, a hundred meters easy."

"Yank or Mex?"

"He is *gringo*, I think. Much yellow hair like girl. Talk on little radio. No hear good, too far, but words sound *inglés*." She'd retrieved her *serape* and was putting it back on as she spoke.

I said, "They do love their electronics." I glanced at my watch. "That would have been just about ten o'clock; maybe he checks in on the hour. I can't think of any reason a *gringo* would be up here except to help them get me. Well, Cody. So I guess I'm entitled to get him if I can. Did he have a rifle?"

"*Sí.*"

"A real rifle or an assault rifle?"

She frowned, not quite sure of the distinction. "It was long gun with telescope and the handle to be pulled and pushed, very *anticuado*. Old-fashion."

"Hey, a bolt-action job with a scope. Well, that figures; it's good sniper country. Okay, I can use that gun." I took out the flat little Russell knife and checked the edge; but Jo Beckman hadn't dulled it significantly with her surgery. "You wait here, please," I said to Antonia.

She shook her head quickly. "I come with, *por favor*. Very quiet, Antonia, stay back enough, okay?"

I frowned at her for a moment. That she knew more than she was telling was obvious. She'd led us to this vantage point without hesitation; clearly she'd been in the area before. She was keeping something from me, and any sensible pro would have strangled her on the spot rather than run the risk of having her, loaded with guns, behind him. I saw that she knew exactly what I was thinking and found it amusing. Anyway, I liked the kid,

240

and too much suspicion can be counterproductive, and to hell with it.

"Sure," I said. "You'd better carry this damn conspicuous hat of Cody's for me. Next guy I impersonate, I hope he goes in for berets or small black beanies. Where do I find this cigarette-happy character?"

Antonia took the hat and rifle. Something had changed between us; my gesture of confidence had made a difference, although I couldn't have said how.

She said, "If you make to the right, *a la derecha*, and climb only fifty meters, maybe, and progress around hill, you will see big stone with tree behind. He is there. *Vaya con Díos, amigo.*"

I couldn't help remembering that the last Mexican citizen who'd bid me go with God was the one who'd sent me into this elaborate mousetrap. But you have to trust somebody; and the man was exactly where she'd said he would be. I wished for a nice dark turtleneck and some durable pants and some silent shoes, or at least just the silent shoes; but there was a considerable breeze rustling the brush and grass of the hillside, and he wasn't really listening for footsteps. He didn't expect to have to deal with anything close enough for him to hear it. He was just looking off to the south and west, every so often making a careful scan of mountains and valley with a pair of big binoculars, 7×50s by the look of them. Night glasses, suggesting that he'd been up here watching for us since before dawn; he was getting bored and tired now.

As Antonia had said, he had shoulder-length blond hair streaming out below a wide-brimmed hat, General Custer style. Well, poor Custer lost his scalp at the Little Bighorn or the Greasy Grass or whatever you want to call it. I waited for a good rushing gust of wind, pitched a pebble beyond him, and while he was half-raised looking that way, got an arm around his face from behind and cut his throat with the three-inch Russell blade, learning that the flat, little all-steel knife, while very good for concealment, became quite slippery when wet. Well, you can't have everything.

An odd, low, warbling birdcall made me look around, still holding him. Antonia was crouched on the slope above me.

"Make okay?" she whispered. "*Bueno*. I come down, hey?"

I shrugged. If she wanted to see a dead man, that was her concern. Sliding down to me, she had her look, her face quite without expression, which must have taken some doing. I mean, when you sever a man's carotid and jugular you get a lot of blood and it isn't nice. Antonia didn't even gulp once. She just reached out her hand for the knife I still held.

"I clean."

"Not if you're going to jab it into the ground like I've seen some dodos do it. I spent a lot of time putting a good edge on that blade."

"You think *estúpido*? Clean with grass, okay?"

While she was busy, I planted the guy back where he'd been, seated against his rock. Checking, I found that he carried no IDs, not even phony ones. A right-hip holster held the same model four-inch-barreled Colt as I'd found in Cody's paper-bag collection. His binoculars were kind of messy; but I found a clean handkerchief in his pocket with which to wipe them, and hung them around my neck. His hat, which had come off, I put back on his head, tipped over his eyes. His little two-way radio, fortunately, had escaped the flood; a red indicator light showed that it was turned on and, presumably, receiving, although there seemed to be nothing to receive at the moment. I hooked it onto my belt with the clip provided. Then I turned my attention to the rifle leaning against the rock beside him.

In this day of complex automatic weapons, there's something beautifully simple-minded about a bolt-action rifle, basically just a steel tube with a removable plug at one end fastened to a piece of wood. This was a Ruger M-77 with a barrel that looked very slim and clean because there was no front sight to mar its lines; there was no rear sight either. There was only the big variable telescope, one modern accessory I'm happy to adopt since it makes long-range shooting much easier. I hoped the dead man had sighted it in carefully; there was no way for me to check it out now.

I wasn't too happy about the caliber: .243, or 6mm. With its little, 100-grain bullet—there are lighter slugs but for a man-sized target like Horace Hosmer Cody he'd have picked the heaviest generally available—the .243 is a marginal cartridge as far as I'm concerned, losing a lot of its punch beyond three hundred yards where a 180-grain, .30-caliber projectile is effective well past six hundred. But at least I had a rifle, which was a relief; this was not good pistol country. A half-gallon canteen of water let me rinse myself off a little better. There was also a half-full quart Thermos of coffee lying beside the green backpack in which he'd brought his géar to this viewpoint. Inside the pack I found a box of .243 cartridges, which I pocketed, 100-grainers as I'd guessed, and two sandwiches done up in neat little baggies. I poured a cup of coffee and handed it to Antonia, who gave me my hat and my well-cleaned knife in return.

"Ham or cheese?" I asked.

"*Queso, por favor.* Here, you drink a little."

We stood there eating the dead man's sandwiches and passing his coffee cup back and forth since, inconsiderately, he'd only brought the one that came with the Thermos. It was callous of us, I suppose, but it had been a long, dry, hungry morning, and I've seen dead men before; I was only surprised that the girl could take it so casually. Most girls I'd known wouldn't have eaten for a week after being exposed to such a horrible sight. As if reading my thoughts, she wiped her mouth and looked down at the body approvingly.

"You kill good," she said calmly. "Like Indian. Maybe join tribe, hey?" She flashed a grin at me to show it was a joke.

"Just waiting for an invitation," I said. "What tribe?"

Her grin faded. "No more tribe. All fat and stupid and frighted. You, me, we make new tribe. Go warpath, scare shits from everybody, ha!"

I said, "Well, first we'd better get the hell out of here, before they start calling up their boy and get no answer."

She said, "Wait. You come to see Piedras Negras. *Por favor*, the little spyglass?" When I gave it to her, she peered through it for a moment. "Yes, look down there."

243

She pointed. There was no village. There was only a clearing among the tumbled black blocks of stone, a small amphitheater, far below us to the south; and at first I thought I saw three fat men in formal black suits walking around it in an odd, drunken manner, which didn't make sense. I put the liberated binoculars to my eyes. I had to give one ocular some spit and a swipe with my own handkerchief before I could focus. Then the magnified scene became clear, and I could see that the creatures waddling around the clearing weren't men at all, but birds. Very large black birds with ugly red heads. They were pecking at some sprawling objects down there that seemed to have been pretty well picked over already.

"Let me introduce." Antonia's voice, from behind me, was expressionless. "*A la izquierda*, most left, is Señor Enrique Serafin Ruiz. In back, far back, Señor Bernardo Bustamente, who try to run away but not enough fast. More *a la derecha*, right, and more closer, Señor Eloy Miera. And most right, Señor Santos Delgado, who seem to have lose the head, *qué lástima*. . . ."

CHAPTER 27

I studied the distant scene thoughtfully through the liberated binoculars. Instinct told me that casual was the way to play it; the kid was watching me and, pretty tough herself, she wasn't going to respect a man who got all upset about a few dead bodies.

I said, "Well, you can't say Arturo isn't a man of his word. He was paid to direct us to the current place of residence of those truck drivers; and there they are. I suppose that's what Will Pierce and his Millie saw when they drove in there, although the bodies were fresher then."

"*Sí*, much more fresher, much more *zopilotes* eating; more *cuervos*—crows. Very disgusting sight, I think. Horrible, yes? Big joke of Arturo. He say so-proud Yankee woman much *histórico*, much *vomito*, much fonny, much scream and sob. '*Fuck your lousy guns,*' she scream, '*get me out of this dreadful country.*' "

So much for the theory that Pierce had found a clue here. All he'd found was a charnel yard that had turned his handsome, ambitious lady inside out—there would have been a solid black mass of scavengers on the bodies back then, ripping and tearing—and transformed her into a sick, frightened creature concerned only with home and safety. There's a breed of civilized predator that can perpetrate all kinds of ruthless atrocities as long as there's no blood involved; however, faced with true, gory, deadly ruthlessness, these dainty menaces, male or female, invariably react by losing their lunches and scrambling for the nearest exit.

It appeared that Arturo, whose humble abode Mrs. Charles had scorned, had followed the couple to see the result of his big joke and had undoubtedly found it most satisfying. Yielding to his lady's panic, Will Pierce had renounced all hope of retrieving the lost arms—with the drivers as dead as Medina and unable to reveal the hiding place, it wasn't much of a hope anyway. Knowing that they were probably under surveillance, he'd fled with her south to Mazatlán meaning to swing east through Durango and Torreón where they could pick up the main highway back north to El Paso and so complete the detour around the area in which the *insurgentes* operated. However, Mondragon had followed, and they hadn't made it. Scratch one William Walter Pierce, elderly and susceptible and not excessively honest, and one Millicent Charles, whose stomach hadn't been as strong as her ambition.

Antonia had some pertinent questions to answer, of course, but this wasn't the time to ask them. Instead I asked, "Can you find me a spot from which I can study the whole mountainside? I want to see if there are any of this character's friends stationed around here."

"Yes, sure, you follow."

Scrambling along behind her, I noted that she was pretty well loaded down with firearms now, having quietly appropriated the dead man's revolver, which seemed fair enough, since I had his rifle. She found me a better vantage point with good cover near the top of the knoll. It let me survey most of the big bowl through which the molten lava had poured before spilling over into the valley below. I couldn't locate the source of the flow; erosion had pretty well ground down these mountains, leaving no easily recognizable cones or craters. Well, I wasn't hunting volcanos. But it was Antonia who spotted the next watcher, about a half mile along the slope, when he got careless with his binoculars.

"I'm afraid he's a dark-faced local lad," I said after making a careful study through the 7×50s. "And that *bandido* mustache. No open season. Find me a *gringo*, please."

"Yes, I think *Mexicano*." Antonia lowered the little telescope. "But if he hunt you, why you care?"

I said, 'I've got a boss in Washington, sure; but locally I'm working for a gent with a certain amount of clout . . . influence. He can help me get away with a reasonable amount of rough stuff; and nobody on this side of the border is going to worry too much if a bunch of Yankee thugs, who're probably here illegally, and who're certainly carrying illegal arms, and undoubtedly engaged in illegal activities, go and get themselves quietly terminated. Too bad about them. As you say, *qué lástima*, what a crying shame. But we've got four Mexican corpses over there already. To be sure, they weren't real solid citizens, and they died running guns for the revolution, but I'd better not crowd my luck, or the tolerance of my *patrón*, by giving him too much additional Mexican blood to wipe off the record. If that character over there was coming at me with hostile intentions—like the karate lady in the motel in Hermosillo—I wouldn't hesitate to take him out; but as long as I can pick and choose I'll keep on hunting the *extranjeros* and let the *nativos* go." I glanced at her. "That must have been quite a massacre down there. I suppose I should have realized that Medina wasn't going to trust those truck drivers to keep their traps shut after they'd helped him hide the arms, no matter what they promised and how much he paid them. Fine old custom. Hell, the legendary buccaneers of the Spanish Main always slaughtered the crews that helped them bury their treasure chests."

There was a little pause; then Antonia said, "Jorge gorgeous man but not much smart. Trust anybody. Other peoples must think for him always. Sooch a beautiful baby, my Jorge."

I was a little startled. I suppose I'd assumed right along that Jorge Medina, kind of a shadowy figure, had been a moderately clever operator who, even in death, had outsmarted his murderers by withholding from them the merchandise they wanted so badly, the weapons he'd acquired as agent for Will Pierce. But apparently I'd credited Señor Medina with more brains than he'd possessed.

I said, "So hiding the arms was your idea."

She laughed shortly. "Hey, I sit in Jorge's peekup when they talk. I look at tall sneaky *político*, so much handsome, so much

247

stupid, so much ambitious, so much greedy. I think he now crying big tears inside because he must pay first-money to Jorge or there will be no weapons. I see he will never pay second-money like promise, not with other men to help him, no way, José. Take arms, laugh at my poor foolish Jorge. Maybe kill." She shrugged. "I must protect, okay?"

I said, "As a matter of fact, Mondragon apparently never got his hands on the final payment, so he couldn't have handed it over even if he'd wanted to."

"No difference. Money, no money, take guns anyway. Like I say before, I tell Jorge first he big fool to get mixed up with man like the Cody you call Pierce. Much big dealer, use Jorge for risk while he for safe, always. But my Jorge no listen, he want rich. Shiny car for him; for me pretty dresses, shoes. I say to him, how many cars you drive dead, how many shoes I wear dead? You think deal guns with crazy *insurgentes* is game like baseball, football? But my Jorge no listen." She gave her expressive shrug again. "So he want rich, I try make rich. I tell what he do, careful no hurt the big pride, you know. Very proud man, my Jorge. I make think idea all his, you know. Say how smart, how brave. Sit in peekup while he makes negotiate with Arturo. Negotiate, right?"

"Negotiate is correct," I said.

"Sooch big word. Antonia no come with to Bahia San Cristóbal to get weapons from ship, man's work, ha! Wait at Piedras Negras with peekup hide in rocks. Wait. So much wait. But now come the four big empty *camiones*, Jorge signal all hiding done safe, such relief, imagine."

She was getting to the tough part, and the narration was slowing down; I had to keep nudging her along.

"I can imagine," I said.

"Jorge pay off men. Money for the load, the drive, the unload. And the keep quiet. Much money for the *silencia*, yes? Tell men leave trucks here at Piedras Negras, ride to El Mirador in peekup, never tell, promise. Much promise. Promise on the blood of the Christ, the nails of the Cross, the robe of the Virgin, the gray hairs of the mother, ha! I go bring peekup, stop twenty

248

meters away, men turn from Jorge and come to ride, my Jorge shoot Miera first like I tell him, most big and dangerous. I, Antonia, shoot Ruiz who try to grab and use for shield. No more shoot from my Jorge on knees, cry like baby, sooch a gentle man. Bustamente run, I shoot not much good with little gun so far. I shoot Delgado very good and go finish Bustamente. Finish Miera, too, tough man, not die so easy. Leave moneys on dead men for Arturo like bargain."

Well, it was what I'd sensed, wasn't it? The kid was dangerous, a natural killer. Considering my own profession, I was hardly in a position to criticize. In fact, I found it an intriguing picture, professionally speaking: the slim, pretty, brown girl with the big dazzling grin shooting three men with her toy .22 and then calmly finishing off a fourth who'd been badly shot by her incompetent lover—not to mention working out the homicidal plan in the first place and selling it to the handsome, weak-kneed Medina. On the other hand, I'd learned that what I'd sensed about her, what had disturbed me, had apparently been the danger-aura of past deaths, not of deaths to come, including mine. At least I could hope so. As far as moral judgments were concerned, this was no place for them, and they're outside my field of competence anyway.

I said, "You mean Arturo was in on it?"

She shrugged. "He find to drive *camiones* bad men he no like and promise no interfere, *si*? For that we leave the moneys we pay the drivers." She giggled. "Better he should get from deads than me. Much *sangre*, blood, not nice. Jorge very much the sick, very much the unhappy, say he should never have let persuade—persuade?—such a terrible thing, we must leave terrible place *pronto*. I have much trouble make him finish plan, but is necessary, I make him see. He drive one big truck to place near Kino; I drive him back in peekup. Do same three more times, Jorge cry all the time, sick again, such a lovely, sensitive fellow. Call Antonia ugly names, leave Antonia in Kino, poosh out of peekup, say take bus, walk, fly, he never want to see Antonia again, bad, bad girl. Then he go with other drivers and be stupid kill. All kill." She spread her hands in a questioning gesture. ''Why Jorge say rich if blood make sick? Never rich without blood, everybodies know. Not peoples like us. Why hate Antonia only try to help? Sooch beautiful, foolish man I love, all dead now.'' Her voice was harsh, and when I glanced at her, I saw that she was crying silently; then she sniffed, cleared her throat softly, swiped the rough *serape* across her face, and said, ''You see the one by dead cottonwood?''

''I see him.''

''That one is *gringo* for you.''

I'd already determined that, mostly by the hat: Yankees seem to crease and wear their hats differently from Mexicans, who manage to make everything they put on their heads so squarely look like stock movie *sombreros*. The range was too long for a shot with the .243, although a well-sighted-in 7mm or .30 Magnum could possibly have reached that far effectively; but it was too early to start shooting anyway.

''Lead the way,'' I said. ''Take us well behind your nearby countryman; we don't want to risk alerting him.''

The radio on my belt cleared its throat. ''Alpha, Alpha. This is Gamma calling Alpha.''

''Come in, Gamma.''

Fortunately the gent from whom I'd got the thing had set the intercom volume quite low; but it was still a startling amount of sound to be hit with when you were trying for stealth. I should have anticipated it, of course. Blame the crack on the head, or just plain stupidity. I sank down among the rocks and fumbled with the controls, reducing the volume of the next transmission. I saw that Antonia remained standing, in the shelter of a bush, glassing the nearest sentry, the Mexican, to see if he'd been disturbed. Well, at least somebody in this idiot expedition had a few brains.

The radio whispered, ''Gamma reporting. Stationed at pass, keeping red GMC truck under surveillance, as instructed, heard vehicle approaching. Maintained cover, watched four-wheel-drive Subaru station wagon appear, color silver; although how the hell anybody got such a low-slung little heap up that lousy road is beyond me. . . .''

"Never mind the irrelevant comments; continue report."

"Yes, sir. Vehicle stopped, driver got out, female. High brown boots, snug white jeans, loose blue shirt, lots of Indian jewelry. Examined GMC, tried door, found it locked. Studied ground, started to follow tracks of subject and female companion, which unfortunately brought her too close to my station. Figured I'd better get the drop on her before she spotted me. Took her by surprise, no trouble, although she was packing a loaded Beretta nine emm emm. ID in the name of Joanna Charles Beckman, M.D. Instructions?"

"Handcuff her and hold her there. Don't come in. Repeat, don't come in. Subjects should be getting close to us here; indications are they left the pickup you're watching several hours ago. We don't want any suspicious traffic on the road to spook them. Stay clear."

I had the voice identified now, even though the fidelity of the tiny speaker left a good deal to be desired, particularly at the low volume I was using. Alpha was Marion Rutherford, the big, boyish gent called Tunk whom I'd first seen through the telescope at Cananea and later encountered very briefly, at close range, in Hermosillo before young Charles blew the lights out— well, my lights, at least—with the same 9mm Beretta that had, apparently, just been taken from his sister. I realized that I was disappointed; I'd been hoping for another voice.

"Received and understood. Gamma out."

The radio went silent. After a little, Antonia, who'd come to crouch beside me, asked, "What Alpha, Gamma?"

"They're using the Greek alphabet for code names. Alpha, beta, gamma, delta, epsilon, and that's as far as I remember it. Why they don't just call the guys Joe and Bob, I don't know. Some people simply have to be fancy."

She was studying my face intently. "We go help your medical lady?"

I drew a long breath. I said, "We don't perform heroic rescues of irrelevant females around here, small fry. She got herself into trouble; she can get herself out. That goes for you, too, as I told you. Nobody invited either of you babes on this picnic;

251

you're both just excess baggage as far as I'm concerned. Now let's see about the *gringo* under the tree. . . . What the hell are you grinning about?"

"Good man," Antonia said.

It was clear that she'd expected me to chicken out; she'd thought I'd drop everything and rush off breathlessly to get the nasty handcuffs off my beloved. Well, I wasn't sure how much love was involved—after all, except for a sweet quickie in front of the fire, I hardly knew the woman except as my stern doctor and efficient nurse—but the impulse had been there, all right. I'd tried to kid myself that I should find out what the hell Jo was doing here, but it really didn't matter, and it was impractical anyway. I had more important concerns right here. Didn't I?

"Good man, hell," I said. "Just pure golden bastard clear through."

"Good bastard," Antonia said. "We go kill *gringo* now?"

252

CHAPTER 28

CROUCHING behind a rock, watching the man under the dead tree, I wondered how many other lookouts they had stationed around—three seemed already redundant, indicating either that somebody was pretty nervous, or that he didn't trust his observers not to go to sleep, or both. Then I wondered how the kid planned to go about it.

"Is my turn," she'd said.

We'd paused for breath in a little stand of aspens that overlooked the skeletal cottonwood that was our target, over a hundred and fifty slanting yards below us. I'd taken out my knife to recheck the edge; but she'd placed a hand on my wrist.

"Is my turn, *hombre*. You go down to big gray stone, easy shoot if I have *problema*, okay?"

There was a nice eagerness in her small face. She wanted the job very badly; but I wasn't happy about her request. This wasn't a training mission put on to break in the rookies, for Christ's sake. The fact that she'd once been lucky enough to overcome some unarmed men in a few blazing seconds of gunfire didn't mean she was qualified to tackle a trained, armed agent like, probably, the character under the dead tree. If I let her go, and she goofed and forced me to shoot to bail her out, we'd wind up in a general firefight sooner than I'd planned. On the other hand . . .

On the other hand, she was a unique specimen in a world of tender ladies who couldn't bear the thought of guns or violence. Keeping her leashed would be an offense against nature, like calling a beagle off a rabbit or asking a good pointer to ignore a covey of quail. Besides, I might as well learn if she was really up to the job before I sent her off to deal with General Southpaw.

I said, "Okay, I'll be by that rock if you need me. Good hunting."

Now I was waiting to see her or hear her, but the mountainside remained undisturbed. Well, I told myself, that just meant she was making her approach properly, meaning invisibly and silently. The man under the tree made a careful sweep with his binoculars, which seemed to be identical to the ones I'd taken from his colleague. He leaned forward to pour himself a cup of coffee from a camouflaged Thermos that I also recognized—hell, they might as well be wearing uniforms, the amount of standardized equipment they were packing, but the weapon leaning beside him was an automatic M-16 assault rifle, not a scope-sighted Ruger bolt-action. This was a dark-haired specimen who kept it cut fairly short, as opposed to the flowing George Armstrong Custer hairdo of the other. No hat.

He threw his head back and raised his elbow high to drain the coffee cup. There was a small, solid thud, the sound of something hard and sharp burying itself in something moderately soft. Well, to be honest, I'm not that good at sounds; I'd caught the glint of the throwing knife before it struck. The man dropped his cup. His mouth opened, but no scream came out, just a barely audible—at my distance—gasp of pure agony. Then there was a rattle of dislodged stones beyond him, and a blanket floated into sight, spread out like a cast net. It dropped over his head. Antonia was right with it, wrapping up his head like a presentation grapefruit and holding the muffling *serape* in place with one arm while the other hand groped for and found the weapon buried under the armpit, wrenched it free, and drove it home a second time. By the time I reached her, she'd laid the man down, freed the *serape*, and put it back on. She was squatting beside him, wiping her blade on his shirt. She looked up at me. Her eyes were strange and shiny; for a moment she was just another dangerous predator crouching over its kill, not quite human. Or very human, depending on your definition of humanity.

"So, *amigo*?" she whispered.

"Muy bien, guapa," I said.

She giggled abruptly. "Your Spanish accent, it is much awful! And I am not your *guapa*. But I do okay, you think?"

I didn't feel it was the right time to point out that she'd been very lucky—we'd been very lucky—that the man hadn't screamed; and that we don't like that throwing-knife routine even when silence is not required. There's a lot of bone in a human body, and slipping a blade accurately between the ribs is difficult enough at contact range. From ten or twelve feet away, it's strictly a game of chance.

"You did fine," I said.

But she'd been testing me; now she lowered the boom. "So much boolsheet you talk!" she said scornfully. "No give more sooch crap, never! Antonia do all wrong, yes? Is plan to come in fast, use *serape* to confuse, blind, make silent, then *cuchillo*, knife, but last five meters all loose rock, impossible to move quiet. So instead make big gamble with the throwing, sorry. A little fright, maybe; very nervous girl, Antonia."

I said, "Sure. Terrible girl. But the job got done, which is what counts, right?"

She shrugged. "If you say." She looked down at the body. "Why we kill him, anyway?"

She was really, as I'd said, a terrible little girl; here she'd killed a man simply because I'd told her the season was open on Yankees of a certain persuasion without really understanding why he was needed dead.

"I told you," I said, "I want to get a certain gent good and mad. Mad enough to commit himself openly instead of hiding in the woodwork the way he's been doing. In the meantime, it reduces the odds a bit, and they surely do need shrinking. Horatius at the bridge facing the whole Etruscan army had nothing on us."

She wasn't interested in any legendary old Romans and their legendary old problems. "Where you think Mondragon hide?"

I gestured toward the jumble of black stone blocks far below us. "Oh, they've probably got him waiting down in that mess somewhere, ready to move in with his boys to do the machete-work and take the credit as soon as his *gringo* allies get us pinned down for him. But let's not worry about him yet; first let's find another sniper."

"Sniper?"

"They're bound to have at least one more scope-sighted rifle backing up the short-range boys with the automatic M-16s, like this one and the Mexican gent we bypassed. Those two men, and the one whose gun I'm packing, were too high to do any good immediately; obviously they were parked up here to watch, pass the word when we appeared, and then slip down the mountain to take us by surprise if the boys down below goofed and let us get forted up somewhere. But they'd have at least one rifle down where it could get into action right away. Since they seem to go in for standardization, their sharpshooter is probably packing a .243 like mine. That means we don't have to worry about any really long-range marksmanship—no half-mile miracles—since with that small caliber, if he knows his stuff, he won't let them station him much more than three hundred meters from the action."

I frowned at the big bowl below us; hell, maybe the whole thing was an ancient crater with one side blown out by the original explosion to form the wide notch by which the road entered from the valley below. I started working the binoculars very slowly across the areas where a sharpshooter might be stationed.

I spoke without lowering the glasses: "I figure that originally they were working on the theory that, following Arturo's instructions, Cody would drive innocently to the picturesque little native village of Piedras Negras to interview some truck drivers about some arms—not knowing that Arturo was playing a joke on him as he had on Will Pierce, and there was no village, and the drivers were dead. So they set their elaborate trap accordingly, using enough men so there was no chance of the old coot escaping them again. There's a detail that may be bothering them a little now; they know you're with me, you heard the man on the radio mention my female companion. Presumably they got the word from Arturo, who'd also have let them know that Señorita Antonia Sisneros is quite aware that Piedras Negras is no center of population, just an overgrown rock pile, and that, while she's a little shy about admitting it, she's got particularly good reason to know that Señor Enrique Serafin Ruiz and Company, while present, are not in condition to be interviewed. But to hell with that, they don't care what game you're playing, holding out on me, letting me waste my time trying to get information from a bunch of dead truck drivers you shot yourself. . . ."

"Kill so many is hard to say. Afraid you have disgust for Antonia."

I said, "Cut it out! You saw me shoot that woman in Hermosillo; you knew damn well that a few dead bodies wouldn't bother me. What's the real reason you played along with Arturo's little joke?"

She said a bit sulkily, "If you know men dead, you no come where Mondragon wait, help me kill him."

I said, "As a matter of fact you were wrong there; I'd have come even if I'd known there was no information about the arms to be had. I told you, I'm tired of being chased; I'm ready to do a little chasing. Anyway, the boys might have worried that you'd spill the beans to Cody, and he'd give up on Piedras Negras, and they'd have all their trouble for nothing, except for the fact that they found our pickup. Clearly Mr. Cody is still coming, limping along feebly on foot. He wouldn't have left the vehicle if he'd received discouraging information from you and decided to give up on this expedition. So the orders went out to keep the boys in ambush position. . . . Only they didn't expect us to make as wide a detour as we actually made, and they don't seem to take their red-alert status very seriously, judging by the ease with which we've slipped up on a couple of them already. We can thank the fact that they think they're dealing with a sick old man and a silly young girl with a .22 pistol who may be sudden death on unarmed truck drivers—if Arturo has told them that much of your story—but can obviously be no serious threat to fine, clean-cut, well-armed, American boys skilled in all the arts of secret mayhem.''

"You no like fine American boys?" Antonia was frowning a little, puzzled. "You no like your country, *hombre*?"

I grinned. "My country's great," I said. "It's just some of my countrymen who aren't so terrific, particularly when they start wandering around other people's countries. It's a scary thing, the number of Americans who'd blow their collective stacks if a lousy outlander came to the U.S. and had the nerve to start telling us how to run our country, but who feel they have a perfect right to tell him how to run his." I shrugged. "This particular bunch of improve-the-dumb-foreigner jerks, who've been trying to give you Mexicans a change of government they think you need even if you're too stupid to know it, seem to've got their *cojones* caught in the international wringer. They're trying very hard to get out of the pinch with their balls intact by eliminating, or getting Mondragon to eliminate, everyone who might be in a position to tell Washington about their busybody international activities. They had Pierce killed, that was easy. Now they're after Cody, but the old guy is giving them a hell of a run. By now they're desperate enough to give Operation Cody the big treatment—they must have brought a dozen armed men across the border, not to mention the Mexican allies—but unfortunately for them there's a slight mixup of identities. They've set their fancy trap for a wounded old fox, and we're going to give them wolf all the way. . . . There's our rifleman.''

I pointed. It was the logical place for a sharpshooter, on the southern point overlooking the gap in the crater wall. From there he could cover the main road out in the valley and the little side road heading up into Piedras Negras—it passed right below him—and he might even be able to cover the whole length of the track into the rocky clearing where the bodies lay, although from our vantage point high up on the opposite wall of the great bowl it was hard to tell what kind of a view he had that way, toward us. He was reasonably well hidden, but it was one of the most likely places for him to be and, keeping the glasses on it steadily for several minutes, I'd finally spotted a movement when he got fidgety and changed position over there.

He was much too far away to reach with a bullet, of course, even with a heavier gun than the one I'd liberated. I'd have to work my way clear around the basin and find a vantage point on the ridge above the point—behind him, since he was facing north—that gave me a clear shot of, I hoped, no more than a couple of hundred yards since I was using a totally unfamiliar rifle, and although, working for an organization like this, the previous owner had undoubtedly sighted it in carefully according to his own theories, I had no way of knowing what they had been.

"Delta One."

Tunk Rutherford's voice came softly over the little radio on my belt, as well as from the one on the dead man's belt. I made a gesture, and Antonia unclipped that and hooked it onto the top of her jeans.

"Delta One. Hey, wake up, Sam, let's have your eleven o'clock check-in. . . . Delta One. Delta One. Alpha calling Delta One. Sammy, where the hell are you?" There was a little pause; then Rutherford spoke again: "Delta Two. Delta Two."

"Delta Two is here. See nothing, hear nothing, have nothing to report." The voice had a strong Spanish accent: this must be the dark-faced gent we'd bypassed. "You wish I check on Señor Gainer? I mean, Delta One?"

"Yeah, get over there, will you, Lupe, and let me know what's going on. . . . Delta Three. Delta Three. Delta Three, this is Alpha calling Delta Three. . . . What the fuck is going on up on that fucking mountain? Alpha calling Delta Three. Come in, Willy, damn you! Alpha calling Delta Three. Shit . . . Delta Four, can you see either One or Three from your post? Are you there, Delta Four?"

Antonia had slipped away to retrieve the gear she'd shed

to make her stalk. Now, returning, she picked up the dead man's M-16 and held it out, gesturing toward the various buttons and levers. Wordlessly, listening to the radio, I showed her how to cock it, switch it from safe to full- or semi-auto, and replace the magazine when empty. Meanwhile the radio kept on talking.

"Delta Four. Dammit Hank, come in. . . ."

"For Christ's sake let a man zip his pants, Tunk." The new voice sounded slightly breathless. "Into each life a little urine must fall. This is Cramer, I mean Delta Four, what do you want besides my eleven o'clock?"

"What's wrong with peeing at your post, Dumbo? If you've got to be delicate about it and go off somewhere, take the two-way with you, dammit! Now listen, something's haywire, neither Sam nor Willy are answering. The chances of both of them having radio trouble aren't real big, if you know what I mean."

"You think that old fart is cruising around up here with a silent raygun or something?"

"That old fart didn't need a raygun to get away from us once, and he's stayed ahead of us even though he keeps leaving bloody footprints everywhere he walks. Maybe he's carrying a pot of chicken blood to make us think we hit him harder than we did. So you watch it, and don't let him catch you squatting to shit or something."

"What about Lupe?"

"If you'd been listening like you should, you'd know that Delta Two is okay; he's heading over to check on Sam. You slip over and see what's wrong with Willy, but for Christ's sake watch yourself."

"Kind of funny if he got One and Three and skipped over Two, Tunk? Maybe he's got something against us *Americanos*."

"We don't know he's got anybody, yet, if there is a he. Maybe it's a magnetic disturbance or something in this volcanic nightmare and they just aren't coming through. Get over there and check, on the double. No. I take that back. Take it easy and watch your back all the way."

"Delta Four out."

After a moment, Rutherford's voice came again: "Gamma, Gamma, this is Alpha calling Gamma."

"Right here, Tunk. I mean Alpha. I've been listening. What's on your mind?"

"Leave the GMC and the Subaru, get in your own heap, and bring the prisoner to HQ. There's something funny going on, and I don't want you way off there in left field. Watch it, watch it, watch it. The rest of you guys stay where you were put, and remember, if somebody's got Sam or Willy, he's got their radios, so be kind of careful what you say on the air, hear?"

An unidentified voice I hadn't heard before grumbled: "Aren't you overreacting, Tunk? Hell, it's just one old goat with a hole in his back!"

"One old goat who got Ralph and Coonie in El Paso and took your gun away, hotshot. And you seem to have forgotten that we're also dealing with a cute little Indian bitch who shot four men dead with a lousy .22, right over there in those rocks, and left them for the buzzards."

Somebody else laughed. "Hey, Tunk, isn't that the dame who got the drop on you in that motel in Hermosillo . . . ?"

"Alpha, Alpha, Delta Two is call Alpha."

"Alpha here. Report."

"Sí, señor. Señor Gainer has the throat very much cut, with very sharp knife, I think a small one."

There was a moment of silence; then an unidentified voice in the radio said, "Shit!"

Rutherford's voice said, "Continue report."

The heavily accented voice of Lupe, known as Delta Two, said, "Señor Gainer's food is eat by others, I think, his coffee is drunk, and they have take his weapons, ammunition, field glasses, and radio. Two people, big man in boots, small woman in moccasins. Man do killing. They come from north, leave to south, I think pass well behind where I station. I follow now, maybe?"

Apparently one of Mondragon's men did not know how to

261

read signs after all; perhaps he just hadn't been present at the ambush near Cananea.

Rutherford's voice said, "Okay, try to track them. Watch out for Delta Four heading your way; we don't want any misunderstandings."

"Delta Two is out."

"Delta Four, you heard that?"

"I heard it. I'm still tangled up in these fucking rocks; I'll be looking in on Willy in about fifteen minutes. Who the hell ever heard of a Texas millionaire making with a shiv like a lousy greaser . . . ? Sorry about that, Lupe. Four out."

Antonia tapped my shoulder. "He big liar. No fifteen minutes, see right over there!"

I looked where she was looking. At first I could see nothing but a brushy mountainside; then a bush shook a little more vigorously than could be accounted for by the erratic breeze. Delta Four, named Hank Cramer, the man who'd been caught with his pants open. Apparently he wasn't great on respect or discipline, but he did have a few brains; he was the one who'd noted that we'd moved from Anglo to Anglo, bypassing the Mexican ally, Lupe. And now, knowing that we had at least one radio and were undoubtedly listening in, he'd broadcast a false ETA, hoping that if we were still hanging around it would make us take our time about slipping away, maybe giving him a chance to surprise us.

"Goddamn smarty-pants," I said. "Let's get out of here."

"No kill him?"

"Bloodthirsty, aren't you?" I shook my head. "Let's stay with the easy ones as long as we can. This guy is tricky and alert, we'll let him go."

She said, patting the M-16, "I take little *maquina* and, what you call them, clips. You take other gun, okay?"

It was a pleasure to work with a female who had a real regard for weapons. I grinned. "Well, it's a cinch you can't pack any more hardware; you're already loaded like a burro. Sure, I'll bring the revolver, just in case we have to fight a real war some time. Lead the way. Put me over there behind that sniper, if you can." Her eye for terrain was better than mine, and I wasn't too proud to take advantage of it.

"First I think we go down, okay?"

"Sure, this high country seems to be getting a bit crowded."

Weighed down with a long gun and four short ones counting the .22 that was wearing a hole in my ankle, plus an assortment of .38 and .243 ammunition, plus a walkie-talkie, I felt like John Wayne or Sylvester Stallone heading off to retake Vietnam single-handed. Well, double-handed. Despite her burden the kid slipped through the brush ahead of me like a ghost. I had a hard time moving as silently, but we got away without attracting the attention of Delta Four. We were well down the slope, making our way down a steep gully, when he came on the air with the bad news.

"Tunk, dammit, the bastards got Willie! Another knife job, but I think the dame did it this time; Willie had a couple of long black hairs in his fist. Radio gone, guns and ammo gone. Christ, even if they didn't bring any of their own, they've got a goddamn arsenal by this time. Anybody who walks up on them careless is going to get blasted back into yesterday. . . . Hold the phone; I hear something!"

The radio was silent. Waiting in the brush where we'd stopped to listen, with the girl crouched beside me, I watched a battered green Jeep come into sight from the valley below. It was the ugly old honest-to-Pete Willys article, topless, made before they fed it hormones and rounded off the corners and plastered it with chrome and racing stripes. It didn't even sport a rollbar, and the windshield lay flat on the hood. I studied the tall man behind the wheel, bushy black hair sticking out from under a khaki cap, dark glasses. Gamma. Even at the distance, I recognized him. I'd last seen him in El Paso, in a Safeway parking lot, manhandling Horace Cody into position for his runty partner to apply the handcuffs—but apparently he could manage his own bracelets if he had to. The woman beside him was wearing them.

I caught the glint of metal when she raised her hands to push back a lock of her short brown hair, windblown in the open vehicle. Jo Beckman. I didn't want to look at her, she was just a pawn in this high-powered chess game, and it was something I had to keep clearly in mind. I looked anyway, watching the old jeep turn left and disappear among the blocks of black stone.

CHAPTER 29

Antonia had been peering through the little pocket telescope I'd lent her. She hadn't bothered to confiscate the binoculars of the man she'd killed, even though the larger glasses would have provided her with better optical assistance; perhaps she'd been unwilling to burden herself with the additional weight. Without comment, she lowered the glass as the jeep, with Gamma and his prisoner, drove out of sight among the rocks below.

I said, "Let's keep moving. I want to be in position to take out that marksman before the *mierda* hits the *ventilador*. We can listen as we go."

As we continued down the gully, Rutherford's voice spoke urgently from the radio: "Delta Four, Delta Four, where the hell have you got to? Alpha calling Delta Four. Over."

After a moment, he got an answer, "Keep your shirt on, Tunk. Four here. It turned out to be just Lupe I heard coming, but I didn't want to take any chances."

"What does Delta Two have to say?"

"According to the tracks—this stony ground makes for mean tracking, Lupe says—they made a big loop behind his station and slipped up on Willy, the girl sneaking in for the kill this time while the man covered her. They seem to have quite an act going, those two, like a pair of hunters taking alternating shots, real polite and sportsmanlike. There's something screwy about it, Tunk."

"What bothers you, besides the fact that they seem to be pretty good?"

"They're too damn good; hell, they act like a team of high-priced hit men. Sam was a pretty sharp guy for a longhair, and Willy was no dope either. And this bald old coot who's spent most of his life counting his money and has a bullet in him, and this crazy young squaw who, according to the description you passed around, doesn't weigh a hundred pounds soaking wet with a full belly . . . this weird pair of killers is supposed to be loping around this vertical damn scenery like a couple of mountain goats taking out our trained and experienced men like kids popping pigeons off the roof of papa's barn. I don't believe it. The girl, maybe, if there's a tribe of half-pint Amazon warriors hiding somewhere in this lousy country, maybe with those legendary headhunters down in the Barranca del Cobre. Maybe she's a natural they dug out of the bush somewhere. Maybe. But the man, like I say, I don't believe it! Sick or well, that's no millionaire senior citizen we're up against. He didn't learn his killing moves drilling any oil wells."

The man—Delta Four, Hank Cramer—was too smart; maybe we should have ambushed him as Antonia suggested. Or maybe it was better this way. I have no real objection, in a tricky situation, to having people laboring under the delusion that I'm Superman; it tends to soften them up nicely.

Rutherford was getting impatient. "Get to the point, Four, or get off the air!"

Cramer spoke with equal impatience: "Wake up, this character is no goddamned oilman, and he didn't come here to Piedras Negras for any information. I don't say that isn't why he was in the neighborhood or that he'd turn down a line on those missing weapons if somebody gave it to him on a platter, but once he got the idea we'd set a trap here—Arturo must have let something slip—he came for us instead of avoiding us. That should tell you something. The son of a bitch is fucking hunting *us*! And Mrs. Cramer's little boy Henry wants out, Buster. Tell Sigma to blow his fucking bugle and get us to hell away from here, and I don't mean next Saturday."

After well over a week in Mexico, I'd finally heard somebody other than myself speak the word I'd been told to listen for, unprompted. Of course it had been spoken in English, not Spanish, and it could be a simple coincidence; but I tapped Antonia on the shoulder as a signal to stop. This I had to hear. Besides, the pace she was setting, I needed to catch my breath.

Rutherford's voice asked sharply, "Are you scared of one man and a little girl?"

"Were you born a meathead or did you have to work at it? Do you think they'd be cruising in here so calmly, the two of them taking on the lot of us, if they didn't have plenty of backup waiting to move in on signal, maybe even official backup? What's our authority for being here on the wrong side of the border with guns, automatic weapons yet, just about as illegal as you can get? And I'll bet those nice, friendly Mexicans we've got helping us—Lupe, and that slick Mondragon character who's hiding in the rocks with his armed gofers and calling himself a general— aren't real popular with the local government. I've seen a Mexican jail, thanks! What the hell good are we doing here anyway? So Mr. Saturday wants Cody, there's no Cody here, there's just a pro with a phony beard and a white suit playing homicidal games with us, while the real Horace Hosmer Cody's lying in some hospital all bandaged up and full of antibiotics probably, with a private room and pretty nurses around the clock. . . ."

He was a smart man, and he'd figured most of it out, particularly the impersonation; he'd realized that, the way I was operating in rough terrain, I couldn't be badly wounded and couldn't be elderly and therefore couldn't be Cody. Of course, like all clever logicians, he'd followed his logic a little too far. He'd given us credit for too much common sense, deducing erroneously that we wouldn't have tackled these odds unless we had reinforcements standing by, maybe even Mexican government reinforcements. Well, that last was a good thought for him to have and pass around. As a matter of fact, I'd been considering pulling a bluff along those lines if the situation became sticky. I only wished his theory were correct.

Suddenly another voice came over the air, curtly: "Delta Four, this is Sigma. You are ordered to report to headquarters immediately. Acknowledge! Over."

It was a voice I hadn't heard here before. Coming out of the tinny little speaker, with the volume turned to a whisper, it didn't come through clearly enough for me to tell if I'd heard it elsewhere. I glanced around quickly.

"Is anybody close enough to hear if I make it a little louder?" I whispered.

"Is safe. No peoples close. Have you know this Sigma . . . ?"

"Shhh!"

Cramer's voice, reproduced more loudly than it had been as I adjusted the control, spoke elaborately: "Yassuh, Boss Saturday, suh. To hear is to obey."

"Delta Four, we do not indulge in these identification routines for your entertainment. If you absolutely must transmit again, which I do not recommend, please observe prescribed radio discipline."

I thumbed the volume back down to its former whisper, having heard all I needed to.

Antonia watching my face, "You know this man. He is one you seek?"

I nodded. "Now get me over behind that damn sniper, quick."

"How close you need?"

"I can do it from three hundred meters, but I'd prefer two hundred."

She shouldered her M-16 again and took off. I left the choice of route to her; she was really very good at finding us gullies and arroyos and clumps of brush and stands of small trees that let us move silently in the right direction without being spotted. When you come across a real expert who wants to help you, don't be proud, let him. Or her. Suddenly I heard the tiny speaker of the radio at my belt whisper my own name, my real name. I'd been Cody so long, off and on, if never very convincingly, that it came as a shock.

"Helm, Helm. This is Sigma calling Matthew Helm. Over."

Antonia glanced at me quickly over her shoulder. After all the horsing around, I'd almost lost track of who knew me as

Cody, who as Helm, and who as both; but I did remember that, having seen Cody and me together in Kino Bay, she belonged in the last category.

I shook my head. "Don't stop. Keep moving."

We were closing in on the sniper's position now, moving cautiously down the ridge at the end of which he was stationed. The sharpshooter and Antonia and I didn't have the area to ourselves by any means; as we made our approach very cautiously, Antonia pointed out to me three armed men stationed below us, one of whom, well ahead, I hadn't spotted for myself. Almost a mob scene. Apparently, before Delta Four had made him realize my identity, while he still thought he was dealing with the real Cody who couldn't get around very well, the man who called himself Sigma had expected us to use the direct, short, easy approach from the south and had stationed his men accordingly. The rough and circuitous route we'd actually taken had caught him with his troop dispositions skewed in the wrong direction.

The radio spoke: "Mr. Helm this is Sigma again. Please come in. We know you have two of our walkie-talkies and are undoubtedly listening. We can dispense with the impersonation nonsense now, can't we? As you've heard, even men who've never seen you have realized at last that you're a substitute. Where is the true Horace Cody? I suppose he is the patient who is being so carefully and conspicuously guarded under your name in that cottage in Kino Beach; well, we'll deal with that problem later. Right now I want you, wherever you are, to step out into plain sight with your vicious little Indian friend, raise your hands, and wait until my men come to disarm you and bring you to me. You have one minute. We're holding the handsome lady who recently took care of you, probably in more ways than one, after you were shot. Dr. Joanna Beckman. If you don't respond, you will hear her suffer. Over."

I tapped Antonia on the shoulder. "This is good enough," I whispered.

"Is more than three hundred meters."

"Not much more, and from here I've got a straight shot at

269

him without too much brush and junk in the way. That rock will give me a good rest.''

Abruptly a woman's voice that I recognized very well came out of the little speaker, somewhat breathless: "This is Jo Beckman. This is Jo Beckman. I'm sorry . . .''

Sigma's voice intruded sharply: "Never mind that, say what you were told to say!''

"I'm sorry, sorry, I was a damn fool to come here and get myself caught like this; you mustn't endanger yourself for me. . . . Ahhh!'' There was a brief pause after her involuntary cry of pain, then her voice came strongly again, not speaking to me: "You'll have to do better than that, you sadistic bastard!''

Antonia, beside me, whispered, "Hey, brave lady.''

Sigma's voice said, "Just a small burn on the hand with a cigarette, Mr. Helm. We *can* do better if we must. Or worse.''

It was a beautiful day for it, for just about anything except skiing, with a warm, bright sun shining down from a deep blue sky untouched by pollution. The breeze of the morning, that had been helpful to me above, could have created a problem here since I didn't know how wind-sensitive the 100-grain .243 bullet might be; however, it was blowing from the south, and I'd be shooting north, so the effect shouldn't be significant, not like a crosswind. I had good cover and a good rest. I was using Cody's big hat, well mashed down, for a cushion under the rifle, since a gun fired off solid, unyielding rock generally won't shoot where it's sighted. It was better to concentrate on these technical details. As I've said before, we don't play the hostage game, and he shouldn't have tried it. He really shouldn't.

I looked down the ridge, which curved slightly so that I could see my target across the curve. He was sitting on a rock behind a screen of brush that shielded him well from the front and sides, not so well from the rear. With the telescopic sight set to its maximum magnification, 9X, he came in sharply. One of the camouflage boys, at least to the extent of a hunting cap and shirt. I hadn't seen him upright, so I couldn't tell what he was wearing below the waist or how tall he was; but I thought he was a fairly small man. He was wearing some kind of big glasses, perhaps

270

shooting glasses. As I'd expected, his rifle and scope looked just like mine. Maybe they'd bought them by the dozen and got a break on the price.

I checked around. There seemed to be nobody on the opposing ridge covering the entrance from the north, perhaps because it would be a very long shot from there to any area of possible action, too long for the small-caliber weapons this outfit seemed to like. From where I lay behind my rock, I couldn't see two of the three men we'd spotted on the way down, but the one Antonia had pointed out to me was still in sight, leaning against a boulder below us thinking himself hidden by the spring foliage of a nearby cottonwood. Another of the blue denim boys, but wearing a tan cowboy hat. He was within range, if I stretched it a bit, and I debated taking him instead of the sniper, but he was carrying only an M-16, which made him the lesser threat. He could wait.

I nudged Antonia. "Time for you to go, *guapa*. Slip over this ridge, climb down the other side, the valley side, and put yourself in good cover near where the road comes out of the basin. Mondragon should be departing soon. You can take him as he comes out."

"How you know he leave?"

"I've seen him in action, sweetie. He gets nervous. When things go wrong, he pulls out his men at the first excuse and takes off flying. I'm about to make a few more things go wrong. . . . Let them come in close and hose them down good for me, baby."

She studied me for a long moment; then her lips formed a smile. "Hear this man! *Guapa*, sweetie, baby! Maybe he like Antonia a little. Good man, fight good, drive good, shoot good. Love lousy, I bet. Antonia teach some time. What you say, *Americano*, see you in *iglésia*?"

"That's right, honey. See you in church. . . . Oh, Antonia?"

She'd started to move away. She stopped and looked over her shoulder. *"Sí?"*

"Where is it?"

She regarded me without expression for a moment. "You ask?"

"You know what I ask. Medina might not have taken you on the man's work of loading and hiding the arms, but he'd certainly have consulted you beforehand about where was the best place for them."

"So you afraid Antonia be kill and never tell."

"Sure. Goddamn nuisance, Antonia, good riddance. But I must know where those weapons are concealed. So tell me, and then you can go get yourself blasted with my blessing, good-bye."

She was watching me carefully. "So cold the blood, hey, no like Antonia one little bit, just want stupid guns, okay?"

"You said it, baby."

She gave me her wonderful big grin. "Very mean fellow, this man. Look for the Rincon de la Aguila, hey. Maybe there, maybe not. Antonia terrible liar. Now I go kill a general, *con su permiso*?"

She leaned forward and kissed me lightly on the lips and was gone with the black assault rifle slung across her back, muzzle down. Alone I felt a strange sense of loss—strange because I usually prefer to operate alone, but I was going to miss working with this pretty, ruthless little hunting partner.

CHAPTER 30

WAITING, holding the M-77 ready, I thought about what Antonia had told me, but the name meant nothing to me. The Rincon de la Aguila, the Cave of the Eagle. Well, if it existed, and I thought it did, even though she'd had to kid me about it a little in her fashion, somebody could undoubtedly find it. And if they could, one of my goals in Mexico, the guns that were wanted by everybody, had been achieved. She was attending to the second, Mondragon, wanted by Ramón. I merely had to achieve the third, Sábado, wanted by Mac. . . . But there was no point in thinking about that, I'd done all the necessary thinking, and my approach was working.

I'd had some luck, of course. The fact that old Cody had been smart and tough enough to get away in El Paso after I'd escaped death near Cananea, leaving a lot of elaborate cover-up plans in ruins, had driven my subject to this all-out effort to save himself by exterminating us both, even coming to Mexico with a full team to make sure that this time the job got done properly—as he'd made clear, the fact that he was here dealing with me instead of Cody, whom he'd expected, only meant that he'd take care of Cody instead of me later, and to hell with the bodyguards around the house in Kino Bay, he had enough manpower to overwhelm any bodyguards. But that had been the luck of it, getting him to Mexico, and particularly to this desolate part of it, where I didn't have to be too careful about the way I dealt with him. Tackling him on his home grounds would have been a much more delicate operation; I could hardly have used this direct, homicidal approach back there. But as I said, it was working. I'd already got him mad enough to reveal himself over the air instead of remaining silent in the background the way he liked. Just a little more pressure and I'd have him in the open where I could finish the damn job.

So there was really nothing to be gained by thinking about it; from now on it was merely a matter of taking the breaks as they came. I reflected instead upon the interesting fact that the eagle, which has always seemed to me the most masculine of birds, is feminine in Spanish.

Then a woman's half-choked cry of pain came over the radio, followed by the voice of Sigma: "Last chance, Helm. Just another little cigarette burn, on the cheek this time, but I have a very good butane lighter here, a miniature blowtorch. I'll give you another sixty seconds. If I don't have a sighting report from one of my men within that time, the lady will find that this is indeed a very bad day at the Black Rocks. . . ."

They all seem to work from the same corny script by the same lousy writer. This Sigma character seemed to be reading his part from a Xerox copy lent him by Ramón's executive officer, Captain Luís Alemán, who'd played the same Torquemada role opposite a different leading lady a week or two back. The only change, hardly demonstrating great creative originality, was that Sigma, or Saturday, or Sábado, was using fire with his threats, while the brave captain had employed steel.

I found the rifleman in the telescopic sight. I waited until he leaned a bit to the right to look at something below. I added pressure to the trigger, gradually, the way you do, until the rifle fired. Although the report was sharp, the recoil of the .243 was surprisingly light; I guess there's something to be said for the smaller calibers. I only lost my target out of the scope for an instant, the time it took me to work the bolt and chamber a fresh round, but it wasn't needed. I was aware that, at the shot, the sharpshooter—well, the would-be sharpshooter—had lurched up and out of his brushy place of concealment. Now he was standing unsteadily among the rocks below it, still holding his rifle; then he dropped the weapon and stumbled away down the open slope in an odd, aimless fashion. I could have put another one into him, but the second shot would have located me definitely for anybody still uncertain as to the source of the first, and I was fairly sure that the first had been good enough. I saw that his camouflage cap was missing.

I knew him now; that is, I'd seen him once before, in that Safeway parking lot in El Paso. He was the other half, the smaller half, of the Mutt-and-Jeff team that had arrested Horace Cody. After three uncertain steps, his knees folded and he pitched forward and rolled a few yards down the hillside and lay sprawled there, unmoving. I noted that his pants carried the same camouflage pattern as the shirt and the missing cap. The cap worried me a little, since its disappearance could indicate that I'd made a head shot, and I'd aimed considerably lower than that.

A voice I didn't recognize spoke without expression: "Sigma, Sigma, this is Delta Five. We just lost Georgie Peterson, I mean Lambda. At least he looks dead from here. A long rifle shot from somewhere on the ridge above and behind him."

"Helm, you murdering maniac . . . !" It was a screech in the little walkie-talkie. Sigma must have continued to hold down the transmit button in his fury although the next words were not addressed to me, or maybe they were in a way: "Pull her boots off, Rutherford. . . . All right, all right, just the right one will do. And the sock. Now, hold her like that!"

I told myself that lots of people had had their tootsies toasted; it had even happened to me. A scar or two down there wasn't a lifelong trauma. Nevertheless, it was with a certain vengeful satisfaction that I swung around to pick up the man below me in the scope; I could hurt people, too. He made it simple for me; he'd stepped out from his cottonwood to look up at the ridge, trying to figure out exactly where my first shot had come from, but it isn't easy to locate the source of a single reverberating report in rocky terrain. I centered the crosshairs low, about six inches above his belt, and held a little to the right since I was now shooting across the wind. I waited for the radio to transmit Jo's next cry. When it came, as my answer, I pressed the trigger gently and the .243 fired again.

The man below responded in a very satisfactory manner; he let out a strange bubbling howl that was clearly audible even three hundred yards away. He clapped his hands to his face and fell forward, rolling back and forth on the ground, still shrieking with gradually diminishing vigor. Under normal circumstances, I prefer a clean and instant execution; but here, as I say, the gruesome result of my shot was satisfactory—it should impress the troops—except for the fact that it indicated that the rifle was, as I'd guessed, shooting much higher than I'd figured, even taking into account the fact that downhill shots always tend to go high.

Sigma's voice screeched tinnily: "Helm, you madman, I'll make this bitch wish she'd never met you."

She was undoubtedly wishing that already, but you can't run an outfit like ours if you're going to be at the orders of every creep with a prisoner and a butane lighter. I took the walkie-talkie from my belt at last. I pressed the transmit button and spoke into the mike, slowly and clearly.

"Mondragon, Mondragon. This is Matthew Helm calling General Carlos Mondragon. Don't bother to answer, sir, just listen. We don't want you or your men, and there are certain people coming who'd hate to find you here and have to figure out what to do with you. Get your boys to hell away, right now, please, while we're closing out this rogue Yankee agency that's been using you for its own purposes. In other words, sir, please be so good as to *vamos pronto*, or as we say in America, haul ass soonest. Understood?"

I thought it was a pretty good speech, hinting at limitless forces at my disposal.

"Yo comprendo," the radio said softly. Whether it was

Mondragon himself or a spokesman, I didn't know, since I'd never been closer to the self-styled general than a quarter of a mile or heard him speak.

Sigma's voice came out of the little speaker: "General Mondragon, don't be stupid, your revolution hasn't got a chance without our help. Sit tight, we'll have this little problem solved in a minute."

There was no answer from the revolutionary camp. I could no longer hear anything from the last man I'd shot; a glance that way told me he'd stopped thrashing around and lay quite still, facedown in the dirt down there, with a dark area surrounding his head. *Forbearance is not a virtue,* Mac had said. It was time to depart. I'd almost left it too late. As I slipped away, crouching, there was a chatter of automatic fire from up the ridge, and a single bullet glanced off the stony hillside to my left and headed off into space with the nasty wavering sound of a ricochet. Somebody'd cut loose with an M-16 burst at several hundred yards, probably not even hoping for a hit, just letting his friends know he'd seen something to shoot at. I heard a faraway shout.

"There he goes! Heading down the east slope. Cut him off below!"

After all the scratchy electronic verbiage I'd been listening to, it was kind of nice to hear an honest-to-God human voice for a change. I let the man above catch a few glimpses of me as I slipped and slid down the slope—once I showed myself long enough for him to try another burst that took some leaves off a nearby bush—then I went flat in the brush and crawled back upward again by a slightly different route. It took me five careful but breathless minutes to return to the friendly rock from which I'd done my previous shooting, making it on my belly where the cover was poor and on hands and knees when it was better.

As I hid myself where I'd have a clear shot at him as he passed, I saw movement far off across the basin; a small blue pickup truck nosed out of a cleft in the jumbled black rocks followed by a brown van that I recognized: Mondragon was pulling out. I'd thought he wouldn't stick, not with people dying all around him. Well, he was no business of mine now; Antonia was on her own, which undoubtedly suited her just fine. Vengeance isn't something to be shared. I set the Ruger in a safe place. It was going to be close work here, too close for a telescopic sight. I took out one of the revolvers I'd liberated. I knew just about where the man would have to be taken, and with a four-inch barrel, the liberated .38 was a little better suited to the range than my own two-incher.

I heard him coming; he was taking few precautions and making no real effort to be silent. After all, there was no danger, he'd seen me running away, down the side of the ridge; I was probably close to the bottom by now. Of course, there was supposed to be a girl with me, and he didn't have her located; but either he'd forgotten her, or he was chauvinist enough to figure he could handle any dames dumb enough to get in his way. Crouching in the brush, I saw him stop to check his bearings: yes, this was the spot. He approached my rock and bent over to pick up something that glinted in the sunshine: an empty .243 cartridge case, confirming the fact that he'd found the right trail. Sticking it into his pocket, he studied my tracks briefly and started downhill after them.

I had the confiscated revolver cocked, waiting. He was in canvas combat boots, jeans, and a camouflage shirt and hunting cap; a stocky gent with a round, red face and a scraggly red beard. He made it easy for me again; everybody was cooperating very nicely. First, he bent over to pick up and pocket a second cartridge case; then he straightened up and stood quite still, listening. The sound of automatic rifle fire reached us from the other side of the ridge; apparently Antonia had seen her man—I hoped she'd let him come well within range—and opened up. My man was a perfect target, standing there; he was dead, and it was time to go on to the next, only the damn gun hadn't fired and wouldn't fire. I don't mean there was anything wrong with the mechanism. There was something wrong with me. That week-old crack on the head, I suppose. But it was getting to be too much, dammit. I don't mind a little killing in the line of business—you might even say it is my business—but this was

278

getting ridiculous, if I may use the word in such a gory connection.

I'd taken the precaution of turning off my walkie-talkie so it wouldn't betray my presence; but I heard the one on Redbeard's belt clear its throat.

"Kappa, Kappa, this is Theta. I think I'm just about below you. What's that shooting I hear? Over."

Redbeard freed the radio and held it to his mouth, speaking softly but not inaudibly. "It's on the west side of the ridge, I don't know what the fuck it is."

"Somebody's surely raising hell with an M-16. Over."

"Never mind that," said Kappa. "Any sign of our man down there? Or the girl?"

"Not any."

"Well, watch yourself, the guy's probably gone to cover. The bastard's slippery as a snake. I didn't see the dame, maybe they've spilt up and somebody's got her cornered over there, I hope. Don't get trigger-happy now; I'm coming your way."

"To hell with you, Buster. You worry about your trigger and I'll worry about mine. Theta out."

Redbeard, alias Kappa, started to clip the little radio back onto his belt; then he saw me, because I'd stood up to let him, and froze. I could see him consider his chances with the assault rifle, but he was holding it carelessly by the sight that looks like a carrying handle—maybe it is; they do funny things in the military—and there was no way he could get it into action before I shot him to pieces.

I said softly, "Lay down the radio and don't dream of touching the transmit button. Place the M-16 and your Colt beside it. I've already killed three men today and a fourth won't bother me a bit, so any games you want to play, have at them."

He followed instructions very carefully and straightened up. "Listen, you murdering bastard . . ."

I said, "I don't burn women with blowtorches and I don't work for anybody who does. Or for a megalomaniac who thinks he knows better than Washington what my country's foreign

279

policy ought to be; a wild-eyed character who, when he's caught playing Secretary of State without a briefcase, tries to kill and torture his way clear. Don't talk murdering to me, Buster. Including this elaborate rattrap, there have been three attempts on my life since I left the U.S. I figured that since you boys are so useless at killing—hell, you can't even finish off an old man with a big, bleeding hole in his back—you'd like to have an expert show you how. Come over here and sit on that rock. I suppose you're going to be brave and refuse to get on the two-way and call in your pal below."

"Fuck you, mister."

"That's okay," I said. "When you don't come to him and don't answer the radio, he'll come to you. While we wait, you might as well get out the handcuffs you characters seem to carry and snap them around your wrists. In front is okay. That's a good boy. Squeeze them good and tight and let me hear them click. Now tell me how the hell we're going to stop this nonsense."

"Who the hell are you?"

"I'm the guy a guy named Rutherford tried to trap and kill, with Mexican help, near a little town called Cananea. I'm the guy a guy named Rutherford tried to kill, with Mexican help, in a bigger city called Hermosillo. And now he's got you boys trying it here, and I'm getting kind of fed up with it," I said. "You're in a bad spot, *amigo*. You've got me on one side and I'm not a very nice fellow when I get mad. And on the other side you've got the Mexican authorities, and you know how they are. The old *ley de fuga* still works down here, Mr. Kappa. They'll give you a running start and use you for machine-gun practice and report that you were shot trying to escape. If they bother to report. Probably they'll just throw you on the garbage heap with the other stiffs over there and forget all about mentioning you officially." I hoped Ramón and his fellow countrymen would forgive my slanderous statement. I went on: "The buzzards will love you, Mr. Kappa. They'll come sailing in to feed in swarms like the bombers over Berlin. The poor

280

hungry things are getting pretty damn tired of picking over the same old human bones; they want some fresh meat."

I noted that the distant firing had stopped after some final, desultory pop-pop-popping. I hoped the kid had got clear unhurt; if she had, they'd never catch her. If she'd accomplished what she intended, and I was willing to bet she had, they probably wouldn't even chase her very hard with Mondragon dead. And with the arms located and Mondragon dead, that was two-thirds of my job done.

"Kappa this is Theta, what's keeping you?"

Redbeard glanced at the radio on the ground ten feet away. I shook my head. He looked at my gun and licked his lips. "What the hell are you trying to say?"

I said, "Bail out, friend. Take a running jump out the door and pull the ripcord. This plane is going down in flames. . . . Shhh, here comes your buddy looking for you as I told you he would. If you warn him, you're dead, and I'll hunt him down, too; more meat for the *zopilotes*. Let him come in, talk it over with him. You can both walk away from this, if you walk in the right direction. Otherwise you'll stay here for good."

He had one of those red faces that always look like a bad sunburn, and those orangy whiskers, and small blue eyes that didn't look very trustworthy, but I couldn't guess who had more reason to mistrust him, Sigma or I. Probably I did. Probably, even if he did say he'd play along, he'd be lying. There's always loyalty to the organization to consider even if the top man is no prize; in any war, more men fight for their ships or units than for their country, and very few fight for their officers.

The man below clattered another pebble; he was closer than he had been. I picked up the gear Kappa had laid down at my request, emptied his revolver and stuck it back into his holster, and turned off his walkie-talkie and hung it on his belt. I checked the condition of his M-16, ready, and stuck the .38 I'd been holding, long since uncocked, under my belt. The assault rifle was the more impressive weapon; a man might be reckless

281

enough to charge a lousy little revolver, but he'd at least hesitate a bit when confronted with the ugly black military killing-machine.

I looked for a suitable spot in which to lie in ambush this time. The other side of the little clearing looked good. As I stepped forward a bit and paused to check it out from that angle, something struck me hard in the back, on the left side. I was even aware of blood spraying out of the exit wound just above my belt. Everything was suddenly very remote, the ratty brush around me, the stony slopes, the blue sky, the bright sun. It seemed as if I were moving in slow motion as I threw myself down—threw, hell, I kind of floated to the ground. I was aware of a very distant report as I fell, and I heard a second bullet go past, and I knew that I'd made the mistake you seldom survive, the error of overconfidence. I'd thought I had it all figured out. I'd decided that the guy running this show was a creature of habit; all his men packed M-16s with twenty-round magazines and .38 pistols with four-inch barrels. All except the snipers, who carried .243 bolt-action rifles with 3x–9x telescopic sights.

But the son of a bitch had loused me up. In addition to the toy .243s, he'd brought one *real* rifle, probably a .30 Magnum, and he'd given it to a man who knew how to use it and stationed him on the point of rocks to the north, on the other side of the entrance, from which he could cover most of the action area including—if his range tables stretched well past six hundred yards—the spot from which I'd chosen to do my shooting. This marksman must have spent a frustrating half-hour while his colleagues died, as he watched me through his big scope and waited for a clear target. He'd probably cursed savagely when I headed down the slope, wishing he hadn't been quite so perfectionist and taken a hope shot, but I'd come back and finally given him the motionless, unobstructed aiming point for which he'd been waiting.

The man with the red beard was running for cover, awkwardly because of his handcuffed hands. It was too bad, I'd tried to save his life, but we give no freebies. If they wanted me, they'd have to pay the full price on the tag. I cut down Kappa

282

with a lengthy burst; my trigger finger took a long time to react to the cease-fire command. Then I lay there waiting for Theta, but he never came, at least not as long as I remained conscious, which wasn't very long.

CHAPTER 31

I'D worried a bit about penetrating Sigma's headquarters, but it turned out to be no problem at all. They took me right to it. The only problem was surviving the ride. Unfortunately my unconsciousness, presumably a reaction to the shock of the bullet wound, didn't last long enough to help. I awoke, in a dim sort of way, aware of little else than the pain, when Theta rolled me over to disarm me; I heard him comment happily, to the driver of the Japanese jeep that had managed to grind its way up to us, on the number of weapons he found. I was glad I'd acquired enough to please him.

Then the two of them grabbed me under the armpits, dragged me roughly to the vehicle, and hauled most of me aboard, leaving my legs dangling. The little pickup-type bed wasn't long enough for all of me, particularly since I had to share the space with the late Mr. Kappa. As an afterthought, they took the handcuffs off him and put them on me, just in case, as they said, the sneaky son of a bitch was playing possum. Getting back down the hill was tricky for the driver but not too bad for me since he had to back down the steep grade very slowly so as not to lose control. At the bottom, we acquired another limp passenger, the second victim of my .243.

"God, we look like one of the meatwagons hauling away the stiffs during the Great Plague," said the man I knew only as Theta. "Never mind Peterson, I heard he's being picked up."

"Damn good thing; we'd have had to lay him across the hood," said the driver. "But I have a hunch Mr. Saturday is going to cure this particular plague pretty damn quick. I mean

Sigma. He's okay, I guess, and goddamn it, somebody's got to get these fucking greasers to straighten up and fly right, but I wish he'd stop playing these crummy Greek word games. Who the shit wants to go around being called Omicron, for Christ's sake?''

Finding the headquarters place was no problem, but the driver was no gentle chauffeur like little Lieutenant Ernesto Barraga of Ramón's *Fuerza Especial*. This hotshot Yankee wheelman had 4WD Grand Prix aspirations, and he sent his vehicle bounding across the roadless basin like a jackrabbit, perhaps figuring that two of the passengers in the rear were in no condition to mind the discomfort and the third had it coming. Then we slowed down to negotiate a narrow cleft between the great stone blocks that brought us into a small, open space, nothing like the wide amphitheater in which I'd seen a few hopeful vultures investigating old bones.

"Here, I'll get him." I recognized the voice. It belonged to the big boy, Marion Rutherford, otherwise known as Tunk or Alpha.

Theta and the driver, Mr. Omicron, had been trying to pull my more-or-less live body out from between the two totally dead ones, but we'd got packed into the limited space pretty tightly, like sardines, during the rough ride, and they were having a hard time prying me loose. The fact that their efforts were fairly painful to me was, of course, irrelevant, so I didn't bother to mention it. Then Rutherford was lifting me out of there like a baby.

"Where do you want him, sir?" he called to somebody.

The shout came back: "Lay him over there beside the woman."

Okay, I'd made it. This was the voice I'd been wanting to hear at close range, without benefit of electronics. Of course, it wasn't exactly the way I'd planned the meeting; I had handcuffs on my wrists and a leg that might not support me if I needed to stand on it, although the toes seemed to be wiggleable, and I might even be dying of internal injuries; but I was here with the man I'd been sent to find and dispose of. The finding, at least,

285

was done. Only the disposing remained. Of course, I also had to live long enough to pass the word about where the arms were located.

I lay for a while with my eyes closed after Rutherford had put me down, waiting for the flames to subside. At last I became aware that Tunk had departed and my man was standing there instead, the man I'd expected to see, the only man he could be, under the circumstances. In El Paso he'd dressed the part of a hip young executive with a smart three-day beard; here, still fashionably whiskery, he was costumed as an outdoors type in a tan poplin Great White Hunter suit, the jacket equipped with enough bellows-type pockets to carry sandwiches for a week. Something held him stiffly erect, still a fine, lean—well, almost—figure of a man. I decided that he was wearing either a corset or a bullet-proof vest or both. There was a Browning Hi-Power belted over the jacket. The belt and pistol holster were of handsome russet leather, and there was a russet leather pouch holding two spare magazines, putting something like forty-two rounds at his disposal, if I remembered the magazine capacity correctly. Fuzzy desert boots at one end and rakish safari hat at the other. Big dark glasses. Sigma, Sábado, Saturday. Well, I had my orders, and if he didn't like his own name I'd be happy to kill him under any name he chose, but it was amateurish of him to stick so stubbornly to the same initial letter.

Seeing my eyes open, he said, "Well, Helm?"

There was nothing I had to say to him; having seen enough, I just closed my eyes again. He kicked me in the side, fortunately the right side.

"You crazy assassin, did you really think you could kill us all with only a girl to help you?" He kicked me again. "Come on, speak up!"

Jo Beckman's voice, from the other side of me, protested: "Stop it, can't you see he's in shock? Are you just going to let him lie there and bleed to death? If you really want to interrogate him, if you have some sensible questions you want to ask him, you'd better stop the hemorrhaging fast or you won't have anybody to interrogate."

"All right, Doctor, I'll have a man bring you a first aid kit and some water. Do what you can for him."

"In these manacles?"

Sigma laughed. Mr. Saturday laughed. Señor Sábado laughed. "Nice try, but it won't work, my dear. It isn't as if your hands were shackled behind you. If you can't manage handcuffed, you're not much of a doctor. . . . Yes, yes, what is it?" Somebody had come running up; I couldn't hear what he said. Sigma said irritably, "Well, what are you waiting for, go fetch him in one of the jeeps and bring him here, fast!"

I could hear footsteps moving away; then fingers were tugging at my bloody shirt and performing some mildly painful explorations. Jo's voice said, "He's gone. Don't take my gloomy diagnosis too seriously, darling; I just wanted to impress the peasants. You're not bleeding enough externally to worry about. Internally is probably another matter, but there's nothing I can do about that. Somebody who knows how and has the proper instruments is going to have to go in and clean out the wound channel and stitch together whatever needs sewing. For the moment, I'll just make a bandage of your shirt since this little kit they brought me is kind of limited, and wrap it around you tightly to keep you from leaking too much." She laughed shortly. "I seem to recall that we've been here before, darling. You seem to attract lead the way a magnet attracts iron."

I opened my eyes to look at her. There was an angry-looking round burn on her cheek and another on her hand; I couldn't see the rest of her the way I was lying. I licked my dry lips.

" 'Darling' is a word I didn't expect to hear," I whispered.

She said, "So you *can* talk, good. Did you think I was going to hate you because you behaved like the callous bastard I always knew you were? Female people who poke around where they're not invited can expect to get clobbered. What they shouldn't expect, what they shouldn't even want, is for male people to drop all business on the spot and stop the world just so the ittle bittle girlie won't get her footsies fried. . . . Ha, I won't even need your shirt. I'd forgotten that big, phony bandage I put on you last night. I'll just move it down about a foot."

"Jo."

"Yes?"

I whispered, "There's a little gun in my right boot, inside." It served them right. If they'd lifted me carefully and carried me the normal way by the arms and legs when they loaded me into the jeep, they couldn't have missed it, but they'd been too happy dragging and bumping me around, trying to make me hurt. Of course, they'd also found enough firearms on me elsewhere, not to mention my little knife, to keep them from searching further. I went on with an effort: "If nobody's looking, and if you think you can bring yourself to use it when the time comes, slip it out and hide it on you somewhere, please." When she didn't speak, I added: "Incidentally, if you do decide to shoot the bastard, go for the head. I think he's wearing some kind of body armor."

I heard her breath catch. She made no answer but continued dismantling the bulky bandage around my chest.

At last she asked, "Is there anything else you need to tell me?"

"Yes." I'd debated whether or not to put the responsibility on her, but I had a hunch Sigma was leaving us alone deliberately to let us talk. When he returned, he'd simply assume I'd shared any information I carried and go to work on us both, so keeping her in ignorance would give her no protection. I whispered, "If I don't make it and you do, find a man with the *Fuerza Especial* of the Mexican Army named Ramón Solana-Ruiz. They call him *El Cacique*. Tell him that the place he wants is the Rincon de la Aguila. Got it?"

"Rincon de la Aguila. Solana-Ruiz." She'd unfastened my trousers; now she was fussing with the boots as if to pull them off first since the pants wouldn't come off over them. I gave a yelp of pain. She said, "Sorry. I guess I can just leave everything on. Let me just slip your trousers down a bit so I can see what I'm doing here." She lowered her voice. "Incidentally, I got the pistol. It's in my boot now."

"Left or right? In case I have to get it off your dead body in a hurry."

"Left, you creep. They took the other one off so they could roast me, remember? Or maybe you didn't hear . . ."

"I heard. How bad is it?"

Jo laughed shortly. "Just a little blister the size of a dinner plate," she said bravely. "Well, would you believe a silver dollar? As for you, my friend, you have a couple of very neat perforations, back and front. I thought bullets were supposed to expand and make dreadful exit wounds."

"He was shooting at extreme range. The slug had lost a lot of its velocity and didn't hit any bone."

"It must be nice to command such a specialized field of knowledge. You and your guns. Not to mention your girls." She was wrapping me up as she talked, lifting me frequently to slip the bandage under me, an operation that wasn't totally painless. She continued to speak: "What happened to the little Indian girl in the blanket and the ridiculous red shoes? The last I saw of her, she was heading off to find you."

I whispered, "She could be around somewhere, so let's not talk about her, huh? And she carried a pair of moccasins for rough work, if it matters. What brought you here, Jo?"

"We had a little hassle back there in Kino Bay. That man, Greer, whom you left to protect Mr. Cody, he and his men caught a thug snooping around the house. They took him inside to question him. That was the moment the old man chose to come marching into the living room complaining that his everlasting bandage was leaking and a man could bleed to death around the place shouting himself hoarse for help—I guess we'd been too preoccupied with the intruder to hear him. And the prisoner took advantage of the distraction to dive through a window and run. One of Greer's men was about to shoot, but Greer told him to hold his fire, we couldn't afford to arouse the town with gunshots except in a real emergency."

"He was right," I said.

Jo went on: "But the spy definitely saw Mr. Cody with his pajama top off and a bandage around his torso with blood on it. That would let the man know he'd seen the real Cody, the one who had the bullet hole in the body, and that the fugitive his friends were chasing up here was the wrong one, the one with the hole in the head. After I'd patched up the old man again—it wasn't a serious hemorrhage—I didn't have anything else to do there. Actually, Greer's been through a first aid course and can take care of him perfectly well. So I thought maybe it would be a good idea for me to take your car and try to find you and let you know your phony identity had been compromised. But I guess I've had better ideas in my life. . . . Careful now. Mr. Sigma is coming back. Three men with him. The big one, Rutherford, is helping a couple who were just brought in by jeep. They seem to've been wounded, one in the leg and the other in the face.''

Footsteps stopped nearby. Sigma's voice said, ''Take care of this man first, Doctor, he was hit in the eye by some rock fragments. . . . No, my dear, I will not take the cuffs off you, please stop trying to play me for a fool!'' He spoke to someone else: ''Sit down on that rock so she can take a look at you, Trautman. You can talk while she's doing it. What happened?''

There was a pause, and I heard a man protest, ''Señor Sábado, I bleed very bad!''

Sigma said, ''The doctor will get to you shortly, just sit down and wait. What's your name?''

''Hernando, señor. That *muchacha* shoot me, shoot everybody, much angry.''

Sigma's voice said, ''Trautman, I asked you what happened.''

He got no answer; but a male voice I hadn't heard before said, ''Oh, Christ, it hurts. How does it look, Doctor? Is it bad?''

''I can't tell yet. Hold still.''

''I'd like your report, Trautman!'' Sigma's voice was sharp.

After a moment, Trautman's voice spoke again, stiffly resentful: ''The General's dead, sir, and I don't know how many got out of the van, that bitch hosed it down with 5.56mm stuff like she was watering a lawn. . . .''

''From the beginning, please.''

Trautman cleared his throat. ''Well, after I reported that

Mondragon was pulling out and got the word from you to stick with him, liaisonlike, I went back to driving the little pickup for him like I'd been doing. The rest of his strike team, or whatever he called it, that gang of big-hat bandits, was in the van, following behind. Our brave liberator was practically pissing his pants, and I won't say I wasn't kinda nervous myself. Hell, why shouldn't I be, with four of the boys down already and no telling where those crazy killers were going to hit next? But then we were out of those lousy rocks and through the slot and heading down into the valley toward the main road, if you want to call *that* a main road. Everybody started breathing again. She was waiting in the brush to the right of the track. First thing I knew, Mondragon's head came off, practically, blood and brains all over the pickup cab, the windshield going all starry, and I just took a dive out the door and let the heap go on without me. The van went past me, almost hitting me, trying to swerve away from her; she was already working it over with that fucking M-16. Men were trying to dive out the rear, and she was knocking them off like they were clay pigeons thrown from a trap house. A half-pint Indian kid in pants and a blanket, with long black hair, no wild Rambo hipshooting, just kneeling there in the brush with the gun to her shoulder firing careful little bursts and switching magazines and grinning like she was having the most fun ever. How the hell did we get mixed up with these crazies, anyway, sir?''

"Never mind that. Did the girl say anything?''

"Ow, that hurts, Doctor. . . . A name,'' Trautman said. "She called out a name, sir. 'Medina,' she shouted. 'Remember Jorge Medina.' Come to think of it, I guess she yelled it in Spanish first and then repeated it in English, maybe for my benefit. Who the hell's Medina? Anyway, I took a shot at her with my .38, long range for a pistol, but I think it registered, but not hard enough. She turned that M-16 on me, and a slug hit the rock I was using for cover and sprayed stuff all over my face, I thought I was blind. When I could see a little out of my left eye, it was all over. The girl was gone. There was some moaning and groaning from the men still alive on the ground and inside the

291

van—it was leaking red out all the doors—but if any of them had been left ambulatory, as we used to say in the Army, they'd ambulated. This one was sitting in the road watching his leg bleed. I got on the walkie-talkie and asked for a pickup. . . . Doctor, what about my eye?"

Jo's voice said, "Ophthalmology is not my field. . . . All right, I can say that there's probably some damage to the cornea, but I can't tell you how serious it is. I've removed as much of the foreign matter as I dare; I don't really know much about eyes, and I don't want to make things worse. I've bandaged it and you should keep it covered until you get to a specialist, and for heaven's sake don't rub it. . . ."

Sigma interrupted: "All right, all right, never mind the bedside manner. Take him along to the other casualties, Rutherford. Oh, just a minute. . . . Trautman, you're *quite* sure General Carlos Mondragon is dead?"

The wounded man snorted. "The Generalissimo wasn't all that great with a whole head; I shouldn't think he'd be much use with just half of one. Sir."

"All right, take him away." I heard the man leaving with Rutherford's help. I heard Jo ask the wounded Mexican to pull up his pants leg. Then Sigma's boot hit me in the side again; I was happy he wasn't masquerading as a mountain climber or a lumberjack with footgear to match. The desert boots were bad enough. "Lying there with your eyes closed trying to make me believe you're at death's door! What do you think I am, a fool? Maybe you'll die of peritonitis eventually, if you live that long, which seems unlikely, but in the meantime . . . Who is this homicidal Indian girl, and who's Medina?"

It was no state secret. I said, "Her name is Antonia Sisneros and Jorge Medina was her lover, the cautious gent working for Will Pierce who was supposed to bring four truckloads of weapons to a certain rendezvous but arrived with empty trucks since he didn't trust friend Mondragon, I can't imagine why not. Mondragon tried to get the location of the arms from him, but Medina died under interrogation."

"Yes, yes, of course I heard all about that; I'd merely forgotten the name of the Mexican go-between, if I ever knew it. Naturally I held my contacts with Pierce to a minimum and asked him not to burden me with the operational details. And I certainly didn't know this Medina had a girlfriend.''

I said, "Señorita Sisneros is slightly upset about his death; upset enough that she's making a project of taking revenge on everyone responsible. She was terribly disappointed that you had Will Pierce killed before she could catch up with him; she was bound she was going to get Mondragon herself. She seems to come from good vendetta stock; she takes her blood feuds seriously.''

Sigma was looking down at me shrewdly. "If she was that close to Medina, she undoubtedly knows where he hid the arms. And since you seem to have got along very well with her, she probably told you. And I wouldn't be a bit surprised if you shared the information with the handsome lady doctor just now, giving me two people to interrogate instead of one. Meaning that if Rutherford, who likes that sort of thing, gets too rough with you, or you have the bad taste to die of your wound, we don't lose the information irretrievably, since we still have the handsome lady doctor to work on.''

He raised his arm to make a beckoning signal, and I heard the heavy footsteps of Tunk Rutherford returning. I wondered if this large young man was doing Sábado's dirty work now as a reaction to having been teased about his innocent boyish face as a kid, but psychiatry was Jo's department. All I had to do was endure.

CHAPTER 32

THE sun was shining fairly straight down on us from the area of blue visible between the black rocks; it didn't seem to be making much progress across the sky today. I'd have appreciated having Cody's big white hat to shield my eyes, but it had fallen off and got left somewhere. The little sheltered hole in the rocks seemed crowded with men and vehicles. Actually, there were only six or eight men and three or four cars—flat on my back and trying not to seem too interested, I couldn't take an exact census—but penned in by the steep walls they seemed like more of both. Mostly it was a barren clearing, but there were a couple of sizeable mesquites at our end and some scraggly grass and brush. An armed sentry, smoking a cigarette, squatted on his heels comfortably on top of one of the rocks overlooking the scene.

"Take our friend Hernando away; Dr. Becker has him all patched up," Sigma said as Rutherford reached us. "Come right back, Tunk. I have a little work for you here."

I wondered just how he decided when to employ the real name and when the Greek-letter code; there didn't seem to be any real consistency about it. However, it was a minor problem; I had more serious things to worry about, including the big young man who was marching back to us smartly. I was aware that Jo was trying to get the Mexican's blood, and maybe some of mine, off her hands.

"Set Helm up against that rock, I think he's had enough of a nap, don't you?" Sigma said when Rutherford reached us. "I'm disappointed in you, Tunk. I thought you were a better shot than that. Almost a foot low and six inches to the left!'' He laughed quickly. ''Don't mind me, my dear boy, I'm only joking. Let's get this unpleasant business done. There may be some numbness in the left leg due to the wound, and we want him to feel this, don't we? So please be so good as to pull off his right boot and sock and proceed with the treatment.''

At least I could congratulate myself on foreseeing an eventuality like this and getting rid of the hidden weapon that might, in the end, make the difference between survival and otherwise, although in this camp of heavily armed men I couldn't at the moment see how a little .22 could be utilized effectively. I felt the warm sun on my bare foot and saw the big man kneeling beside me with the butane lighter, the kind designed for setting fire to pipe tobacco and other reluctant combustibles. I told myself that, hell, I'd been burned before, what was the big deal? Then the lighter flared and the pain came and I concentrated on keeping the sound effects to a minimum. I'm not an iron man, I can holler with the best, but it wasn't a screaming situation yet.

I heard Sigma's voice: ''Well, Dr. Becker? Excuse me, Dr. Beckman. You can stop it with a word. Where are those weapons?''

Jo said bravely, ''I didn't notice him paying much attention to my moans and groans; why should I worry about his?'' But her voice was strained.

Sigma laughed. He not only laughed, he kept on laughing; it was almost an attack of hysterics. Big Tunk Rutherford crouched beside my foot, holding the lighter and awaiting further orders, his pleasant, boyish face impassive. I saw Jo looking at me, her expression showing puzzlement as well as sympathy, but I couldn't help her; I didn't know what the hell was going on either. After he'd regained control, Sigma had to remove the dark glasses and wipe them with a crisp white handkerchief and dry his eyes. He returned the glasses to his face, refolded the handkerchief, and put it away carefully. He stepped forward and slapped me hard.

''So brave!'' he sneered. ''So stupid! I just had to have the pleasure of seeing the great undercover hero gritting his teeth and sweating, trying not to scream, groaning and grunting, refusing heroically to betray the information. . . . You brainless clown, what do I want with those arms now? I hope nobody ever finds them; I sincerely hope they stay lost forever! Now that Mondragon is dead they are certainly no use to me. The continued hope of them bought me his assistance; I let him believe that, although I didn't know the exact location of the hiding place, I at least knew how to go about learning it. And as it turned out I wasn't deceiving him, I could eventually have got it from you, or Dr. Beckman, or the little Indian girl. But of course I wouldn't have. The last thing I want, now that Washington has withdrawn its approval and started an investigation, is a well-armed and well-publicized revolution here in Mexico. If Señorita Sisneros hadn't killed our tame general, with all he knew about me, I would have had to have somebody else do it as soon as I no longer needed him. But this is a much more satisfactory solution: the great revolutionary hero shot to death by a woman he'd wronged. No suspicion of a Yankee assassination or, for that matter, of a Mexican government execution." He frowned down at me. "Could that be why you brought her here? Perhaps you have a few more brains than I suspected. You do have some friends among the authorities, I believe; you could be acting on their behalf."

He didn't make it a question; and I volunteered no answers to the question he hadn't asked. I was trying to ignore the throbbing in my foot and the various other unbearable agonies I had to bear while figuring the possibility of a break. The big question mark was Antonia. I decided that there wasn't really enough cover here to let her sneak up to us, good as she was at moving silently and unseen; and she was supposedly carrying a pistol bullet anyway. The idea of her being wounded, perhaps badly wounded, was disturbing, more disturbing than I'd expected; after all, the girl really meant nothing to me. We'd never been lovers. What had developed between us was merely a casual relationship—call it a business partnership—of no great significance, right? Anyway, I reminded myself, pistoleers are as bad

296

as fighter pilots for claiming hostiles shot down that weren't. However, I'd better assume the worst and figure out a way of dealing with the situation with whatever assistance Jo could provide, without waiting for help. I became aware that Sigma was speaking again.

"Betrayal," he was saying harshly. "Treachery! Washington is full of cowards afraid of taking effective action. They call it a war, but what they really want to see is just a harmless snowball fight that'll impress the citizens without involving any serious casualties. . . . Snow, ha! Not a bad figure of speech, if I do say so! Snow and grass and all the other vicious substances pouring across our borders; but if anyone takes *real* steps to prevent it, valid political steps, they panic and cut off his funds and try to disgrace him, even if the operation was originally authorized at the very highest level. . . . As I said, treachery. So now they are investigating me! Well, they are going to be disappointed, they are not going to bring me down with the other patriots who've been used as whipping boys recently. They will have no evidence. Nobody has found those ill-fated arms, and even if somebody does find them, there's nobody alive to connect me with them."

I licked my lips. "What about the money Mondragon paid Will Pierce to buy them with, the first payment, the one that was actually made? It was U.S. government money and it came from you, didn't it?"

I didn't really expect him to answer except with another kick; I was surprised when he laughed instead.

"My dear man, anyone unable to juggle government funds skillfully enough to lose a few hundred thousand dollars, or even a few million, where no accountant can find them, has no business accepting an administrative post in our great, confused bureaucracy. I can assure you the transaction is well hidden, and the only man besides Mondragon himself who could have caused me trouble in that connection, Pierce, is dead. And if he should have mentioned me as the source of the money to that assistant whose name had slipped my mind, Medina, well, Medina is dead, too. And shortly Pierce's inquisitive partner, now lying wounded in Kino Bay under your name, will also be dead with whatever suspicions he may have entertained—I doubt that they were ever more than suspicions, but Cody is a persistent old man who was closely associated with Pierce for many years, and why take the risk of having him stumble on something?'' Sigma paused. "Which leaves only you. And the lady. I suppose I shouldn't have tried to be quite so clever, using you in the manner I did. It was a mistake; instead of being useful camouflage you turned out to be a considerable nuisance, but we'll take care of that now.'' He cleared his throat, slightly embarrassed. "Dr. Beckman, I regret this very much, but I think you can see that I have no choice now but to eliminate the two of you.''

Jo said calmly, "As a psychiatrist, I can assure you that's what all murderers say. There's never any choice; they *must* kill.''

He didn't like that. "My dear lady, I am not a murderer, I am simply a realist who understands what has to be done for survival. . . .''

He was interrupted by the sharp chatter of an assault rifle. I turned quickly and painfully to see Antonia on top of the rock on which I'd last seen the sentry; she must have dealt with him silently in order to take his place. She must have taken his M-16 in her usual thrifty fashion, because there was one slung across her back while she held another firmly to her right shoulder as she fired downwards systematically in short bursts, using the sights, at the men and vehicles below. The break had come so suddenly it almost slipped by me, but I recovered a little faster than Rutherford and Sigma, who were still staring at the slender, lethal apparition silhouetted against the sky. I managed to get my right leg up and kick the big man hard in the chest so that he went sprawling. Fortunately I'd been lying on my back in the jeep when they'd decided to handcuff me, and they hadn't bothered to turn me over to get my arms behind; I managed to reach out with my shackled hands and grab one of Sigma's legs. When I pulled hard, he came down, and I dragged myself on top of him.

"Jo, shoot Rutherford!" I gasped. "Never mind this one, I've got him, just empty the whole clip into the big bastard, he's too big to monkey with. Shoot him anywhere, he's wearing no protection. Just shoot him and keep on shooting!"

Sigma was struggling to free himself; he was also trying to reach the Browning on his belt, which wasn't a bad idea. I heard the little .22 automatic go off behind me as I reached the larger pistol, kind of hauling myself up the frame of the man beneath me. My left leg wasn't a hell of a lot of use or, rather, whenever I tried to use it, everything hurt so badly I almost blacked out. But I got one handcuffed hand on the butt of Sigma's weapon and when he tried to pry my hand away I managed to use the other hand and the leverage of the manacles to twist a finger for him until it broke. He screamed and went slack under me for a moment, long enough for me to drag the heavy automatic out of the russet leather holster and raise myself up to hammer it into his face with all my strength. I'd have shot him—after all, that was what I was here for—if I'd known the condition of his weapon, but if he had no cartridge in the chamber it would have been a two-handed job to ready it for firing, hard if not impossible to manage with cuffs on.

The little .22 was still snapping behind me like an angry Pekinese. Across the clearing, Antonia's M-16 was still firing, and other weapons of varying decibel levels had joined the chorus. I wished the stubborn, gun-happy girl would pull out; she'd already given me the distraction I needed. Sigma had gone limp at my blow, so I rolled off him, determined that the Browning did have a round in the chamber, cocked the weapon, and swung it in the general direction of Marion Rutherford.

Jo had the big man stopped. Apparently he'd got to his feet and gone for her, and she'd kept backing away and shooting. Now her gun was empty, and he was just standing there, swaying, bleeding from four wounds that I could see, but there was just too much beef there to be put down by the tiny, 40-grain bullets. He lifted his big hands and started toward her again, and I took careful aim and blew out his brains with the 9mm Browning. I suppose you could say I'd got back at him for trying to trap me near Cananea and siccing Mason Charles on me in Hermosillo, but to hell with that. You can waste your life trying to balance the ledger perfectly. He fell like a tree.

Jo tucked the little gun carefully under her waistband. She turned, took two steps, and vomited. Well, there was nothing I could do about that; she was a grown woman and capable of wiping her own mouth. I laid aside the Browning and fumbled in Sigma's pockets; when he started to come to life I picked up the pistol again and slammed it alongside his head. I continued to search his pockets. We seemed to have been forgotten under our mesquite, but a firefight was still continuing around the parked vehicles. The noise was, if anything, growing in volume. I couldn't understand how one small girl, even with automatic weapons and spare magazines, could stage such a battle, but in order to come to her assistance I had to get my hands free. . . .

"No, it's me!" Jo spoke quickly as, suddenly aware of her presence, I whipped the gun around. She drew a sleeve across her mouth. "Sorry about that. What can I do?"

"Check the big guy for a handcuff key. Skinny little thing with a round shank and just a little sideways nubbin at the end. Kind of a sharp prong sticking out the other end. . . . Never mind, here's one."

It was on Sigma's key ring. Jo held out her wrists and I got the cuffs off her; then she performed the same operation for me.

"Do all handcuffs open with the same key?" she asked.

"Never mind the research, get me Rutherford's M-16, over there. . . ."

"That will not be necessary, señor."

It was a soft male voice I'd heard before, speaking from behind me. I rolled myself over painfully to look, and there was Lieutenant Ernesto Barraga, in full camouflage regalia, the little man I'd thought about very recently in another connection. I suppose it says something about ESP.

Barraga said, "You will not need the weapon, Señor Helm. The situation is under our control."

I said, "Where the hell did you come from?"

"We have always been watching, señor, but it took a certain time to assemble enough men after we saw you wounded. For this, my apologies."

I looked over toward the cars; other little commando types in camouflage suits and berets were disarming Sigma's men. But there was no one on the rock. Then I saw one of Ramón's men kneeling beside a small figure lying at the foot of it.

"Oh, Christ, no!" I said, and got to my feet somehow.

Jo protested, "Matt, you mustn't . . ."

"Shut up and hand me that assault rifle."

I don't know why the Army loves it so. It's not much of a rifle and, unlike the more powerful and longer M-1, now obsolete, it makes a lousy crutch. I wound up emptying the bastard weapon so it wouldn't shoot me, and using it, butt down, as a half-assed cane. I thought of pulling my boot back on but the idea of bending over that far wasn't attractive, and the burn was the least of my worries. With the aid of the M-16, I limped across the open space past the bullet-riddled rolling stock. There were a lot of flat tires and some leaking gas tanks, but this wasn't a movie, so there were no picturesque, blazing fires.

I saw a couple of men I recognized. One was the tall individual called Gamma who'd captured Jo and driven her here; the one who, with a shorter partner named Peterson into whom I'd recently put a bullet, had put handcuffs on Buff Cody a long, long time ago. He was standing with three other sullen men, guarded by well-armed little brown-faced commandos. The second familiar face belonged to Captain Luís Alemán, Ramón's second in command, to whom I owed some bruises and ring-cuts and a certain amount of humiliation. Well, as I said, the ledger is never completely in balance; and I had more urgent matters on my mind.

The man who was kneeling beside Antonia rose as I came up. "Are you Señor Matthew Helm? She ask for you."

"I'm Helm. How is she?"

He shook his head and walked away. I lowered myself to my knees, and it didn't hurt much. There was a much bigger hurt that made my little physical disabilities irrelevant. She looked even smaller lying there. They'd spread the *serape* over her like a blanket. There was a little blood at the corner of her mouth. I found a handkerchief and wiped it away. Her eyes opened.

"So it is you, *gringo*," she whispered.

I said, "Nobody asked you to pull any goddamn sacrifice plays, you dumb little *indio*. Who the hell do you think you are, Joan of Arc?"

She brought her hand out from under the *serape* and touched her chest. "Bullet here from *pistola* kill pretty soon, I think, but I make good shooting first, hey? You okay now?"

"Yes, I'm okay."

Her big eyes watched me steadily. Then she gave me her big white grin. "Beeg liar, always."

"All right, I'm a liar. I stopped one, but I'll get over it, thanks to you. I . . ."

But the grin had faded and something in her face made me abort the sentence. She took my hand with cold fingers and held it tightly for a moment, fighting the pain.

At last she whispered, "Hey, we make pretty good tribe, *amigo*. Go warpath much good. I think I die now, okay?"

She did.

After a long time I released the lifeless hand I'd been holding and felt for the pockets in the coarse cloth of the *serape*. I left the high-heeled shoes but took the partly used box of high-powered .22s. I pushed myself up and turned to see Jo standing there. I noted that she had two boots on now. She was holding a third, and a long stick that had been freshly cut, maybe from a willow, although I couldn't recall seeing any around. She was watching me gravely.

"I'm sorry, Matt."

I said, "I apologize for being rude. In answer to your question, I belive that most Smith and Wesson handcuff keys fit most

Smith and Wesson handcuffs. Maybe all do, I'm not an expert on the subject. But figure it out, when a cop comes in with half-a-dozen prisoners, does he want to spend time trying to remember which key unlocks which thug?''

Jo said, "One of the men made you a better cane than that stupid weapon you're using. If you have to keep walking around when you should be lying down. And you'd better wear something on that foot, but let me clean and bandage it first."

"Never mind all that," I said. "Just hold the boot so I can get into it, if you don't mind. . . . Thanks. Now I suggest you take a walk, Jo. Not far, just down around the bend of the road. I've got something left to do here, and I don't think you want to see it. But give me that little automatic first, please."

Jo licked her lips. "You already have Mr. Sigma's gun, right there under your belt."

I said, "She was in this from the start. I think it would please her if her pistol was used to finish it. Please stand in front of me while I load it; then get the hell out of here."

I fed the tiny .22 cartridges into the diminutive magazine, which I inserted into the butt of the shiny .22 automatic. I pulled back the slide once and let it go forward, checking to make sure a round had fed into the chamber. I apologized to the little weapon. It still looked like a ballistic disaster, but it had worked for Antonia, it had worked for Jo, and somehow I was quite certain it was going to work for me.

"Okay, thanks," I said.

Jo moved away without speaking. Looking up, I saw that Ramón had arrived. He was talking with Captain Alemán, near the little group of prisoners—there were five now; Sigma had joined his captured men. I took a couple of steps in that direction. The trouble with having a sore foot on one side and a bad hip on the other was that it was hard to know which leg to limp on. Ramón came to meet me.

I said, "Mondragon is dead. The weapons are in the Rincon de la Aguila, wherever that may be."

"My Yaquis will know. You have done a good job. No

one . . ." He glanced toward Captain Alemán, the Army representative. "No one will now question the release of the beautiful young *rubia*, supposedly your wife."

I remembered that *rubia* was the word for blonde. I had trouble remembering the blonde in question; my adventures with Gloria belonged to another lifetime.

I said, "I have a feeling she didn't find her role as hostage too arduous."

Ramón smiled pleasantly. "She is a very charming young lady. Shall we leave it at that?" He cleared his throat. "What do you want done with these?"

We moved closer to the captives. I said, "We don't want to give the local *zopilotes* indigestion. The one with the safari suit and the beat-up face is mine. With your permission, of course. I suggest you turn the others loose, you've got enough dead *gringos* on your hands already. But it's only a suggestion."

"What are you going to do with me?"

That was Sigma, moving forward anxiously. He was cradling the left hand with the broken finger like a sick baby. He was looking rather battered, but he was not as badly damaged as he would have been if he hadn't managed to turn his head when I first slammed the gun at his face. As it was, he'd taken one blow on the left cheek, which was badly swollen, and the other on the left ear, which was torn, spilling considerable blood down the side of his Great White Hunter outfit with its empty holster. Well, I was in even worse shape, shot and burned, in the grimy remnants of the second white Buff Cody suit I'd gone through, so I felt no great sympathy for his condition.

Ignoring Sigma, Ramón spoke to Captain Alemán. "Those four *gringos*. Be so good as to procure for them an operational vehicle and tell them that they have twelve hours to disappear. If they are found in this country at . . ." He glanced at his watch. ". . . at two o'clock tomorrow morning, they will be shot."

"As you wish, señor."

The surly Army bastard obviously disapproved; he would have liked to execute everybody in sight, probably including me.

"Now you," Ramón said, turning to Sigma. "I understand those four—all these Americans—were under your command. Let us first establish who you are, señor, and what your business is here in Mexico."

"My name . . ." Sigma hesitated. "My name is Warren Harding Somerset, and I work for the United States government. I advise you to release me immediately!"

I drew a long breath. The name was in the open at last. As the mission developed, Mac's instructions had seemed, at first, slightly incredible, but they'd been quite clear to anyone used to deciphering his doubletalk. I'd been told to find and dispose of a certain Señor Sábado and if this brought me into conflict with Mr. Warren Somerset it was just too damn bad. There was no other way in which I could interpret those orders. I didn't even want to. After all, some effort should be made to keep the accounts balanced, and the man had done his best to kill me, and Antonia was dead.

Looking at him, I thought of the middle name he'd revealed, and wondered who'd choose to name a baby boy after President Harding, not the greatest Chief Executive ever to inhabit the White House.

Ramón glanced at me. "Do you confirm this man's identity, Señor Helm?"

I had the shape of the operation clearly in mind now, and I said, "Hell, no! And if you check with Washington, I'm sure you'll find they never heard of him. Maybe they've got a Somerset somewhere, it would be surprising if they didn't, they've got several Helms, too, but this man's name is Sábado."

"Helm, damn you . . . !"

One of Ramón's men had moved up behind the prisoner. He silenced the outburst with a strong poke from the barrel of his assault rifle.

Ramón looked grave. "We have heard of a Señor Sábado. He has caused my government much trouble. You are sure this is the man?"

I shrugged. "His men called him Mr. Saturday. He was also

305

going by the code name Sigma, perhaps to conceal his real identity."

"Helm, you're mad!" Somerset protested, moving up to confront me. "What are you trying to do to me? You know who I am, we met in El Paso when I . . ."

He stopped, perhaps realizing that reminding me how he'd set me up for murder wasn't likely to help him out of his predicament.

I said, "I can't recall ever meeting you or anybody named Somerset, friend. Ramón, we can settle this very easily. Among the wounded is a revolutionary named Hernando with a bullet in the leg, one of Mondragon's men. Bring him in and let him have a look at this man. Ask him if this is the man they knew as Sábado."

Ramón said judiciously, "Of course, we do not need this evidence to convict him. Anyone who enters my country with machine guns and associates with terrorists can expect to make the acquaintance of our prisons, assuming that we are merciful enough to let him live. However, this elusive Sábado has been a problem long enough; I shall be glad to have it solved." He glanced at Lieutenant Barraga. "Find me the man named Hernando, please."

The little lieutenant saluted smartly and marched off. I stood watching him absently; then Somerset made his move. He took a quick step forward and snatched the heavy pistol from my belt, using his intact right hand.

"Everything's gone wrong since I met you!" he gasped. "At least I'll take you with me, Helm!"

My big worry was the guard. Standing there behind Somerset, if he cut loose with a lot of 5.56mm stuff some of it would be bound to achieve full penetration and hit me. I was relieved to see him moving aside for a safer angle. Somerset was wrestling with the Browning's hammer, which I'd let down in order to carry the weapon in the front of my pants without risking castration. As a southpaw, even though it was his own gun, and presumably familiar, he was having a hard time getting it cocked right-handed. Maybe in his outfit, unlike ours, they didn't practice with the weak hand.

I waited until, having got the job done, he started to raise the weapon. Then, remembering the Kevlar he was wearing, I shot him three times in the face with the little .22 hidden in my hand.

CHAPTER 33

I woke up in a familiar bed in a familiar room with a familiar feminine face looking down at me. Even though there was a small, round Band-Aid on one cheek that hadn't been there before, and on the back of the hand with which she wielded the thermometer, I found myself wondering for a moment if I hadn't just had a simple concussion nightmare, right here in the Schonfeld's beach house in Kino Bay. Perhaps I'd never driven away from this town with a girl named Antonia or met a man named Arturo or shot a man called Sábado. Perhaps the girl named Antonia was still alive back in Hermosillo. . . . But I knew she wasn't.

I licked my lips. "How the hell did I get back here?" I whispered. I had some confused memories, but it was easier to ask than to sort them out.

"Oh, you're with us again," Jo said. "We seem to play this scene over and over, darling."

"Still darling?" I asked.

"Just a figure of speech," she said. "I call all my patients darling. Darlings Number One, Two, Three, etc. You were operated on in a clinic in Guaymas, but it was thought best to hide you here for your convalescence. Too many dead and wounded *Americanos* could cause comment, in spite of your friend Ramón's political influence, which seems to be considerable. He'll be in to see you as soon as he gets all the loose ends tied up tightly. He said to tell you the arms have been found and properly disposed of. He said you might be interested in the fact that the rifles were HK-19s in the 7.62 NATO caliber used by the

Mexican Army. I hope I got that right. He said to thank you for a job well done."

"He's welcome, but not very."

"How do you feel? Up to seeing an important visitor?"

"How important?"

"He says he's your boss. I don't envy him the job."

"Save your pity for the people he bosses."

"I'll send him in."

Then Mac was standing over me. He looked tall from the bed, although he wasn't really a tall man by my six-plus standard. Same gray suit and black eyebrows. Same cold gray eyes.

"You did well, Eric," he said. "Employing the young lady's pistol was a particularly nice touch. No self-respecting U.S. agent would dream of performing an official termination, to use that tired euphemism, with such a cheap and unreliable little weapon. Obviously Señor Sábado was the victim of his dangerous revolutionary associates—well, obviously after our friend Solana-Ruiz rearranged a few facts and swore a few people to secrecy. As for Mr. Warren Harding Somerset, he is on vacation at present, and I am afraid there will be terrible news for his friends shortly. Airplane travel is not as safe as it should be. Something really must be done about it. But I do commend you on executing your mission in a very satisfactory manner."

I was tired of all the fulsome damn praise. Keep the troops happy, ha! Why didn't some of these executive bastards do their own damn dirty work?

I said, "Actually, that crummy-looking little automatic fired whenever it was asked to and didn't blow anybody's hand off. And there's a great deal to be said for using English language, sir. One of these days my ESP is going to malfunction and we'll both screw up badly."

Mac smiled indulgently. It's something I tell him after every job, and all I ever get is that tolerant smile.

"Really, Eric!" he said. "In your wildest dreams, can you see the head of one agency of the U.S. Government boldly ordering one of his operatives to terminate—there it is again!—the chief of another? Allow me a few polite circumlocutions, please.

309

It was not a good situation. The man was powerful and dangerous, with influential friends in Washington, and the Latin American situation was very tense; he could not be allowed to damage our relations with this great neighbor of ours to the south. We could not even afford to have it made public, as he would have been sure to do if he'd been brought to trial, that this wild plan of his had once existed, even to the extent of having substantial sums allocated to it, with Washington approval. Besides, he was simply killing too many people in an effort to cover his tracks. He had to be stopped; and I was sure you would understand, as you did, that if he died as Señor Sábado down here in Mexico, we could easily deal with a missing Mr. Somerset up in the U.S. I find it ironical that this is close to the same removal technique he planned to employ with you and Mr. Cody." Mac paused. "As far as drugs are concerned, I can tell you that certain delicate negotiations have resulted in much improved cooperation from the present Mexican authorities." He looked down at me for a moment. "You're entitled to the usual convalescent leave, of course. When you feel fit enough, please report to the Ranch for evaluation and rehabilitation."

"Yes, sir."

He started for the door and turned. "It occurred to me that you might want to know a little more about the young woman who was killed at the Black Rocks, so I ordered an investigation."

Just about the time you decide you're working for a ruthlessly programmed robot he goes and turns human on you.

"What did you find out?" I asked.

"Nothing. So far we have discovered no record of her before she appeared in Guaymas associated with Jorge Medina de Campo. If you wish, we can continue . . ."

"No." It was better to remember her as a little warrior girl who came out of nowhere, unexplained. "But thank you, sir."

He nodded and left the room. Later in the day I had two more visitors. Horace Hosmer Cody held himself very straight and showed few effects of his wound or his age; he was wearing boots, jeans, a double-breasted gray shirt with snaps instead of buttons, a bolo tie that I recognized—apparently Jo had given him back his lucky piece—and a big hat, which he took off in deference to the sickroom atmosphere. His companion was wearing high-heeled white sandals, yellow linen slacks, and a yellow satin blouse with a blue silk scarf at the throat. I'd forgotten how lovely and adult she could look with her makeup intact and her golden hair smoothly pinned and sprayed into place. When she saw me in the bed, she gave a little gasp of pity and came hurrying forward on her high heels to kiss me lightly on the mouth. I was aware that Jo was standing in the doorway, looking amused.

"Oh, you poor man, what have they been doing to you?" Gloria breathed.

"Shooting me, mostly," I said. "It's practically a national pastime. Hi, Gloria."

"Well, you seem to be in good hands." There was a faint, how-could-you-forget-me-so-soon sharpness to her voice, but it was the mechanical reaction of the truly beautiful woman who expects all men to remain at her feet until dismissed. There had been nothing in the kiss, and we both knew that the little fire that had burned for a moment one night in the mountains had long since flickered out. She straightened up. "Well, I hope you get well soon, Matt. My . . . my husband wants to talk to you."

I watched her go out of the room, followed by Jo. Horace Hosmer Cody came forward.

"Looks like they've been giving you a rough time, son."

"It's a rough life," I said. I glanced at the empty doorway. "Husband? I thought that wedding had been rigged so it wouldn't take."

"That's what the man told her when he was setting me up, but he never bothered to fix it. Just as well; otherwise we'd have to go through the damn ceremony again." He grinned at me. "Still think I'm all kinds of a villain, don't you, boy?"

"Well, half a villain, or maybe just a quarter. You're not an arms smuggler, and you didn't have Pierce and Millicent Charles killed, and I don't think you have any designs on Gloria's life or money, but there seems to be no doubt that you did send the frighteners after her to scare her into marrying you.''

"That's right, and it's a big joke between us." The old man reached out and pulled a chair close so he could sit down. "Ah, that's better. It's hell on a man my age, still a little short of red corpuscles, keeping up with a young wife. What money?''

"What?''

"That little gal's got no money at all, mister. That vampire woman, Millie, got Will Pierce to clean it all out, even the trust funds left to Glory by her mother. He was executor; he could do it, and he did. And lost it all, the damn woman-crazy fool.'' Cody drew a long breath. "I'm a dirty old man, son. I've loved that little gal since she was old enough to start walking. Don't ask me to explain it. Your headshrinker lady friend might know. Never took a step out of line though, all the time she was growing up, that would have spoiled it. I knew, I just knew, son, that sooner or later the time would come when she'd need me, and I'd be right there.''

"And the time came?' I said.

"What was she going to do without money, the way she'd been brought up? Marry some rich slob who'd make her unhappy? Can you see her working a supermarket checkout counter or selling real estate? And here's old Buff Cody with money running out his ears. . . . What was I going to do? I was good old Uncle Buffy to her. She'd have thought I was joking if I asked her to marry me. Should I have told her she was flat broke penniless, and here was a million, two million, five million, and all she had to do was . . . I couldn't goddamn *buy* her, could I? So, what the hell, I scared her. I knew she'd come to me in trouble, she always had when she was frightened or worried. Not a nice thing to do, but who ever said Buff Cody was nice? Anyway, it worked, and she's forgiven me, and we laugh about it now.''

"Have you forgiven her?''

He frowned. "What are you driving at?''

I licked my lips. "If I'd known a girl since she was a baby, and she'd known me, I wouldn't feel too damn happy if she suddenly decided I was capable of murdering her for her money, just on the word of a two-bit thug bribed or intimidated into lying by a two-bit bureaucrat.''

The old man looked at me for a moment; then he smiled thinly. ''I guess you're younger than you look in those whiskers, putting the ladies on pedestals, like plaster saints. There ain't much of that kind of loyalty around, boy. I'd given Glory plenty cause for suspicion; how can I blame her for buying the whole package?'' He cleared his throat, rising. ''Incidentally, she's likely to be a rich woman sooner than she thinks. Had a few problems before and seems like running around with a bullet in the back didn't help them none. But no need for her to know that, yet. Well, take care of yourself, son. Like they say, you'd better, nobody else is going to.''

We shook hands, and he started for the door. I spoke to his retreating back: ''I hate to contradict an old man, but you seem to be a pretty nice guy, actually.''

He didn't turn his head. ''Don't tell anybody, son, or it'll cost me money.''

Then it was evening, and Jo brought in my liquid diet. I wouldn't want to flatter it by calling it a dinner. She'd eaten in the kitchen and brought a cup of coffee to keep me company. She was wearing blue jeans and a loose white shirt with the tails out. No silver. She sat there studying me for a while, and I thought she was evaluating the situation. She was thinking that Gloria was beautiful but meaningless; any woman who let the lovely Glorias of the world bother her was a fool. There had been another girl who could have been much more significant, but she was dead. That left only the two of us, and the question of whether a civilized woman like her could, or should, find any kind of satisfactory relationship with an uncivilized gent like me.

''We'll have that intravenous apparatus out of there in a couple of days,'' she said. ''Easier to get the antibiotics into you that way than stuffing them down your throat. Mean as you are, a girl could lose a couple of fingers. . . . I saw it, you know. The way you teased that man into grabbing the gun, standing

313

there looking as if you were half-asleep, and let him fumble with it awhile, and then shot him.''

"I told you to take a walk.''

She spoke calmly: ''You're a dreadful man, darling. One of these days I'll undoubtedly start disapproving of you very strongly, the way any decent woman would. That's assuming that I'm a decent woman. In any case, professional pride compels me to get you well, first. After that, well, we'll just have to see see how it goes, won't we?''